DATE DUE			

LAST PICK

JASON WALZ

Color by **Jon Proctor**

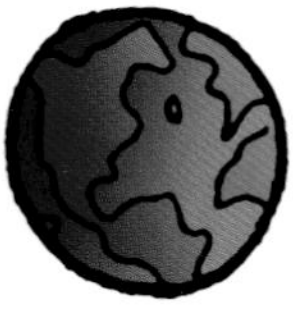

:01
First Second

New York

For Desmond and Emmett.
Take care of each other. Always.

:01 First Second

Published by First Second
First Second is an imprint of Roaring Brook Press, a division of
Holtzbrinck Publishing Holdings Limited Partnership
175 Fifth Avenue, New York, NY 10010

Library of Congress Control Number: 2017957412
Paperback ISBN: 978-1-62672-891-2
Hardcover ISBN: 978-1-62672-890-5

Our books may be purchased in bulk for promotional, educational, or business use.
Please contact your local bookseller or the Macmillan Corporate and Premium Sales Department
at (800) 221-7945 ext. 5442 or by e-mail at MacmillanSpecialMarkets@macmillan.com.

FIRST EDITION

First edition, 2018

Book design by Dezi Sienty, Molly Johanson, and Andrew Arnold
Interior color by Jon Proctor
Cover color by Shelli Paroline and Braden Lamb
Printed in China
Paperback: 1 3 5 7 9 10 8 6 4 2
Hardcover: 1 3 5 7 9 10 8 6 4 2

Penciled with a light blue Prismacolor Col-erase. Inked with a Pentel Brush and
Alvin Penstix in a variety of sizes. Colored digitally in Photoshop.

BY ART WE LIVE

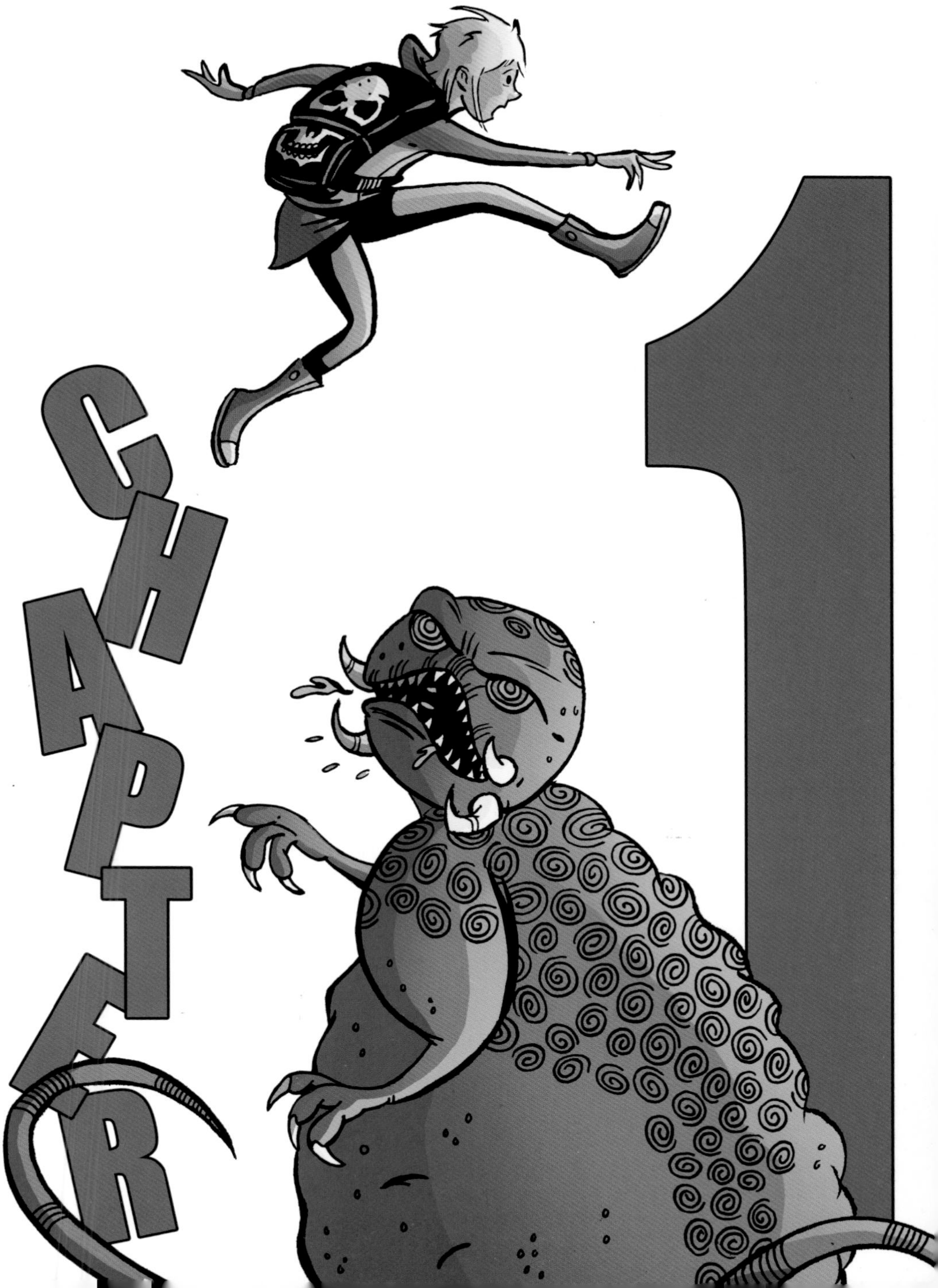
CHAPTER
1

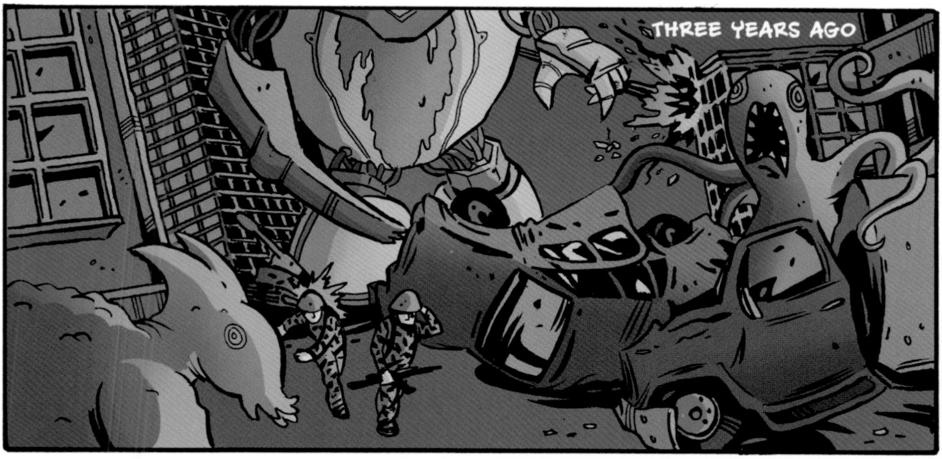
THREE YEARS AGO

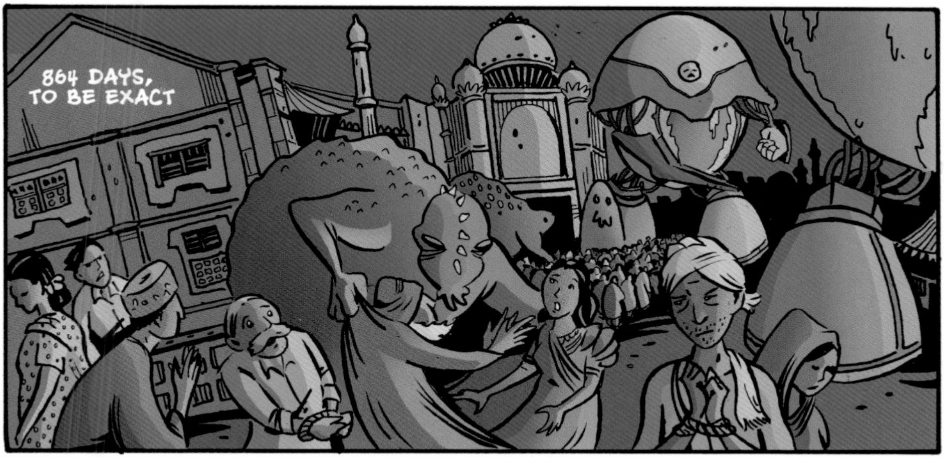
864 DAYS, TO BE EXACT

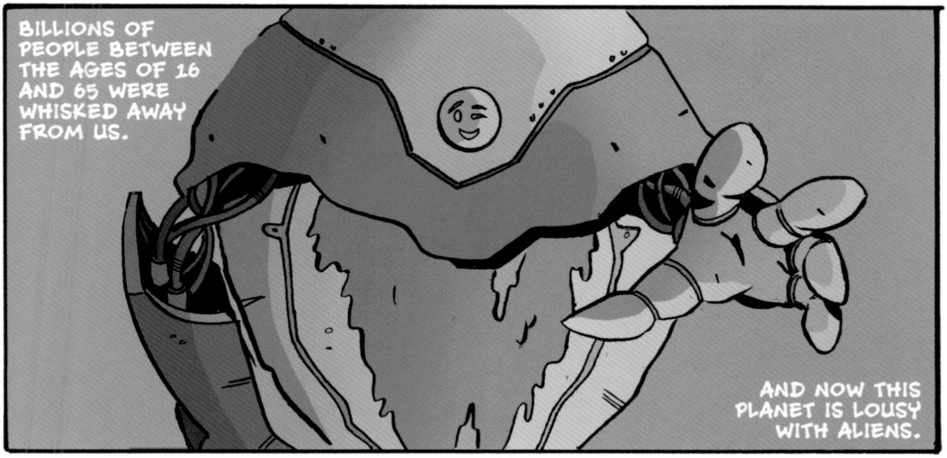
BILLIONS OF PEOPLE BETWEEN THE AGES OF 16 AND 65 WERE WHISKED AWAY FROM US.
AND NOW THIS PLANET IS LOUSY WITH ALIENS.

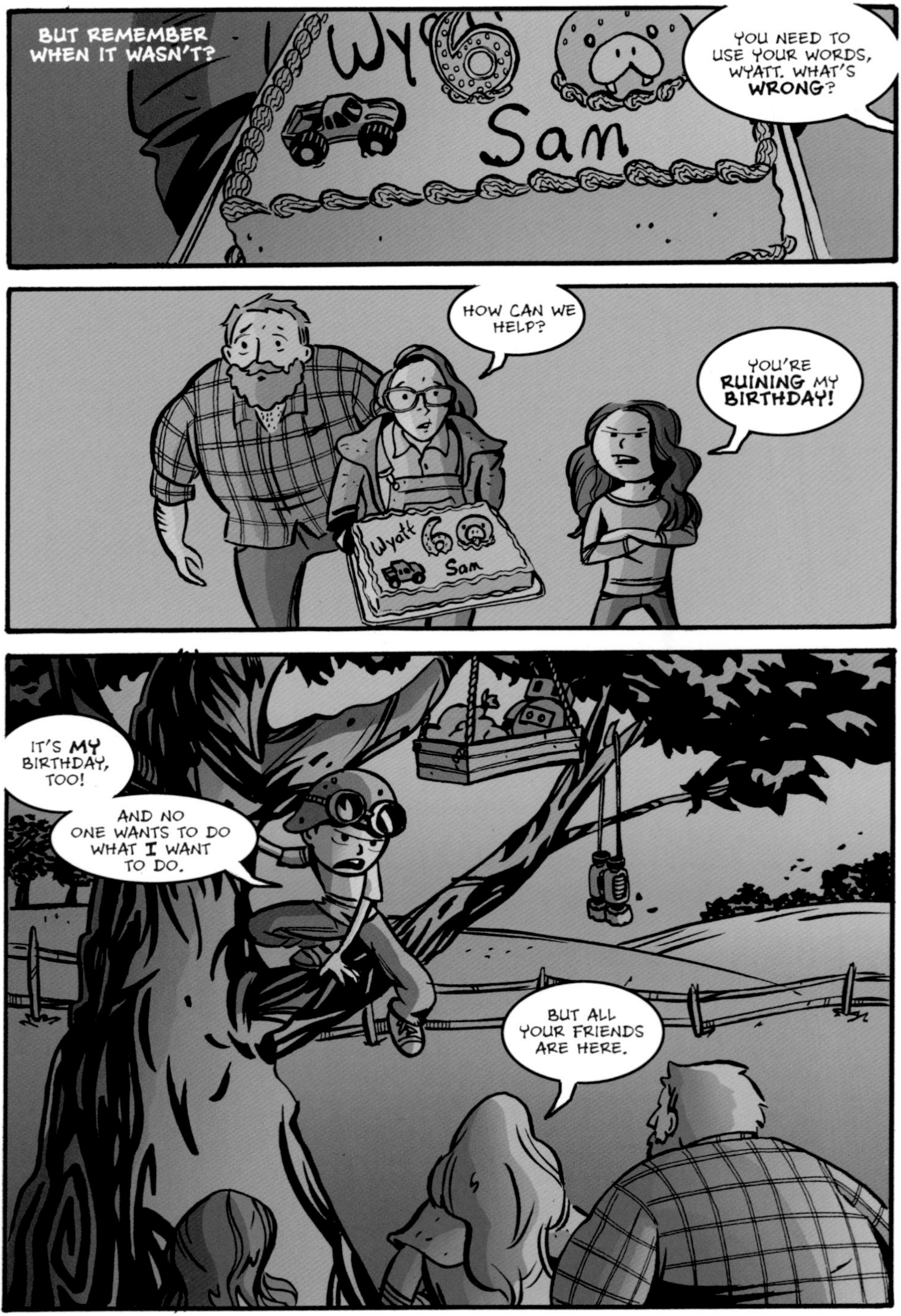
BUT REMEMBER WHEN IT WASN'T?
YOU NEED TO USE YOUR WORDS, WYATT. WHAT'S WRONG?
Wyatt
Sam
HOW CAN WE HELP?
YOU'RE RUINING MY BIRTHDAY!
IT'S MY BIRTHDAY, TOO!
AND NO ONE WANTS TO DO WHAT I WANT TO DO.
BUT ALL YOUR FRIENDS ARE HERE.

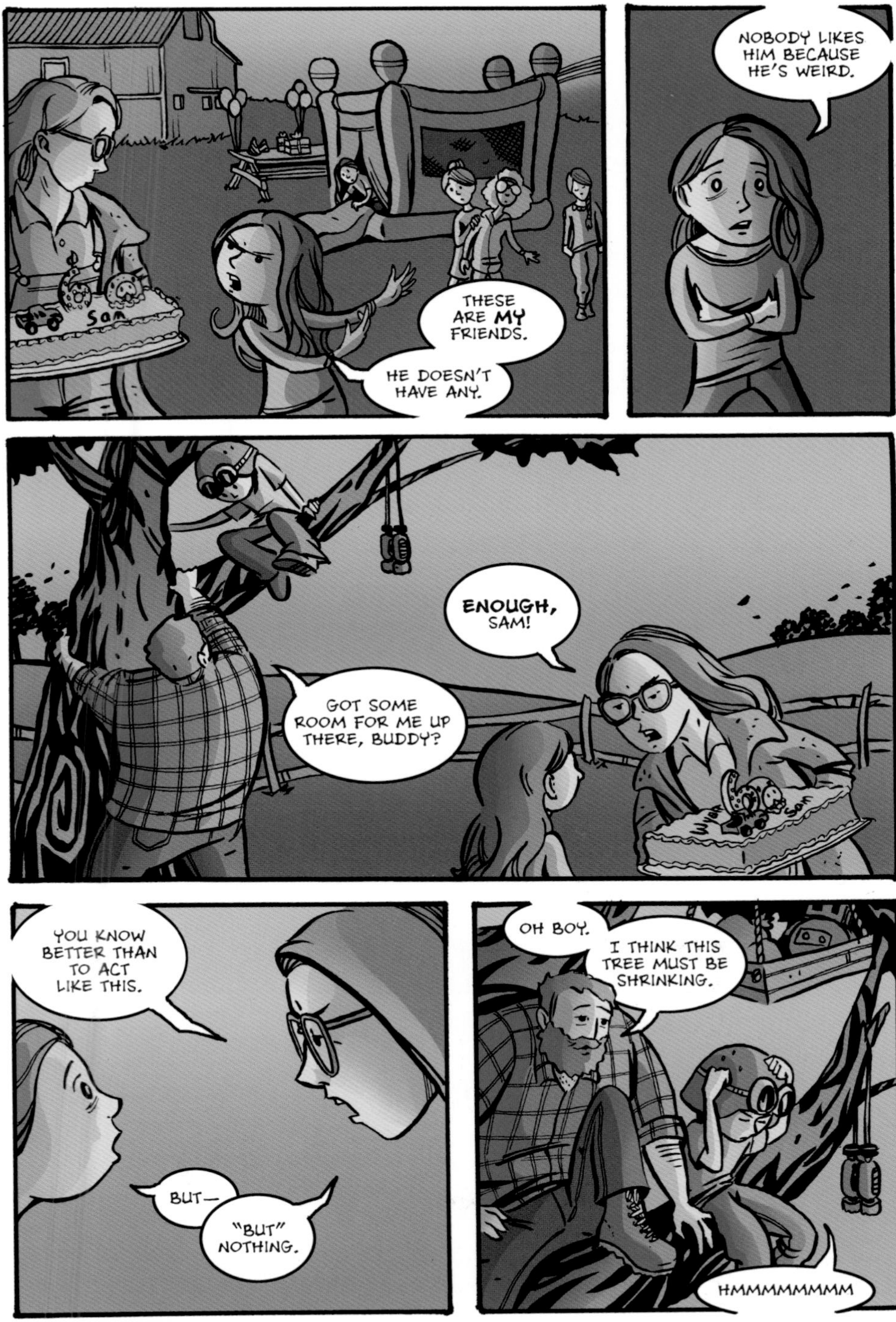
THESE ARE MY FRIENDS.
HE DOESN'T HAVE ANY.
NOBODY LIKES HIM BECAUSE HE'S WEIRD.
ENOUGH, SAM!
GOT SOME ROOM FOR ME UP THERE, BUDDY?
YOU KNOW BETTER THAN TO ACT LIKE THIS.
BUT—
"BUT" NOTHING.
OH BOY.
I THINK THIS TREE MUST BE SHRINKING.
HMMMMMMMM

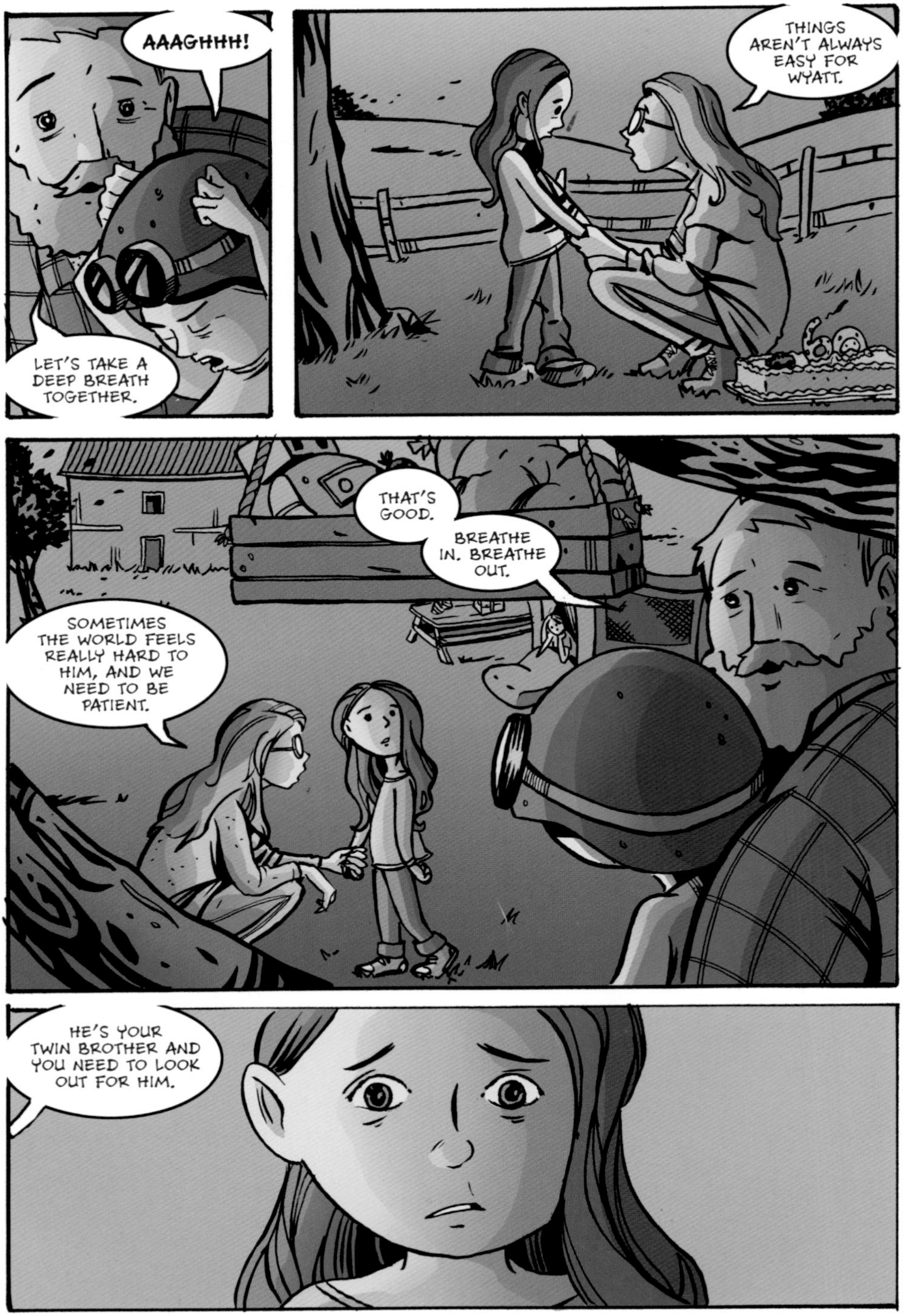
AAAGHHH!
LET'S TAKE A DEEP BREATH TOGETHER.
THINGS AREN'T ALWAYS EASY FOR WYATT.
THAT'S GOOD.
BREATHE IN. BREATHE OUT.
SOMETIMES THE WORLD FEELS REALLY HARD TO HIM, AND WE NEED TO BE PATIENT.
HE'S YOUR TWIN BROTHER AND YOU NEED TO LOOK OUT FOR HIM.

"YOU'RE A TEAM."

YOU THERE, TURD ONE?

THAT'S **BIRD** ONE.

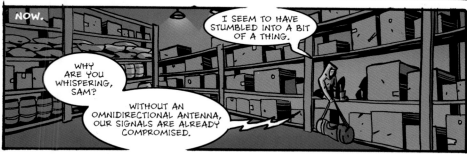

NOW.

I SEEM TO HAVE STUMBLED INTO A BIT OF A THING.

WHY ARE YOU WHISPERING, SAM?

WITHOUT AN OMNIDIRECTIONAL ANTENNA, OUR SIGNALS ARE ALREADY COMPROMISED.

SO IT BECOMES EVEN **MORE** DIFFICULT TO—

FASCINATING. NOW SHUT UP FOR A SECOND.

THERE'S SOME GROSS ALIEN CREATURE THINGY BLOCKING WHAT I NEED TO GET TO.

INTERESTING. TELL ME EVERYTHING ABOUT IT.

Wyatt's

I MENTIONED IT WAS GROSS, RIGHT?

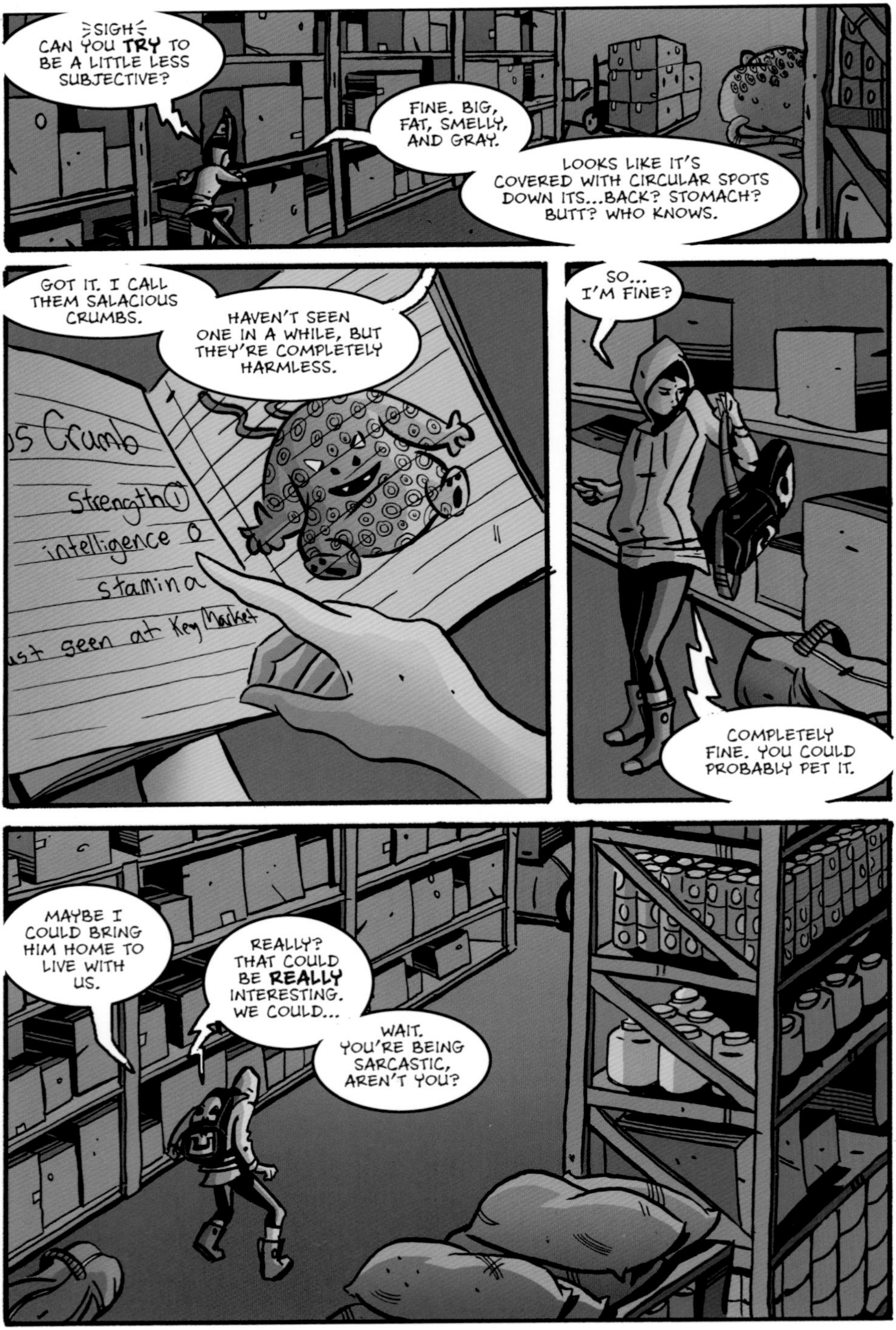

SIGH
CAN YOU TRY TO BE A LITTLE LESS SUBJECTIVE?
FINE. BIG, FAT, SMELLY, AND GRAY.
LOOKS LIKE IT'S COVERED WITH CIRCULAR SPOTS DOWN ITS...BACK? STOMACH? BUTT? WHO KNOWS.
GOT IT. I CALL THEM SALACIOUS CRUMBS.
HAVEN'T SEEN ONE IN A WHILE, BUT THEY'RE COMPLETELY HARMLESS.
s Crumb
Strength 1
intelligence 0
stamina
ust seen at Key Market
SO... I'M FINE?
COMPLETELY FINE. YOU COULD PROBABLY PET IT.
MAYBE I COULD BRING HIM HOME TO LIVE WITH US.
REALLY? THAT COULD BE REALLY INTERESTING. WE COULD...
WAIT. YOU'RE BEING SARCASTIC, AREN'T YOU?

UHM. HEY.
I JUST NEED TO GET SOMETHING FROM THE COOLER OVER THERE.
KEEP COOLER DOOR CLOSED
SLURP
NOM NOM
SO IF YOU COULD JUST STOP STUFFING YOUR FAT FACE FOR A MINUTE, I'LL BE ON MY WAY.
AH. I SEE.
BUT UNFORTUNATELY FOR YOU, LITTLE RUDE GIRL, I'M STILL RATHER HUNGRY.
OH, WAIT. CANCEL THAT.
WRONG ONE.

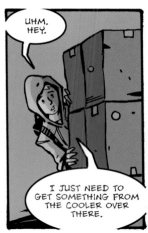

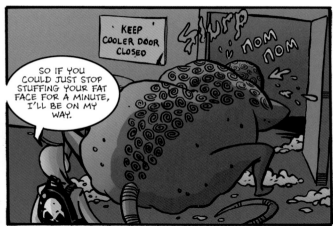

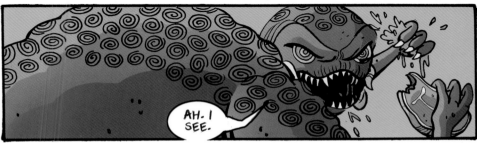

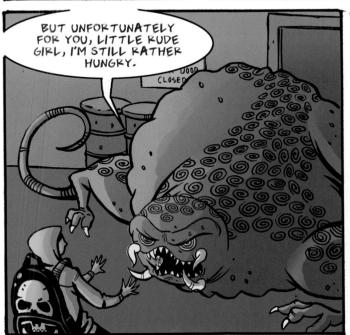

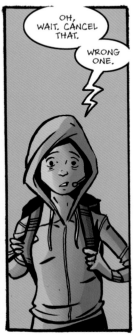

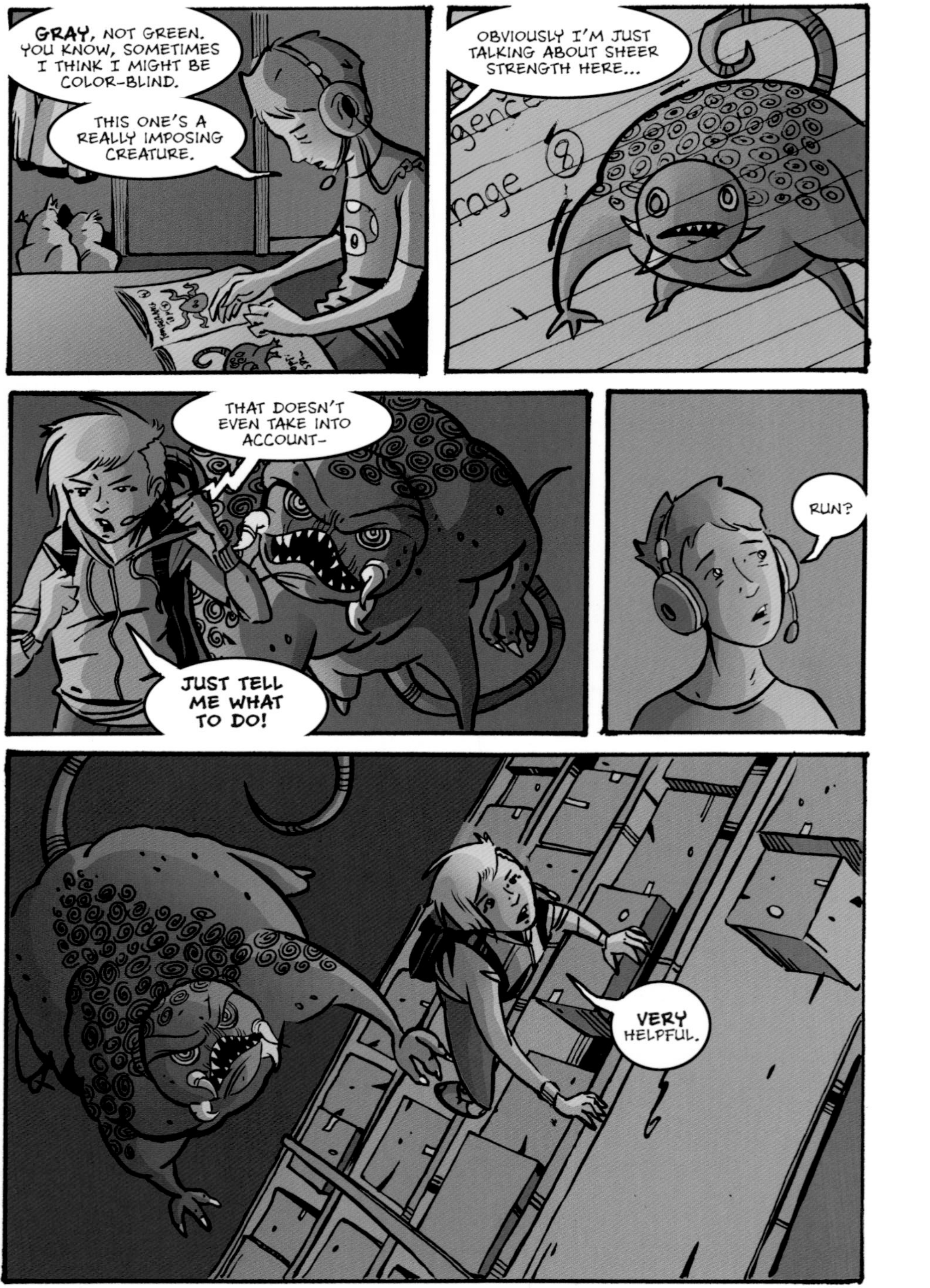
GRAY, NOT GREEN. YOU KNOW, SOMETIMES I THINK I MIGHT BE COLOR-BLIND.
THIS ONE'S A REALLY IMPOSING CREATURE.
OBVIOUSLY I'M JUST TALKING ABOUT SHEER STRENGTH HERE...
THAT DOESN'T EVEN TAKE INTO ACCOUNT-
JUST TELL ME WHAT TO DO!
RUN?
VERY HELPFUL.

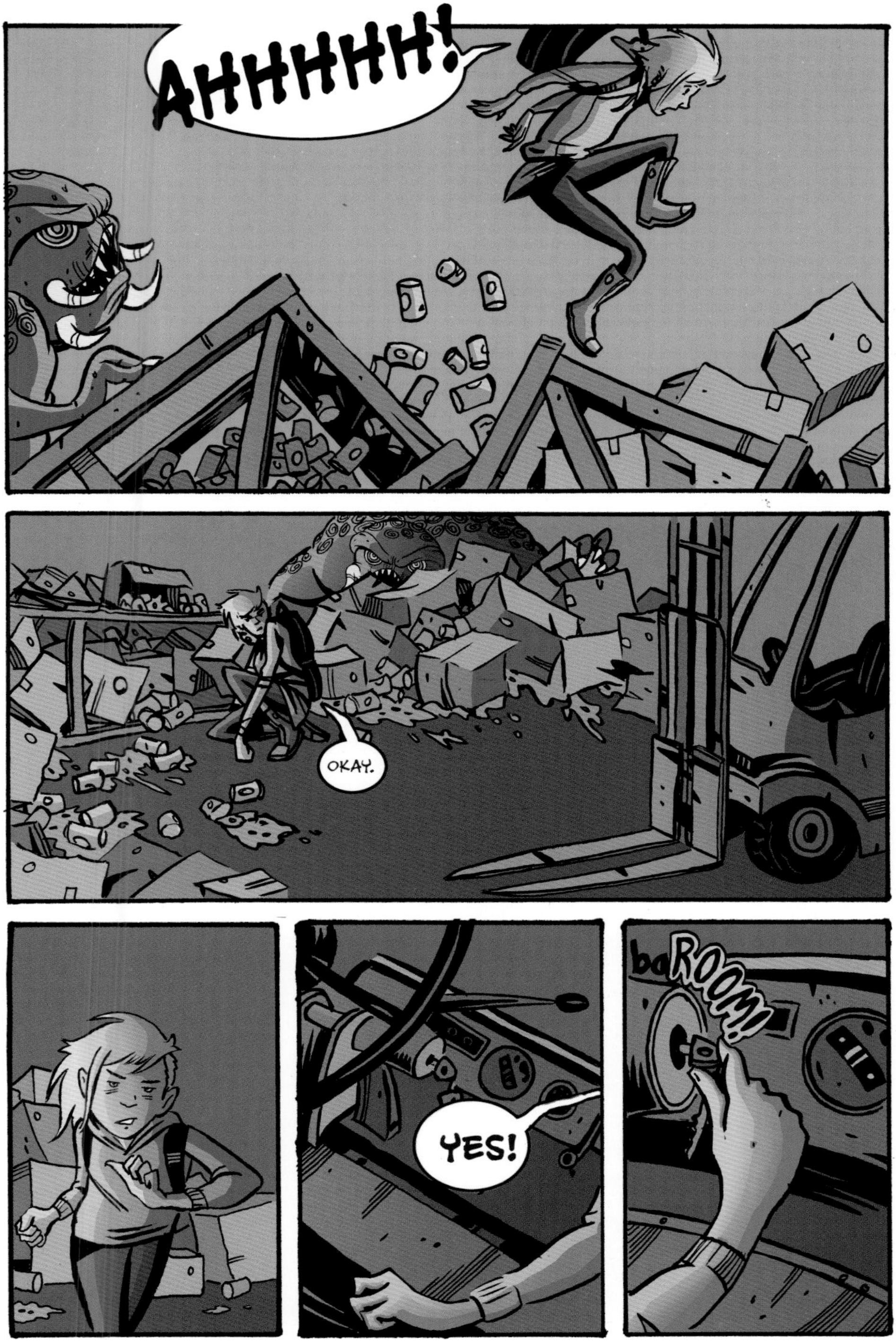
AHHHHH!
OKAY.
YES!
baROOM!

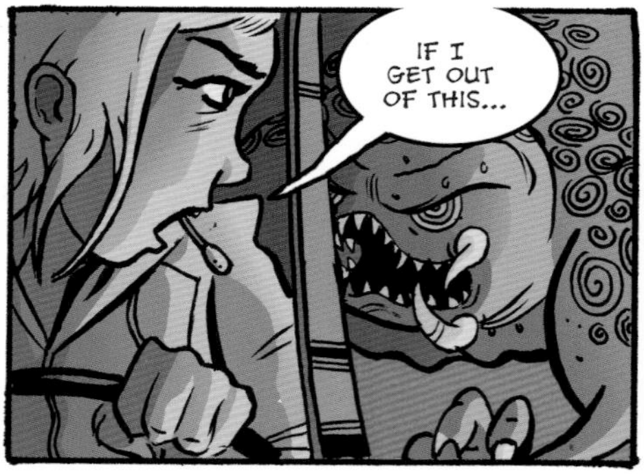
IF I GET OUT OF THIS...

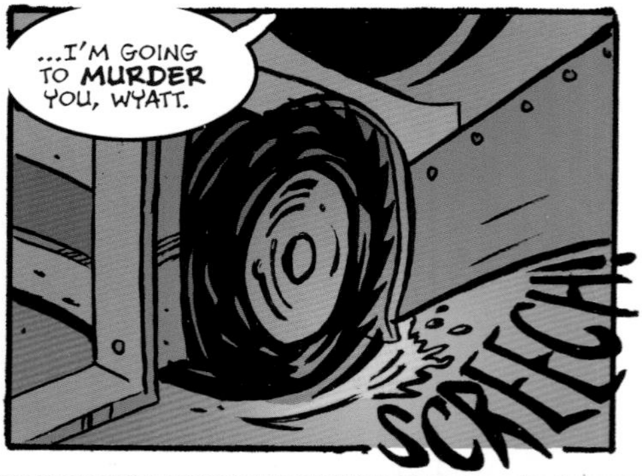
...I'M GOING TO **MURDER** YOU, WYATT.
SCREECH!

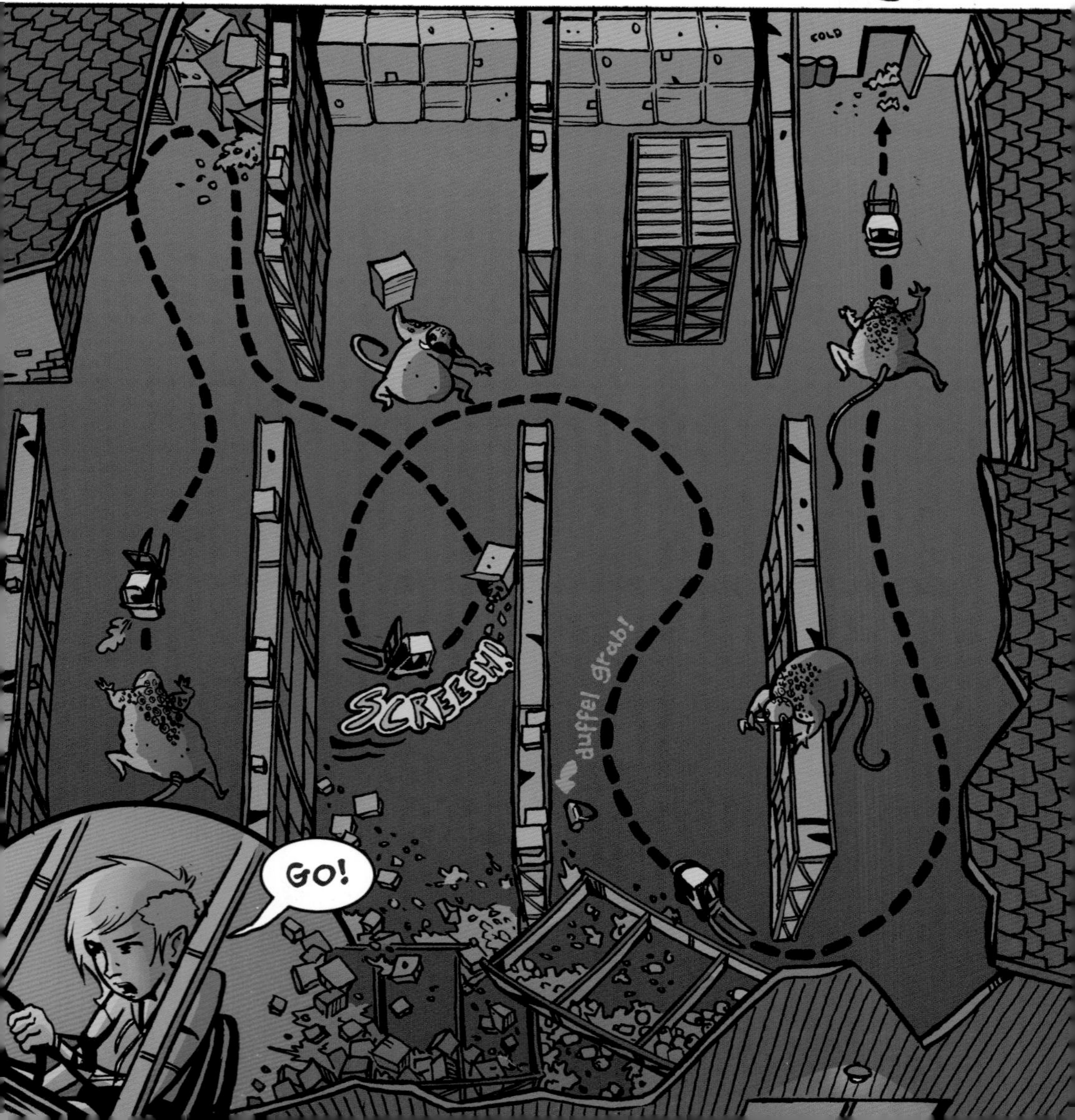
COLD
SCREECH!
duffel grab!
GO!

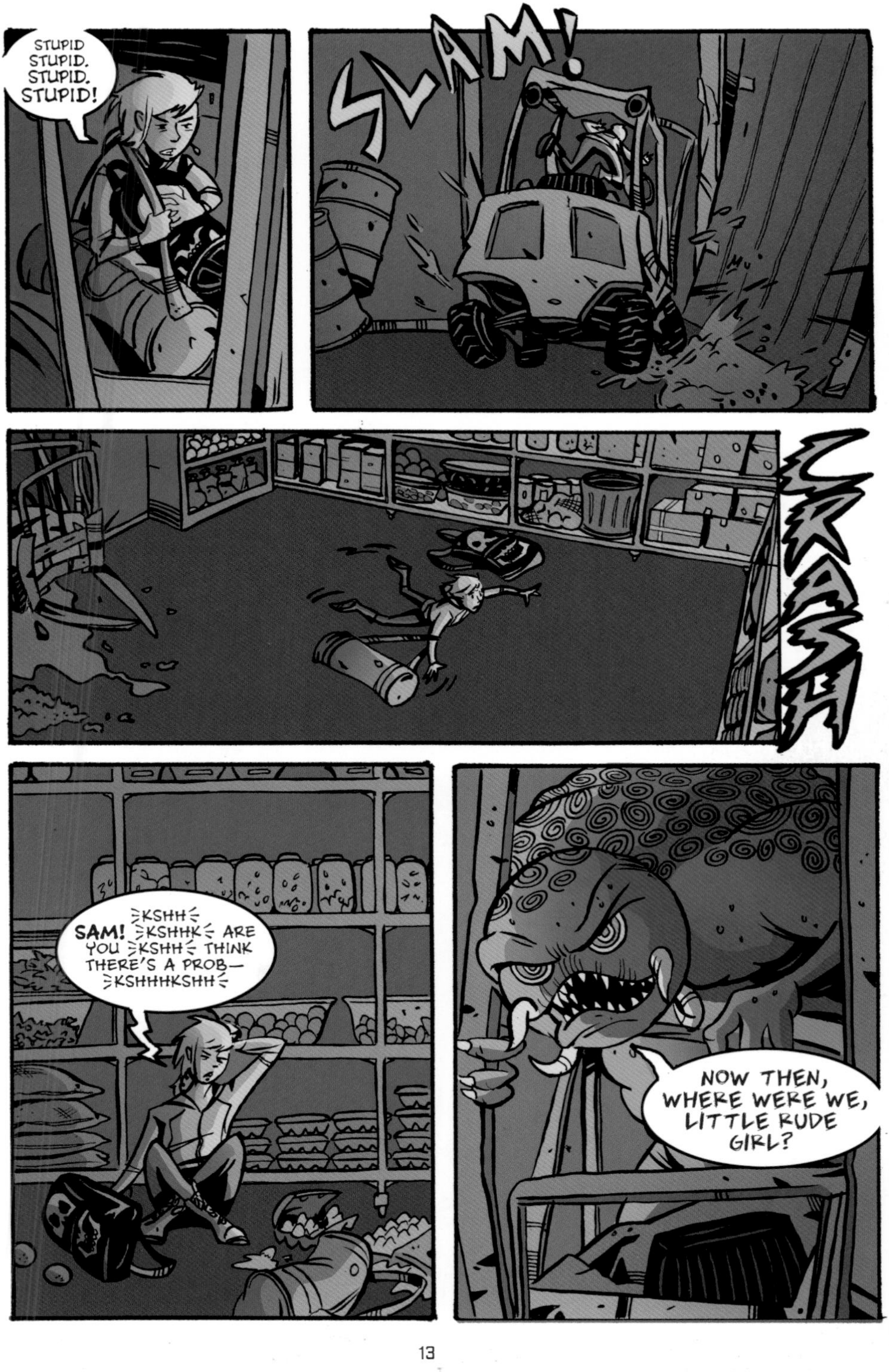
STUPID STUPID. STUPID. STUPID!
SLAM!
CRASH
SAM! KSHH KSHHK ARE YOU KSHH THINK THERE'S A PROB— KSHHHKSHH
NOW THEN, WHERE WERE WE, LITTLE RUDE GIRL?

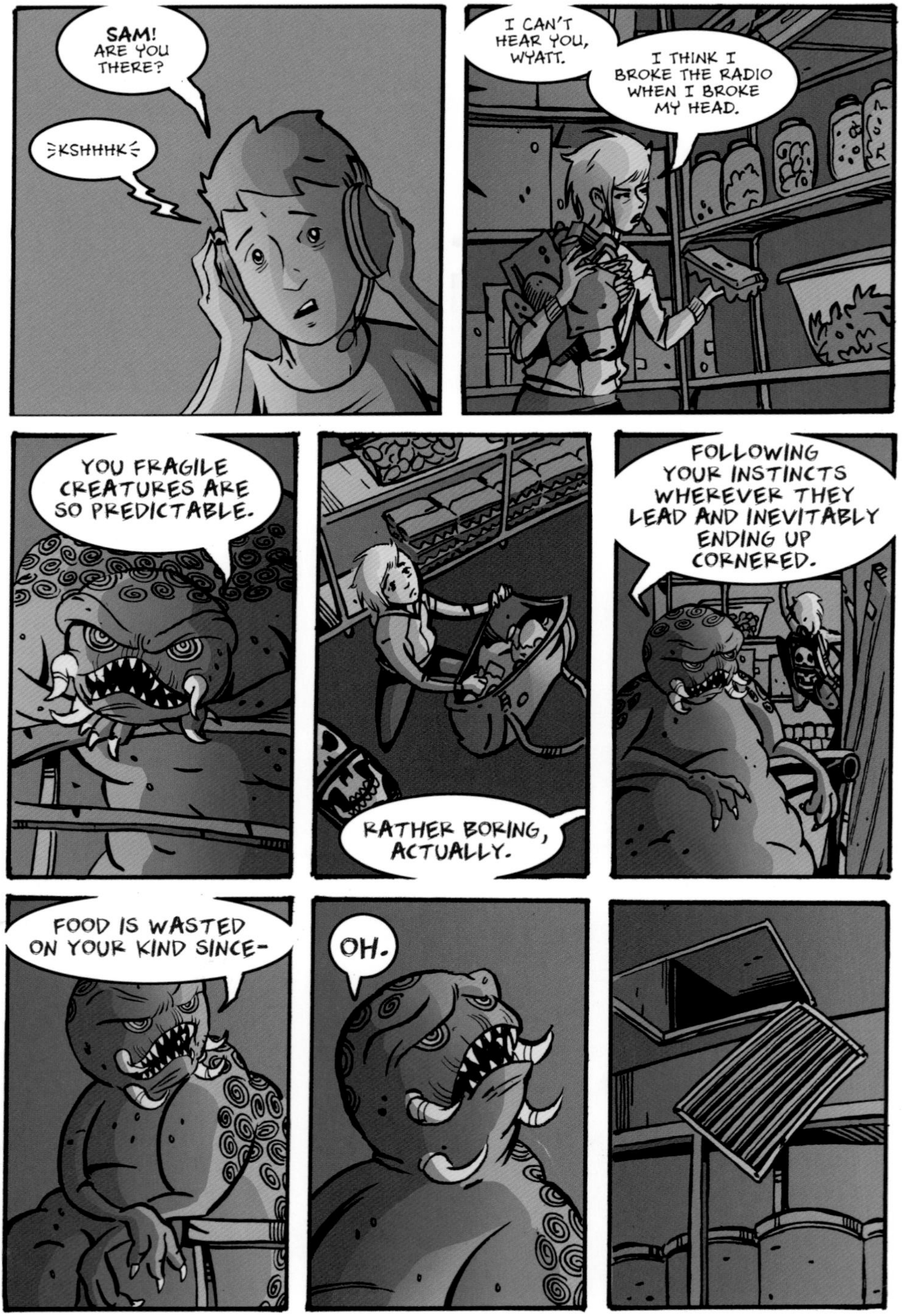
SAM! ARE YOU THERE?
KSHHHK
I CAN'T HEAR YOU, WYATT.
I THINK I BROKE THE RADIO WHEN I BROKE MY HEAD.
YOU FRAGILE CREATURES ARE SO PREDICTABLE.
RATHER BORING, ACTUALLY.
FOLLOWING YOUR INSTINCTS WHEREVER THEY LEAD AND INEVITABLY ENDING UP CORNERED.
FOOD IS WASTED ON YOUR KIND SINCE-
OH.

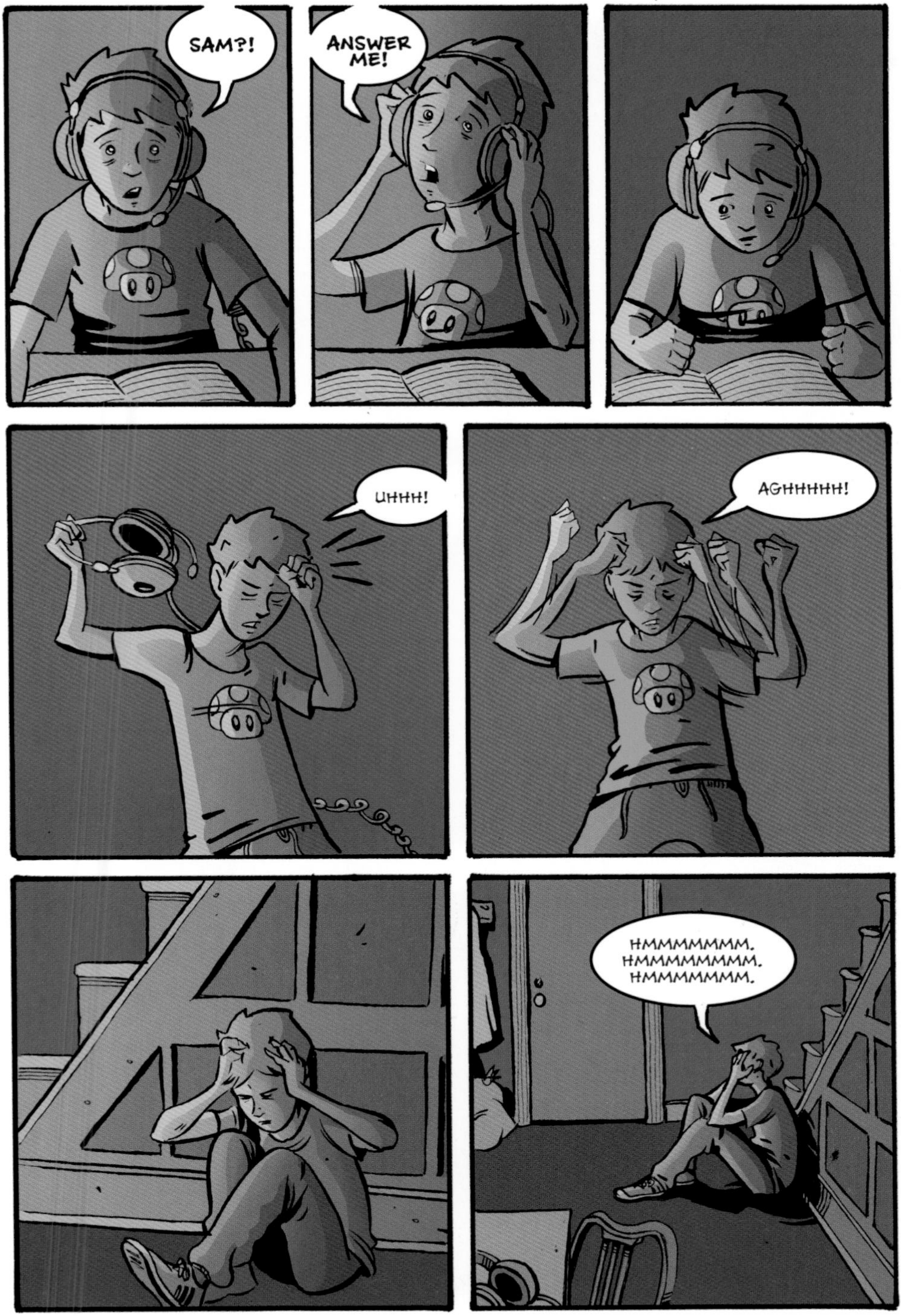
SAM?!
ANSWER ME!
UHHH!
AGHHHHH!
HMMMMMMM.
HMMMMMMMM.
HMMMMMMM.

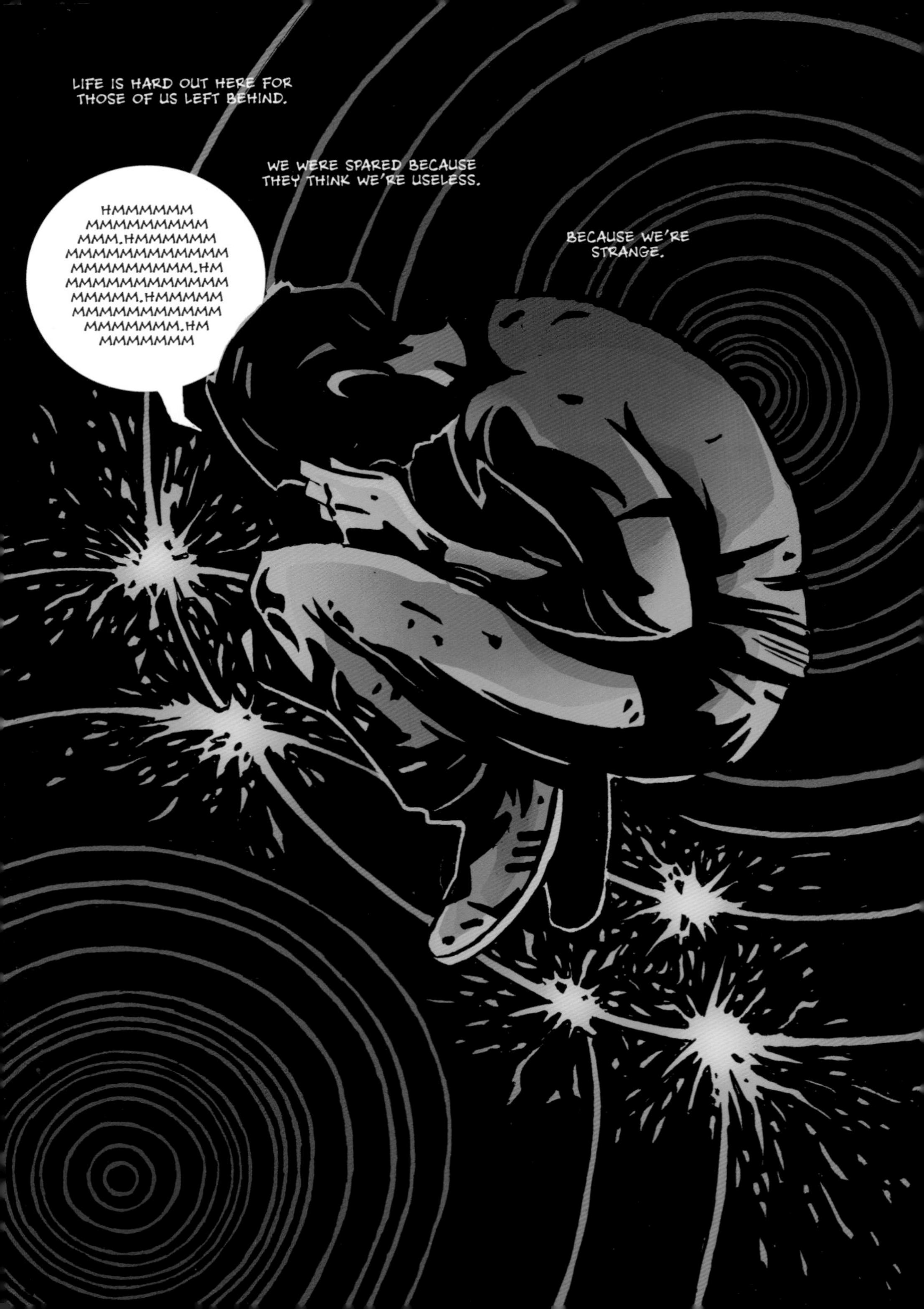
LIFE IS HARD OUT HERE FOR THOSE OF US LEFT BEHIND.
WE WERE SPARED BECAUSE THEY THINK WE'RE USELESS.
HMMMMMMM MMMMMMMMM MMM.HMMMMMM MMMMMMMMMMMMM MMMMMMMMM.HM MMMMMMMMMMMMM MMMMM.HMMMMM MMMMMMMMMMMM MMMMMMM.HM MMMMMMM
BECAUSE WE'RE STRANGE.

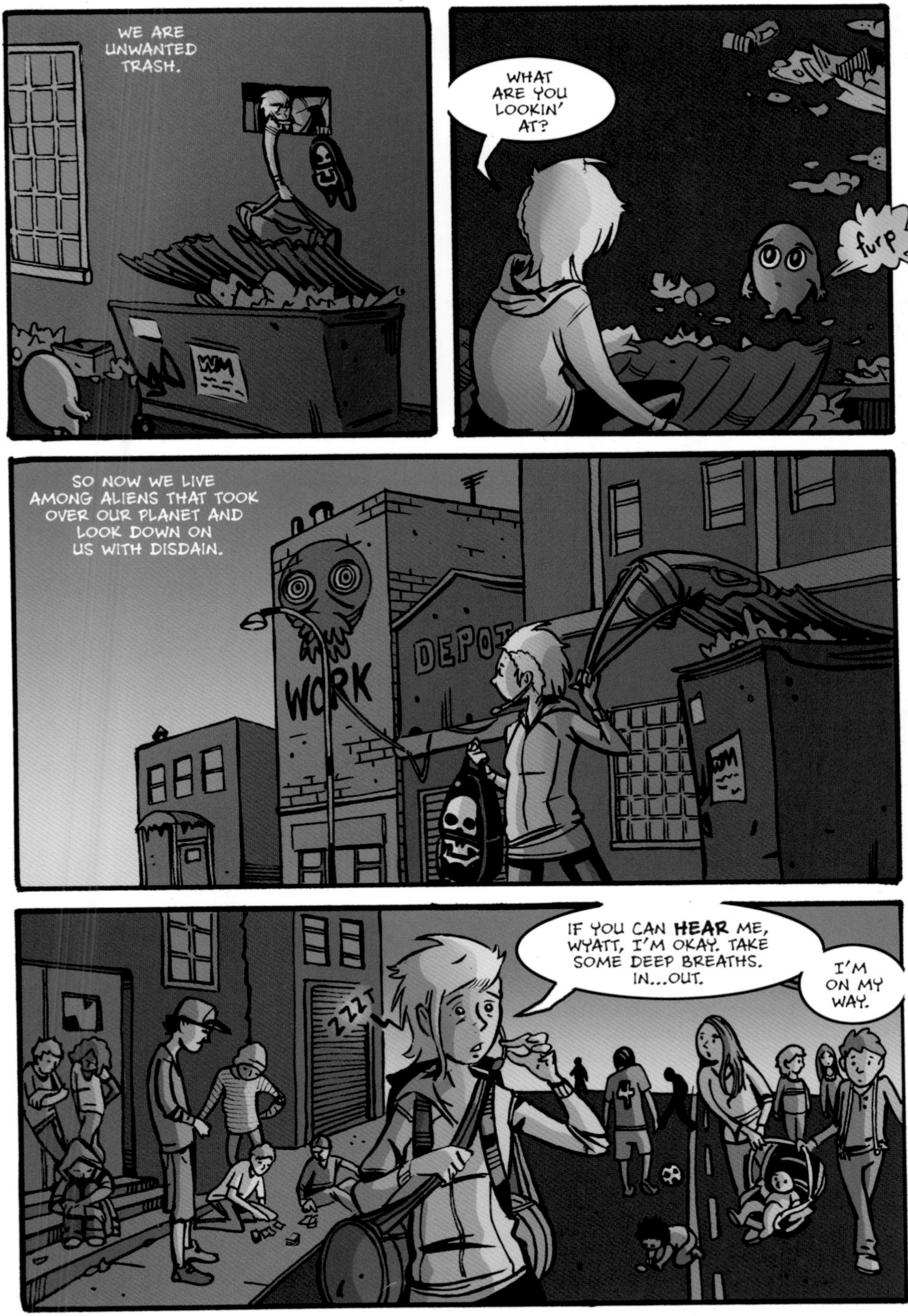
WE ARE UNWANTED TRASH.
WM
WHAT ARE YOU LOOKIN' AT?
furp
SO NOW WE LIVE AMONG ALIENS THAT TOOK OVER OUR PLANET AND LOOK DOWN ON US WITH DISDAIN.
WORK
DEPOT
WM
ZZZT
IF YOU CAN **HEAR** ME, WYATT, I'M OKAY. TAKE SOME DEEP BREATHS. IN...OUT.
I'M ON MY WAY.

WE WERE LEFT BEHIND BECAUSE WE WERE EITHER TOO YOUNG, TOO OLD, OR TOO "DISABLED."

MOM and DAD

ah and Jesse

Kris Thompson Dad

PAULA BRUNER
mother, sister, daughter

I HEARD IT WAS A GIRL.

STOLE FROM THE WAREHOUSE RIGHT UNDER THEIR NOSES.

AS IF WE DIDN'T ALREADY HAVE ENOUGH REASONS TO FEEL BAD ABOUT OURSELVES.

R U USEFUL

BEGINNING TODAY, WE WILL BE REDUCING YOUR WEEKLY RATIONS BY HALF.

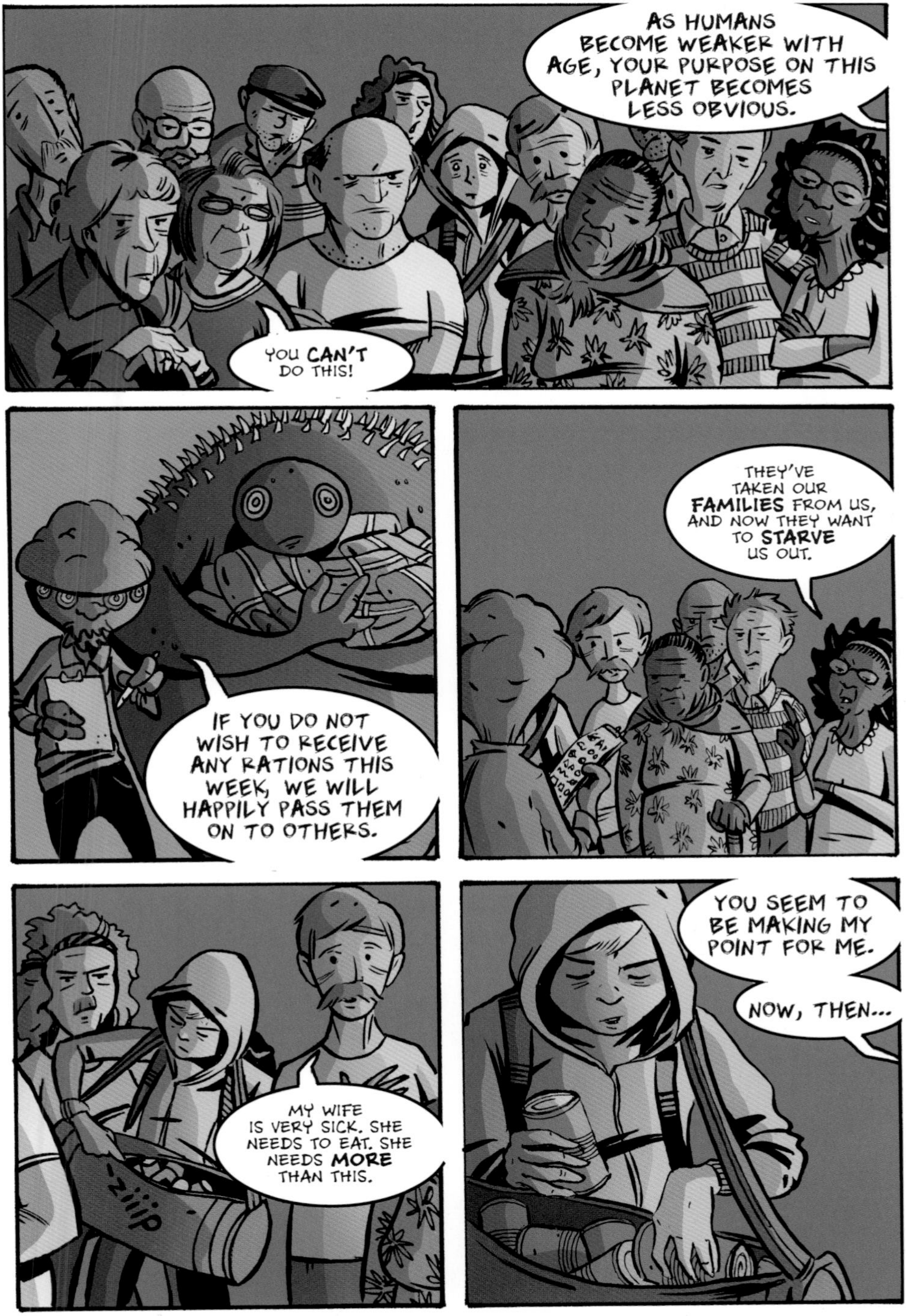
AS HUMANS BECOME WEAKER WITH AGE, YOUR PURPOSE ON THIS PLANET BECOMES LESS OBVIOUS.
YOU CAN'T DO THIS!
IF YOU DO NOT WISH TO RECEIVE ANY RATIONS THIS WEEK, WE WILL HAPPILY PASS THEM ON TO OTHERS.
THEY'VE TAKEN OUR FAMILIES FROM US, AND NOW THEY WANT TO STARVE US OUT.
ZIIIP
MY WIFE IS VERY SICK. SHE NEEDS TO EAT. SHE NEEDS MORE THAN THIS.
YOU SEEM TO BE MAKING MY POINT FOR ME.
NOW, THEN...

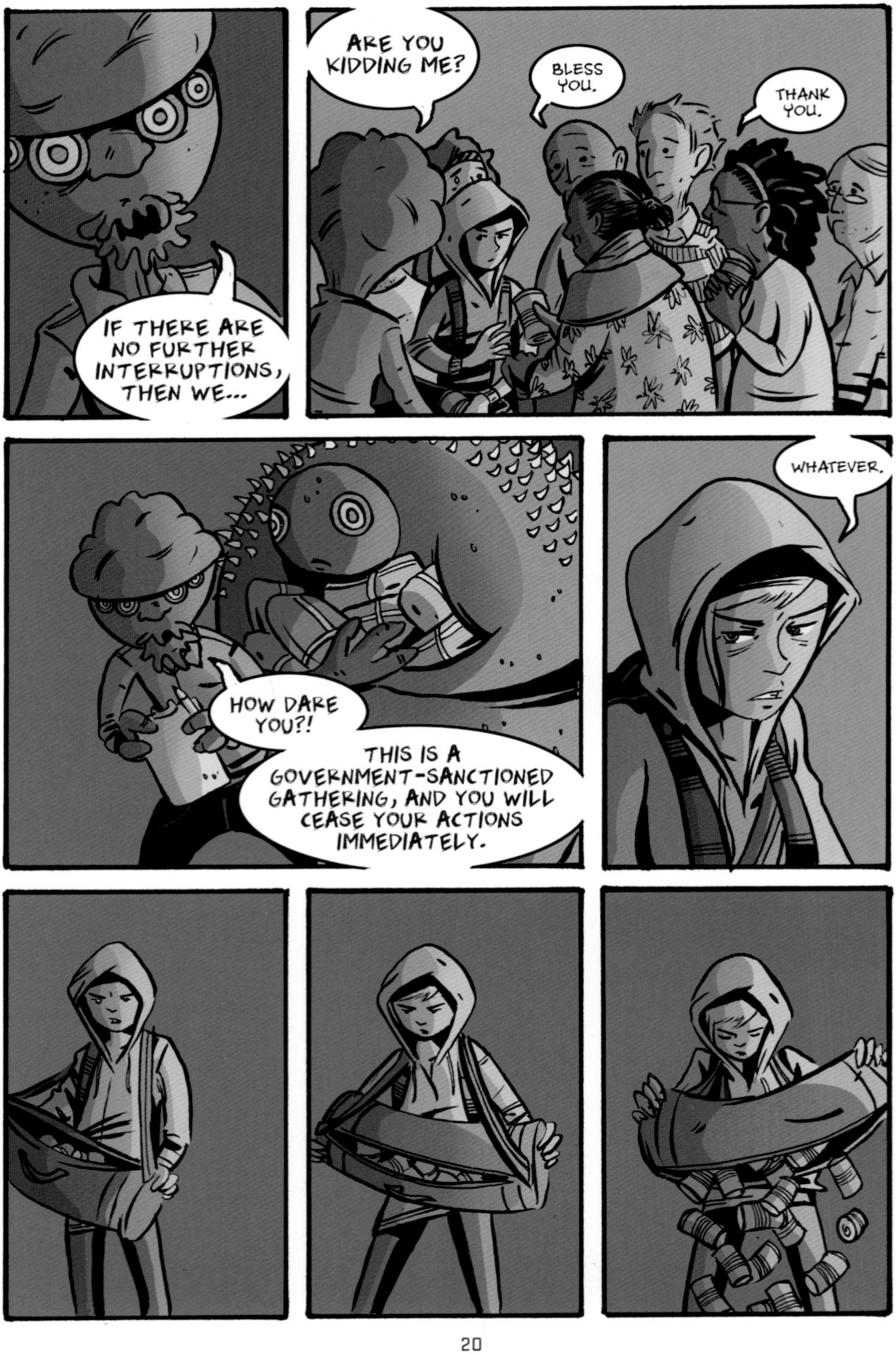
IF THERE ARE NO FURTHER INTERRUPTIONS, THEN WE...
ARE YOU KIDDING ME?
BLESS YOU.
THANK YOU.
HOW DARE YOU?!
THIS IS A GOVERNMENT-SANCTIONED GATHERING, AND YOU WILL CEASE YOUR ACTIONS IMMEDIATELY.
WHATEVER.

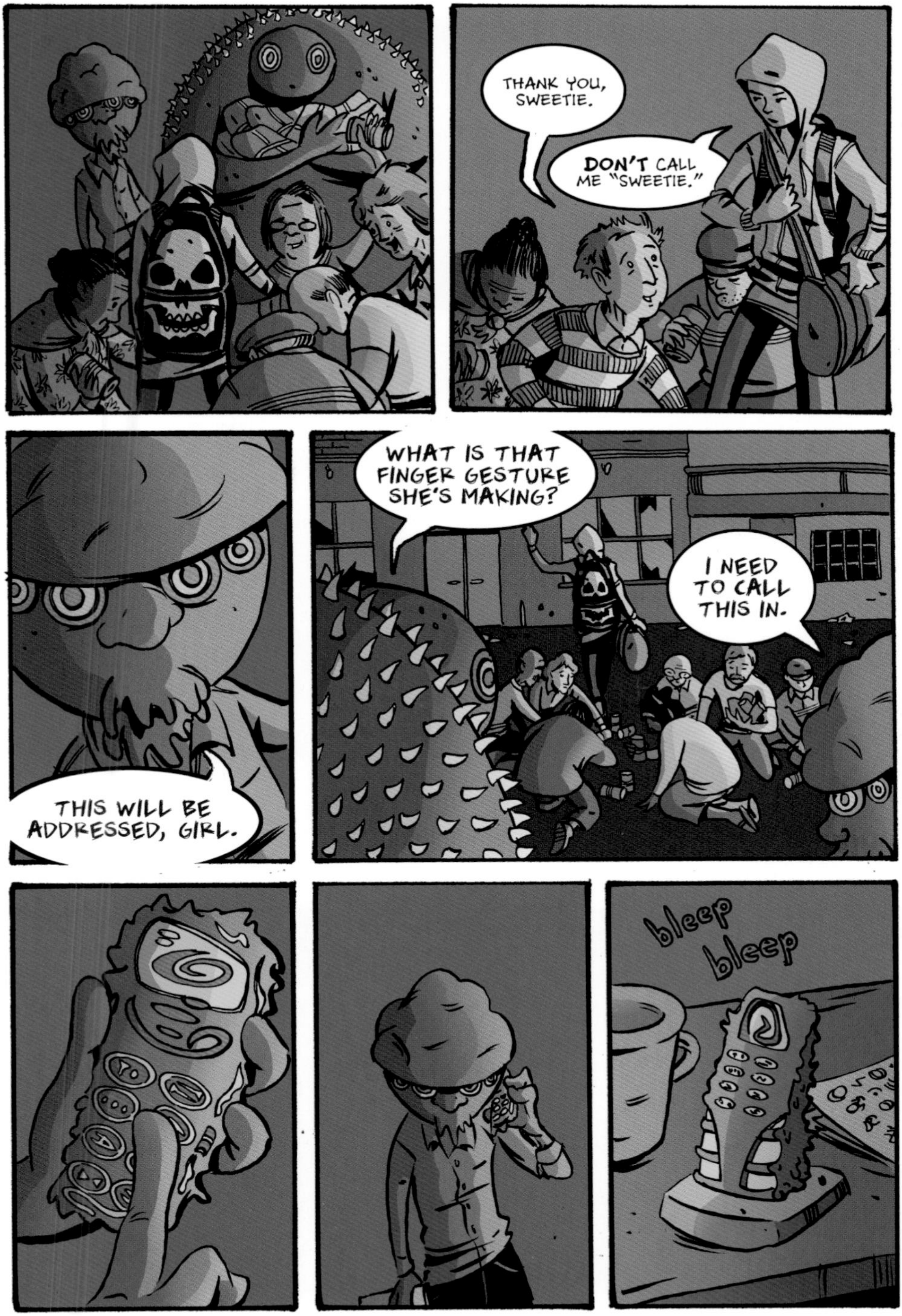
THANK YOU, SWEETIE.
DON'T CALL ME "SWEETIE."
THIS WILL BE ADDRESSED, GIRL.
WHAT IS THAT FINGER GESTURE SHE'S MAKING?
I NEED TO CALL THIS IN.
bleep bleep

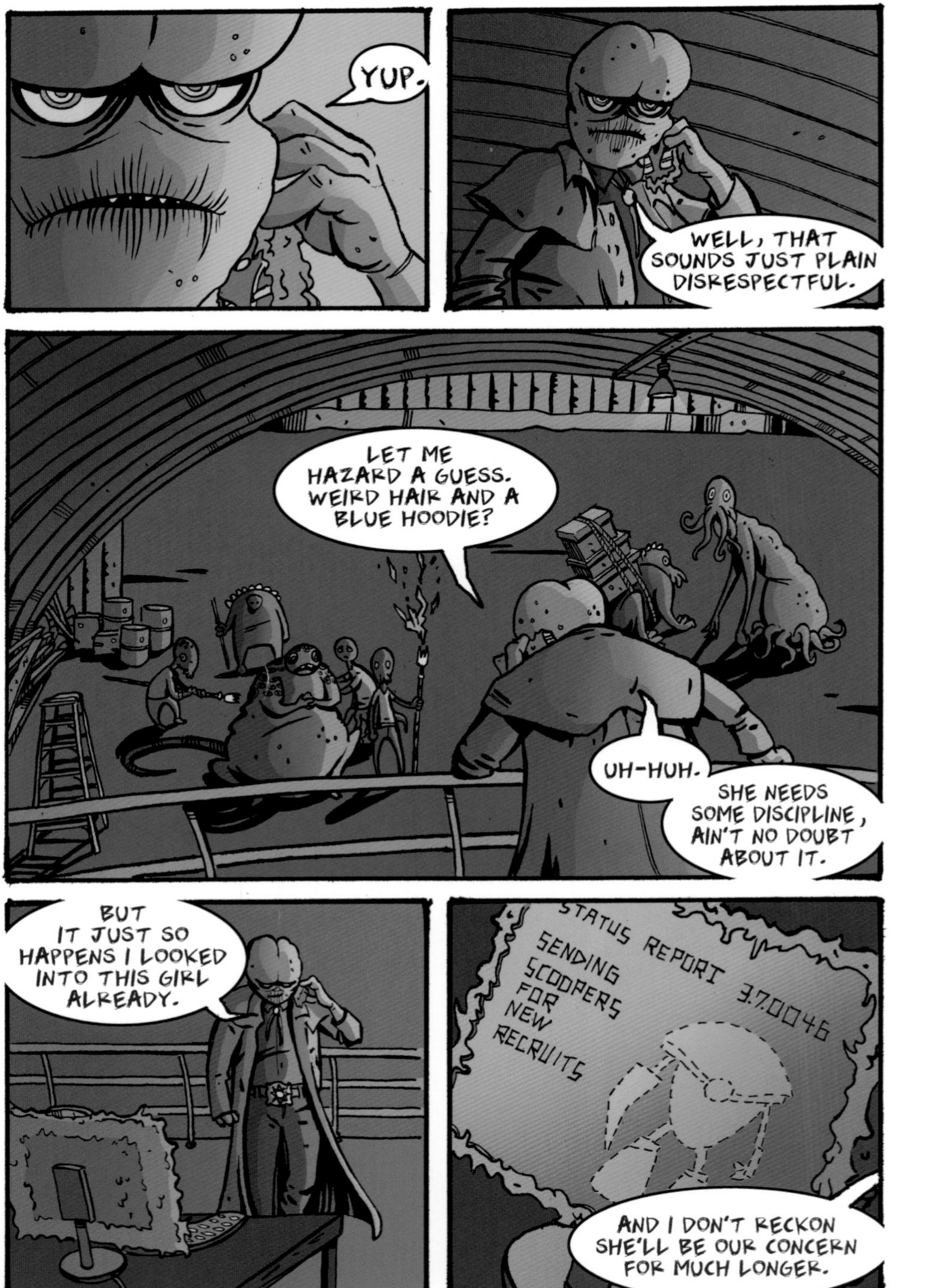
YUP.
WELL, THAT SOUNDS JUST PLAIN DISRESPECTFUL.
LET ME HAZARD A GUESS. WEIRD HAIR AND A BLUE HOODIE?
UH-HUH.
SHE NEEDS SOME DISCIPLINE, AIN'T NO DOUBT ABOUT IT.
BUT IT JUST SO HAPPENS I LOOKED INTO THIS GIRL ALREADY.
STATUS REPORT 3.7.0046
SENDING SCOOPERS FOR NEW RECRUITS
AND I DON'T RECKON SHE'LL BE OUR CONCERN FOR MUCH LONGER.

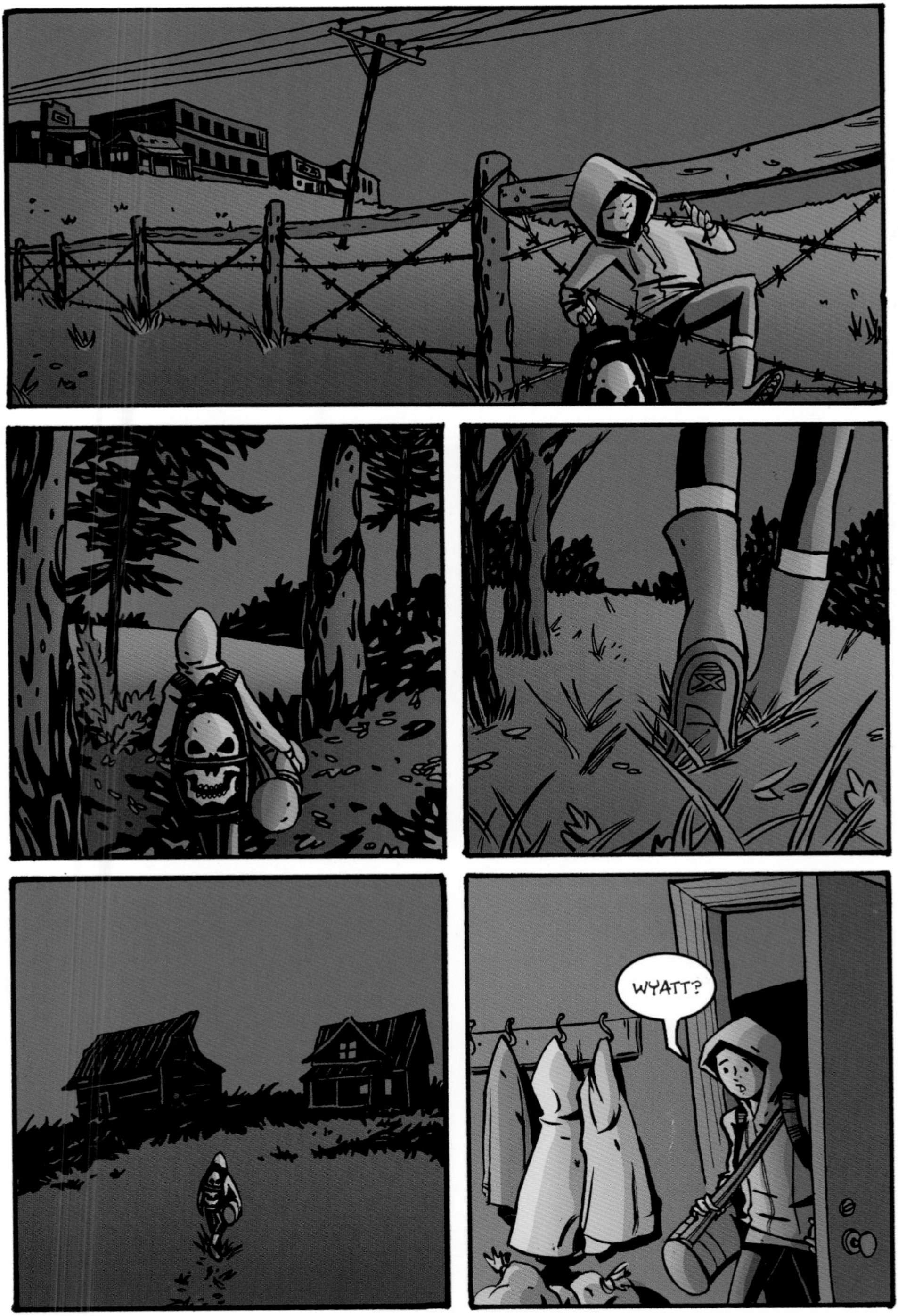
WYATT?

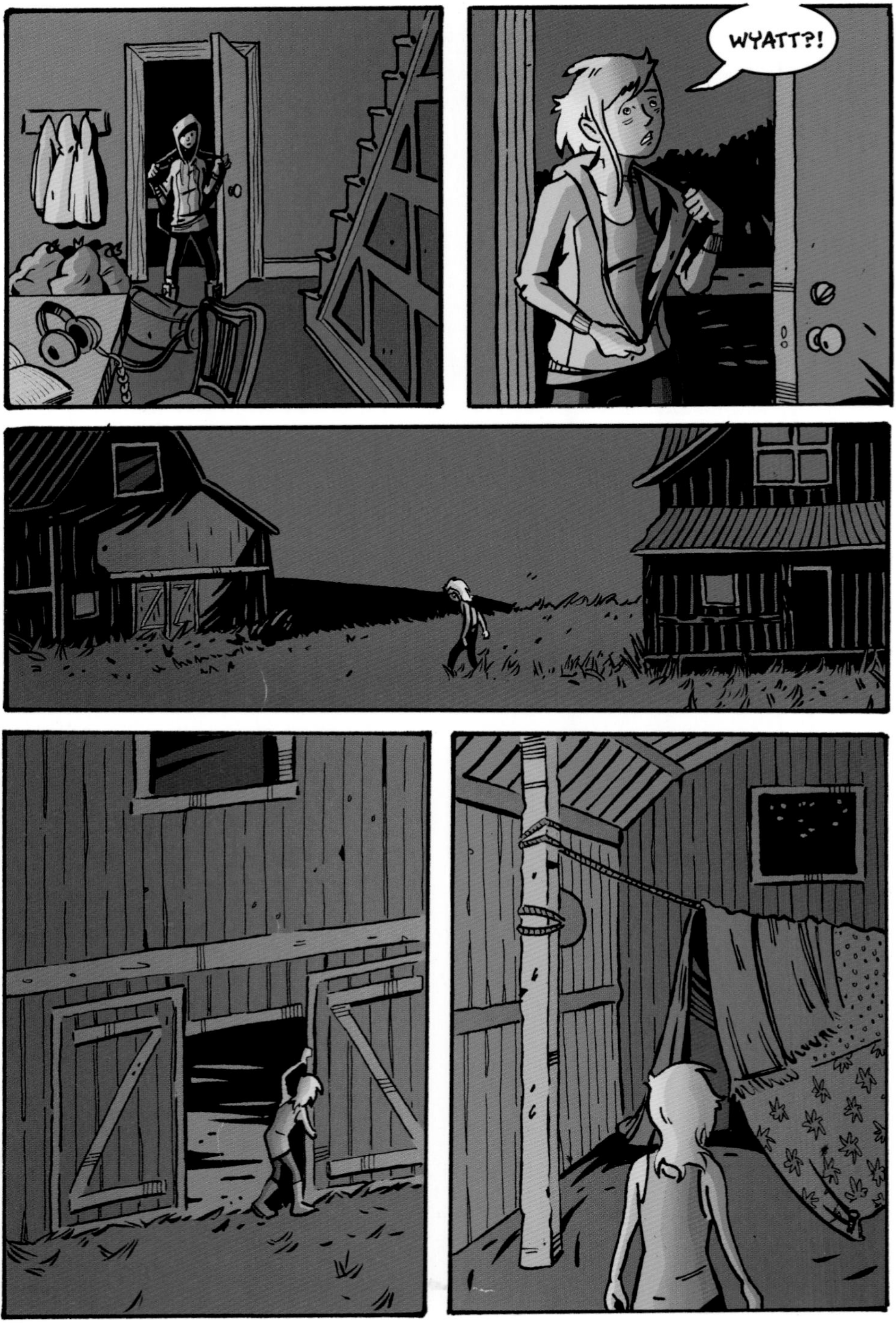
WYATT?!

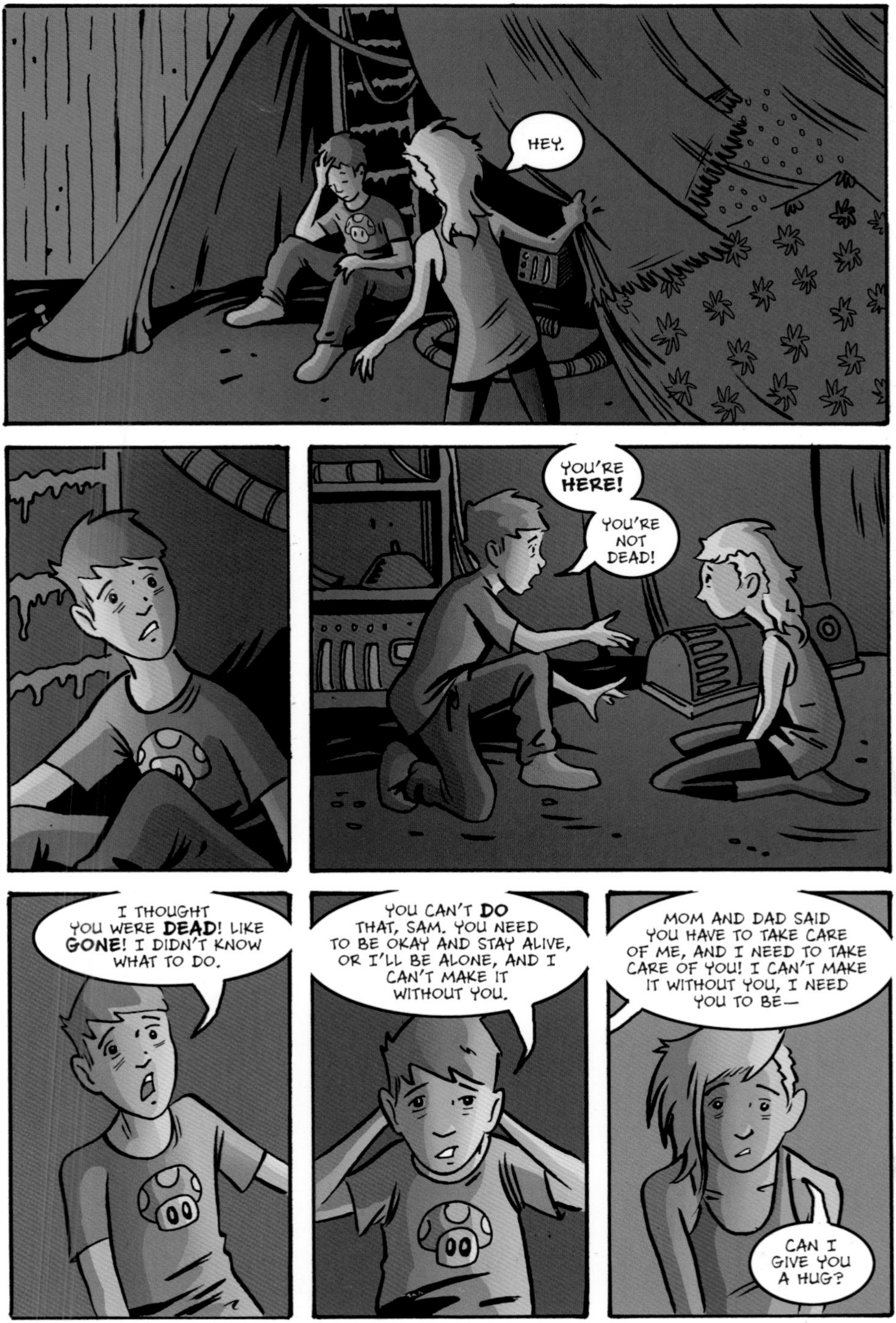
HEY.
YOU'RE HERE!
YOU'RE NOT DEAD!
I THOUGHT YOU WERE DEAD! LIKE GONE! I DIDN'T KNOW WHAT TO DO.
YOU CAN'T DO THAT, SAM. YOU NEED TO BE OKAY AND STAY ALIVE, OR I'LL BE ALONE, AND I CAN'T MAKE IT WITHOUT YOU.
MOM AND DAD SAID YOU HAVE TO TAKE CARE OF ME, AND I NEED TO TAKE CARE OF YOU! I CAN'T MAKE IT WITHOUT YOU, I NEED YOU TO BE—
CAN I GIVE YOU A HUG?

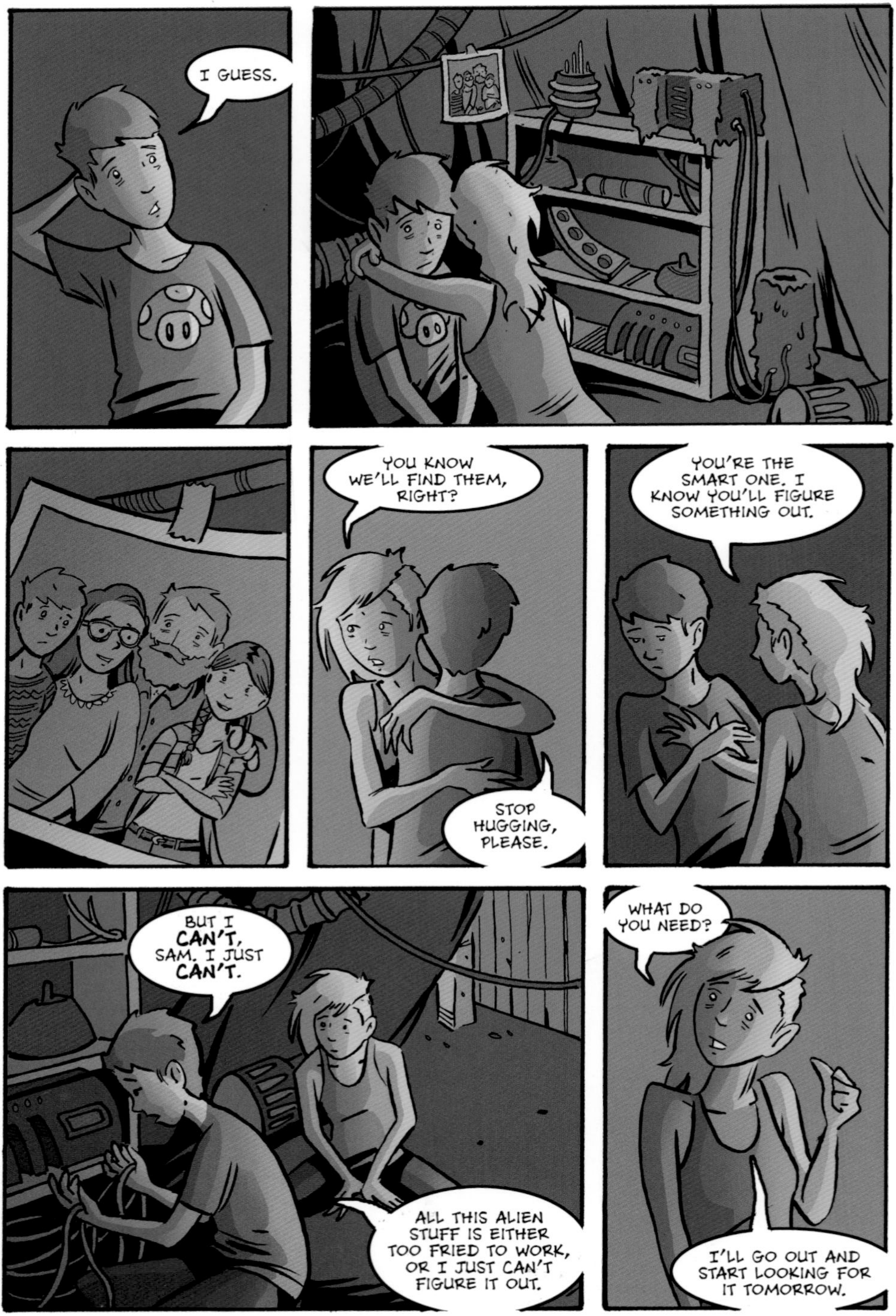
I GUESS.
YOU KNOW WE'LL FIND THEM, RIGHT?
STOP HUGGING, PLEASE.
YOU'RE THE SMART ONE. I KNOW YOU'LL FIGURE SOMETHING OUT.
BUT I CAN'T, SAM. I JUST CAN'T.
ALL THIS ALIEN STUFF IS EITHER TOO FRIED TO WORK, OR I JUST CAN'T FIGURE IT OUT.
WHAT DO YOU NEED?
I'LL GO OUT AND START LOOKING FOR IT TOMORROW.

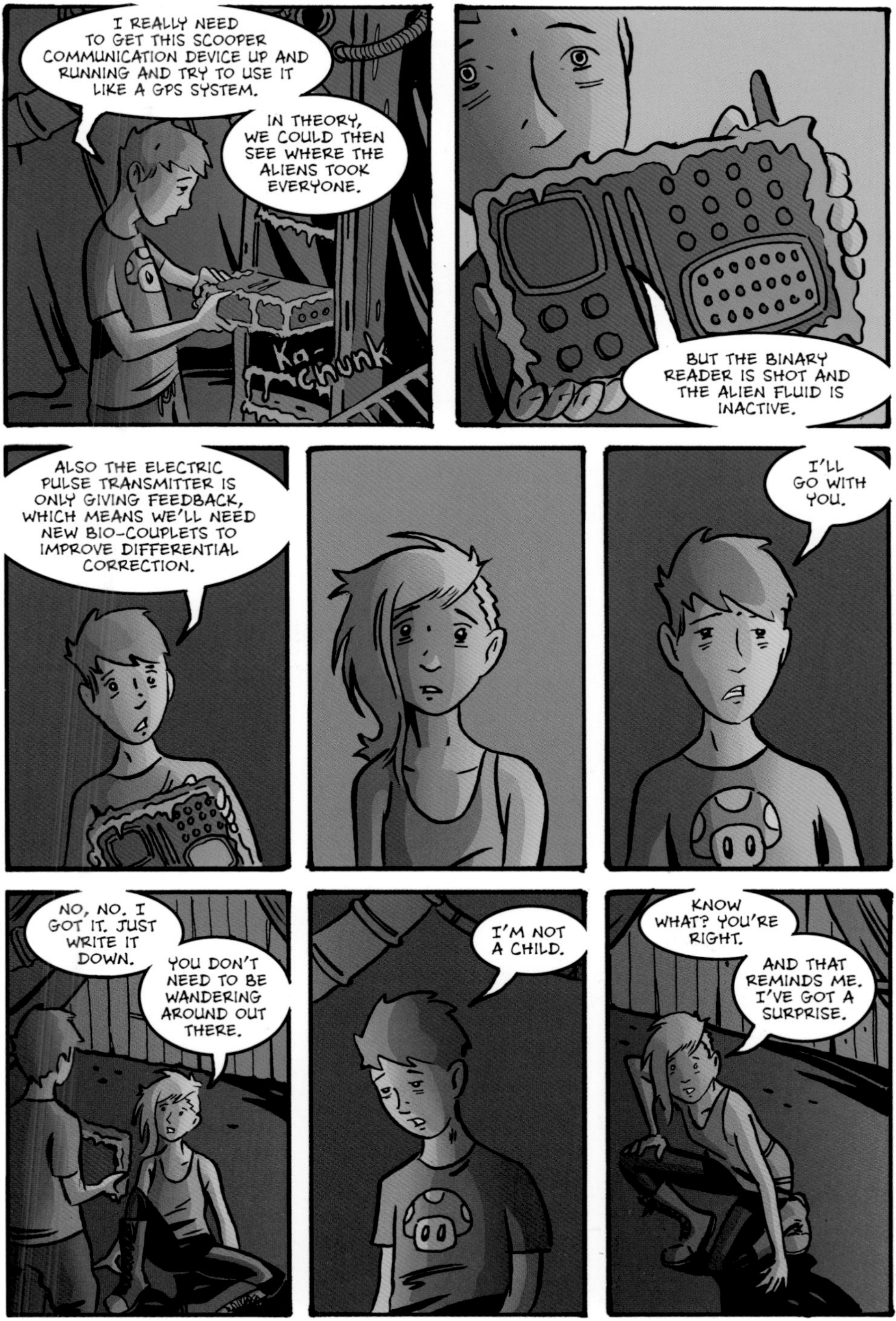
I REALLY NEED TO GET THIS SCOOPER COMMUNICATION DEVICE UP AND RUNNING AND TRY TO USE IT LIKE A GPS SYSTEM.
IN THEORY, WE COULD THEN SEE WHERE THE ALIENS TOOK EVERYONE.
Ka-chunk
BUT THE BINARY READER IS SHOT AND THE ALIEN FLUID IS INACTIVE.
ALSO THE ELECTRIC PULSE TRANSMITTER IS ONLY GIVING FEEDBACK, WHICH MEANS WE'LL NEED NEW BIO-COUPLETS TO IMPROVE DIFFERENTIAL CORRECTION.
I'LL GO WITH YOU.
NO, NO. I GOT IT. JUST WRITE IT DOWN.
YOU DON'T NEED TO BE WANDERING AROUND OUT THERE.
I'M NOT A CHILD.
KNOW WHAT? YOU'RE RIGHT.
AND THAT REMINDS ME. I'VE GOT A SURPRISE.

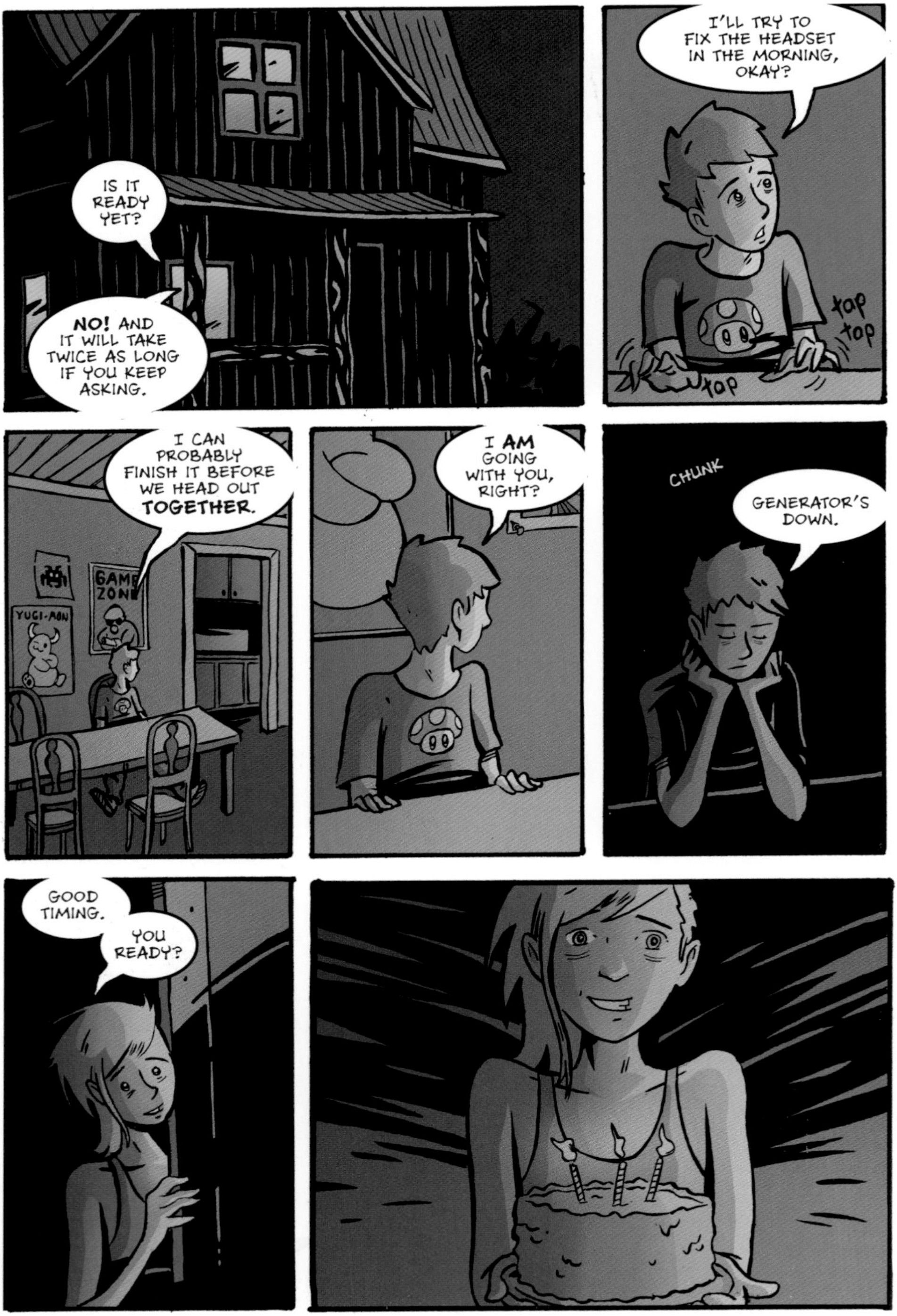
IS IT READY YET?
NO! AND IT WILL TAKE TWICE AS LONG IF YOU KEEP ASKING.
I'LL TRY TO FIX THE HEADSET IN THE MORNING, OKAY?
tap tap
tap
I CAN PROBABLY FINISH IT BEFORE WE HEAD OUT TOGETHER.
GAME ZONE
YUGI-MON
I AM GOING WITH YOU, RIGHT?
CHUNK
GENERATOR'S DOWN.
GOOD TIMING.
YOU READY?

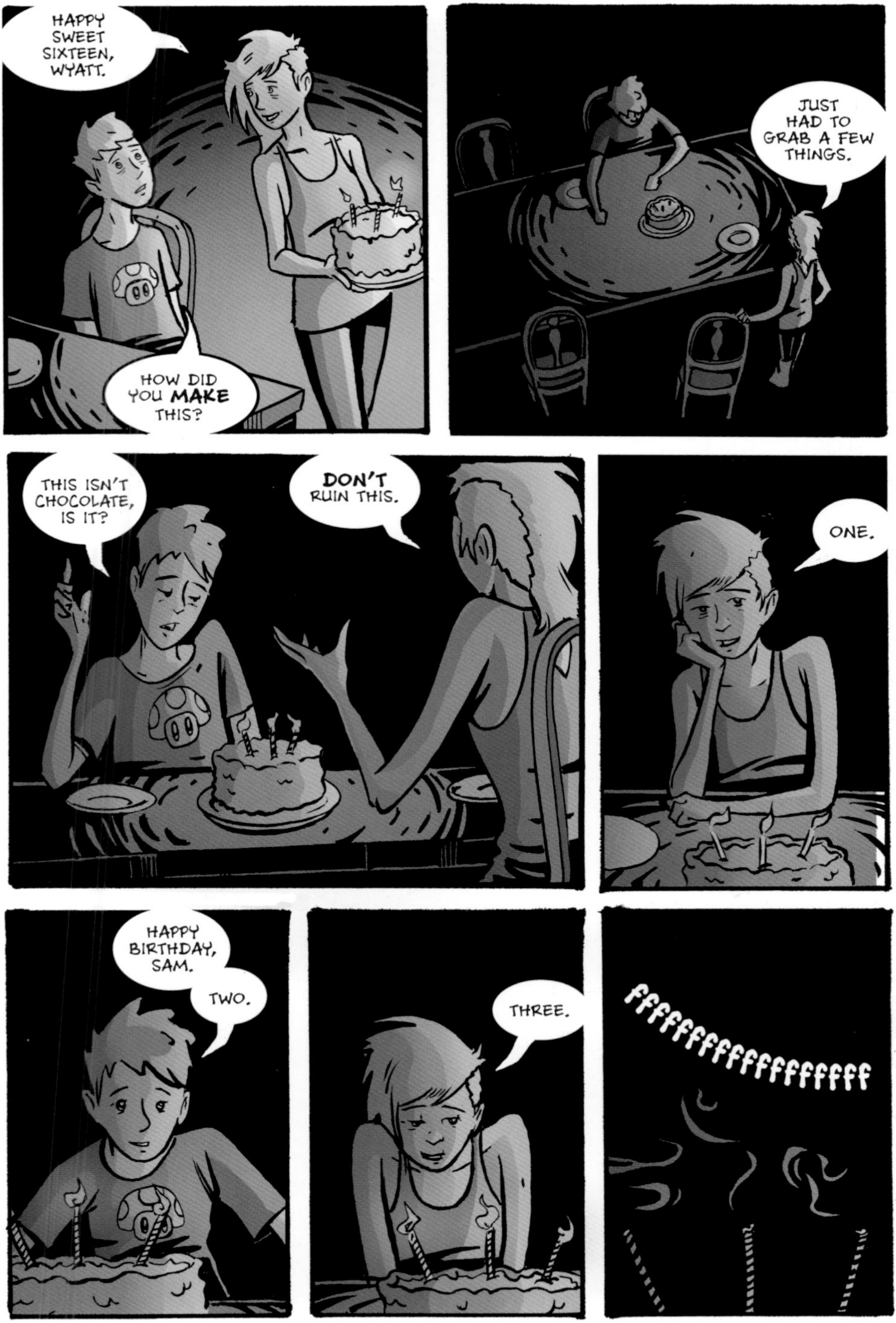
HAPPY SWEET SIXTEEN, WYATT.
HOW DID YOU MAKE THIS?
JUST HAD TO GRAB A FEW THINGS.
THIS ISN'T CHOCOLATE, IS IT?
DON'T RUIN THIS.
ONE.
HAPPY BIRTHDAY, SAM.
TWO.
THREE.
ffffffffffffffffffff

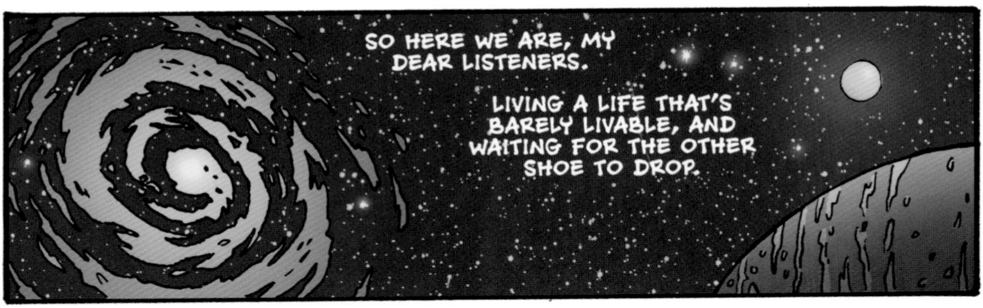
SO HERE WE ARE, MY DEAR LISTENERS.
LIVING A LIFE THAT'S BARELY LIVABLE, AND WAITING FOR THE OTHER SHOE TO DROP.

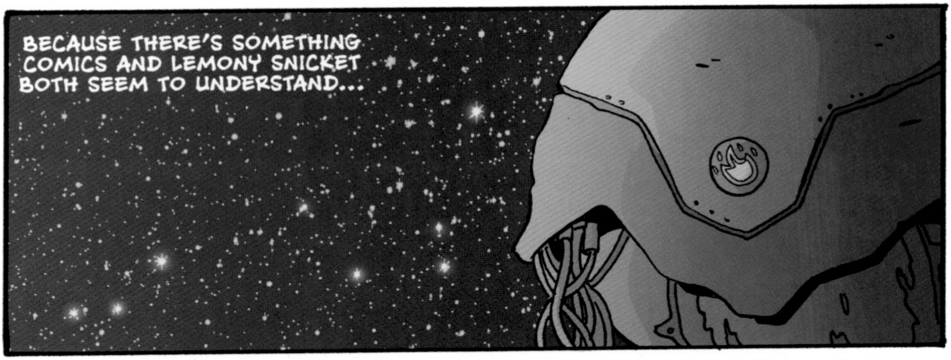
BECAUSE THERE'S SOMETHING COMICS AND LEMONY SNICKET BOTH SEEM TO UNDERSTAND...

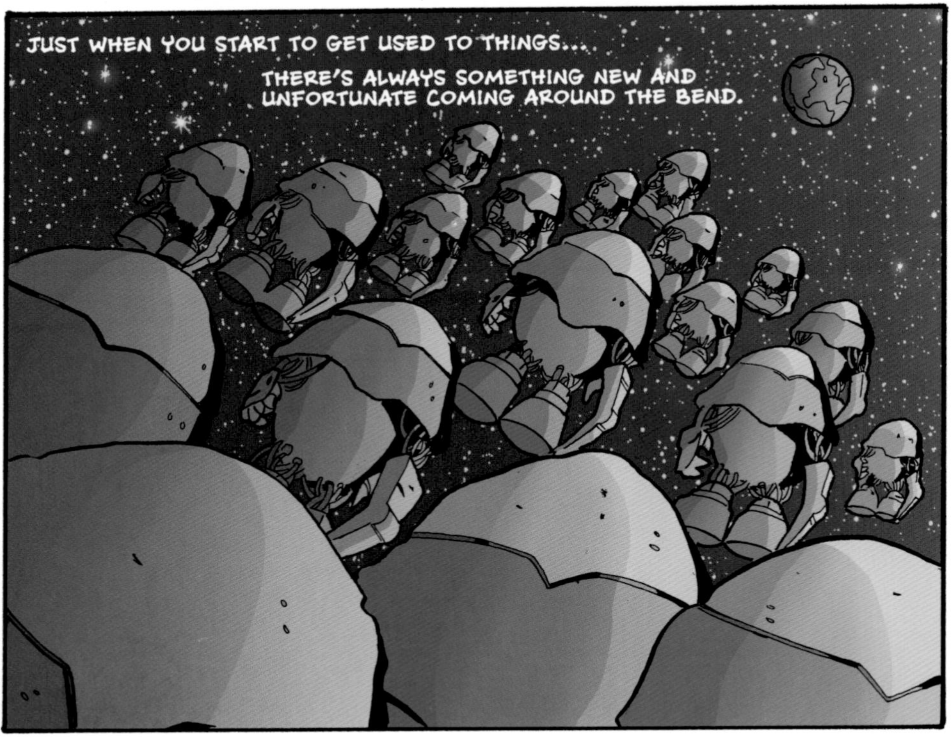
JUST WHEN YOU START TO GET USED TO THINGS...
THERE'S ALWAYS SOMETHING NEW AND UNFORTUNATE COMING AROUND THE BEND.

CHAPTER TWO

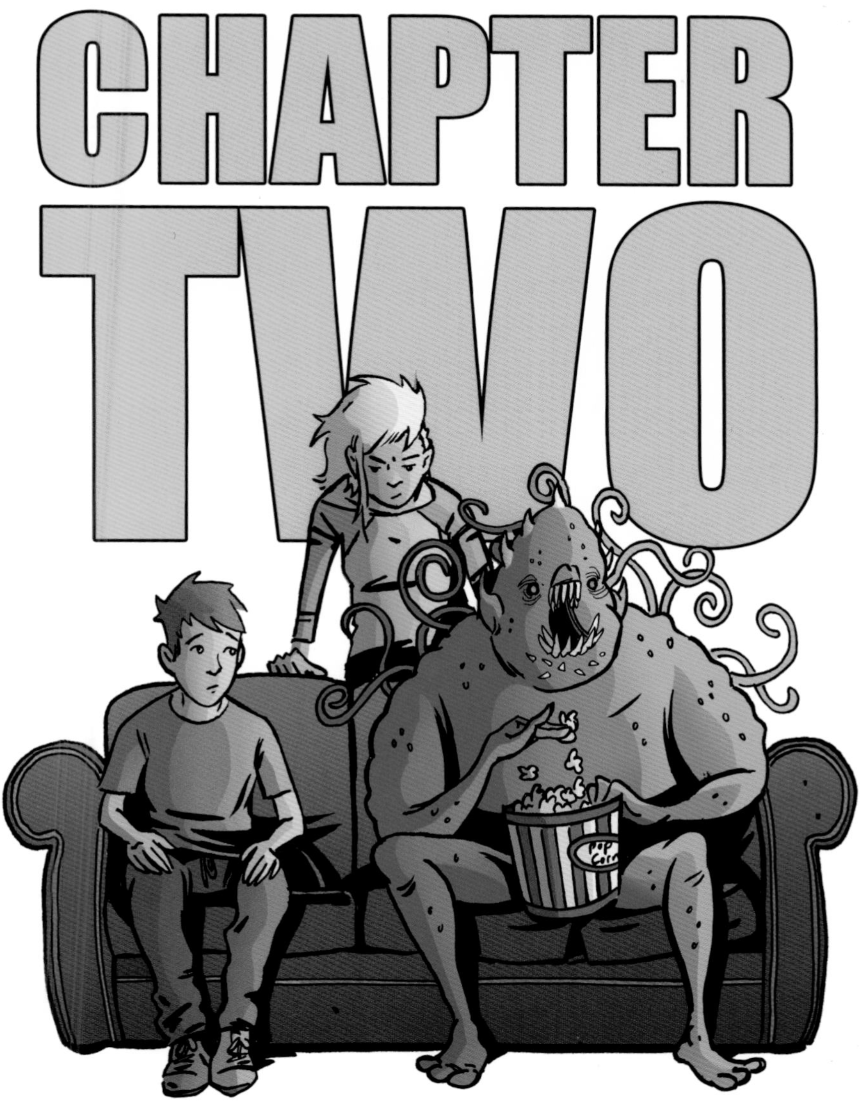

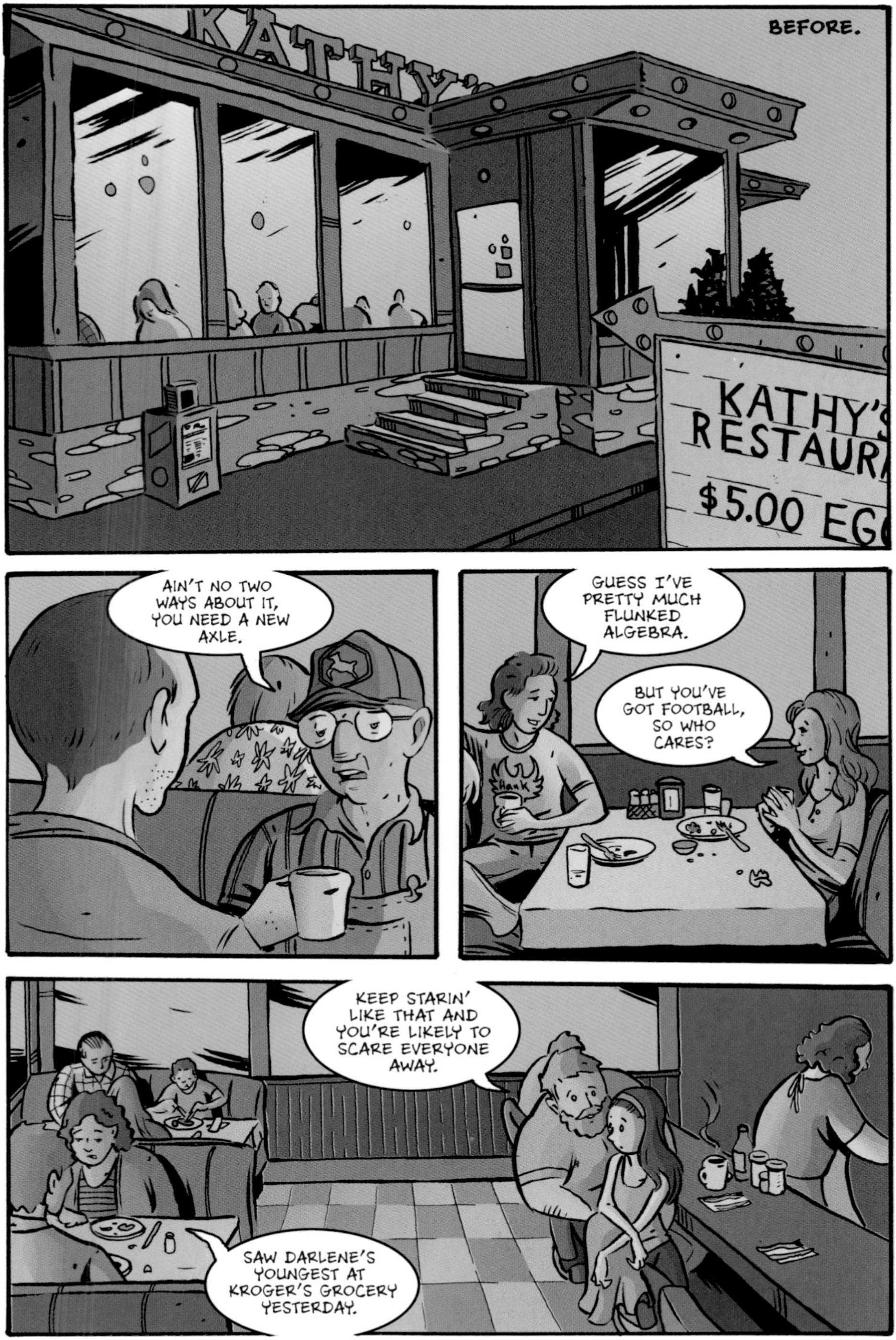
BEFORE.
KATHY'S
KATHY'S RESTAURA
$5.00 EG
AIN'T NO TWO WAYS ABOUT IT, YOU NEED A NEW AXLE.
GUESS I'VE PRETTY MUCH FLUNKED ALGEBRA.
BUT YOU'VE GOT FOOTBALL, SO WHO CARES?
KEEP STARIN' LIKE THAT AND YOU'RE LIKELY TO SCARE EVERYONE AWAY.
SAW DARLENE'S YOUNGEST AT KROGER'S GROCERY YESTERDAY.

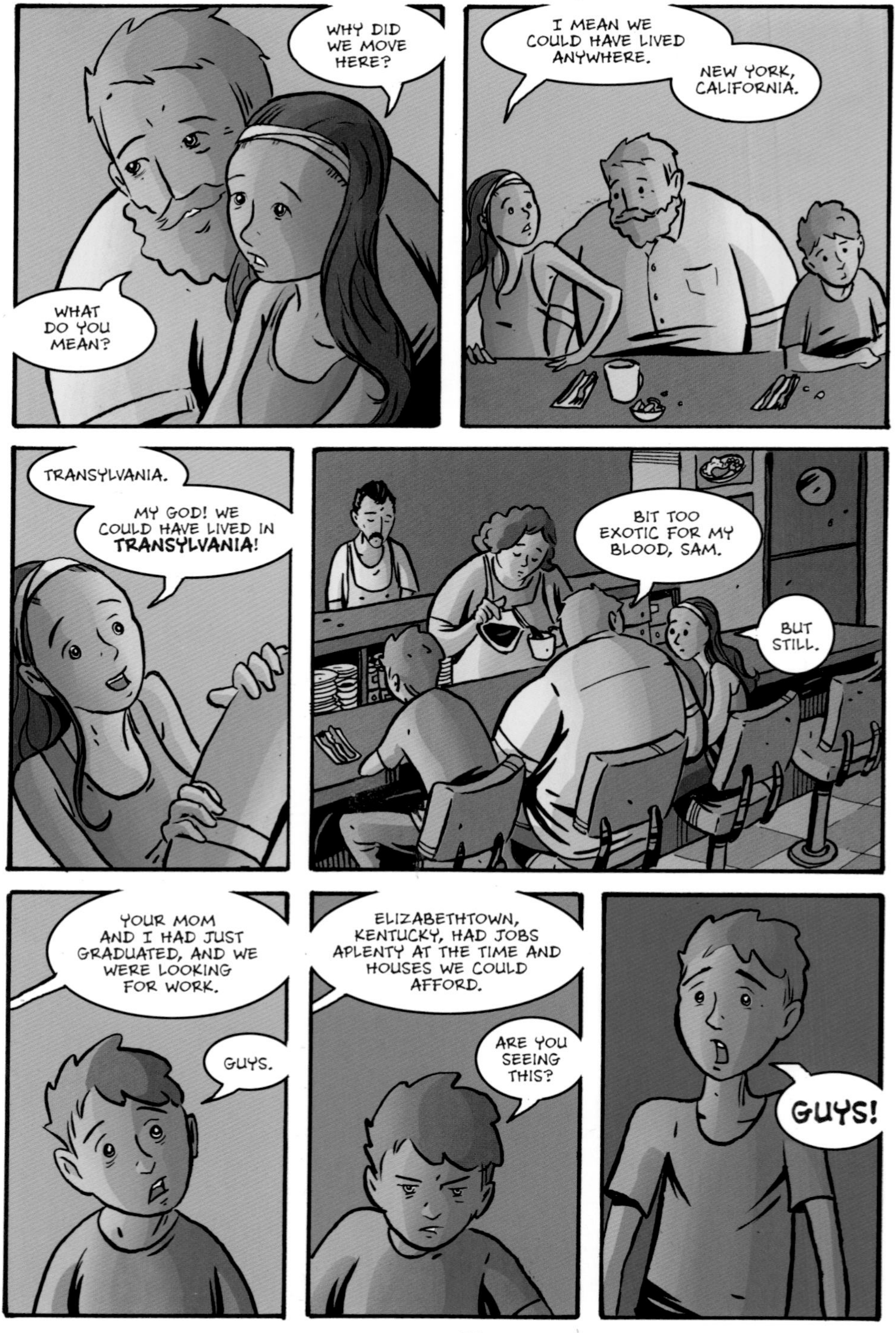
WHY DID WE MOVE HERE?
WHAT DO YOU MEAN?
I MEAN WE COULD HAVE LIVED ANYWHERE.
NEW YORK, CALIFORNIA.
TRANSYLVANIA.
MY GOD! WE COULD HAVE LIVED IN TRANSYLVANIA!
BIT TOO EXOTIC FOR MY BLOOD, SAM.
BUT STILL.
YOUR MOM AND I HAD JUST GRADUATED, AND WE WERE LOOKING FOR WORK.
GUYS.
ELIZABETHTOWN, KENTUCKY, HAD JOBS APLENTY AT THE TIME AND HOUSES WE COULD AFFORD.
ARE YOU SEEING THIS?
GUYS!

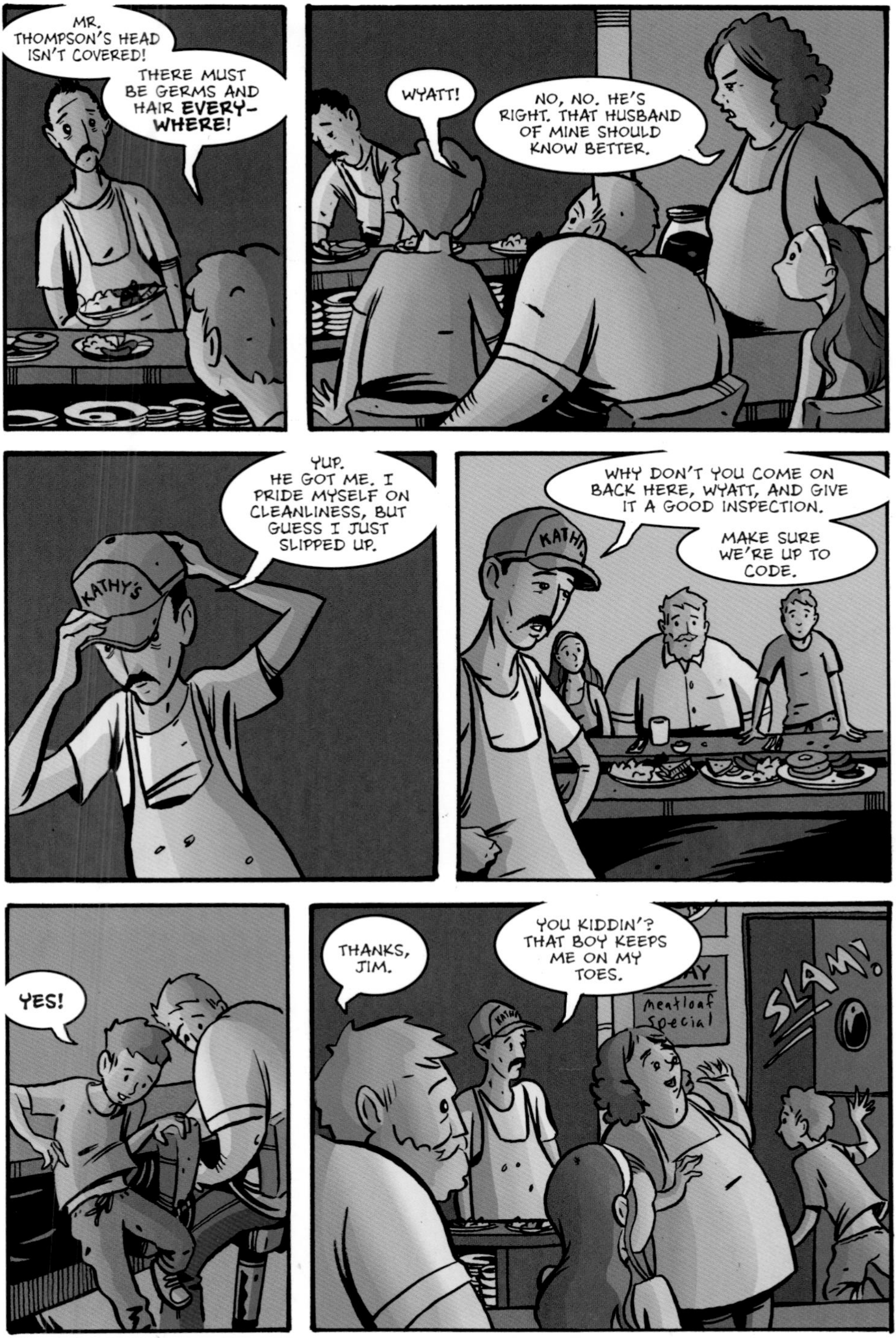
MR. THOMPSON'S HEAD ISN'T COVERED!
THERE MUST BE GERMS AND HAIR **EVERY-WHERE!**
WYATT!
NO, NO. HE'S RIGHT. THAT HUSBAND OF MINE SHOULD KNOW BETTER.
KATHY'S
YUP. HE GOT ME. I PRIDE MYSELF ON CLEANLINESS, BUT GUESS I JUST SLIPPED UP.
WHY DON'T YOU COME ON BACK HERE, WYATT, AND GIVE IT A GOOD INSPECTION.
MAKE SURE WE'RE UP TO CODE.
YES!
THANKS, JIM.
YOU KIDDIN'? THAT BOY KEEPS ME ON MY TOES.
meatloaf special
SLAM!

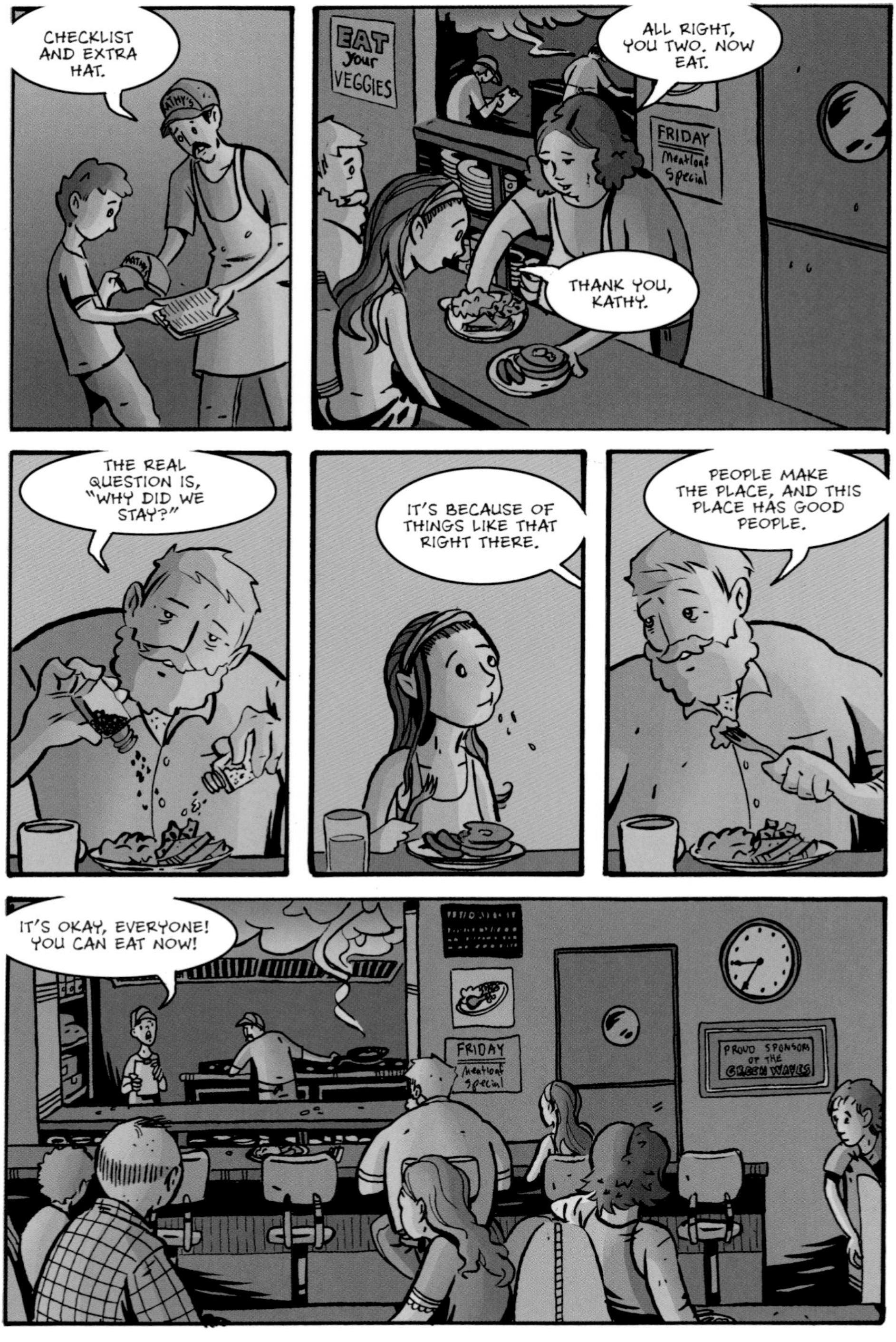
CHECKLIST AND EXTRA HAT.
KATHY'S
EAT your VEGGIES
ALL RIGHT, YOU TWO. NOW EAT.
FRIDAY Meatloaf Special
THANK YOU, KATHY.
THE REAL QUESTION IS, "WHY DID WE STAY?"
IT'S BECAUSE OF THINGS LIKE THAT RIGHT THERE.
PEOPLE MAKE THE PLACE, AND THIS PLACE HAS GOOD PEOPLE.
IT'S OKAY, EVERYONE! YOU CAN EAT NOW!
FRIDAY Meatloaf Special
PROUD SPONSORS OF THE GREEN WAVES

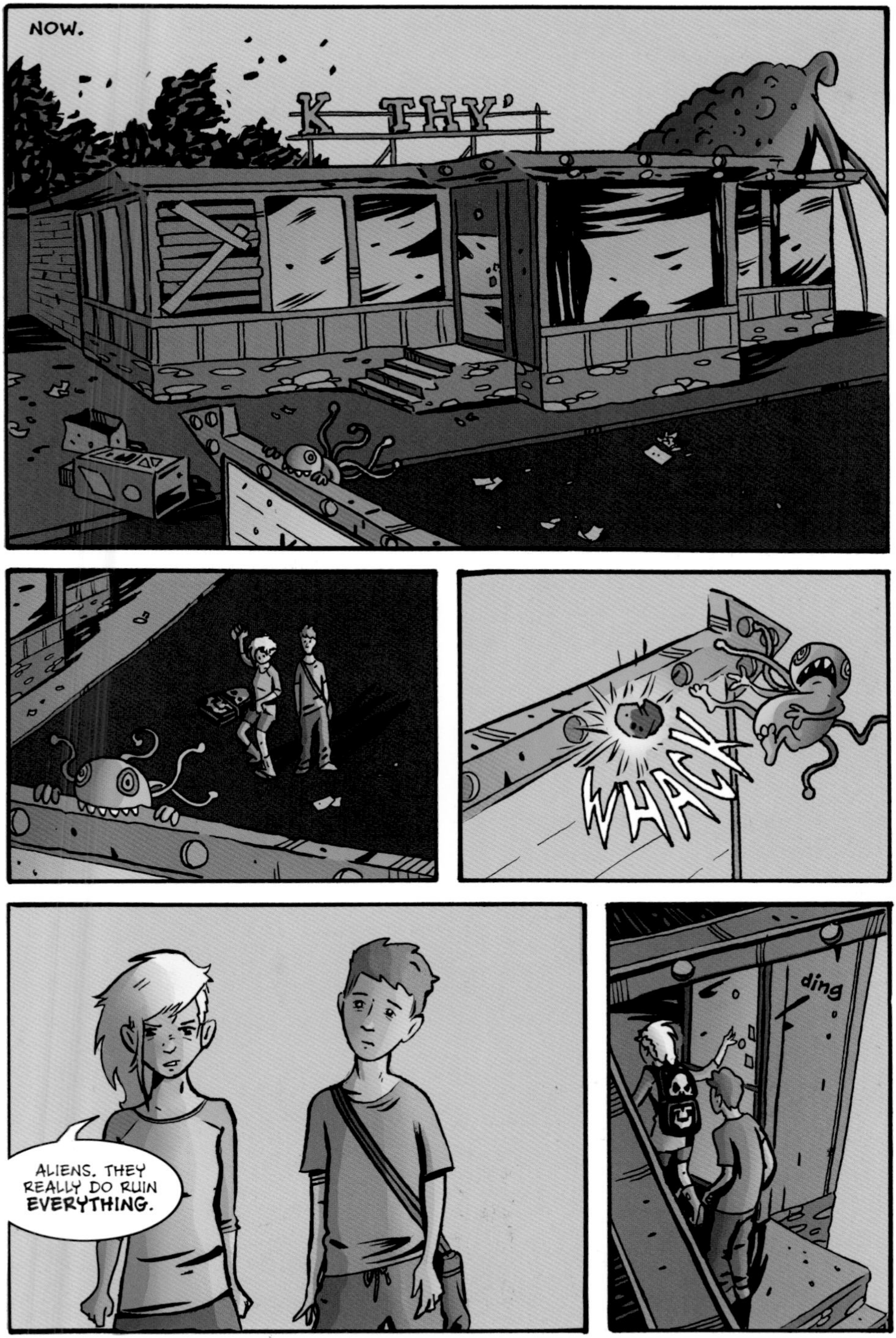
NOW.
K THY'
WHACK
ding
ALIENS. THEY REALLY DO RUIN EVERYTHING.

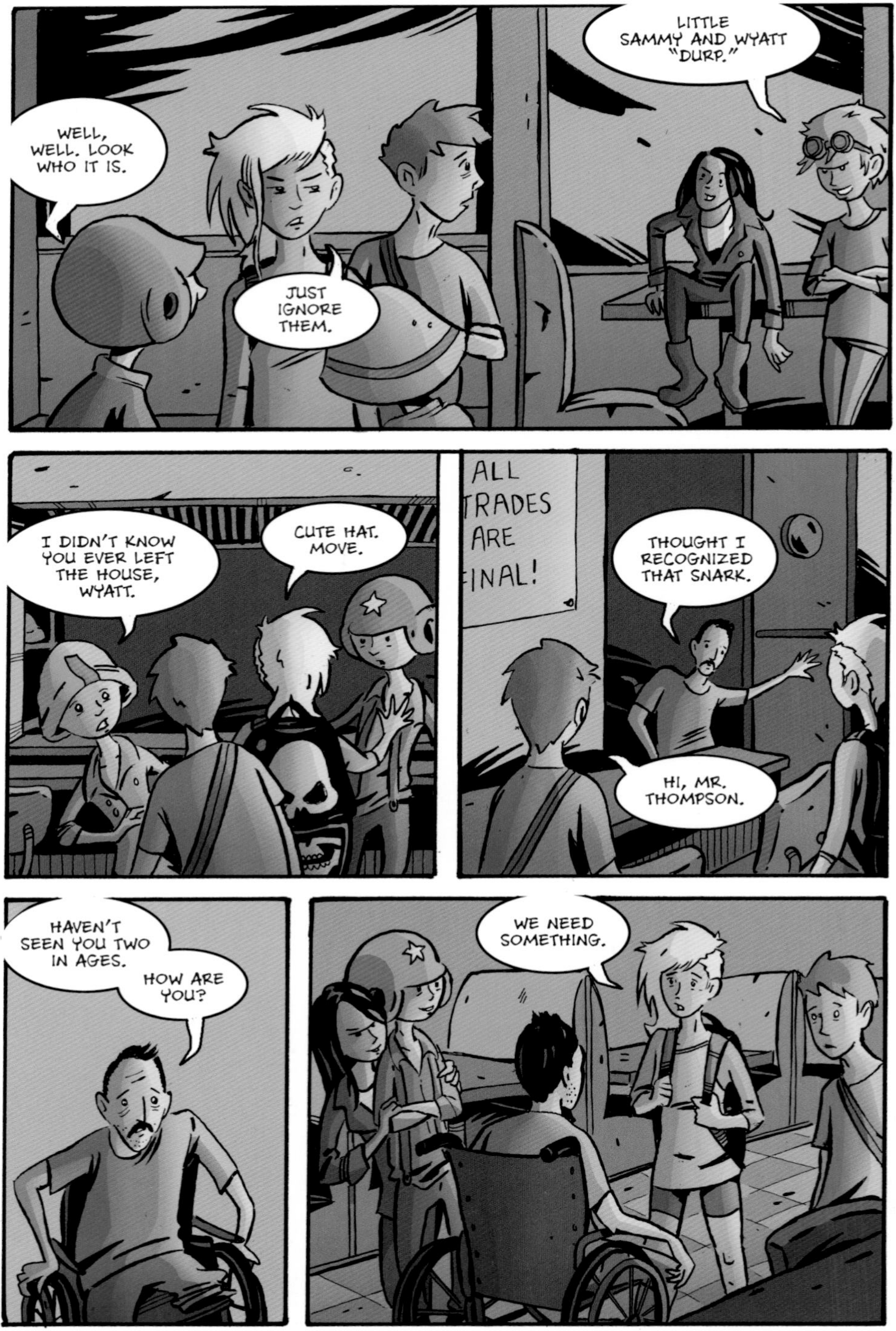
WELL, WELL. LOOK WHO IT IS.
JUST IGNORE THEM.
LITTLE SAMMY AND WYATT "DURP."
I DIDN'T KNOW YOU EVER LEFT THE HOUSE, WYATT.
CUTE HAT. MOVE.
ALL TRADES ARE FINAL!
THOUGHT I RECOGNIZED THAT SNARK.
HI, MR. THOMPSON.
HAVEN'T SEEN YOU TWO IN AGES.
HOW ARE YOU?
WE NEED SOMETHING.

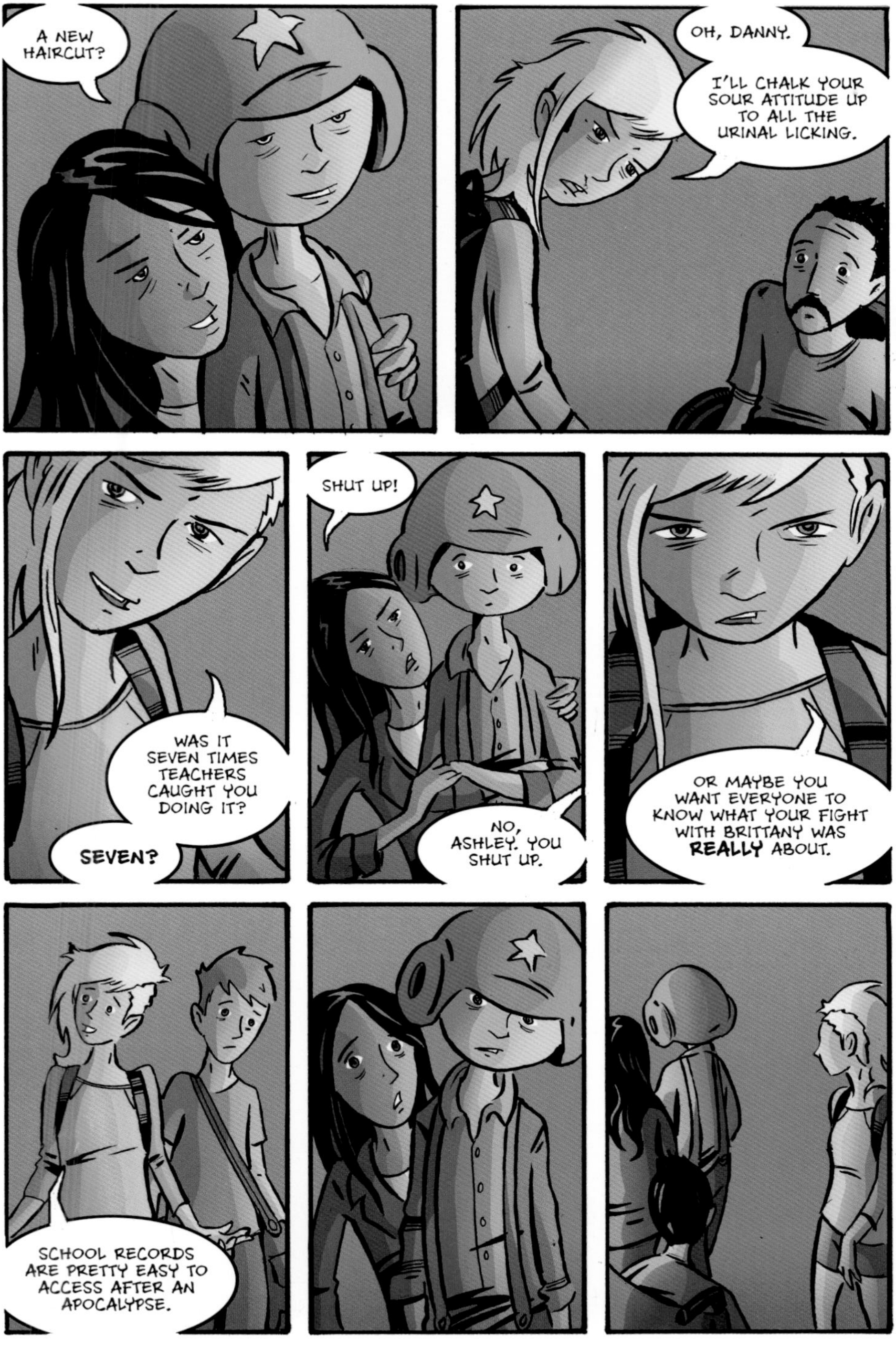
A NEW HAIRCUT?
OH, DANNY.
I'LL CHALK YOUR SOUR ATTITUDE UP TO ALL THE URINAL LICKING.
WAS IT SEVEN TIMES TEACHERS CAUGHT YOU DOING IT?
SEVEN?
SHUT UP!
NO, ASHLEY. YOU SHUT UP.
OR MAYBE YOU WANT EVERYONE TO KNOW WHAT YOUR FIGHT WITH BRITTANY WAS REALLY ABOUT.
SCHOOL RECORDS ARE PRETTY EASY TO ACCESS AFTER AN APOCALYPSE.

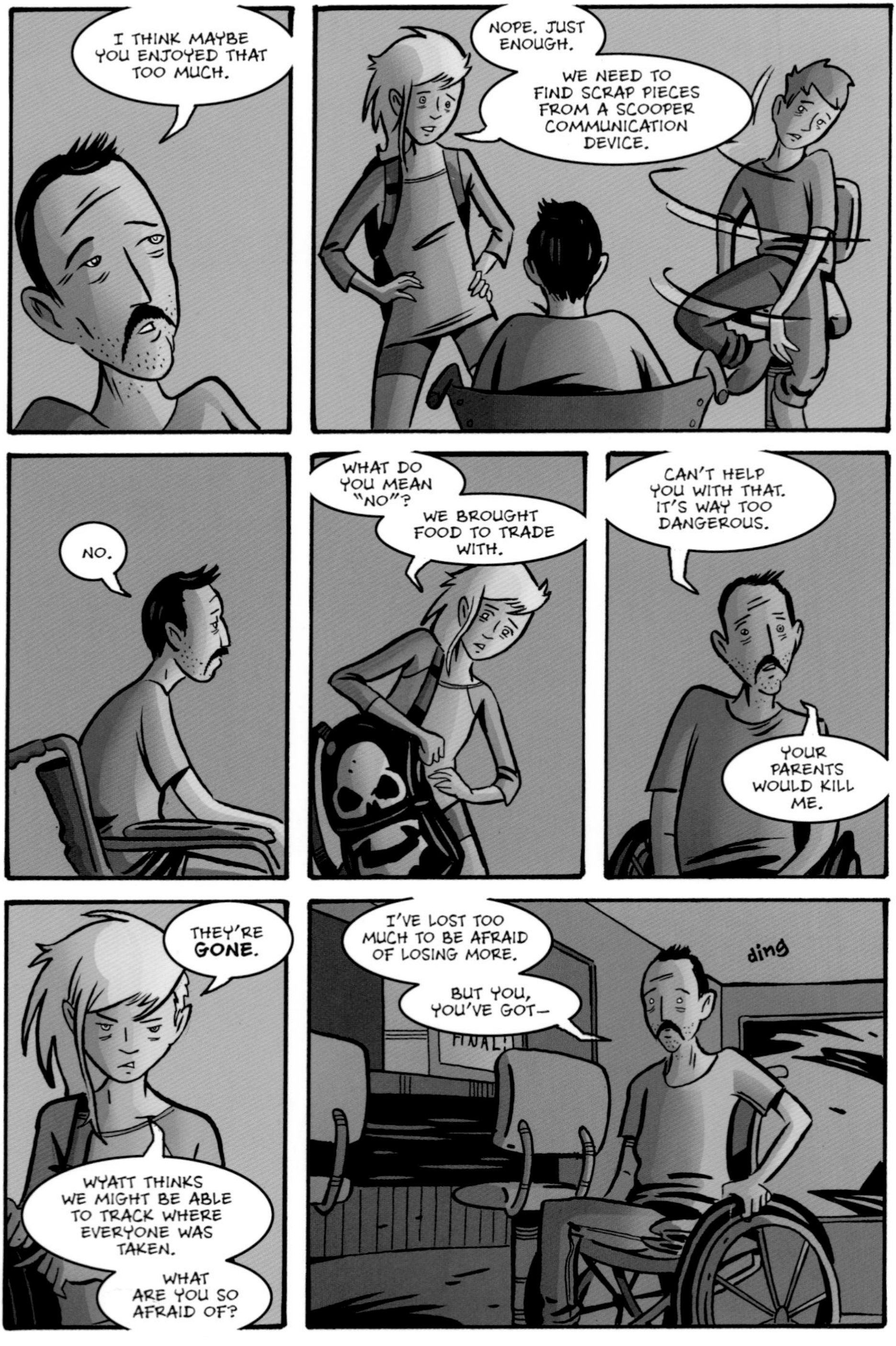

I THINK MAYBE YOU ENJOYED THAT TOO MUCH.
NOPE. JUST ENOUGH.
WE NEED TO FIND SCRAP PIECES FROM A SCOOPER COMMUNICATION DEVICE.
NO.
WHAT DO YOU MEAN "NO"?
WE BROUGHT FOOD TO TRADE WITH.
CAN'T HELP YOU WITH THAT. IT'S WAY TOO DANGEROUS.
YOUR PARENTS WOULD KILL ME.
THEY'RE **GONE**.
WYATT THINKS WE MIGHT BE ABLE TO TRACK WHERE EVERYONE WAS TAKEN.
WHAT ARE YOU SO AFRAID OF?
I'VE LOST TOO MUCH TO BE AFRAID OF LOSING MORE.
BUT YOU, YOU'VE GOT—
ding

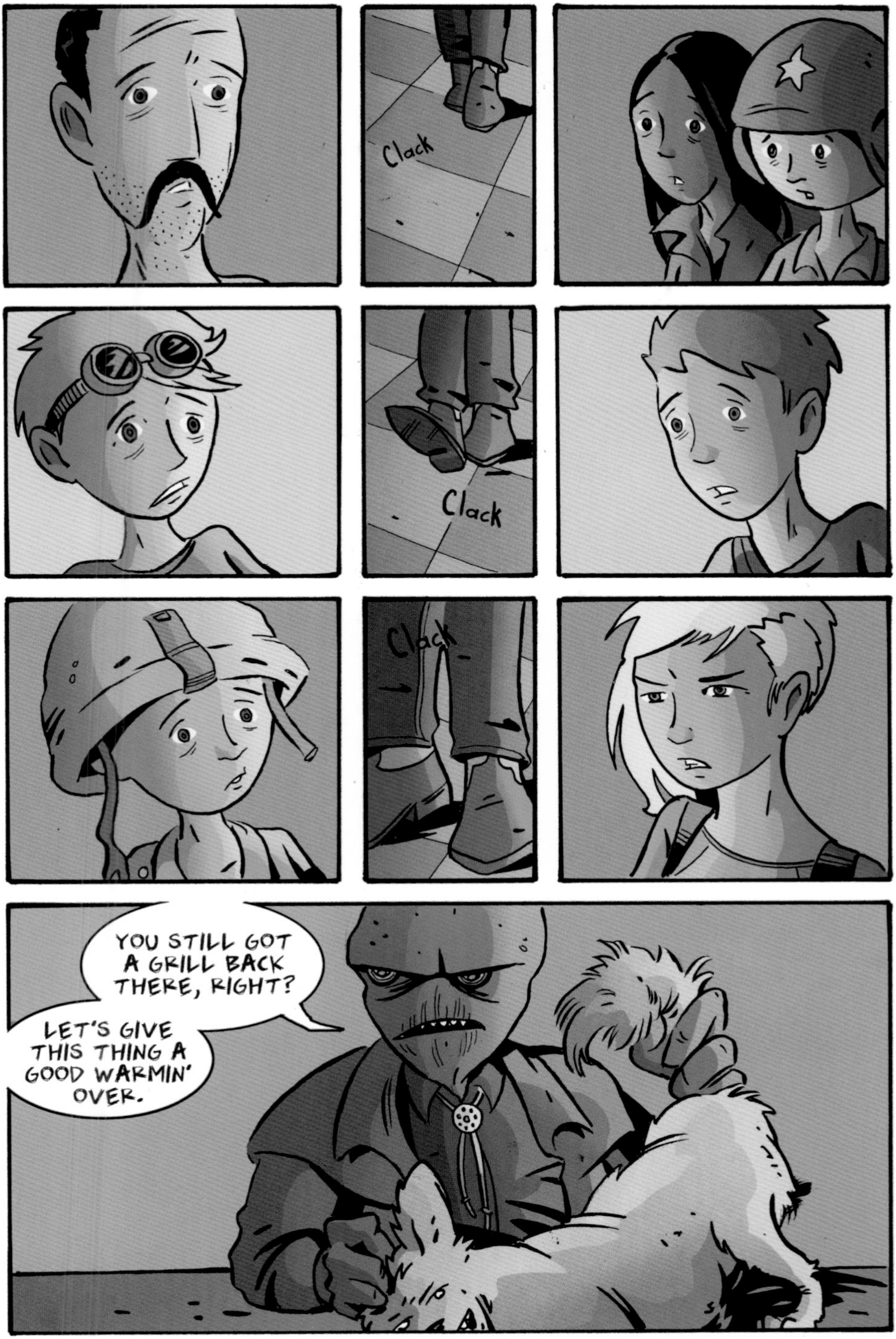
Clack
Clack
Clack
YOU STILL GOT A GRILL BACK THERE, RIGHT?
LET'S GIVE THIS THING A GOOD WARMIN' OVER.

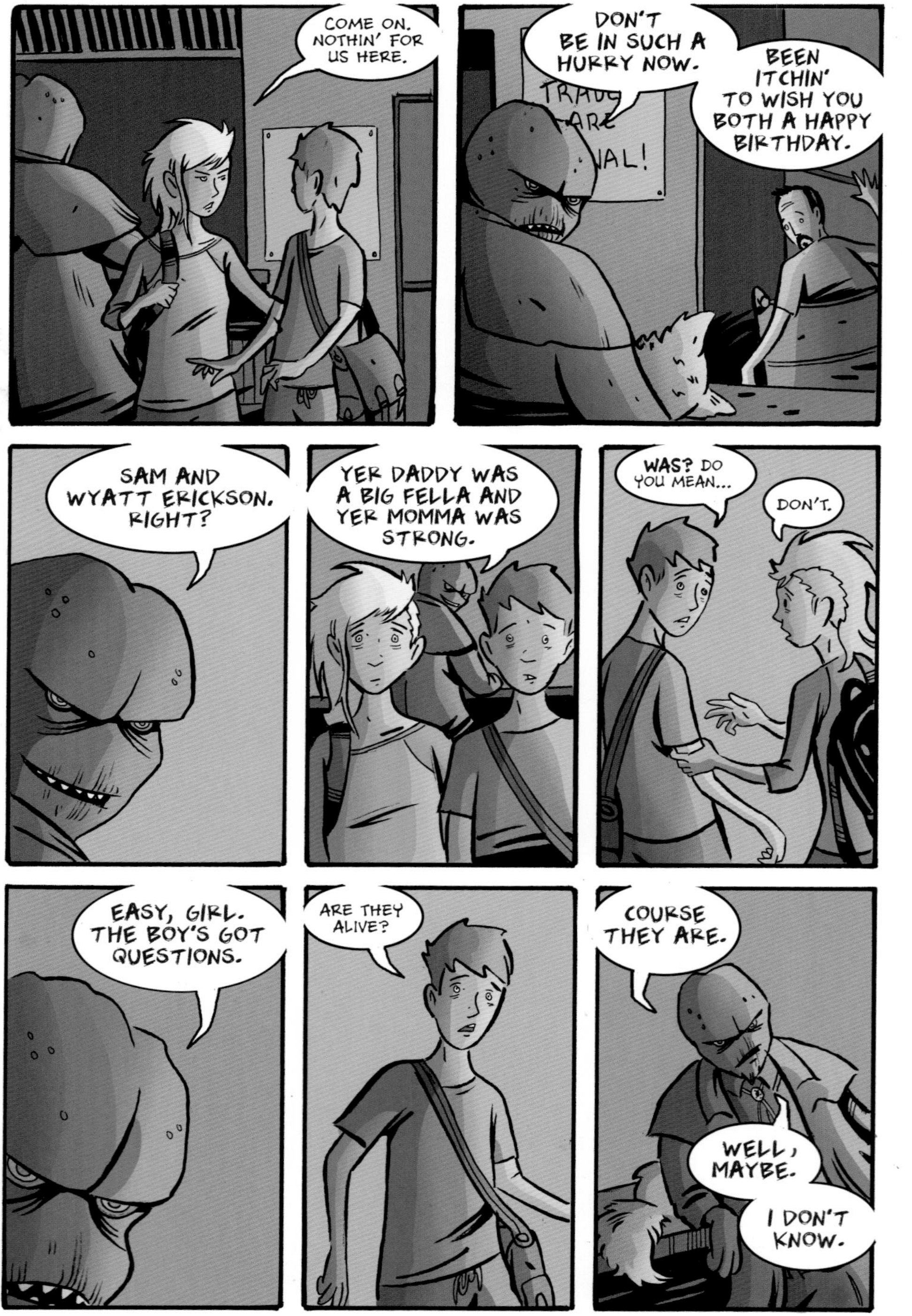
COME ON. NOTHIN' FOR US HERE.
DON'T BE IN SUCH A HURRY NOW.
BEEN ITCHIN' TO WISH YOU BOTH A HAPPY BIRTHDAY.
SAM AND WYATT ERICKSON. RIGHT?
YER DADDY WAS A BIG FELLA AND YER MOMMA WAS STRONG.
WAS? DO YOU MEAN...
DON'T.
EASY, GIRL. THE BOY'S GOT QUESTIONS.
ARE THEY ALIVE?
COURSE THEY ARE.
WELL, MAYBE.
I DON'T KNOW.

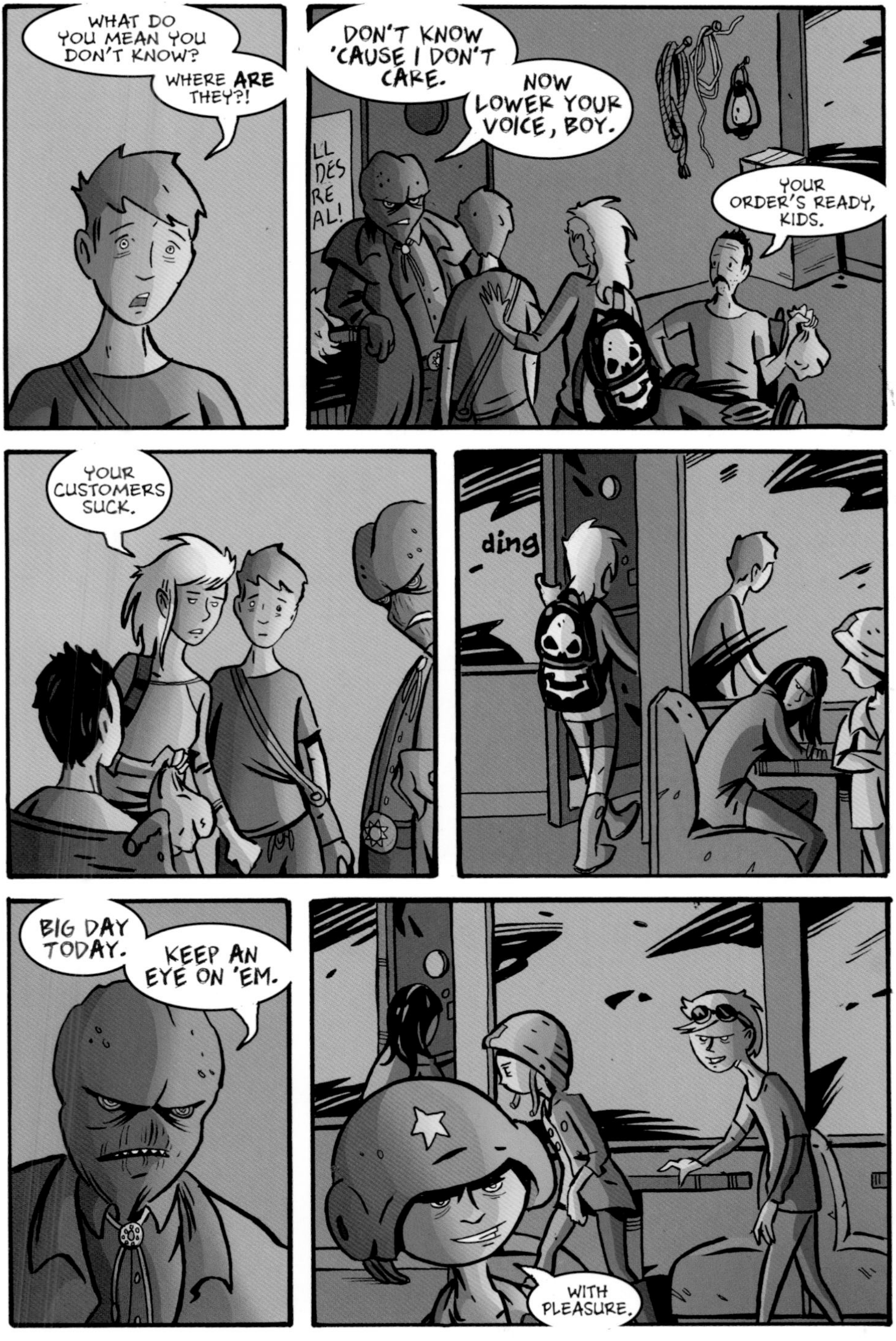
WHAT DO YOU MEAN YOU DON'T KNOW?
WHERE ARE THEY?!
DON'T KNOW 'CAUSE I DON'T CARE.
NOW LOWER YOUR VOICE, BOY.
YOUR ORDER'S READY, KIDS.
YOUR CUSTOMERS SUCK.
ding
BIG DAY TODAY.
KEEP AN EYE ON 'EM.
WITH PLEASURE.

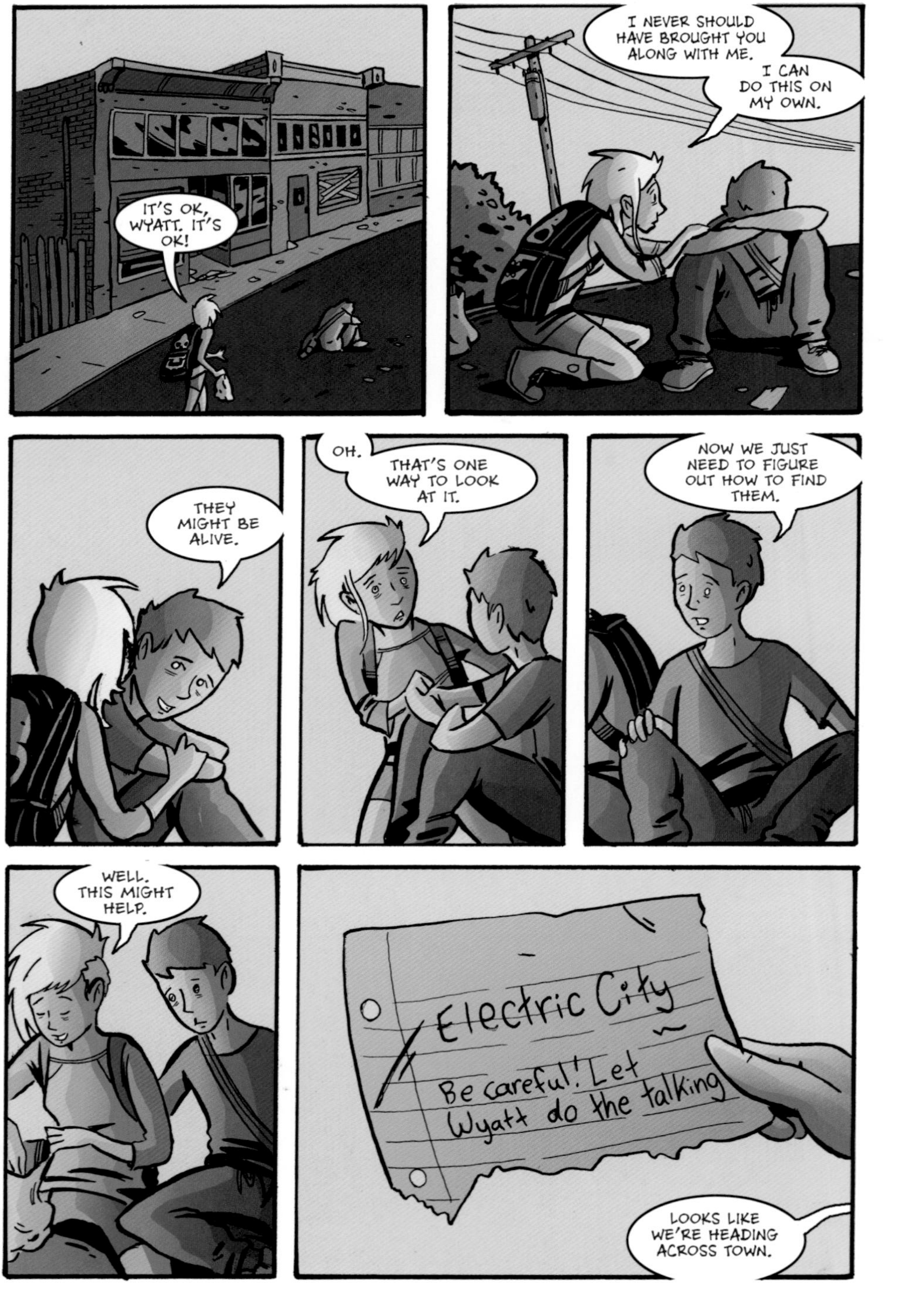
IT'S OK, WYATT. IT'S OK!
I NEVER SHOULD HAVE BROUGHT YOU ALONG WITH ME.
I CAN DO THIS ON MY OWN.
THEY MIGHT BE ALIVE.
OH.
THAT'S ONE WAY TO LOOK AT IT.
NOW WE JUST NEED TO FIGURE OUT HOW TO FIND THEM.
WELL. THIS MIGHT HELP.
Electric City
Be careful! Let Wyatt do the talking
LOOKS LIKE WE'RE HEADING ACROSS TOWN.

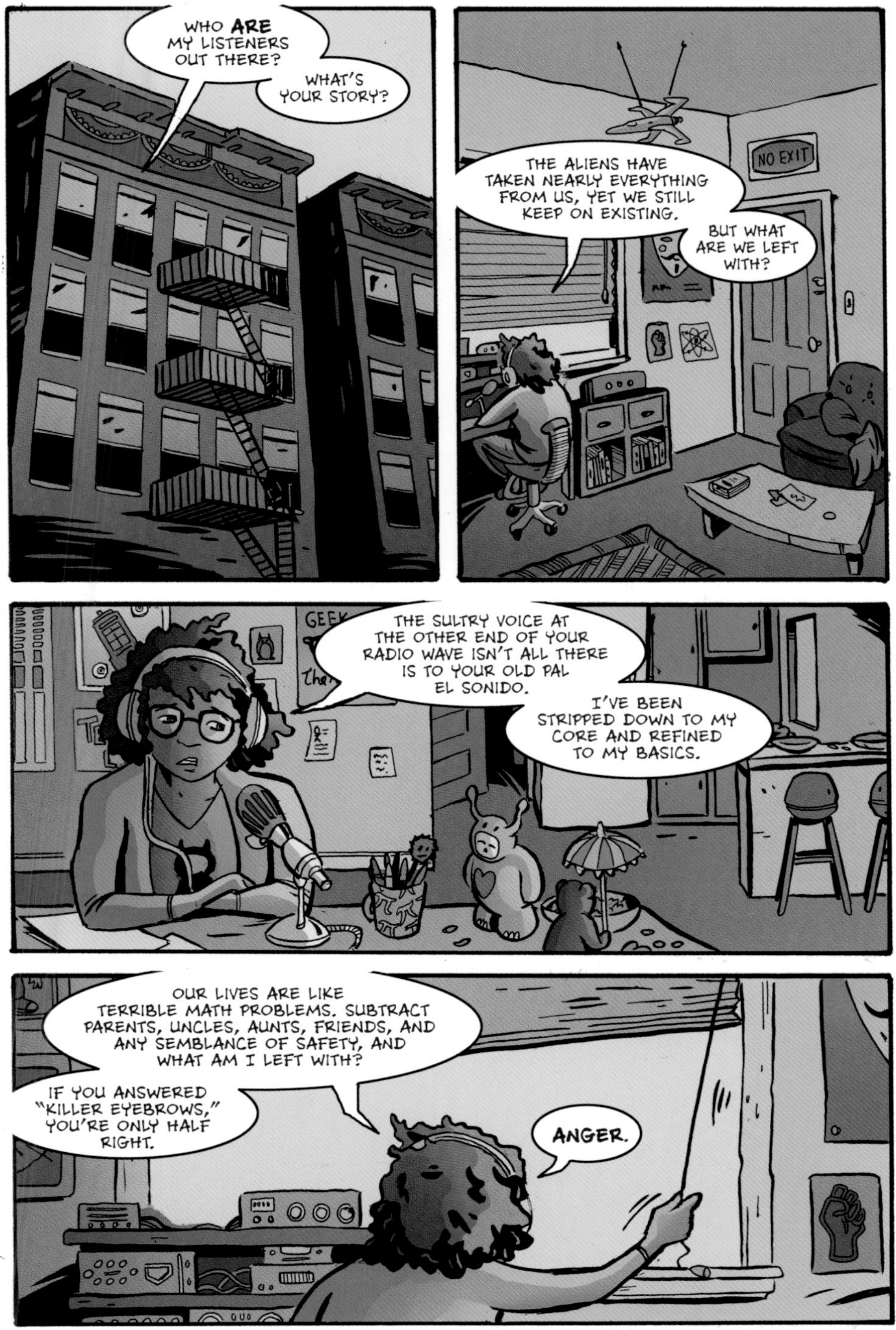
WHO ARE MY LISTENERS OUT THERE?
WHAT'S YOUR STORY?
NO EXIT
THE ALIENS HAVE TAKEN NEARLY EVERYTHING FROM US, YET WE STILL KEEP ON EXISTING.
BUT WHAT ARE WE LEFT WITH?
GEEK
THE SULTRY VOICE AT THE OTHER END OF YOUR RADIO WAVE ISN'T ALL THERE IS TO YOUR OLD PAL EL SONIDO.
I'VE BEEN STRIPPED DOWN TO MY CORE AND REFINED TO MY BASICS.
OUR LIVES ARE LIKE TERRIBLE MATH PROBLEMS. SUBTRACT PARENTS, UNCLES, AUNTS, FRIENDS, AND ANY SEMBLANCE OF SAFETY, AND WHAT AM I LEFT WITH?
IF YOU ANSWERED "KILLER EYEBROWS," YOU'RE ONLY HALF RIGHT.
ANGER.

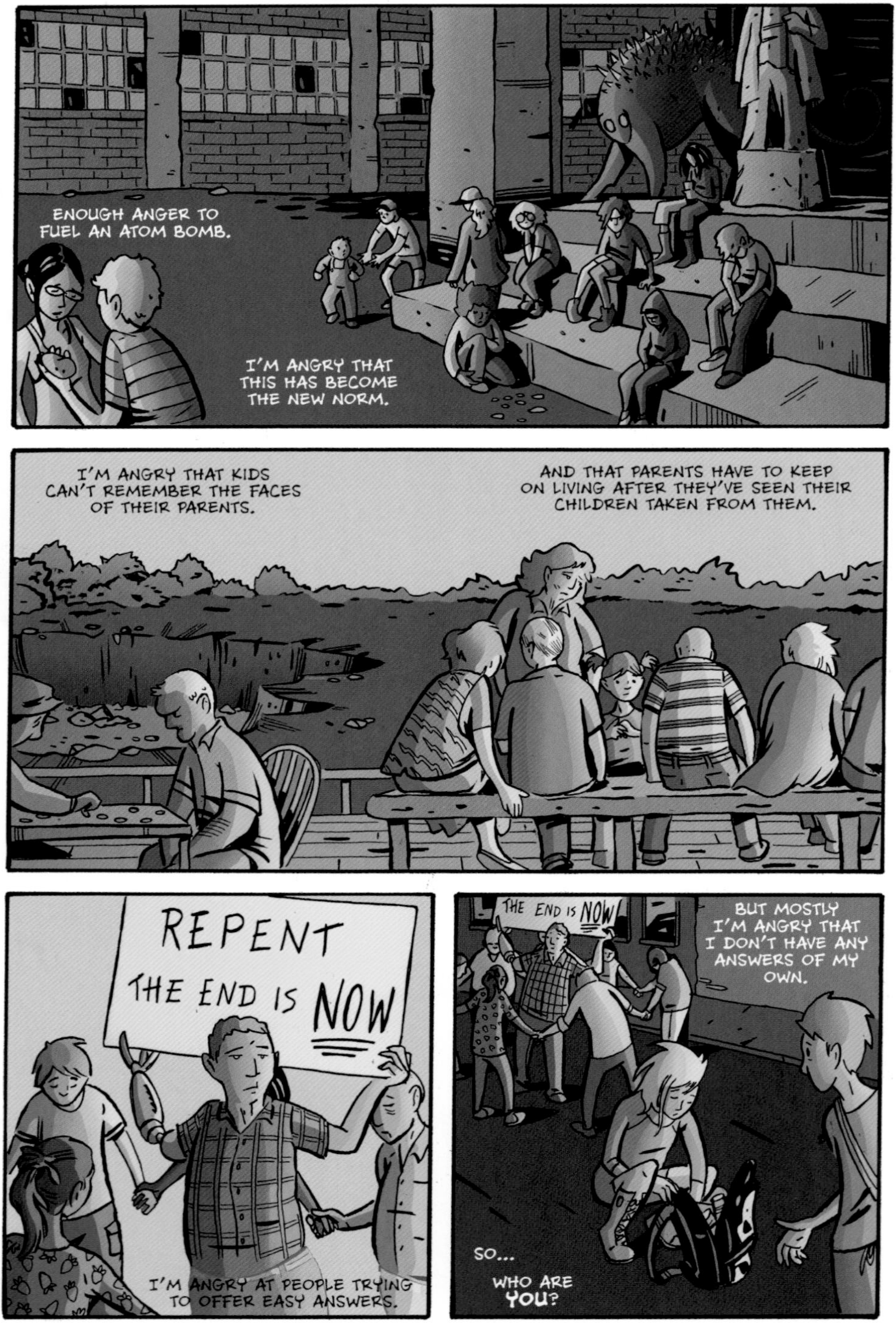
ENOUGH ANGER TO FUEL AN ATOM BOMB.
I'M ANGRY THAT THIS HAS BECOME THE NEW NORM.
I'M ANGRY THAT KIDS CAN'T REMEMBER THE FACES OF THEIR PARENTS.
AND THAT PARENTS HAVE TO KEEP ON LIVING AFTER THEY'VE SEEN THEIR CHILDREN TAKEN FROM THEM.
REPENT
THE END IS NOW
I'M ANGRY AT PEOPLE TRYING TO OFFER EASY ANSWERS.
THE END IS NOW
BUT MOSTLY I'M ANGRY THAT I DON'T HAVE ANY ANSWERS OF MY OWN.
SO...
WHO ARE YOU?

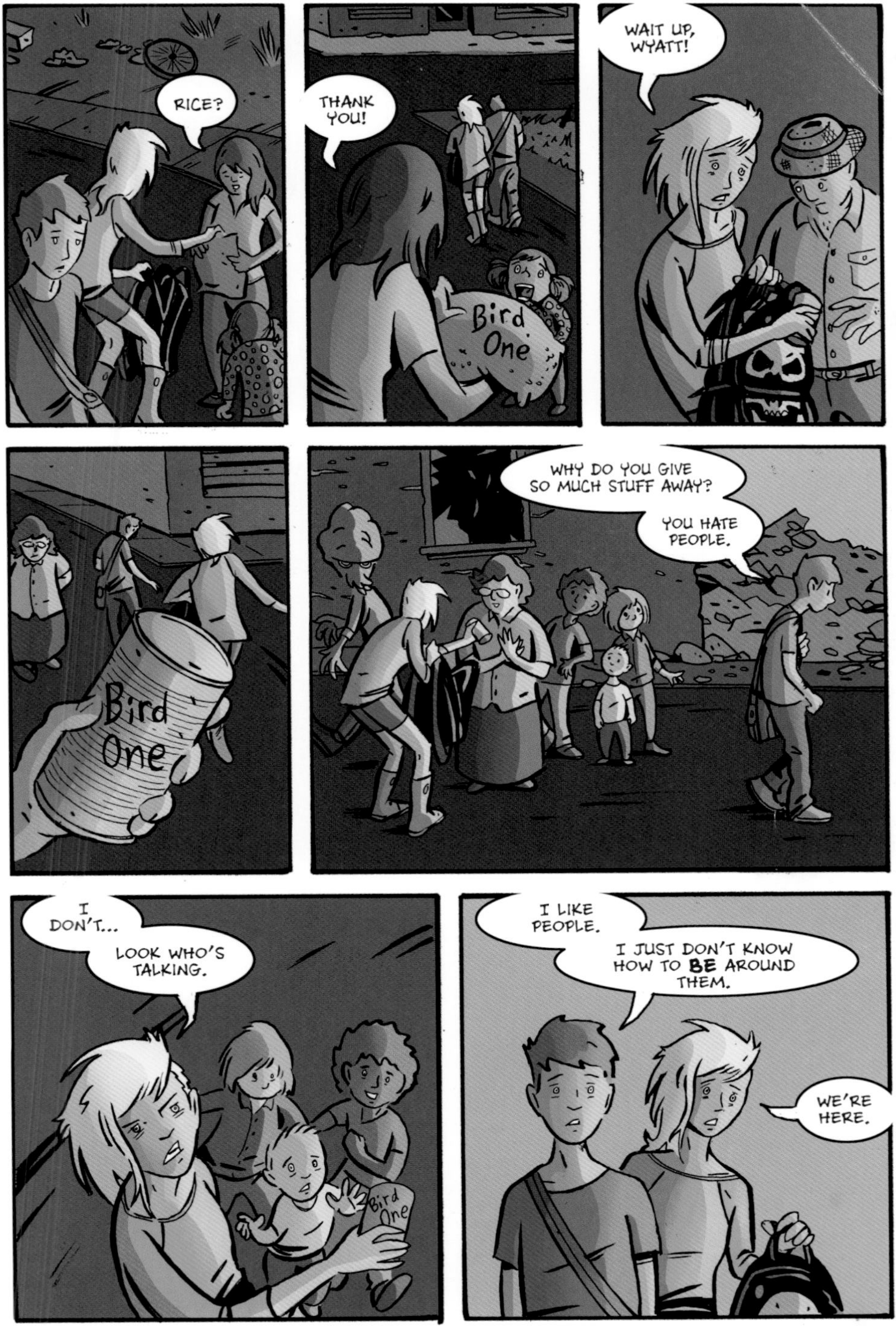
RICE?
THANK YOU!
Bird One
WAIT UP, WYATT!
Bird One
WHY DO YOU GIVE SO MUCH STUFF AWAY?
YOU HATE PEOPLE.
I DON'T...
LOOK WHO'S TALKING.
Bird One
I LIKE PEOPLE.
I JUST DON'T KNOW HOW TO **BE** AROUND THEM.
WE'RE HERE.

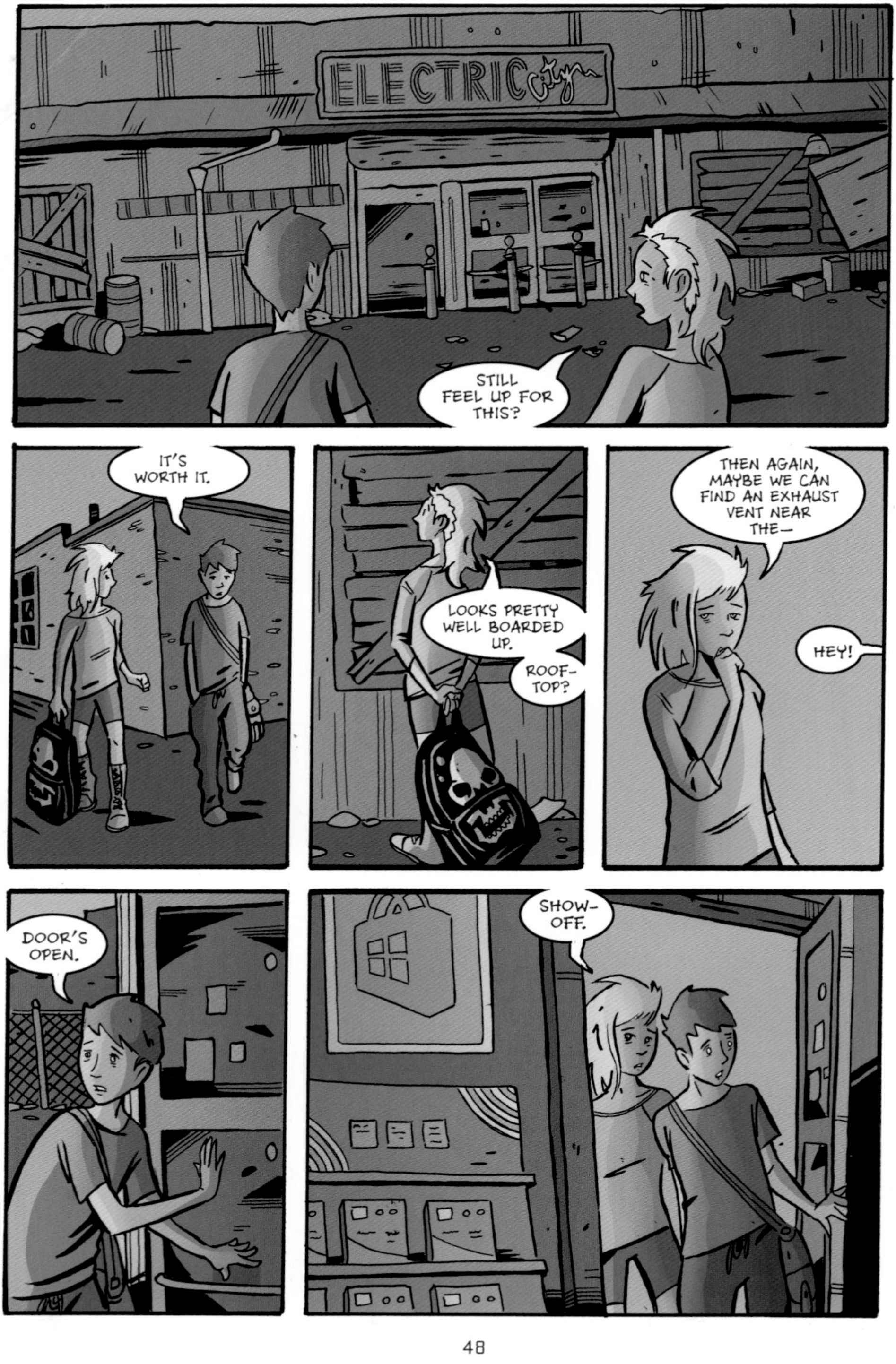
ELECTRIC city
STILL FEEL UP FOR THIS?
IT'S WORTH IT.
LOOKS PRETTY WELL BOARDED UP.
ROOF-TOP?
THEN AGAIN, MAYBE WE CAN FIND AN EXHAUST VENT NEAR THE—
HEY!
DOOR'S OPEN.
SHOW-OFF.

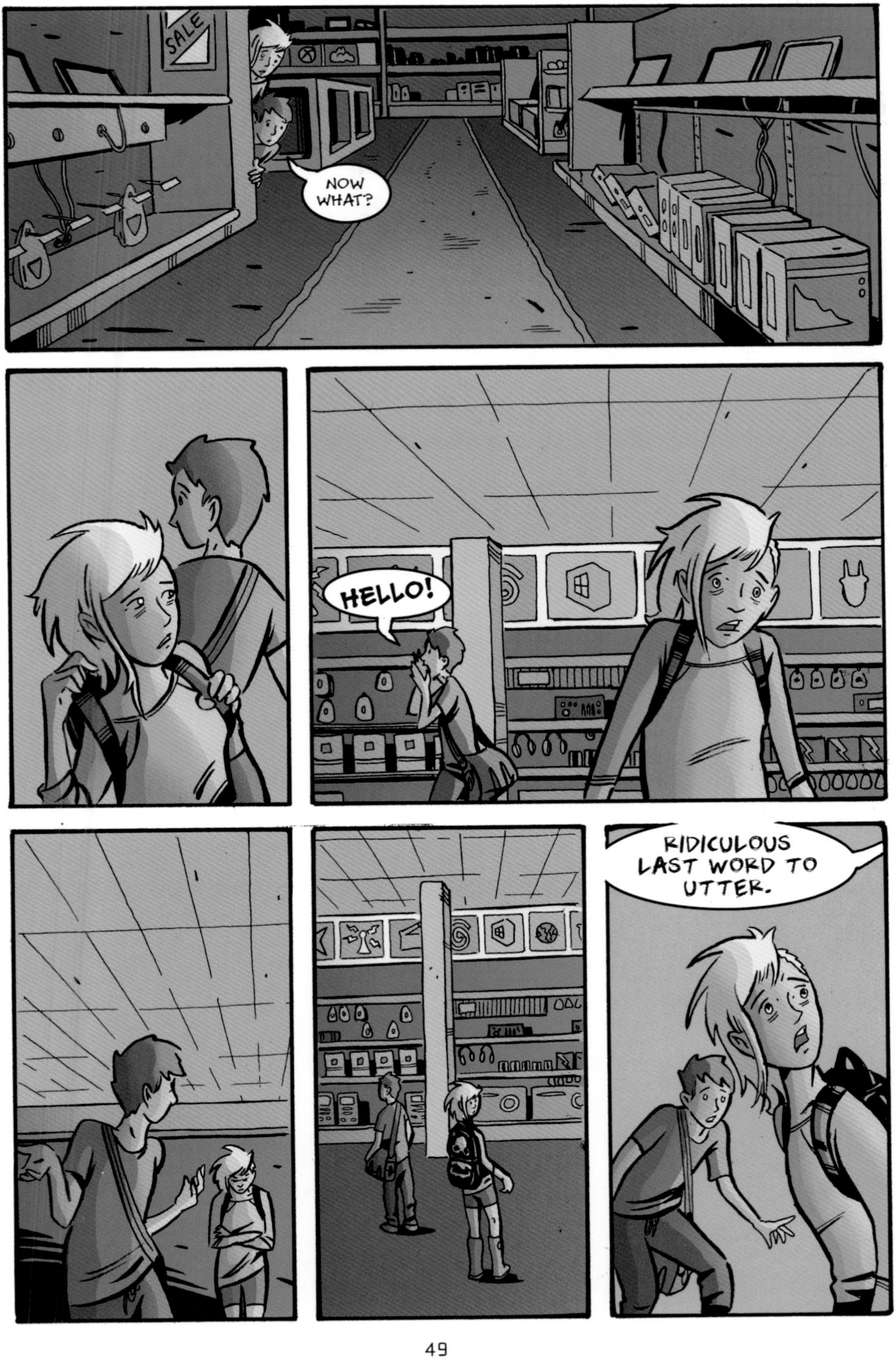
NOW WHAT?
HELLO!
RIDICULOUS LAST WORD TO UTTER.

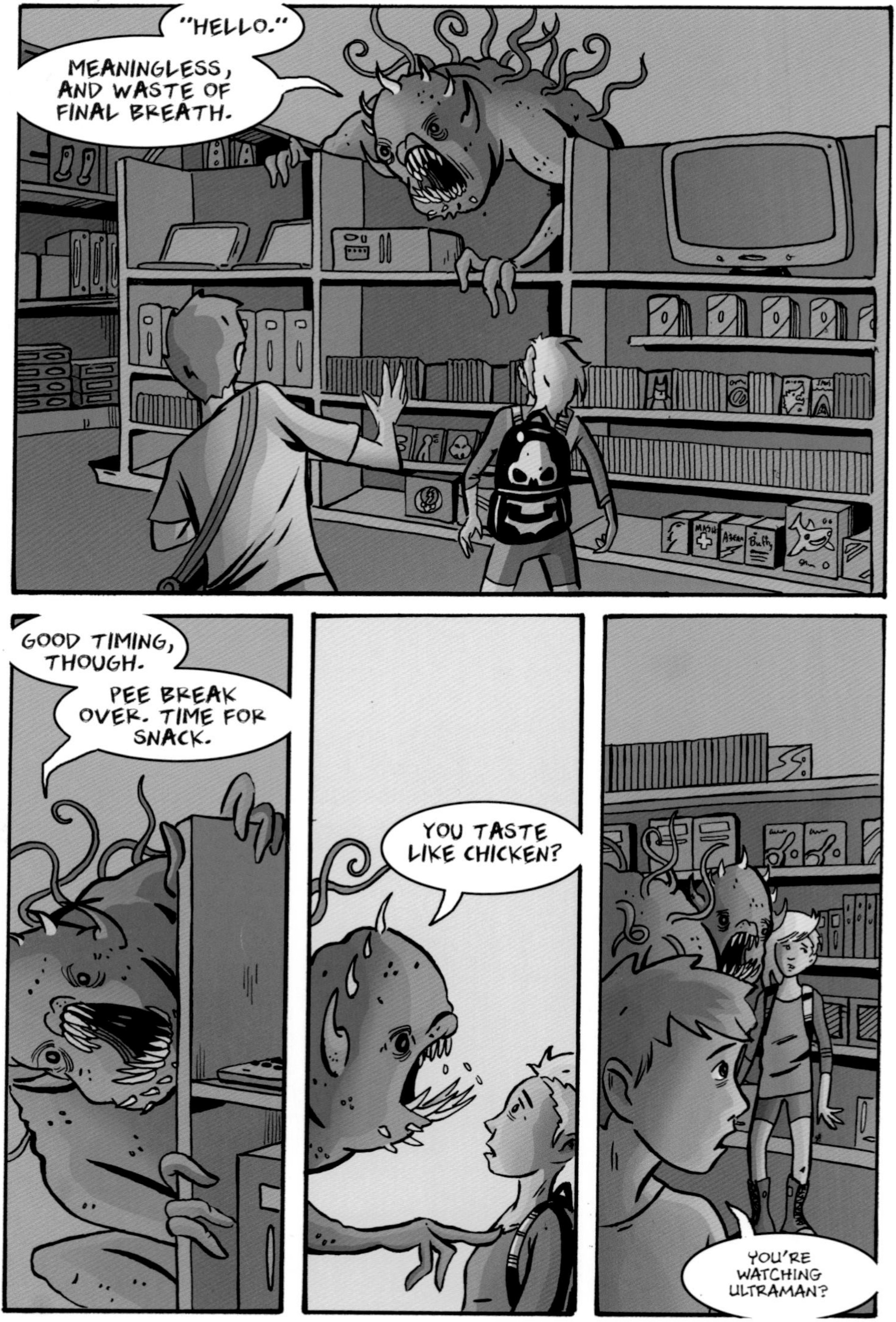
"HELLO."
MEANINGLESS, AND WASTE OF FINAL BREATH.
GOOD TIMING, THOUGH.
PEE BREAK OVER. TIME FOR SNACK.
YOU TASTE LIKE CHICKEN?
YOU'RE WATCHING ULTRAMAN?

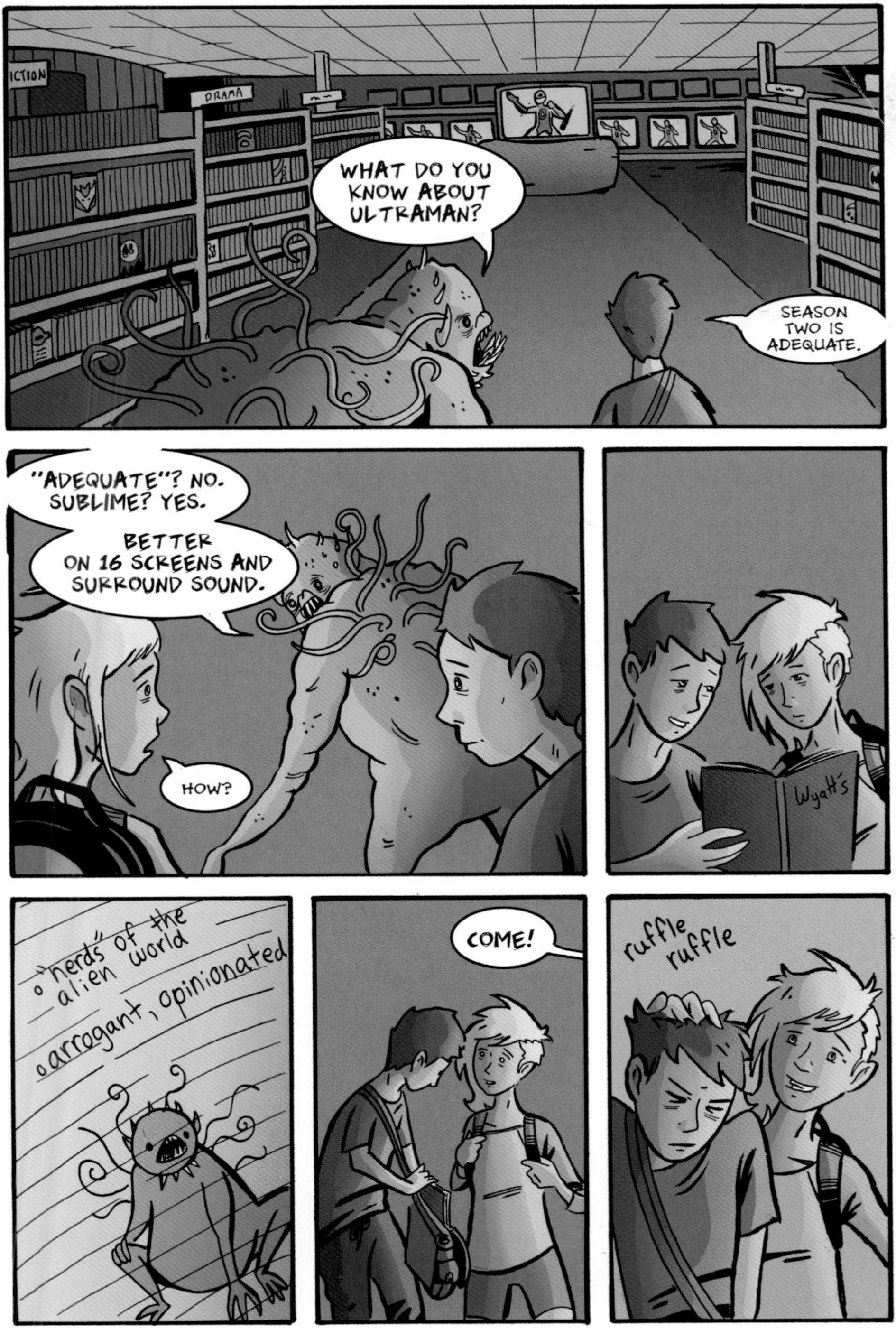
ICTION
DRAMA
WHAT DO YOU KNOW ABOUT ULTRAMAN?
SEASON TWO IS ADEQUATE.
"ADEQUATE"? NO. SUBLIME? YES.
BETTER ON 16 SCREENS AND SURROUND SOUND.
HOW?
Wyatt's
o "nerds" of the alien world
o arrogant, opinionated
COME!
ruffle ruffle

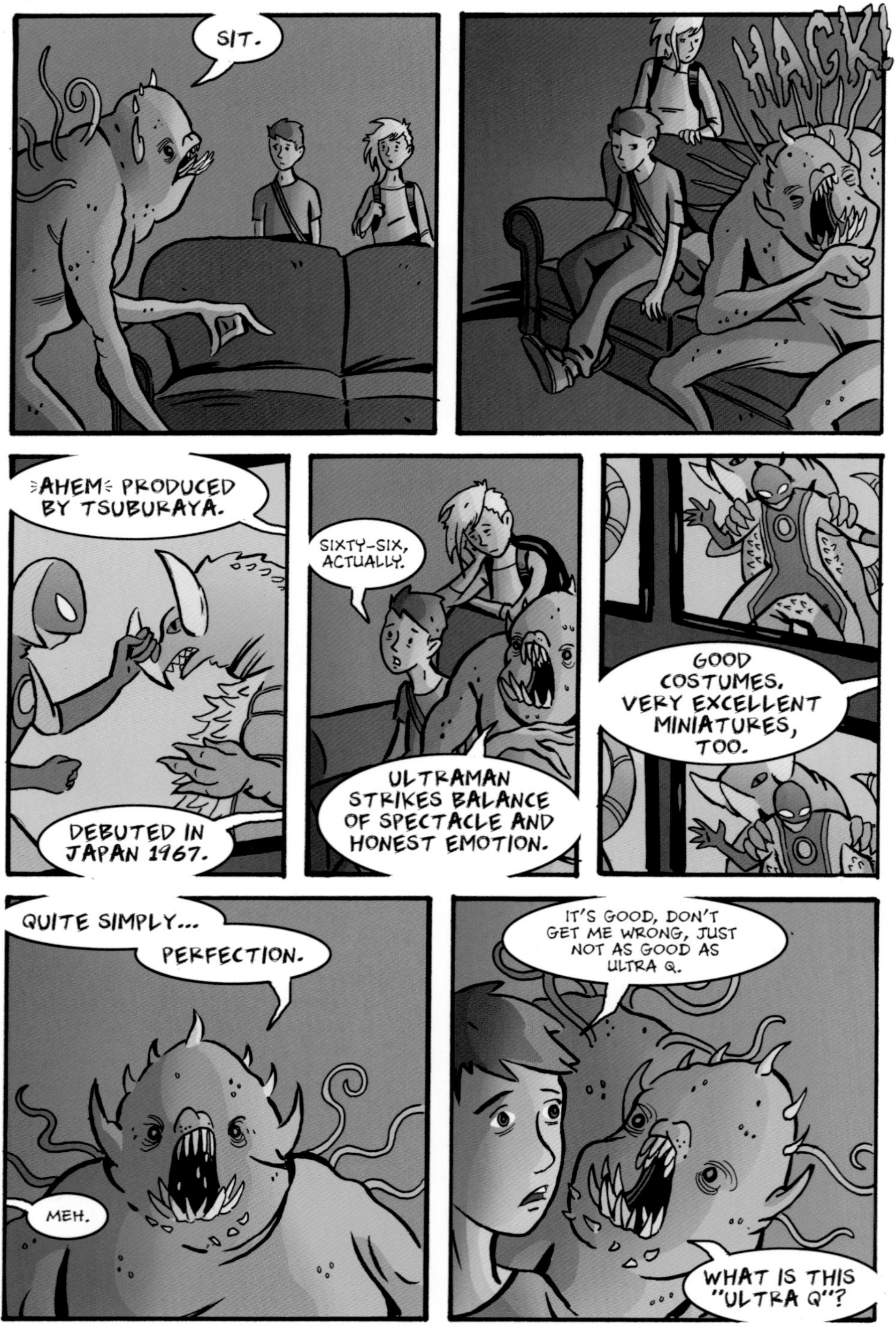
SIT.
HACK!
AHEM PRODUCED BY TSUBURAYA.
DEBUTED IN JAPAN 1967.
SIXTY-SIX, ACTUALLY.
ULTRAMAN STRIKES BALANCE OF SPECTACLE AND HONEST EMOTION.
GOOD COSTUMES. VERY EXCELLENT MINIATURES, TOO.
QUITE SIMPLY...
PERFECTION.
MEH.
IT'S GOOD, DON'T GET ME WRONG, JUST NOT AS GOOD AS ULTRA Q.
WHAT IS THIS "ULTRA Q"?

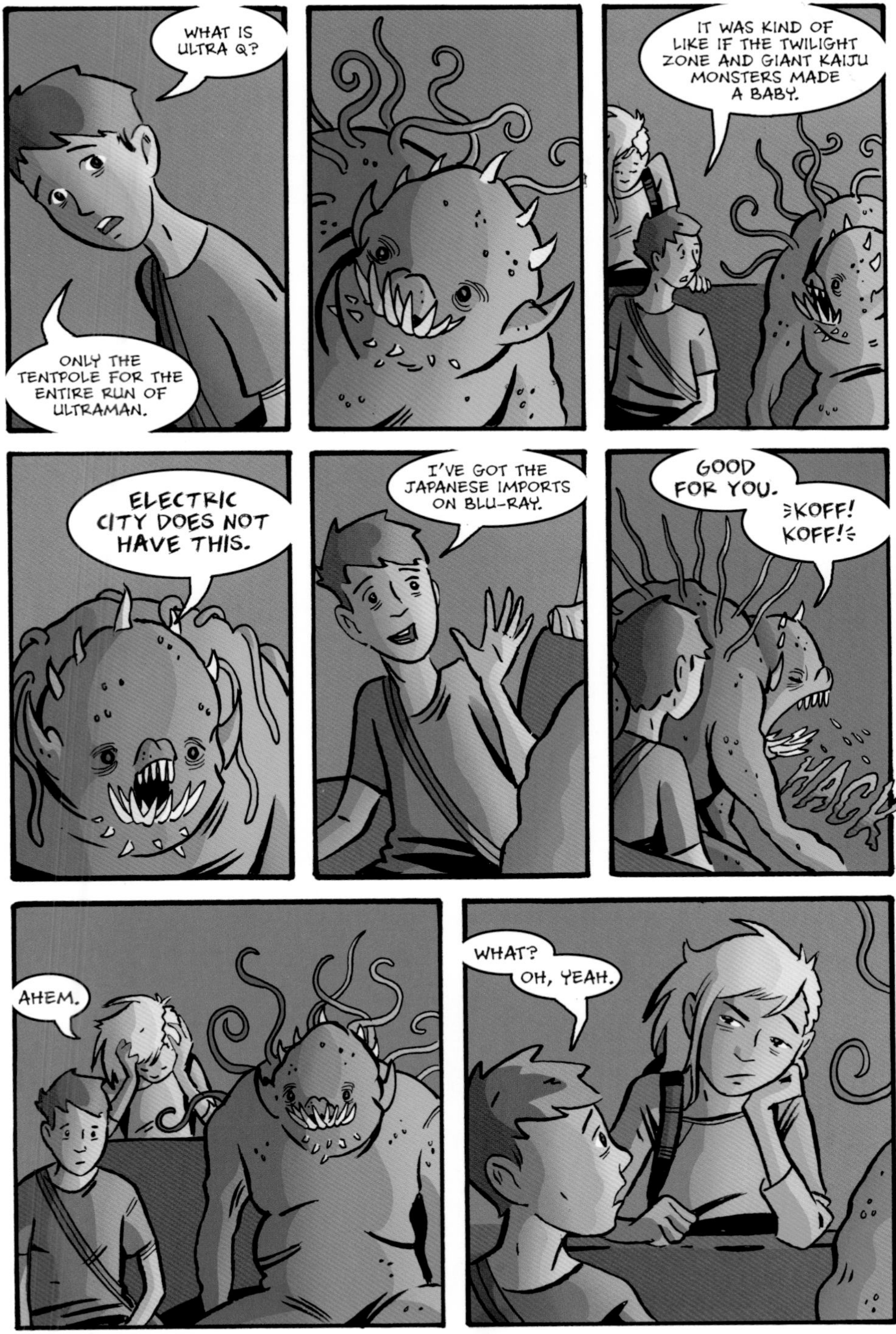
WHAT IS ULTRA Q?
ONLY THE TENTPOLE FOR THE ENTIRE RUN OF ULTRAMAN.
IT WAS KIND OF LIKE IF THE TWILIGHT ZONE AND GIANT KAIJU MONSTERS MADE A BABY.
ELECTRIC CITY DOES NOT HAVE THIS.
I'VE GOT THE JAPANESE IMPORTS ON BLU-RAY.
GOOD FOR YOU.
KOFF! KOFF!
HACK
AHEM.
WHAT? OH, YEAH.

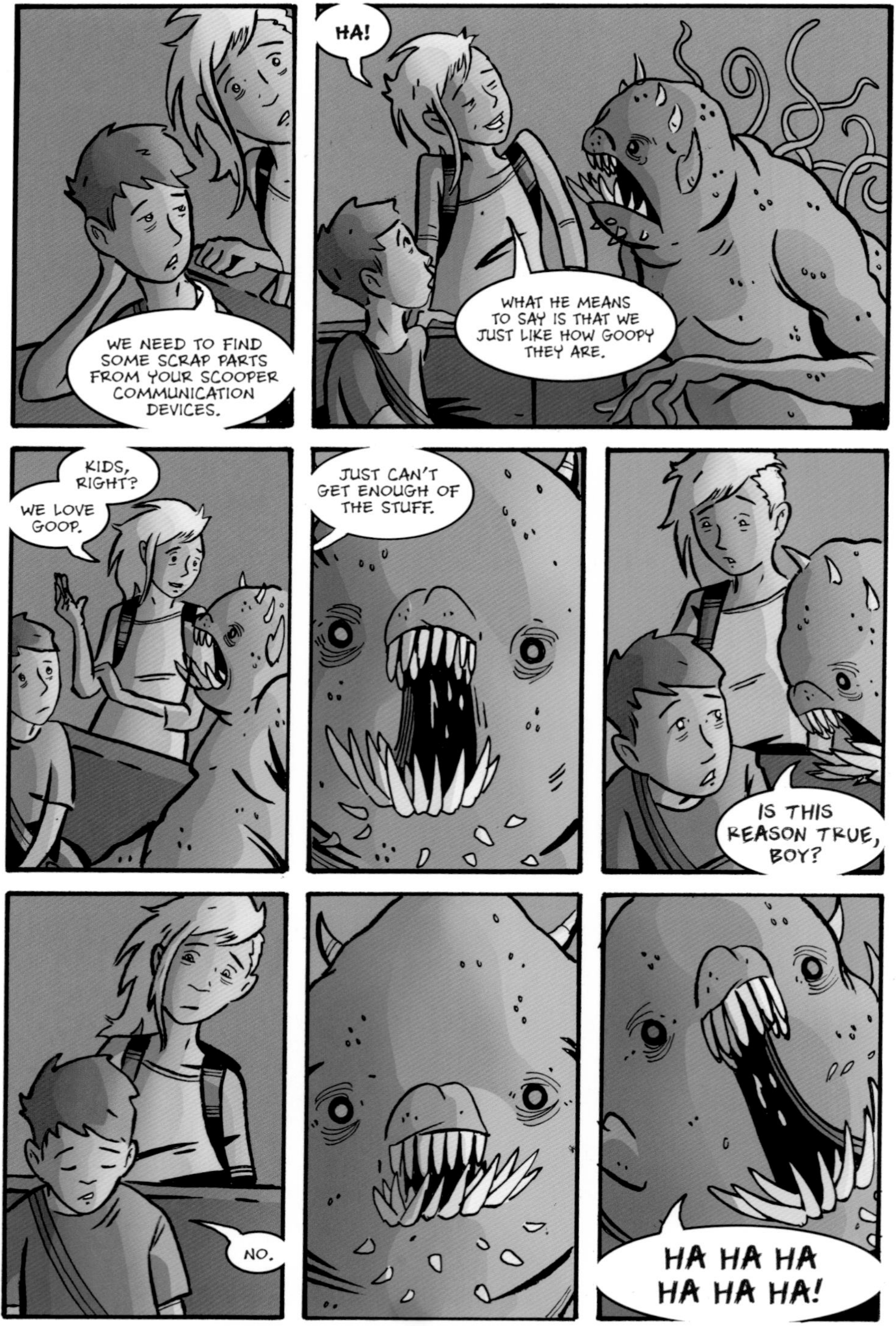
WE NEED TO FIND SOME SCRAP PARTS FROM YOUR SCOOPER COMMUNICATION DEVICES.
HA!
WHAT HE MEANS TO SAY IS THAT WE JUST LIKE HOW GOOPY THEY ARE.
KIDS, RIGHT?
WE LOVE GOOP.
JUST CAN'T GET ENOUGH OF THE STUFF.
IS THIS REASON TRUE, BOY?
NO.
HA HA HA HA HA HA!

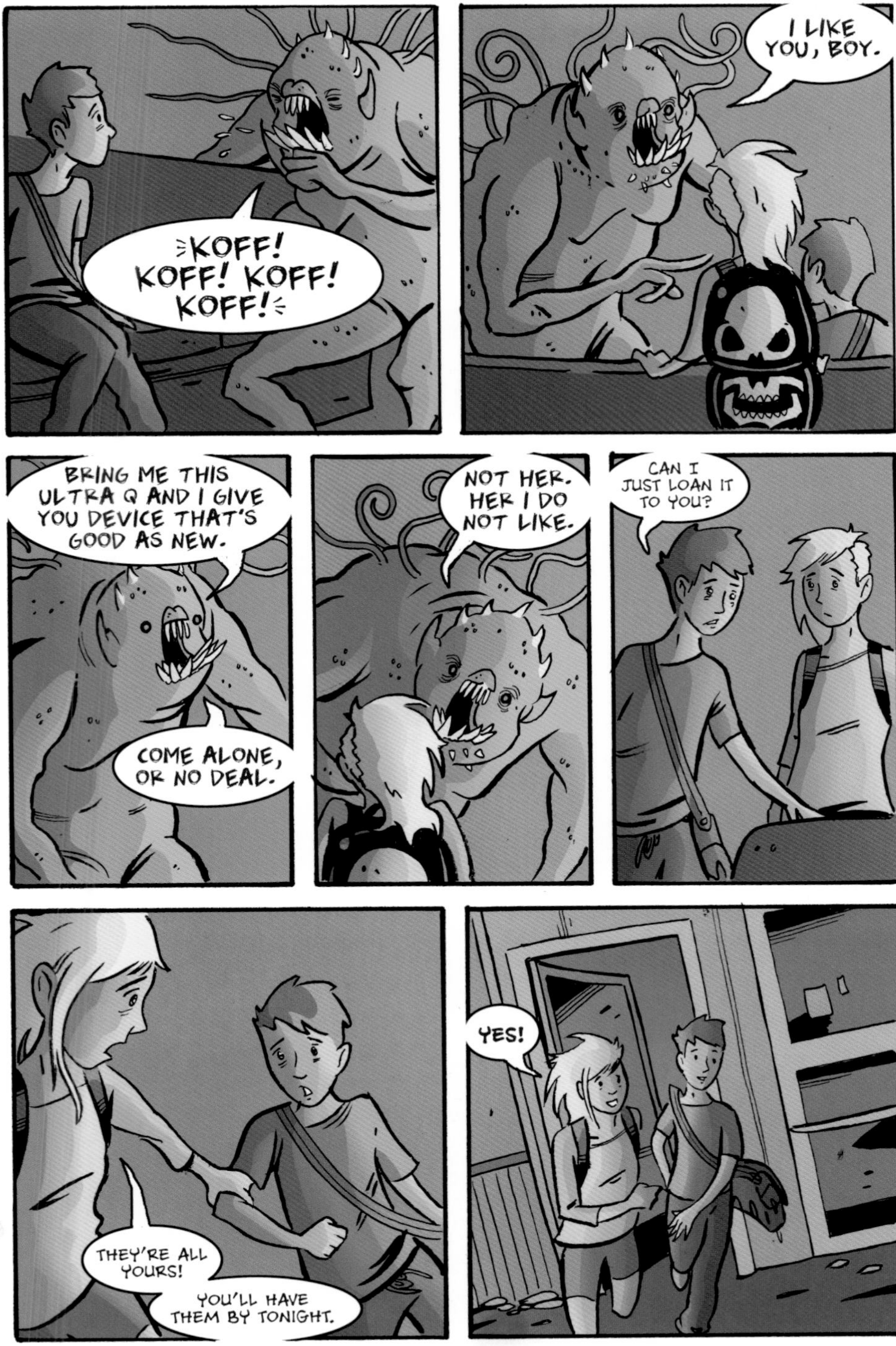
KOFF! KOFF! KOFF! KOFF!
I LIKE YOU, BOY.
BRING ME THIS ULTRA Q AND I GIVE YOU DEVICE THAT'S GOOD AS NEW.
COME ALONE, OR NO DEAL.
NOT HER. HER I DO NOT LIKE.
CAN I JUST LOAN IT TO YOU?
THEY'RE ALL YOURS!
YOU'LL HAVE THEM BY TONIGHT.
YES!

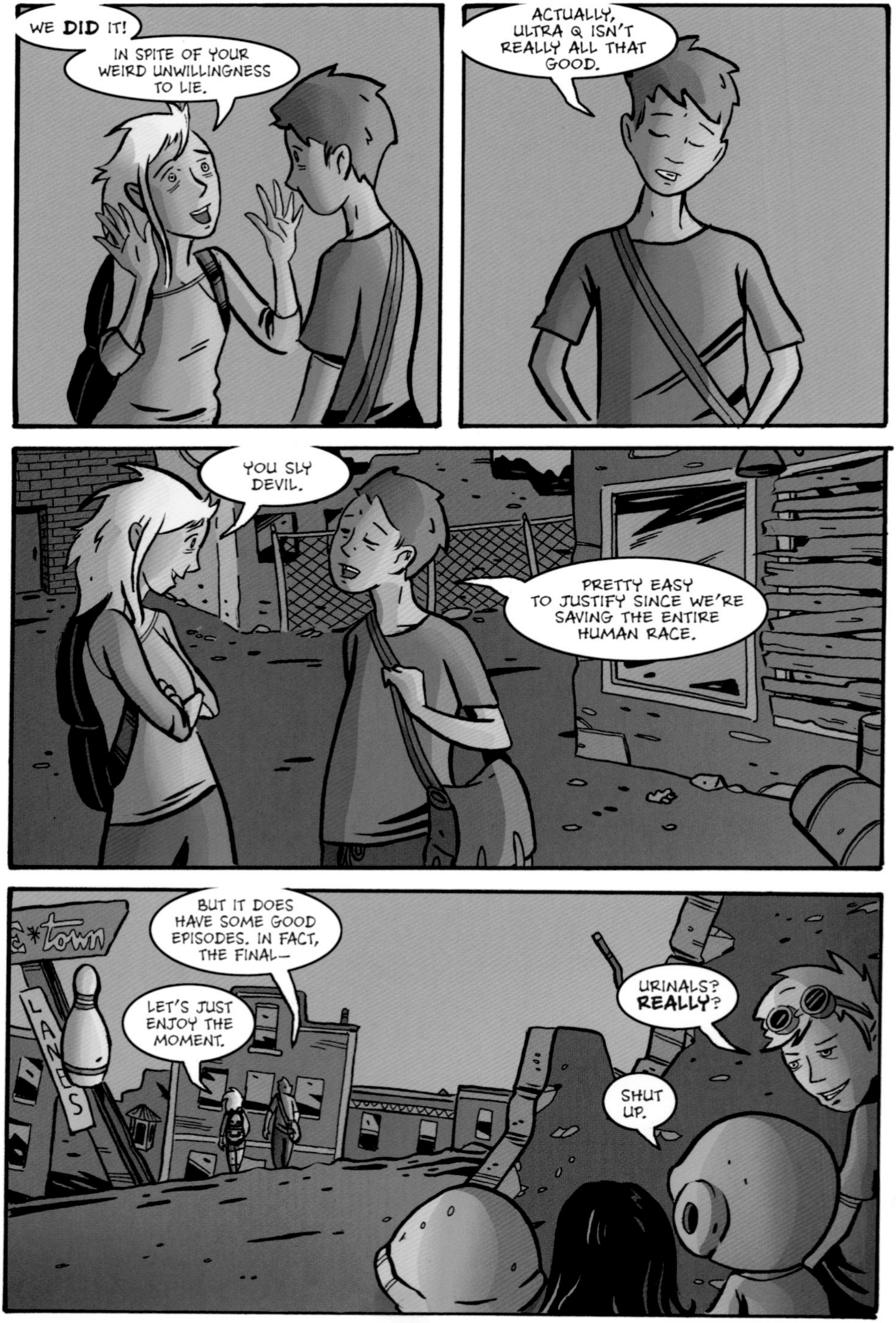
WE DID IT!
IN SPITE OF YOUR WEIRD UNWILLINGNESS TO LIE.
ACTUALLY, ULTRA Q ISN'T REALLY ALL THAT GOOD.
YOU SLY DEVIL.
PRETTY EASY TO JUSTIFY SINCE WE'RE SAVING THE ENTIRE HUMAN RACE.
LANES
BUT IT DOES HAVE SOME GOOD EPISODES. IN FACT, THE FINAL—
LET'S JUST ENJOY THE MOMENT.
URINALS? REALLY?
SHUT UP.

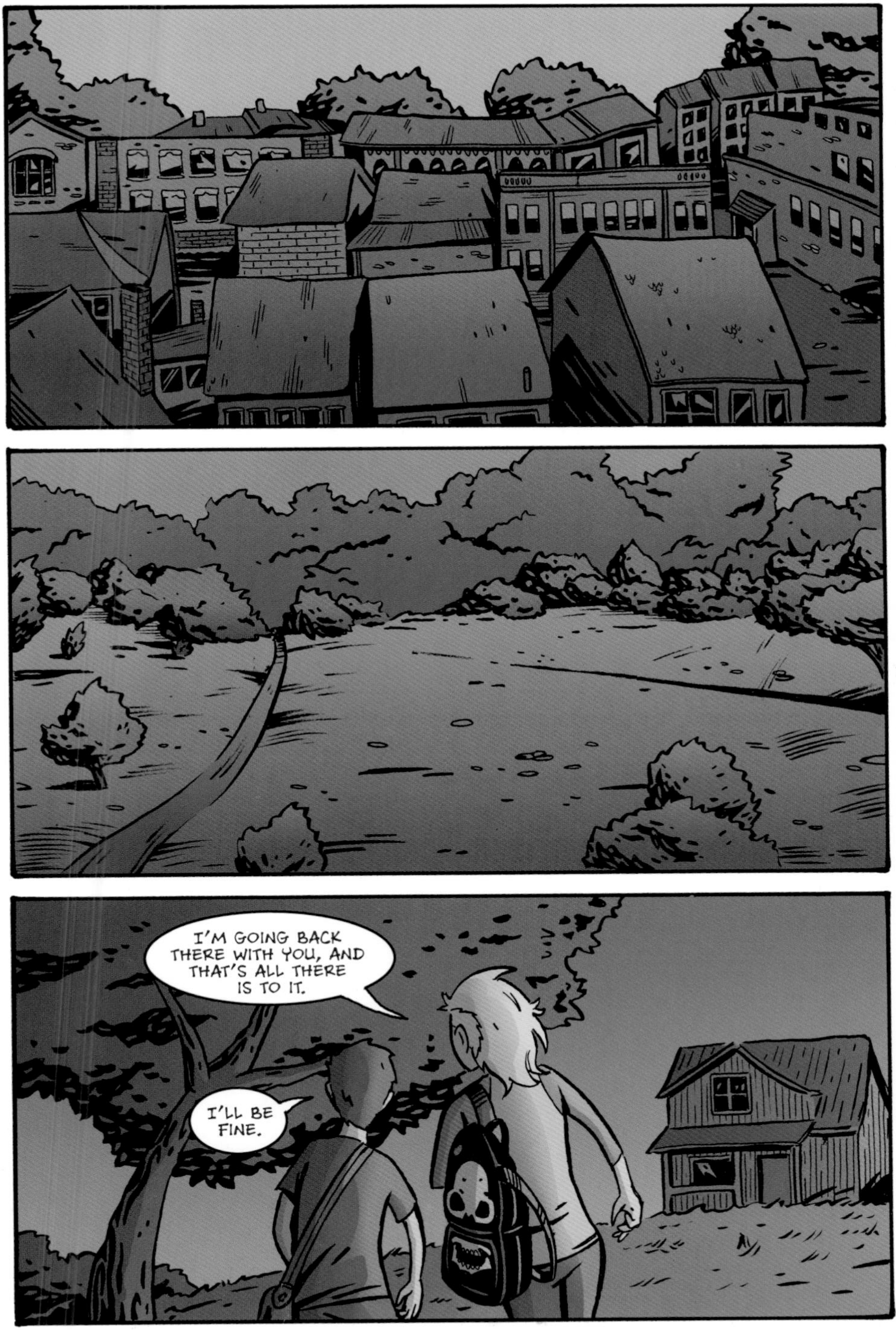
I'M GOING BACK THERE WITH YOU, AND THAT'S ALL THERE IS TO IT.
I'LL BE FINE.

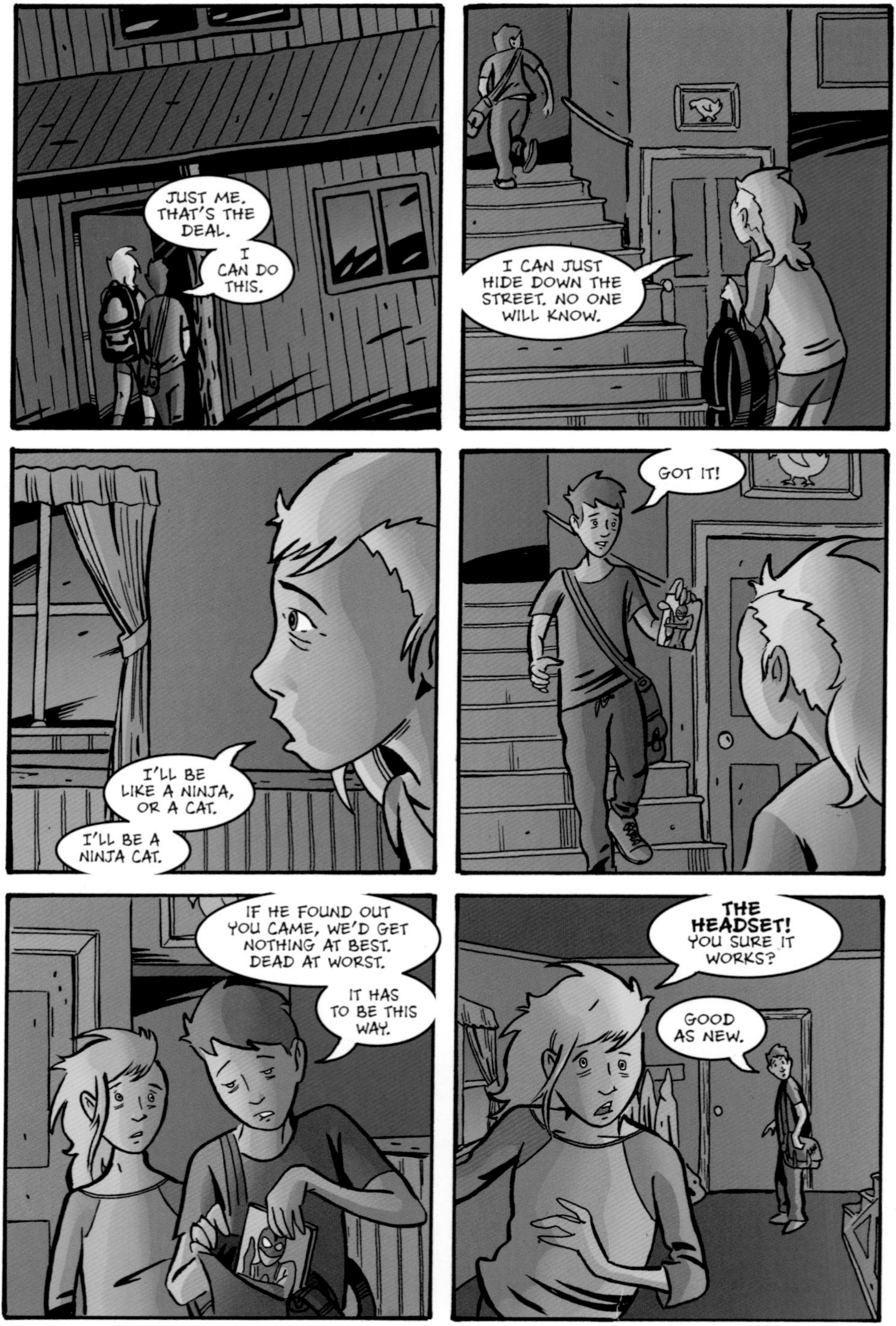
JUST ME. THAT'S THE DEAL.
I CAN DO THIS.
I CAN JUST HIDE DOWN THE STREET. NO ONE WILL KNOW.
I'LL BE LIKE A NINJA, OR A CAT.
I'LL BE A NINJA CAT.
GOT IT!
IF HE FOUND OUT YOU CAME, WE'D GET NOTHING AT BEST. DEAD AT WORST.
IT HAS TO BE THIS WAY.
THE HEADSET! YOU SURE IT WORKS?
GOOD AS NEW.

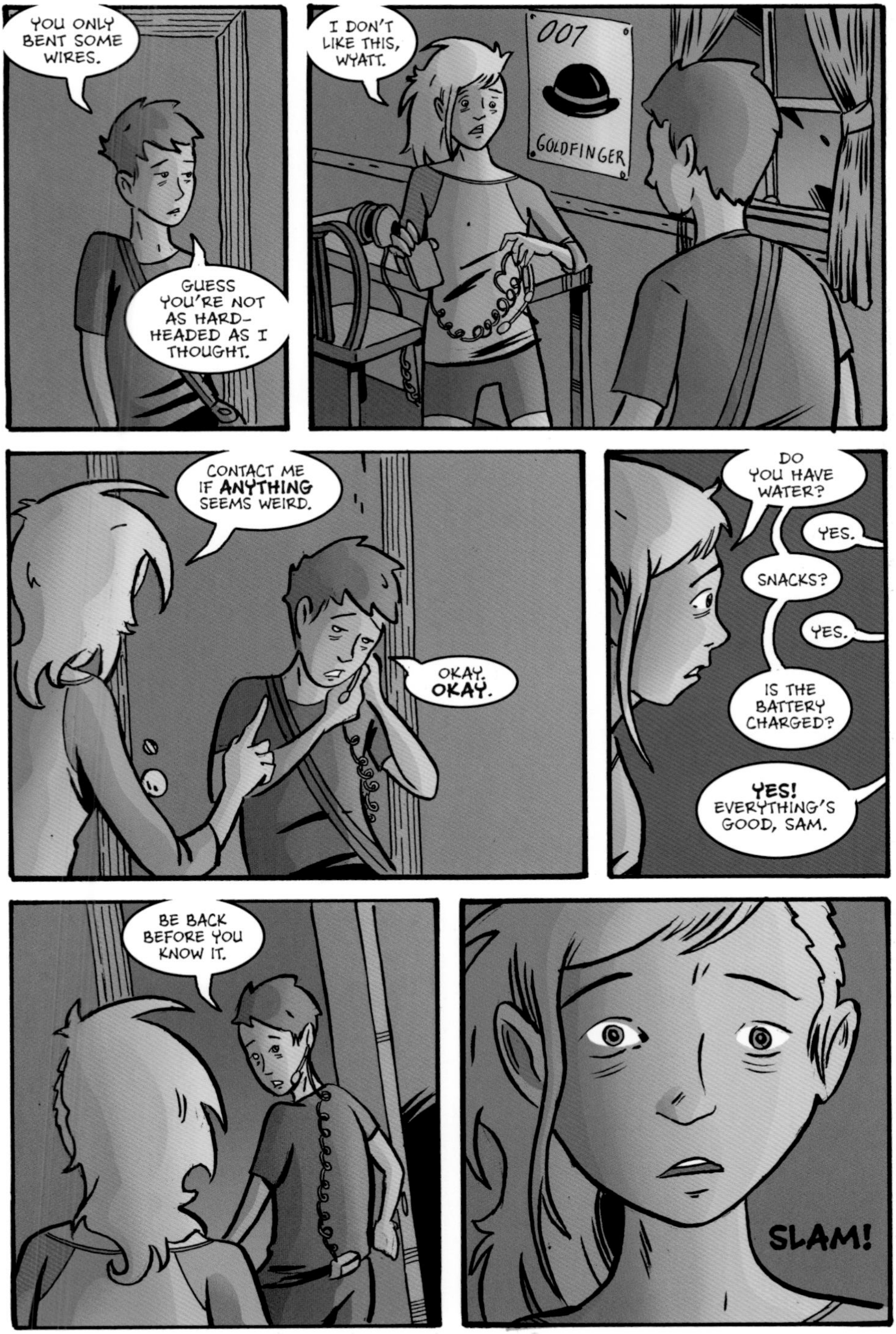
YOU ONLY BENT SOME WIRES.
GUESS YOU'RE NOT AS HARD-HEADED AS I THOUGHT.
I DON'T LIKE THIS, WYATT.
007
GOLDFINGER
CONTACT ME IF **ANYTHING** SEEMS WEIRD.
OKAY. **OKAY.**
DO YOU HAVE WATER?
YES.
SNACKS?
YES.
IS THE BATTERY CHARGED?
YES! EVERYTHING'S GOOD, SAM.
BE BACK BEFORE YOU KNOW IT.
SLAM!

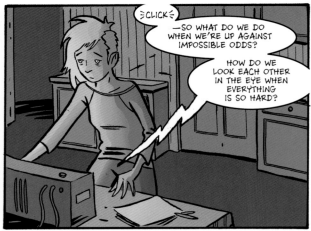

CLICK

—SO WHAT DO WE DO WHEN WE'RE UP AGAINST IMPOSSIBLE ODDS?

HOW DO WE LOOK EACH OTHER IN THE EYE WHEN EVERYTHING IS SO HARD?

IT'S A SMALL WORLD THAT HAS GOTTEN A WHOLE LOT SMALLER.

AS CARETAKERS OF IT...

...IT'S UP TO US TO MAKE THE BEST OF IT.

WANT SOME UNWARRANTED ADVICE FROM EL SONIDO?

JUST DO SOMETHING NICE FOR SOMEONE.

IT'S LIKE DAVID BOWIE ONCE SAID:

"WE CAN BE HEROES, JUST FOR ONE DAY."

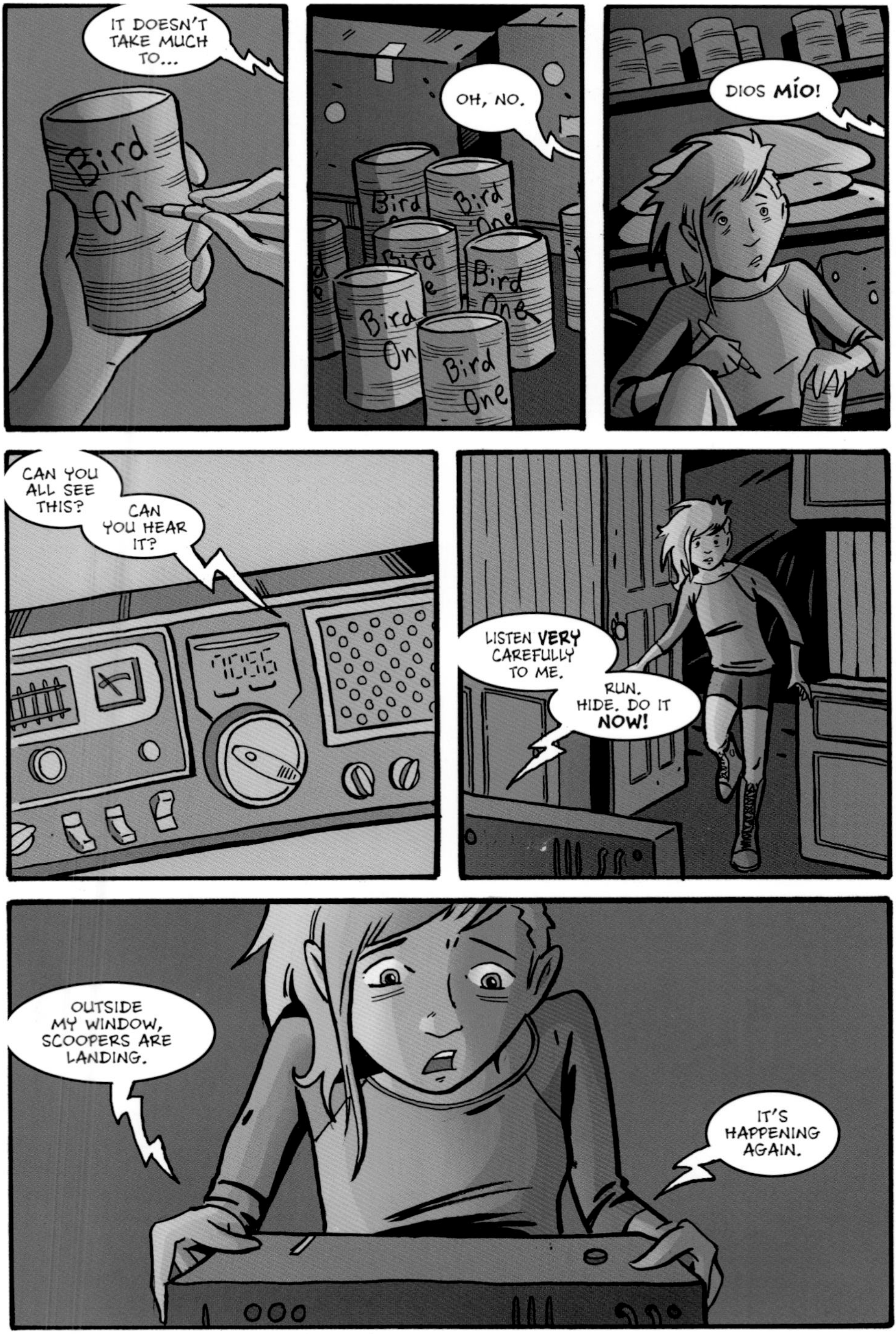

IT DOESN'T TAKE MUCH TO...
Bird On
OH, NO.
Bird One
DIOS **MÍO**!
CAN YOU ALL SEE THIS?
CAN YOU HEAR IT?
LISTEN **VERY** CAREFULLY TO ME.
RUN. HIDE. DO IT **NOW!**
OUTSIDE MY WINDOW, SCOOPERS ARE LANDING.
IT'S HAPPENING AGAIN.

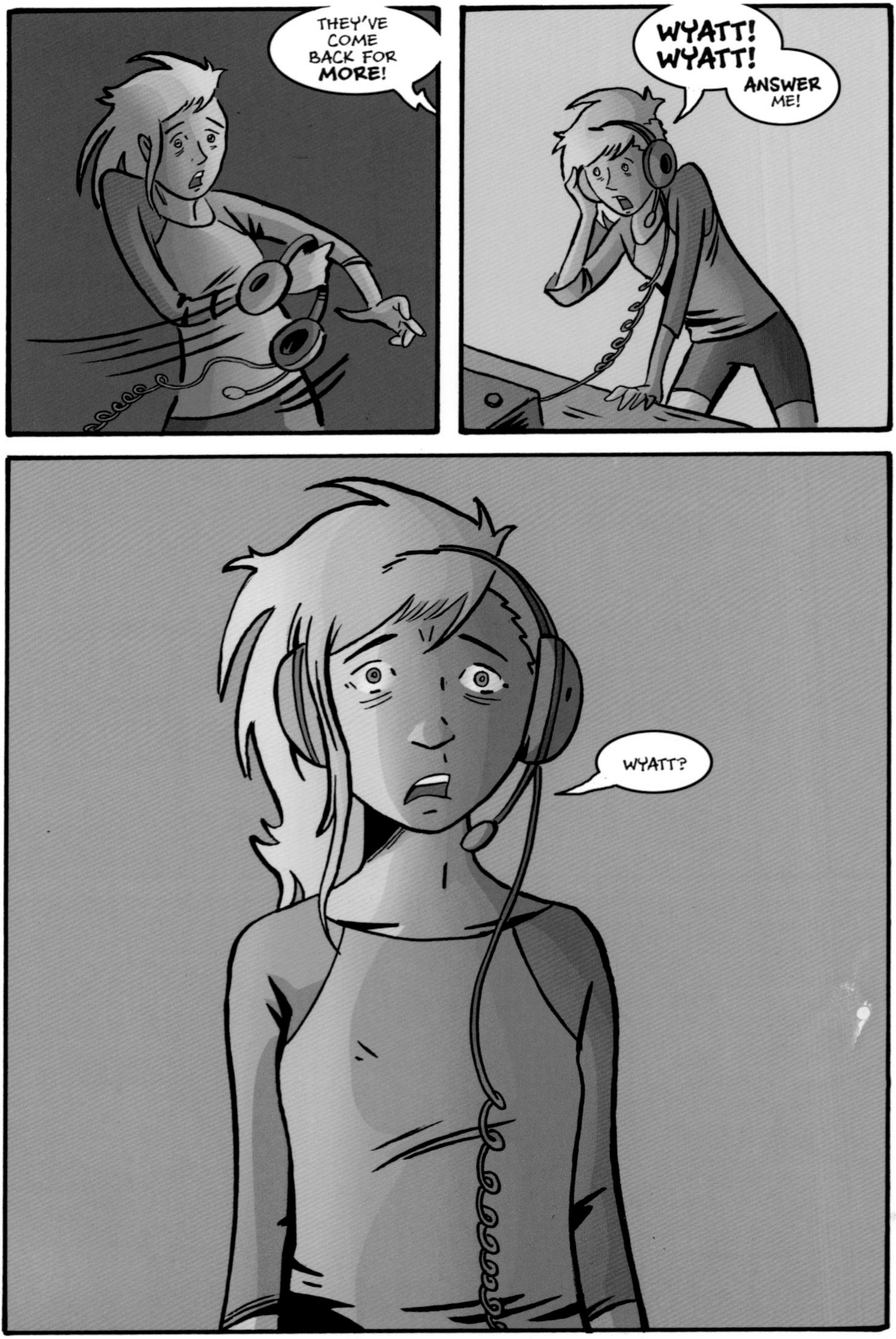
THEY'VE COME BACK FOR MORE!
WYATT! WYATT!
ANSWER ME!
WYATT?

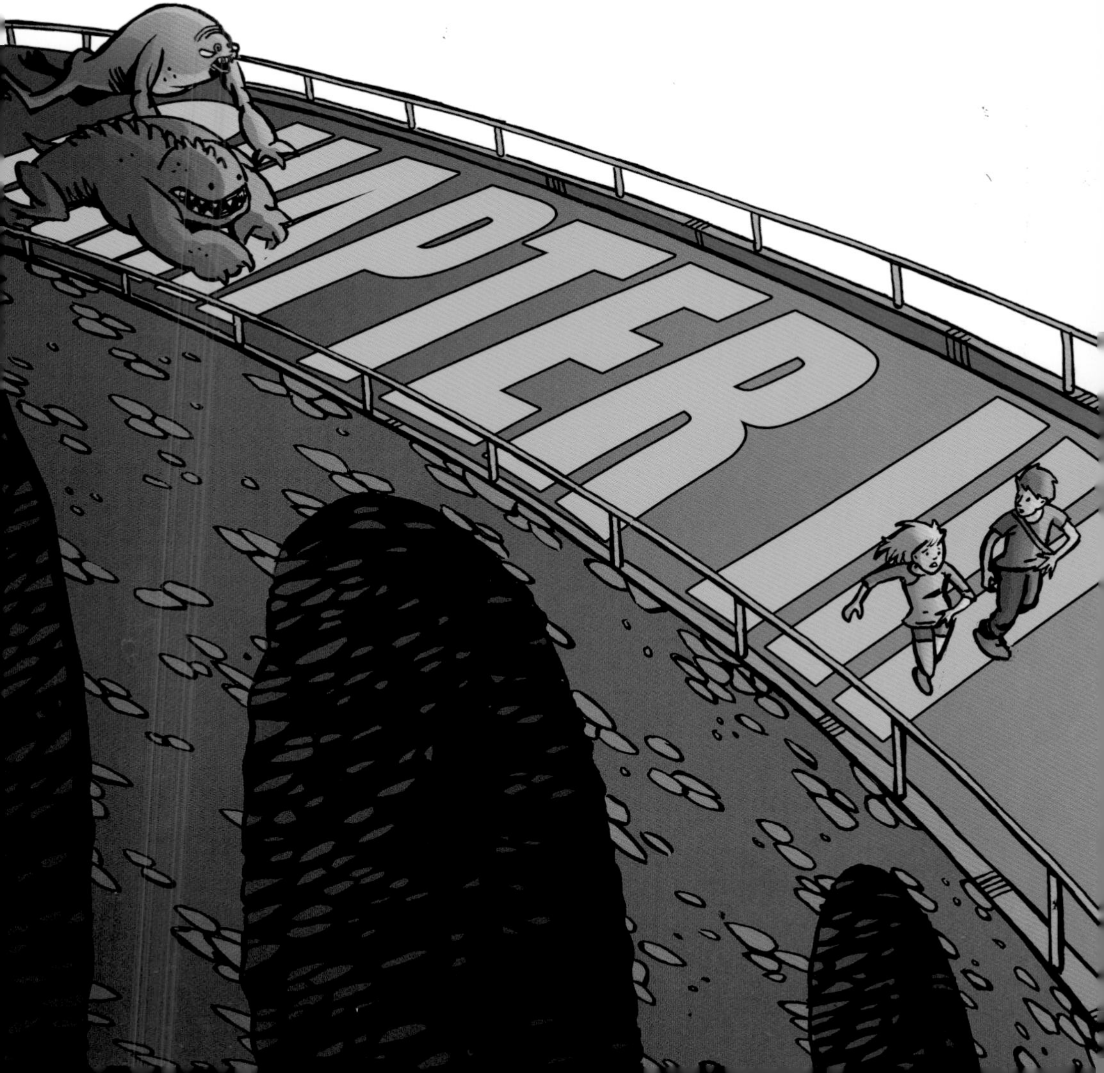

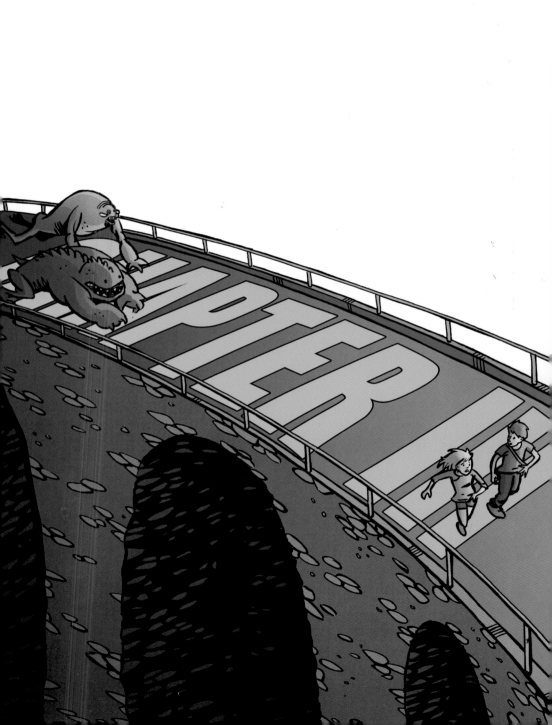

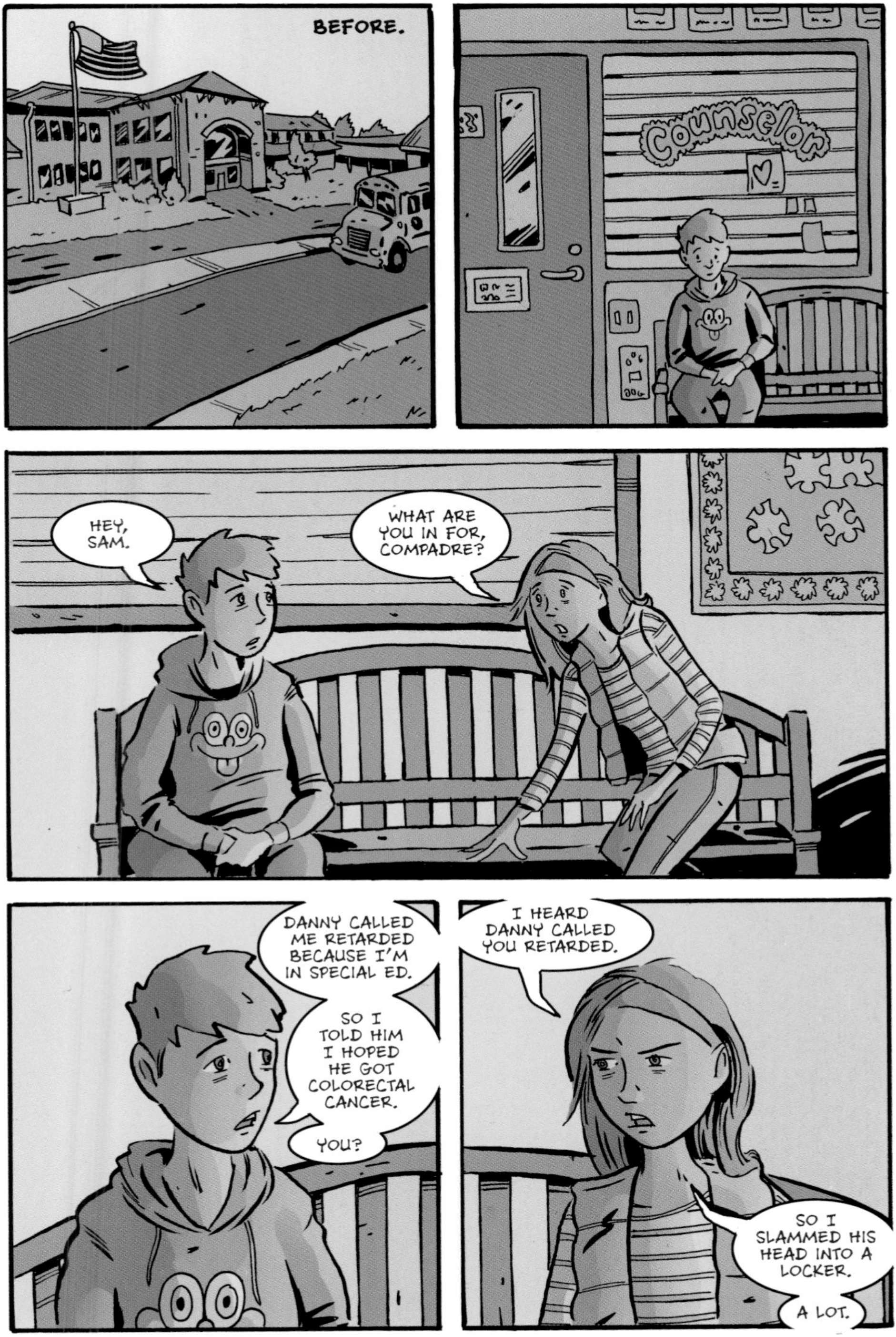
BEFORE.
Counselor
HEY, SAM.
WHAT ARE YOU IN FOR, COMPADRE?
DANNY CALLED ME RETARDED BECAUSE I'M IN SPECIAL ED.
SO I TOLD HIM I HOPED HE GOT COLORECTAL CANCER.
YOU?
I HEARD DANNY CALLED YOU RETARDED.
SO I SLAMMED HIS HEAD INTO A LOCKER.
A LOT.

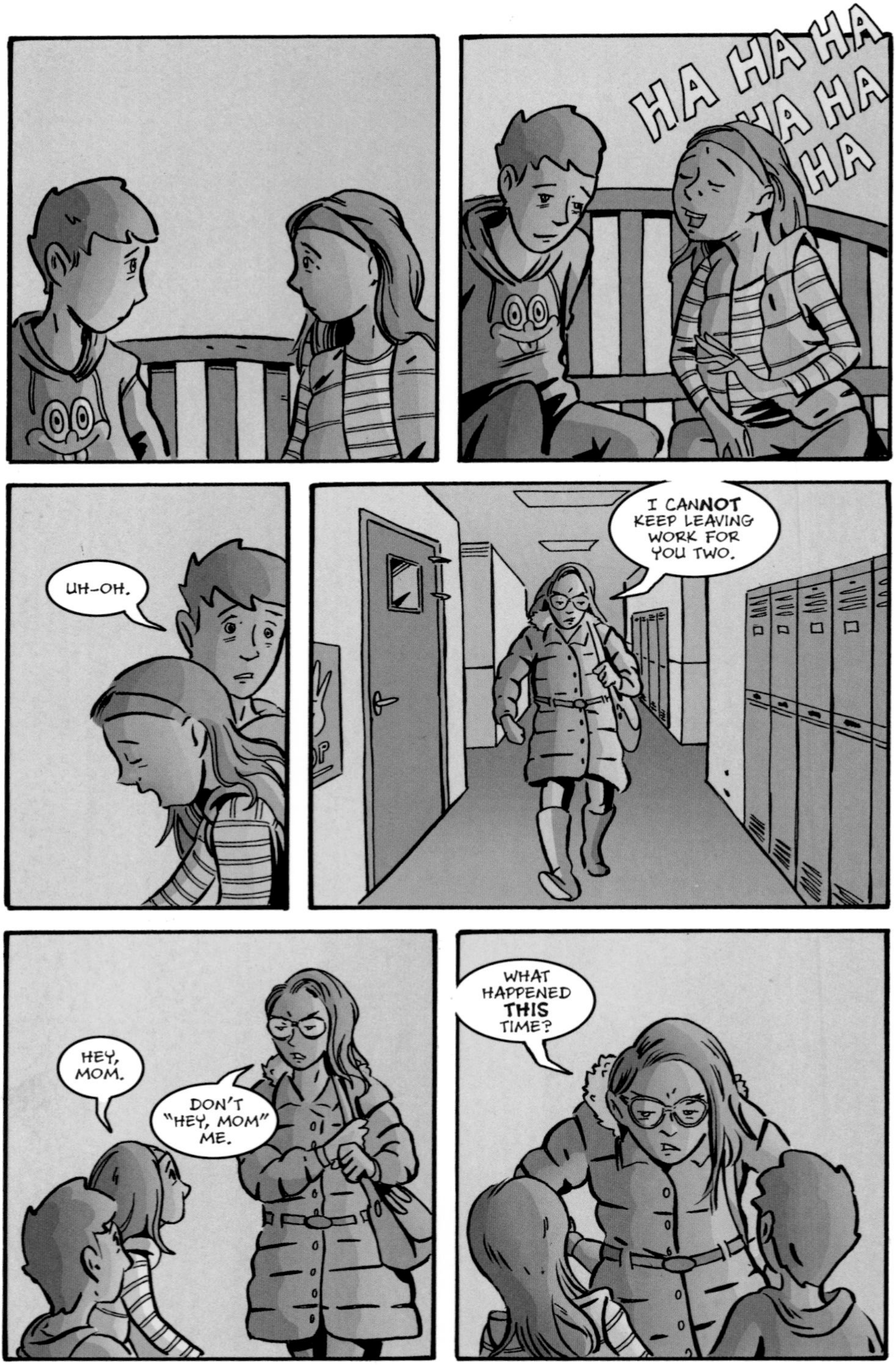
HA HA HA
HA HA HA
HA
UH-OH.
I CANNOT KEEP LEAVING WORK FOR YOU TWO.
HEY, MOM.
DON'T "HEY, MOM" ME.
WHAT HAPPENED THIS TIME?

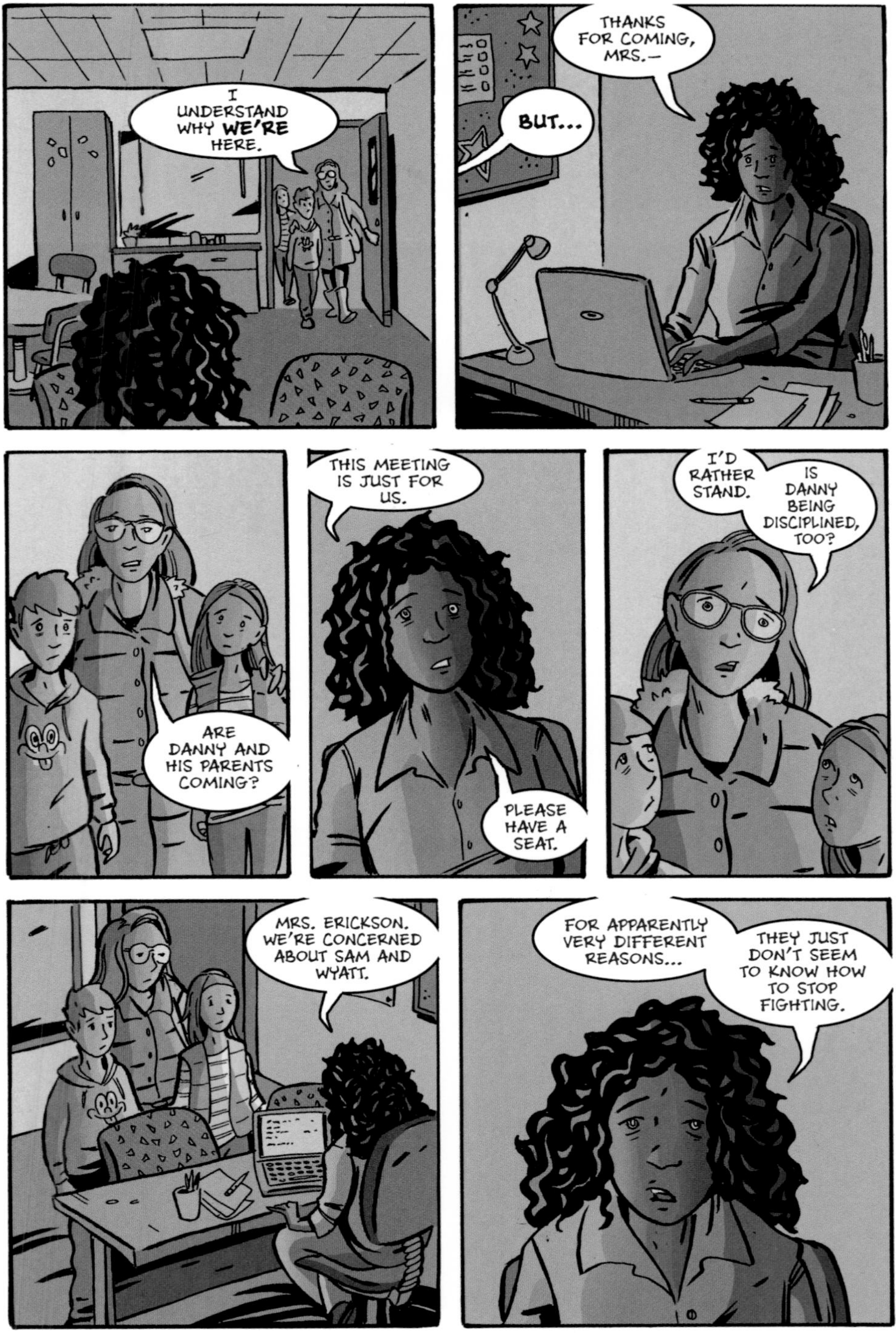
I UNDERSTAND WHY WE'RE HERE.
THANKS FOR COMING, MRS.–
BUT...
ARE DANNY AND HIS PARENTS COMING?
THIS MEETING IS JUST FOR US.
PLEASE HAVE A SEAT.
I'D RATHER STAND.
IS DANNY BEING DISCIPLINED, TOO?
MRS. ERICKSON. WE'RE CONCERNED ABOUT SAM AND WYATT.
FOR APPARENTLY VERY DIFFERENT REASONS...
THEY JUST DON'T SEEM TO KNOW HOW TO STOP FIGHTING.

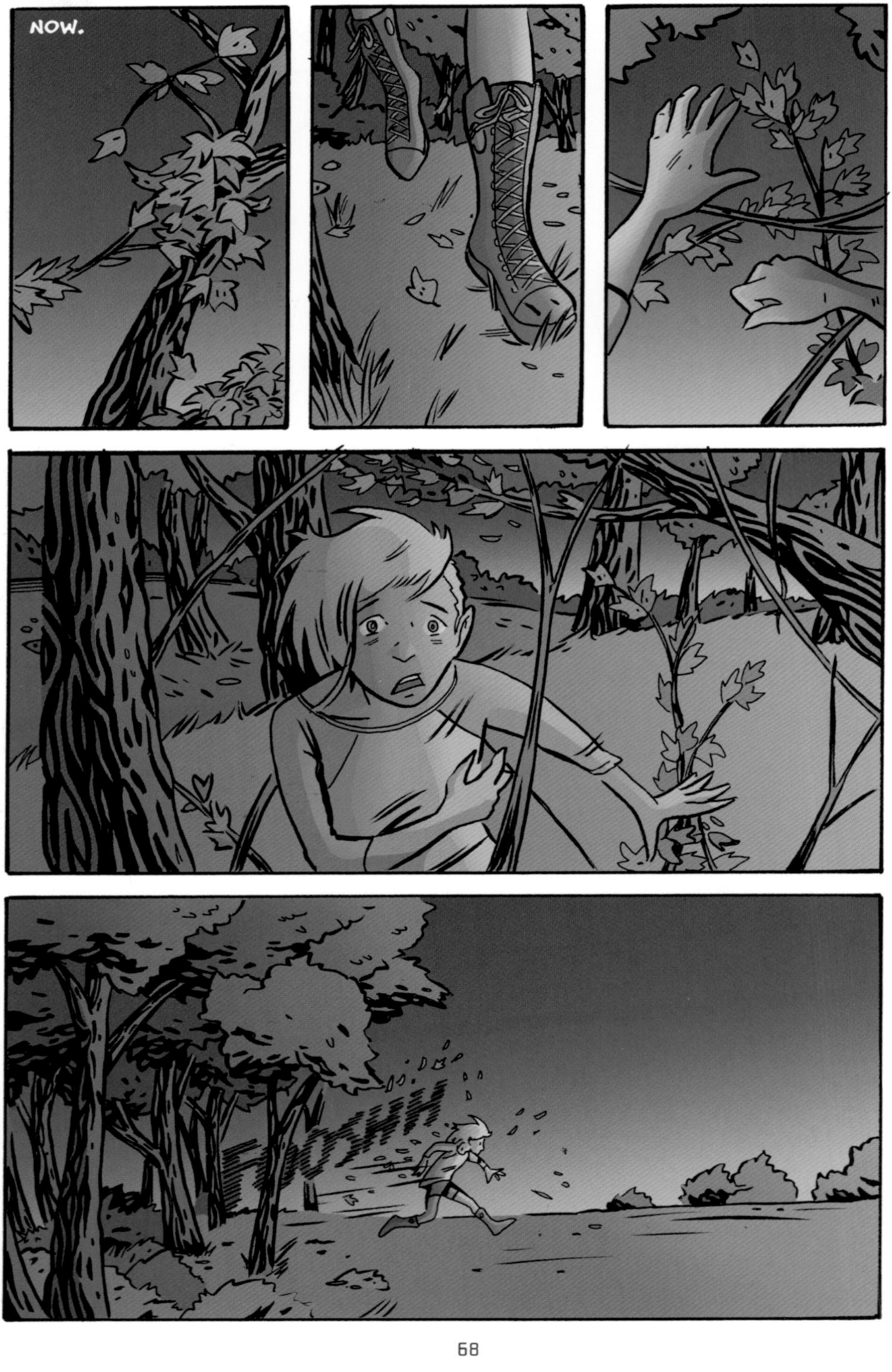
NOW.

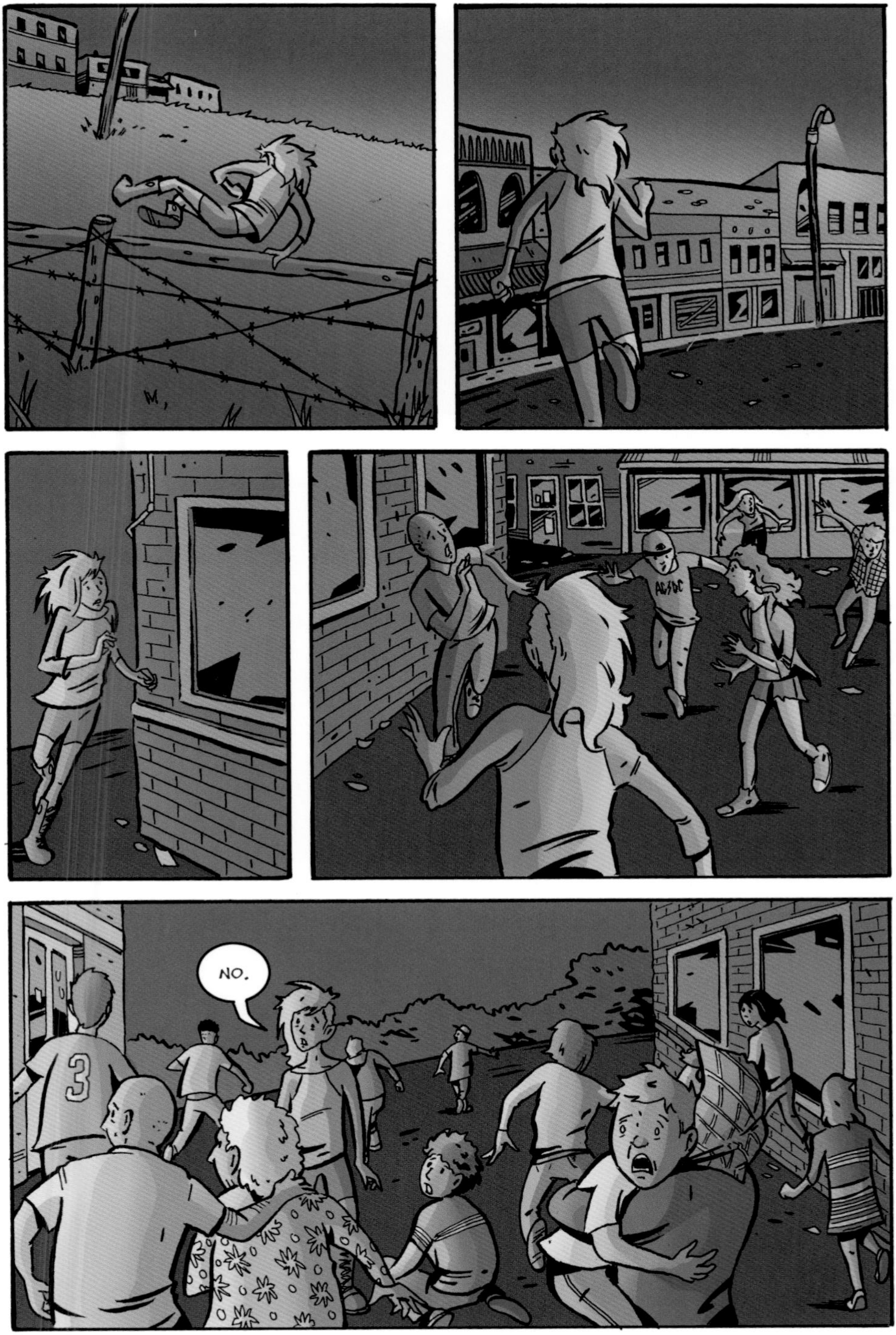
AC/DC
NO.

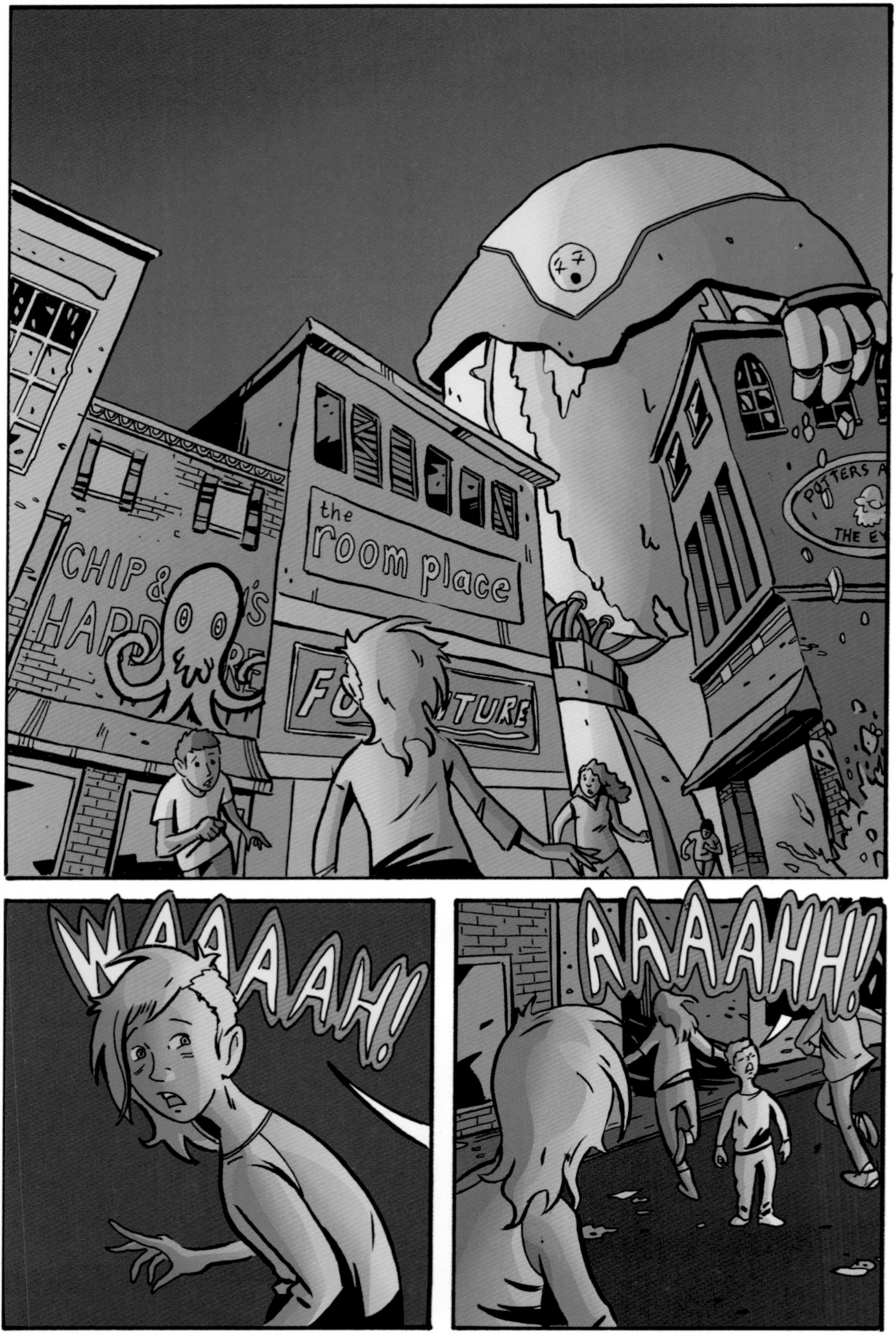
the room place
WAAAAAH!
AAAAAH!

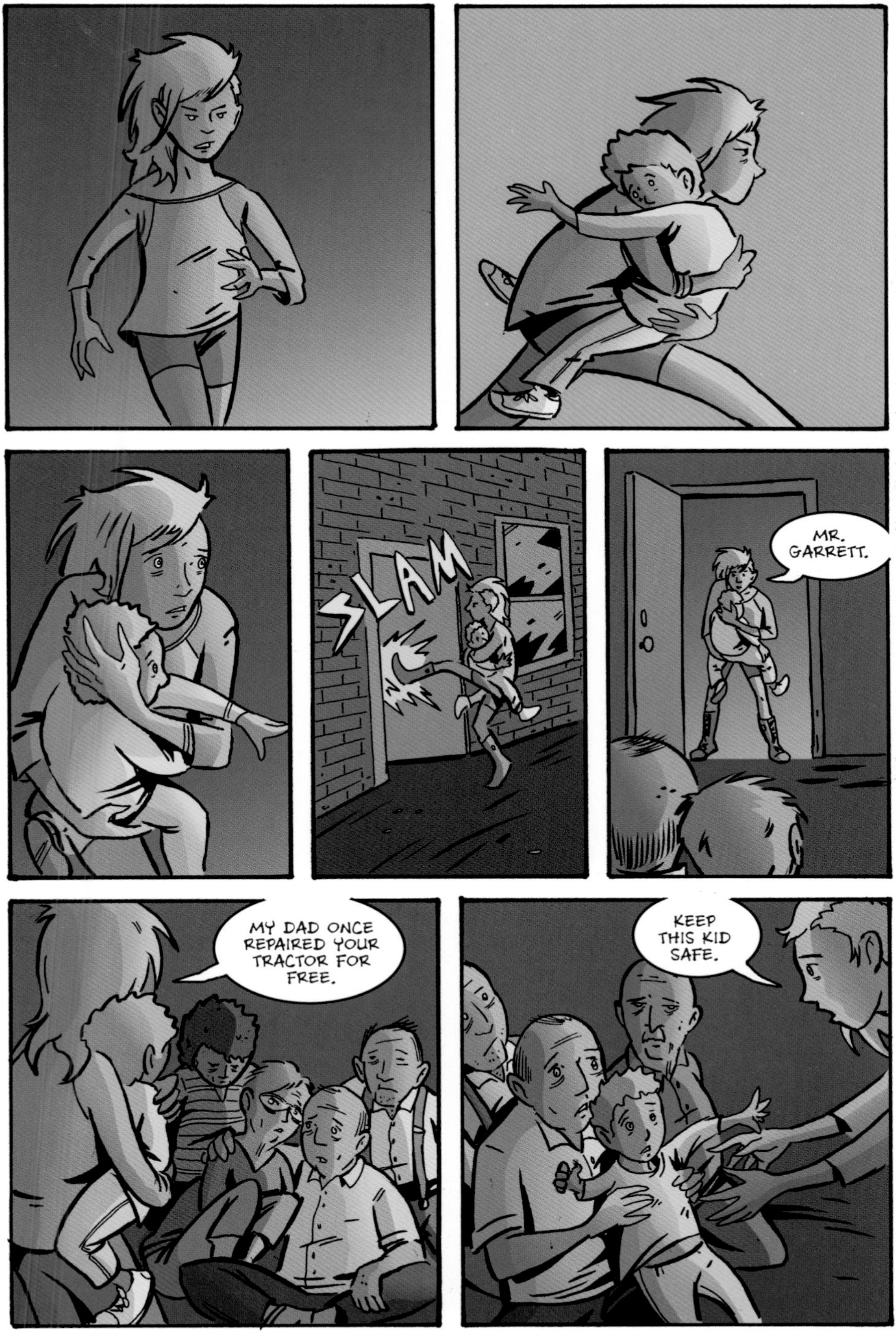
SLAM
MR. GARRETT.
MY DAD ONCE REPAIRED YOUR TRACTOR FOR FREE.
KEEP THIS KID SAFE.

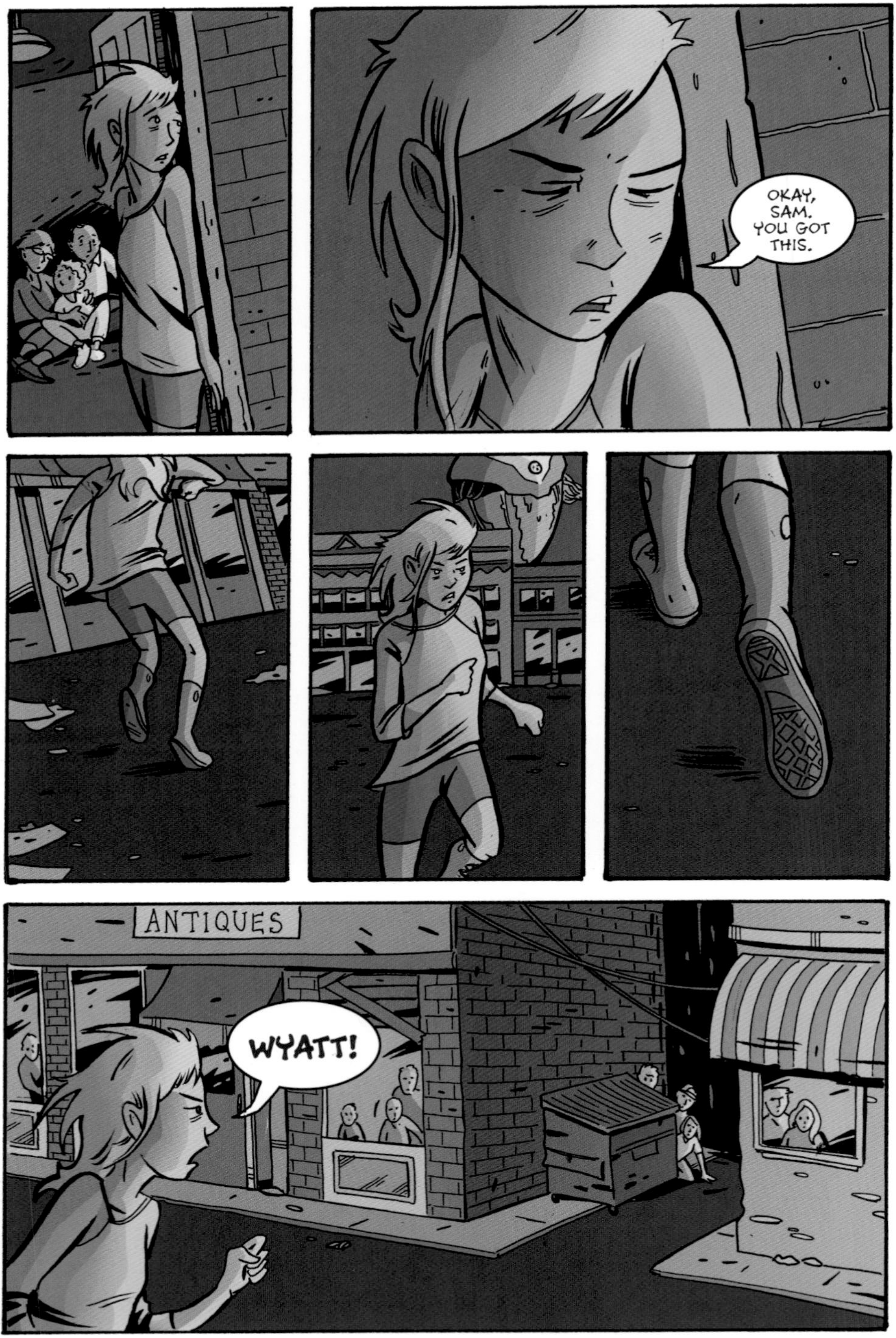
OKAY, SAM. YOU GOT THIS.
ANTIQUES
WYATT!

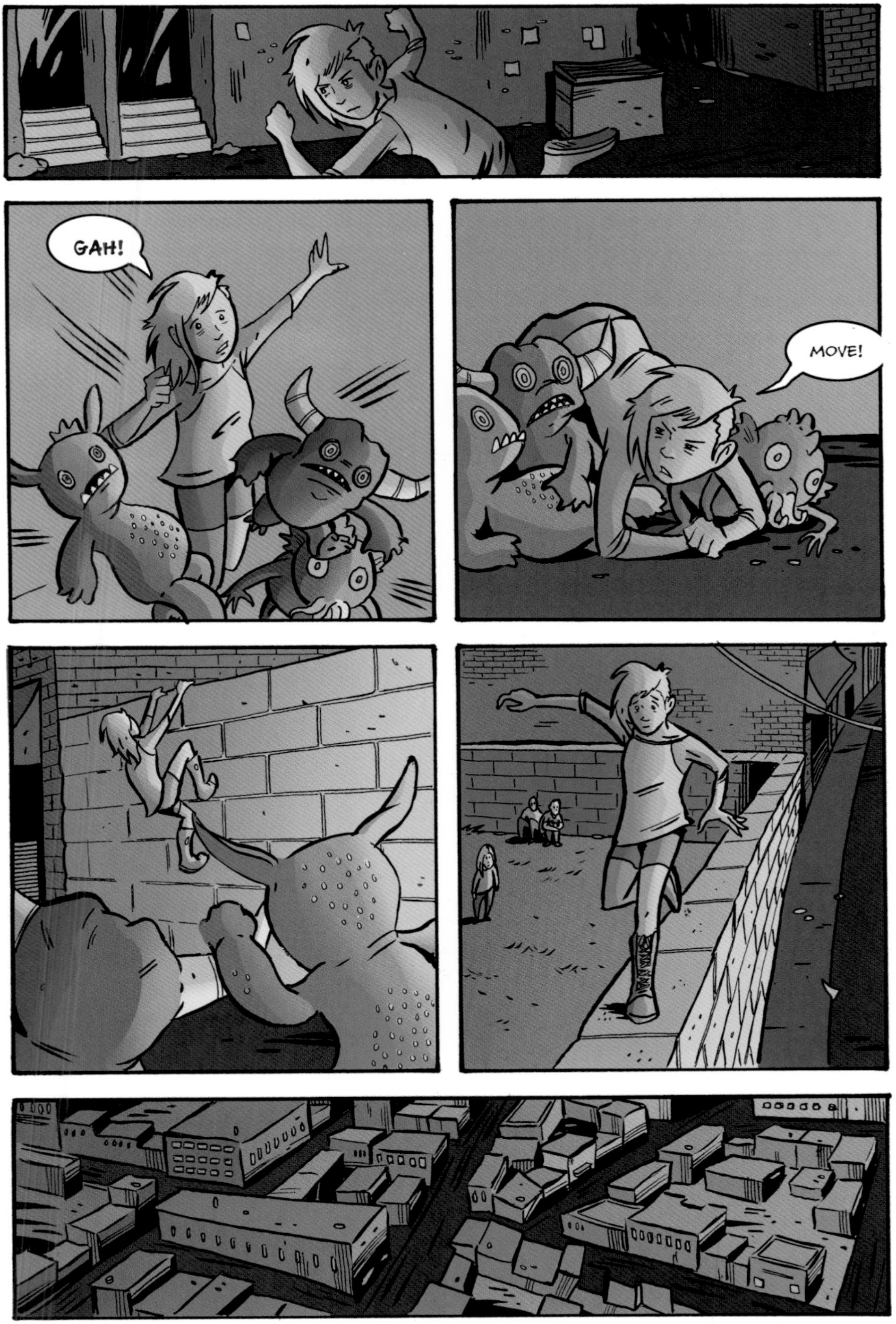
GAH!
MOVE!

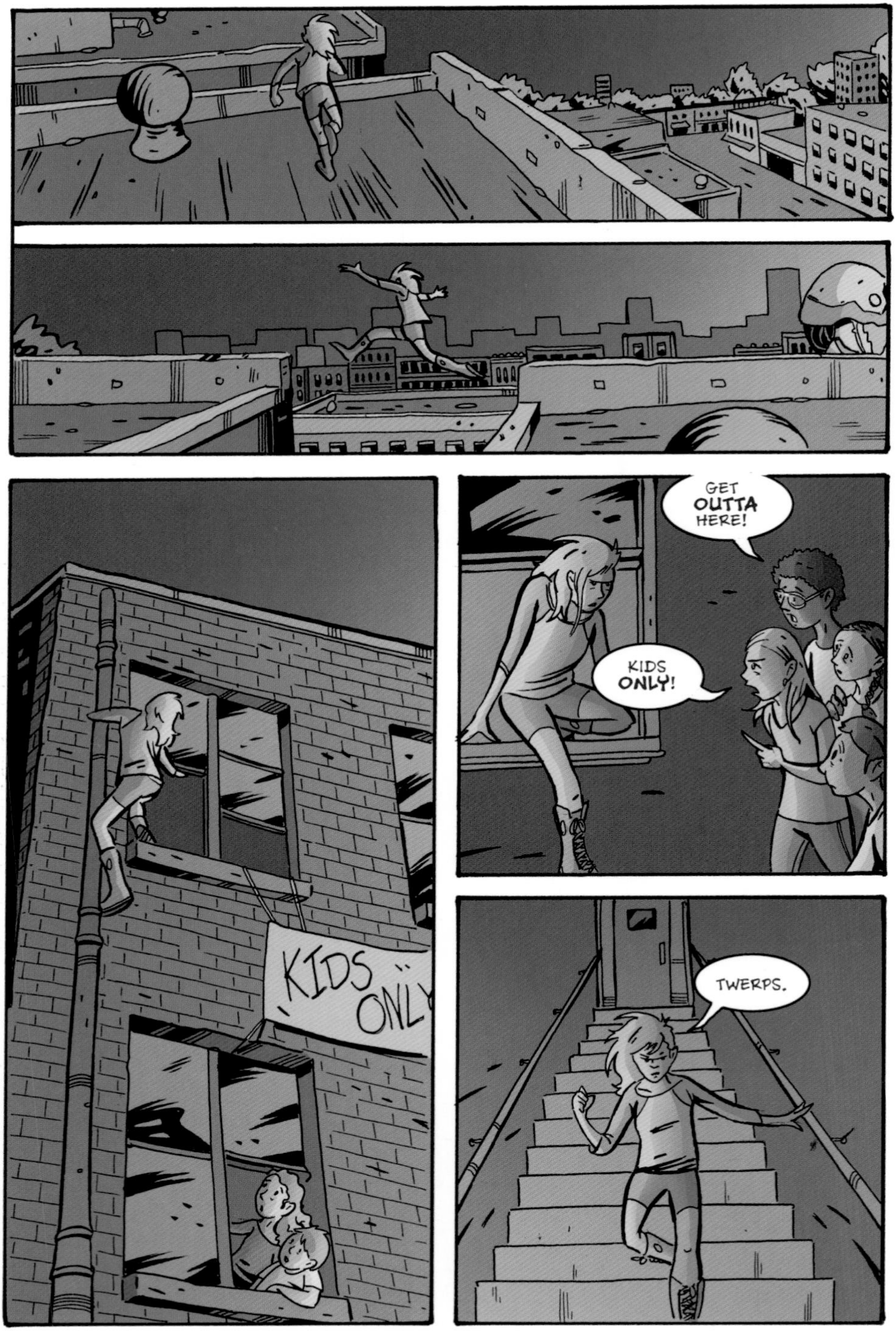
KIDS ONLY
GET OUTTA HERE!
KIDS ONLY!
TWERPS.

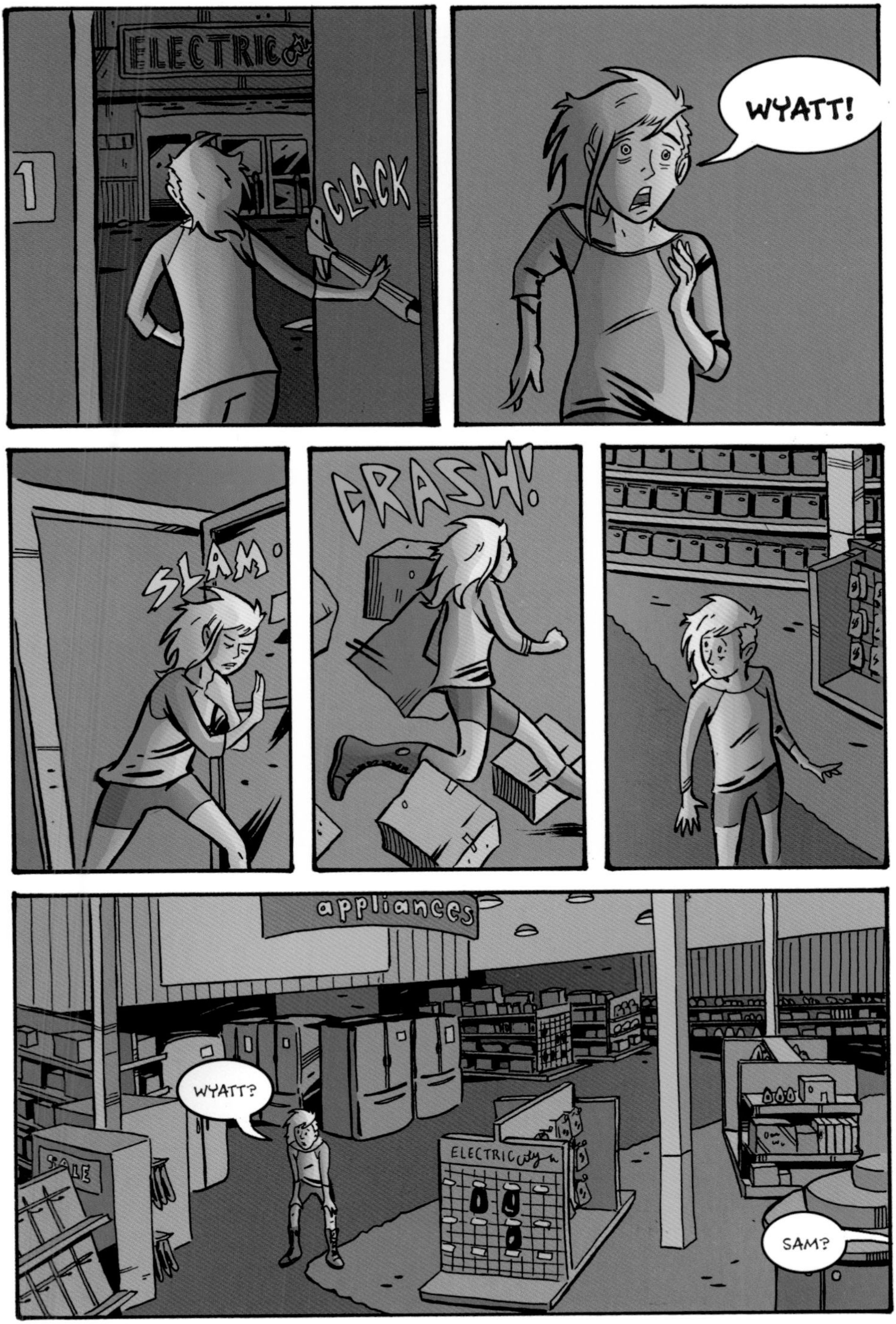
ELECTRIC
1
CLACK
WYATT!
SLAM
CRASH!
appliances
WYATT?
ELECTRIC
SALE
SAM?

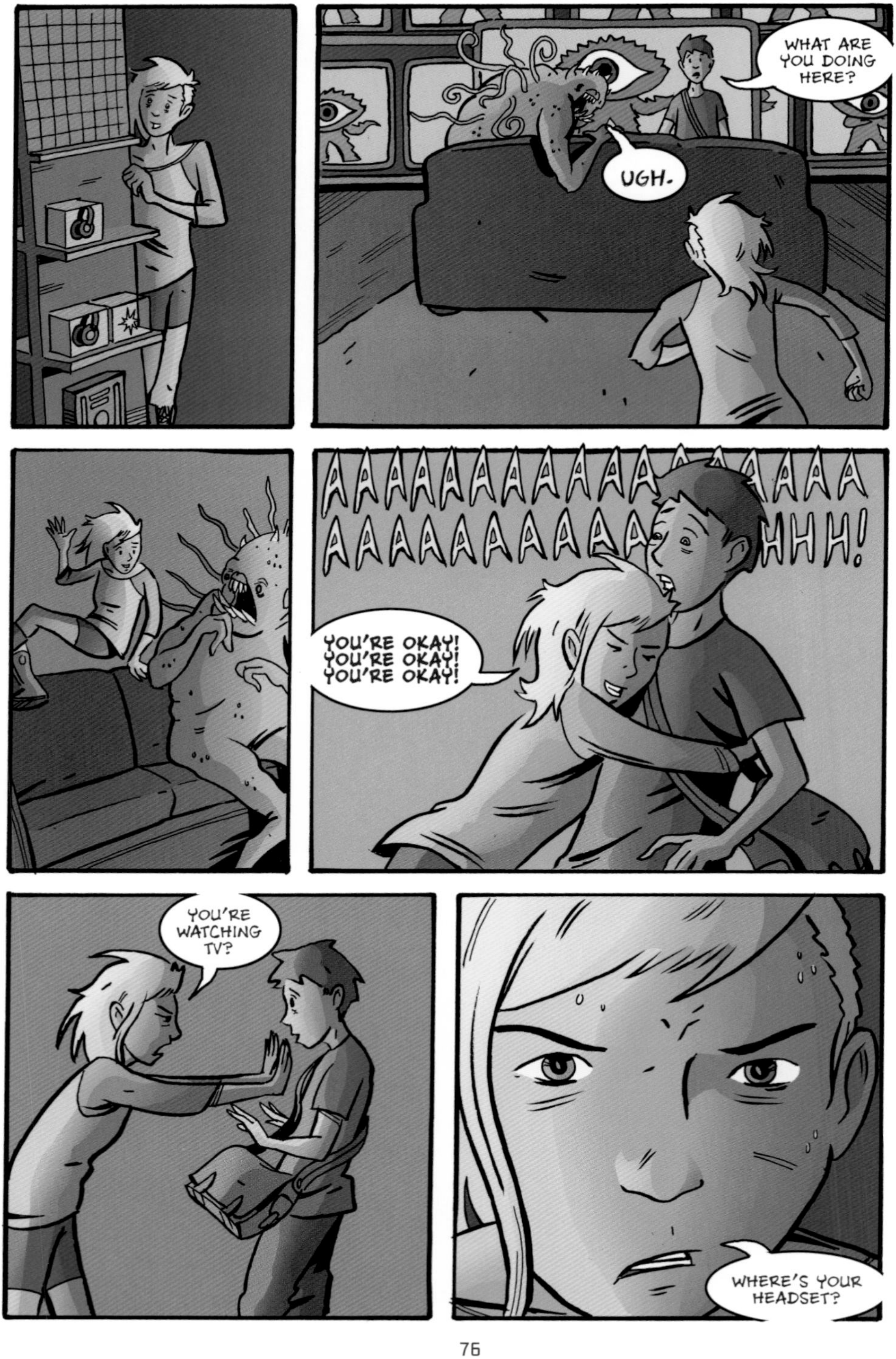
WHAT ARE YOU DOING HERE?
UGH.
AAAAAAAAAAAAAAAAAAA AAAAAAAAAAAAAHHH!
YOU'RE OKAY! YOU'RE OKAY! YOU'RE OKAY!
YOU'RE WATCHING TV?
WHERE'S YOUR HEADSET?

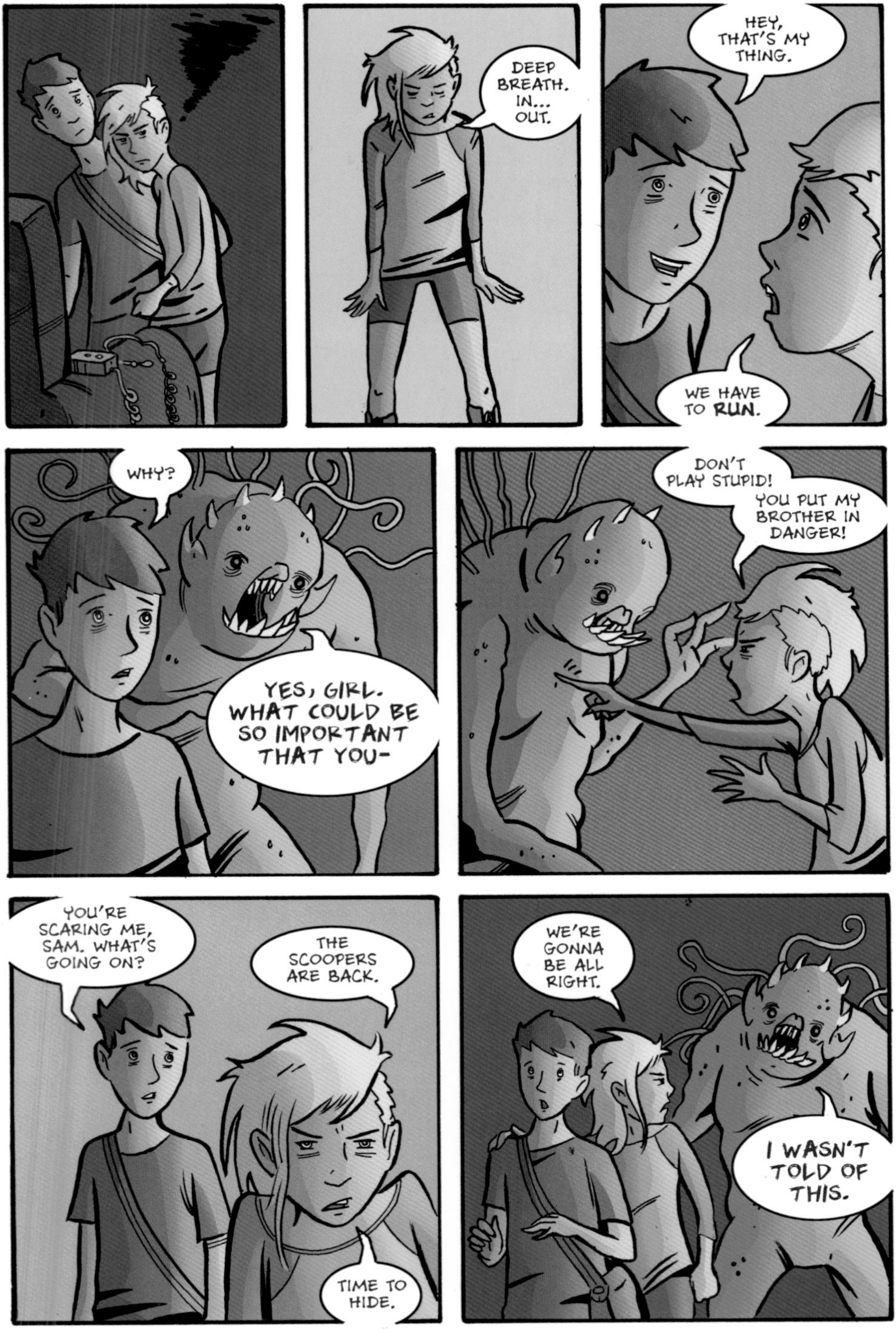
DEEP BREATH. IN... OUT.
HEY, THAT'S MY THING.
WE HAVE TO RUN.
WHY?
YES, GIRL. WHAT COULD BE SO IMPORTANT THAT YOU-
DON'T PLAY STUPID!
YOU PUT MY BROTHER IN DANGER!
YOU'RE SCARING ME, SAM. WHAT'S GOING ON?
THE SCOOPERS ARE BACK.
TIME TO HIDE.
WE'RE GONNA BE ALL RIGHT.
I WASN'T TOLD OF THIS.

I HATE THIS PLANET.

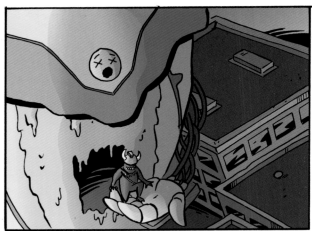

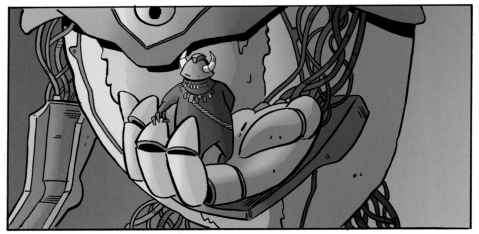

WELCOME TO THE BEAUTIFUL SOUTH, COMMANDER.

LET'S GET THIS OVER WITH.

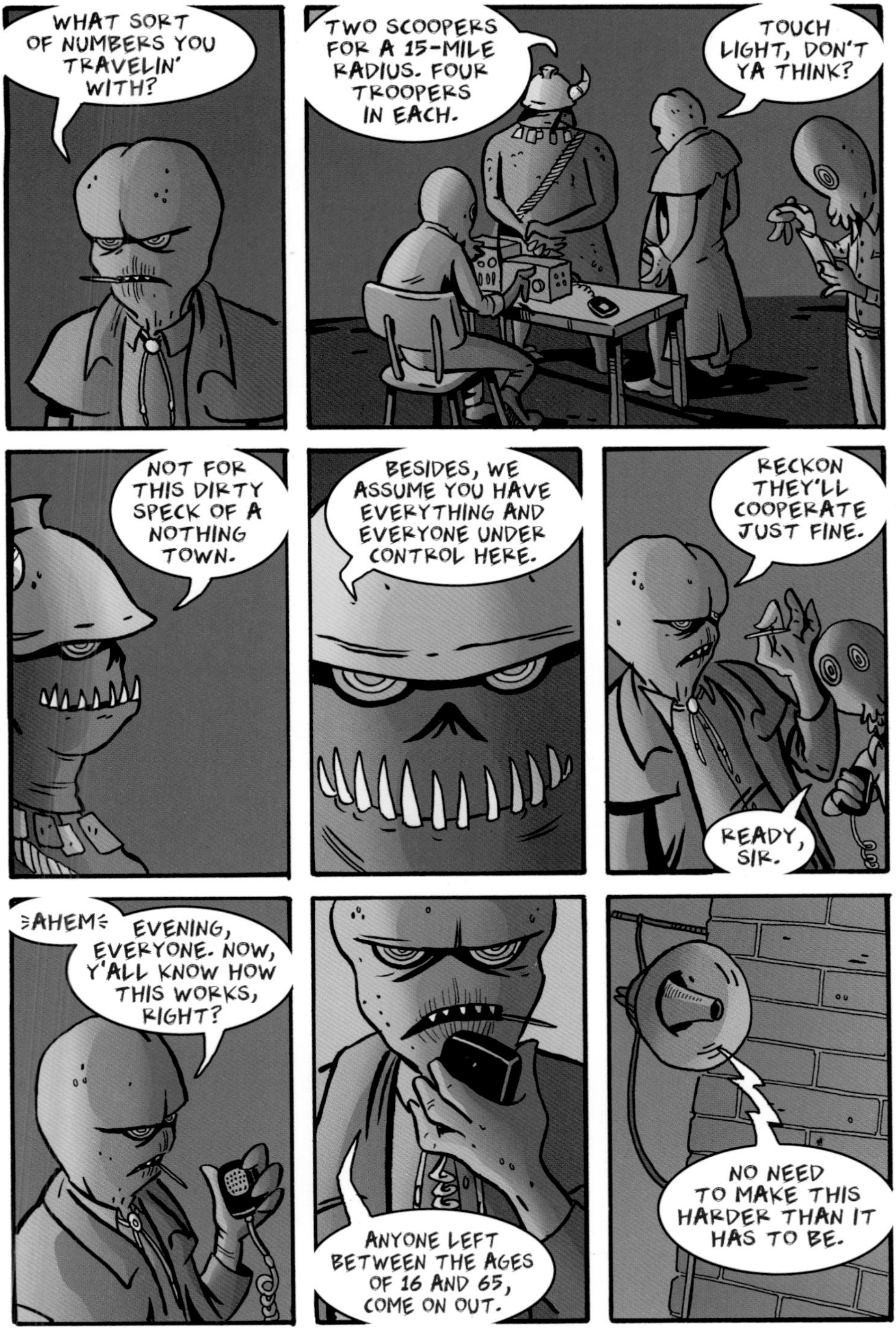
WHAT SORT OF NUMBERS YOU TRAVELIN' WITH?
TWO SCOOPERS FOR A 15-MILE RADIUS. FOUR TROOPERS IN EACH.
TOUCH LIGHT, DON'T YA THINK?
NOT FOR THIS DIRTY SPECK OF A NOTHING TOWN.
BESIDES, WE ASSUME YOU HAVE EVERYTHING AND EVERYONE UNDER CONTROL HERE.
RECKON THEY'LL COOPERATE JUST FINE.
READY, SIR.
AHEM
EVENING, EVERYONE. NOW, Y'ALL KNOW HOW THIS WORKS, RIGHT?
ANYONE LEFT BETWEEN THE AGES OF 16 AND 65, COME ON OUT.
NO NEED TO MAKE THIS HARDER THAN IT HAS TO BE.

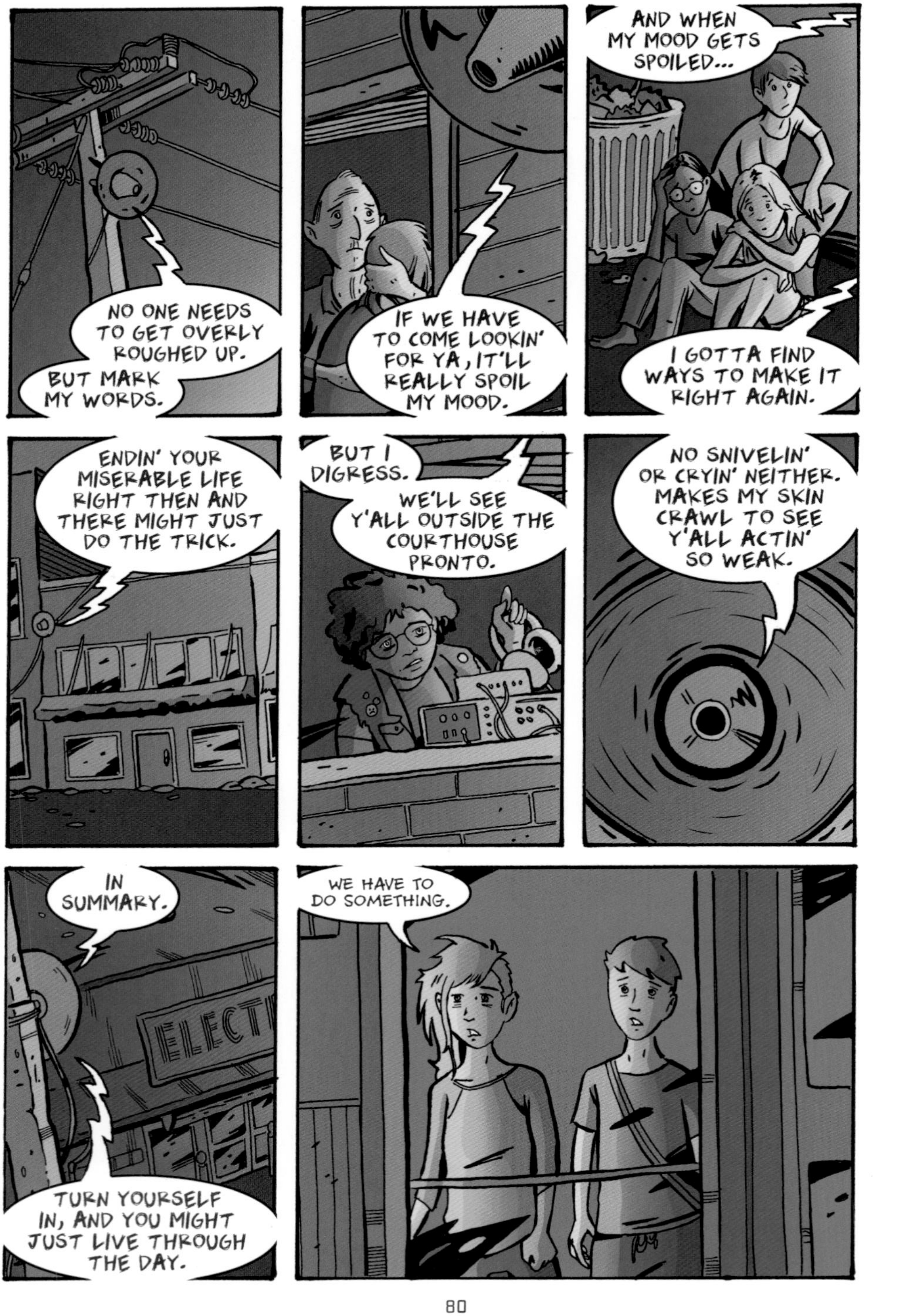
NO ONE NEEDS TO GET OVERLY ROUGHED UP.
BUT MARK MY WORDS.
IF WE HAVE TO COME LOOKIN' FOR YA, IT'LL REALLY SPOIL MY MOOD.
AND WHEN MY MOOD GETS SPOILED...
I GOTTA FIND WAYS TO MAKE IT RIGHT AGAIN.
ENDIN' YOUR MISERABLE LIFE RIGHT THEN AND THERE MIGHT JUST DO THE TRICK.
BUT I DIGRESS.
WE'LL SEE Y'ALL OUTSIDE THE COURTHOUSE PRONTO.
NO SNIVELIN' OR CRYIN' NEITHER. MAKES MY SKIN CRAWL TO SEE Y'ALL ACTIN' SO WEAK.
IN SUMMARY.
TURN YOURSELF IN, AND YOU MIGHT JUST LIVE THROUGH THE DAY.
ELECT
WE HAVE TO DO SOMETHING.

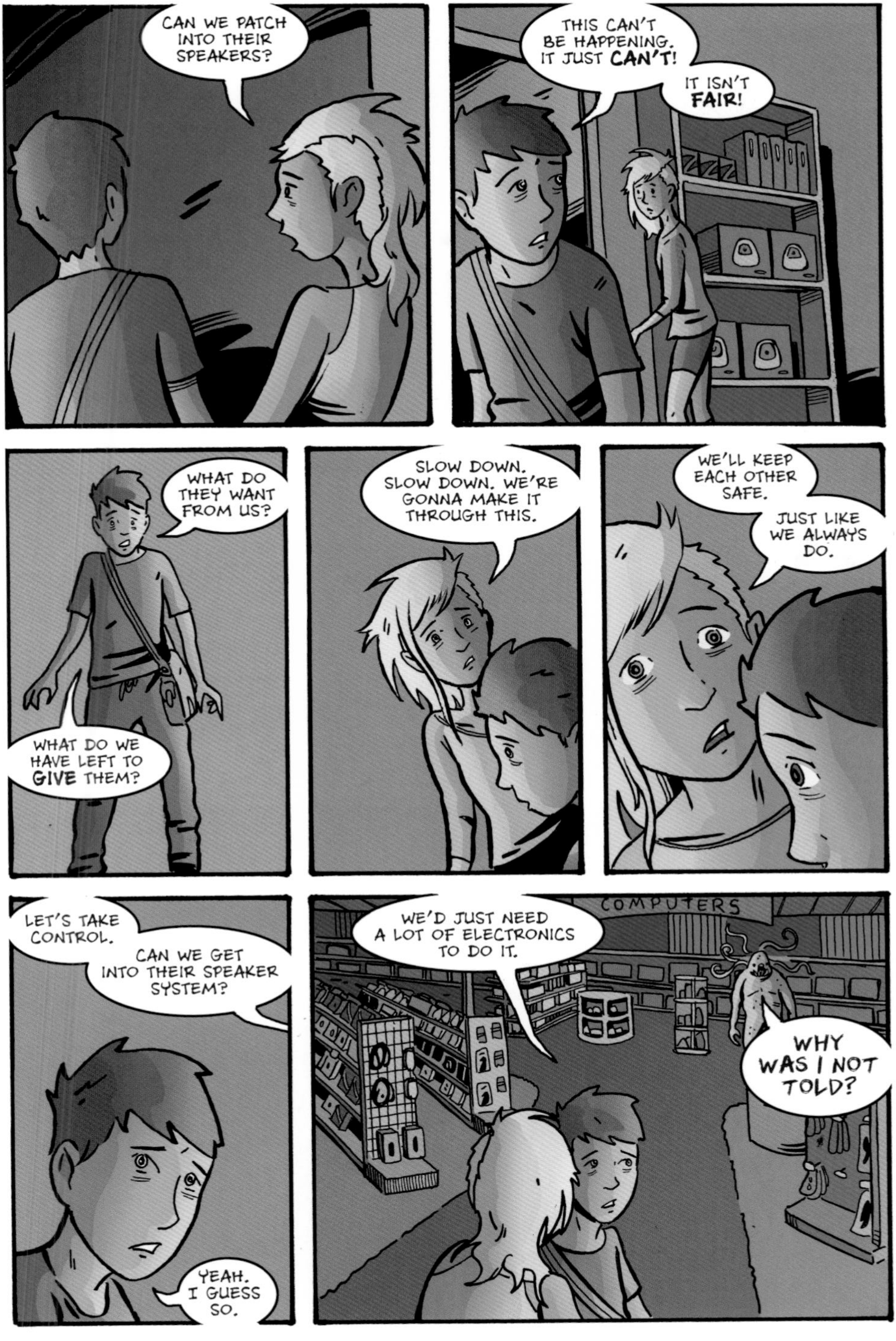
CAN WE PATCH INTO THEIR SPEAKERS?
THIS CAN'T BE HAPPENING. IT JUST CAN'T!
IT ISN'T FAIR!
WHAT DO THEY WANT FROM US?
WHAT DO WE HAVE LEFT TO GIVE THEM?
SLOW DOWN. SLOW DOWN. WE'RE GONNA MAKE IT THROUGH THIS.
WE'LL KEEP EACH OTHER SAFE.
JUST LIKE WE ALWAYS DO.
LET'S TAKE CONTROL.
CAN WE GET INTO THEIR SPEAKER SYSTEM?
YEAH. I GUESS SO.
WE'D JUST NEED A LOT OF ELECTRONICS TO DO IT.
COMPUTERS
WHY WAS I NOT TOLD?

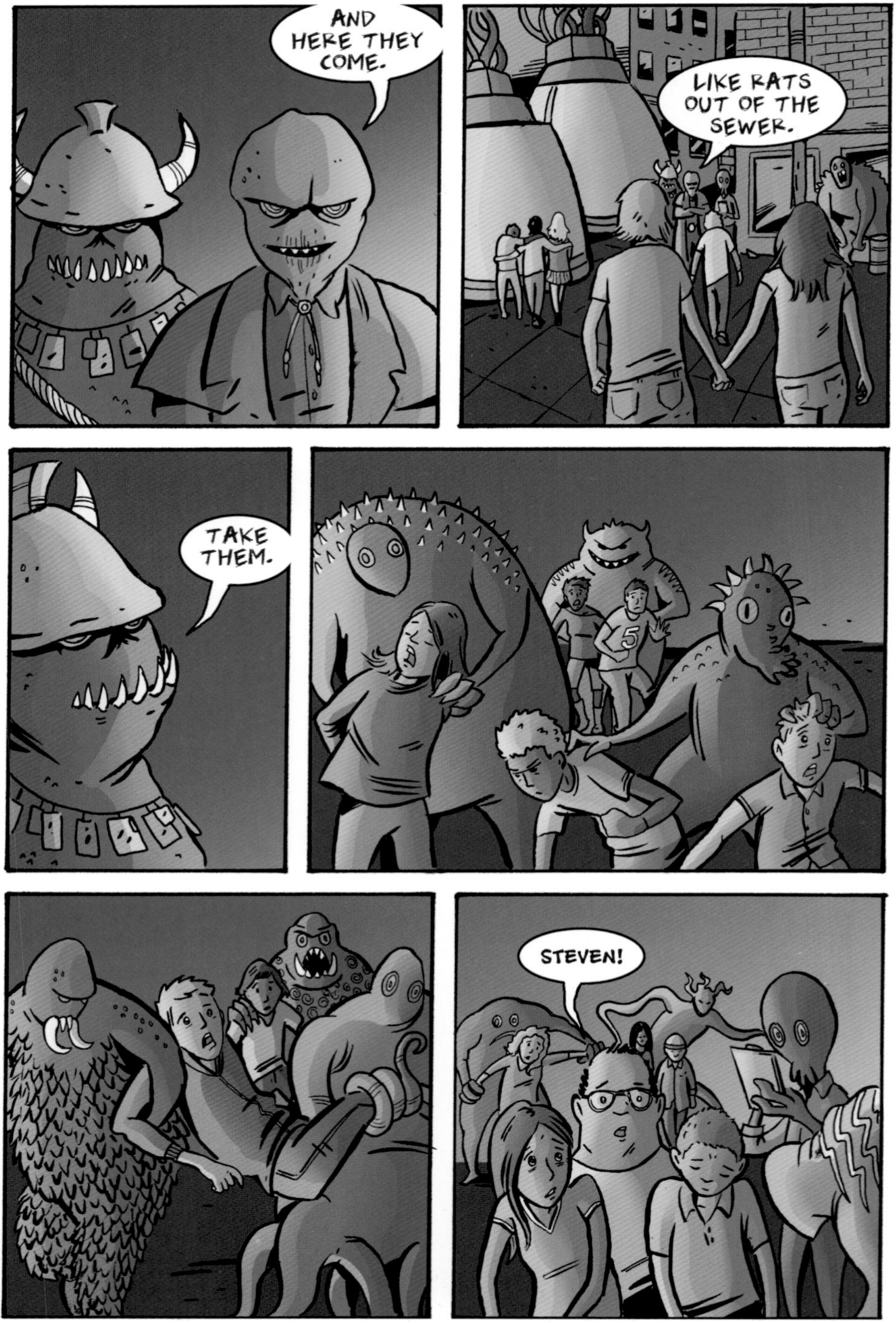
AND HERE THEY COME.
LIKE RATS OUT OF THE SEWER.
TAKE THEM.
STEVEN!

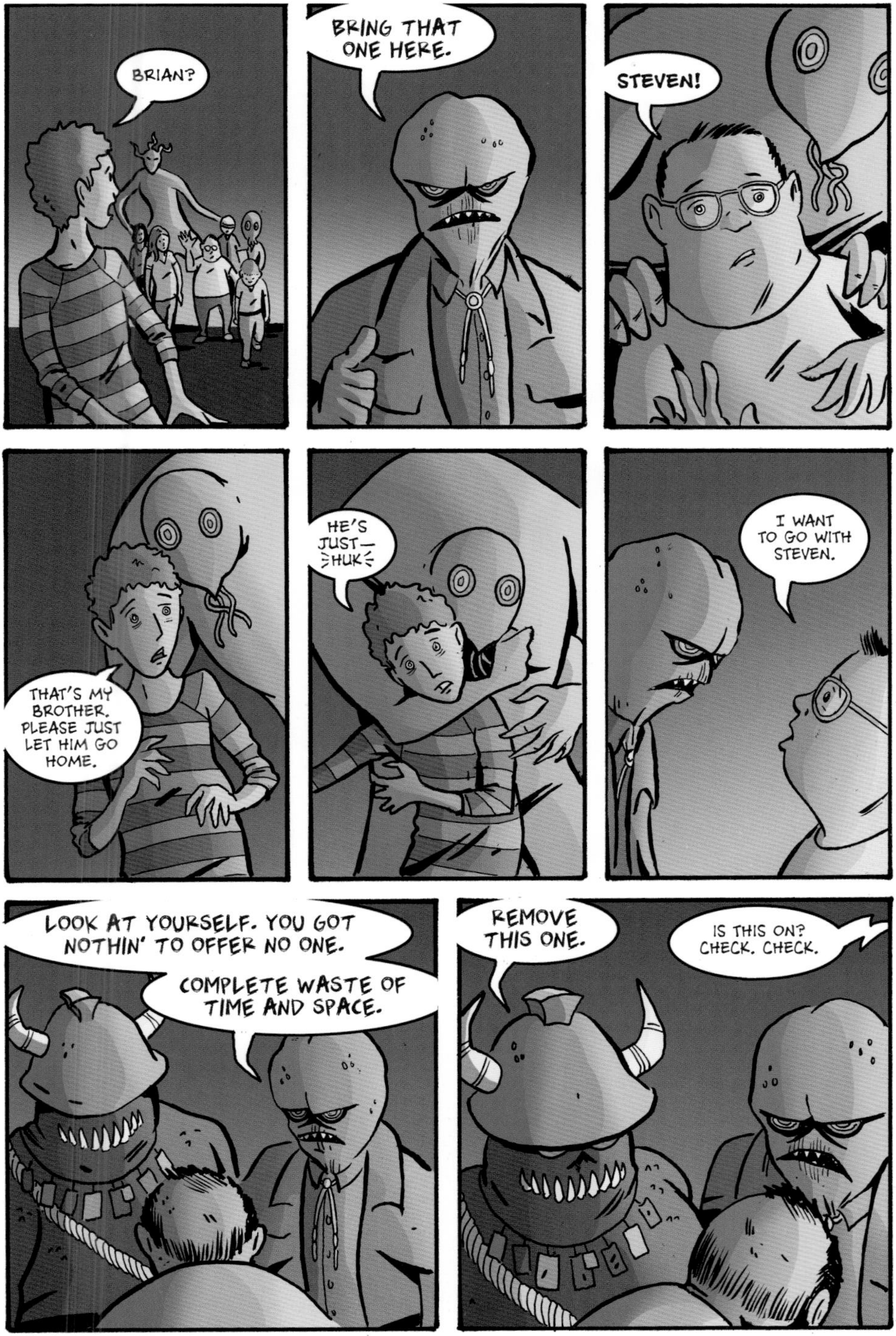
BRIAN?
BRING THAT ONE HERE.
STEVEN!
THAT'S MY BROTHER. PLEASE JUST LET HIM GO HOME.
HE'S JUST— HUK
I WANT TO GO WITH STEVEN.
LOOK AT YOURSELF. YOU GOT NOTHIN' TO OFFER NO ONE.
COMPLETE WASTE OF TIME AND SPACE.
REMOVE THIS ONE.
IS THIS ON? CHECK. CHECK.

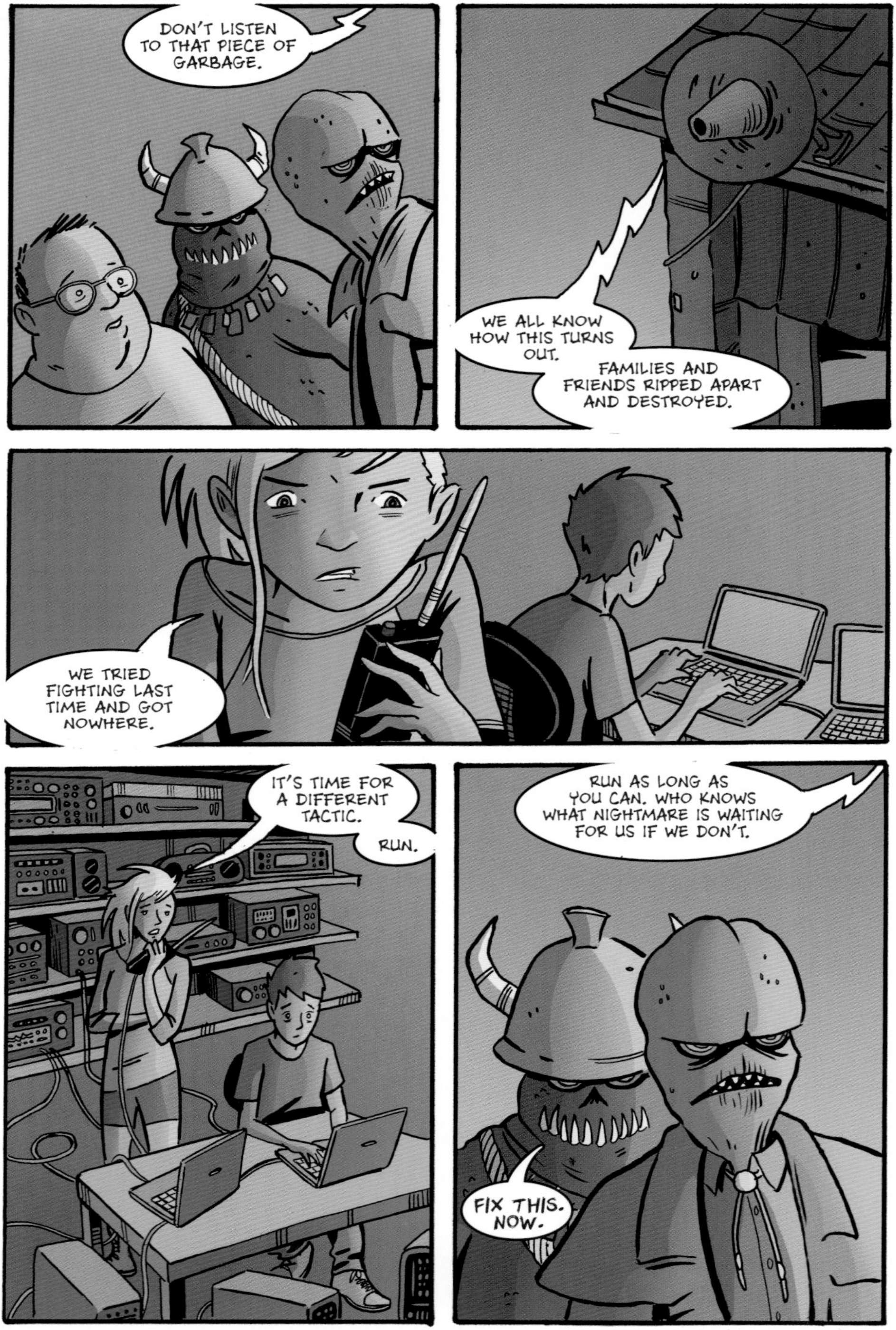
DON'T LISTEN TO THAT PIECE OF GARBAGE.
WE ALL KNOW HOW THIS TURNS OUT.
FAMILIES AND FRIENDS RIPPED APART AND DESTROYED.
WE TRIED FIGHTING LAST TIME AND GOT NOWHERE.
IT'S TIME FOR A DIFFERENT TACTIC.
RUN.
RUN AS LONG AS YOU CAN. WHO KNOWS WHAT NIGHTMARE IS WAITING FOR US IF WE DON'T.
FIX THIS. NOW.

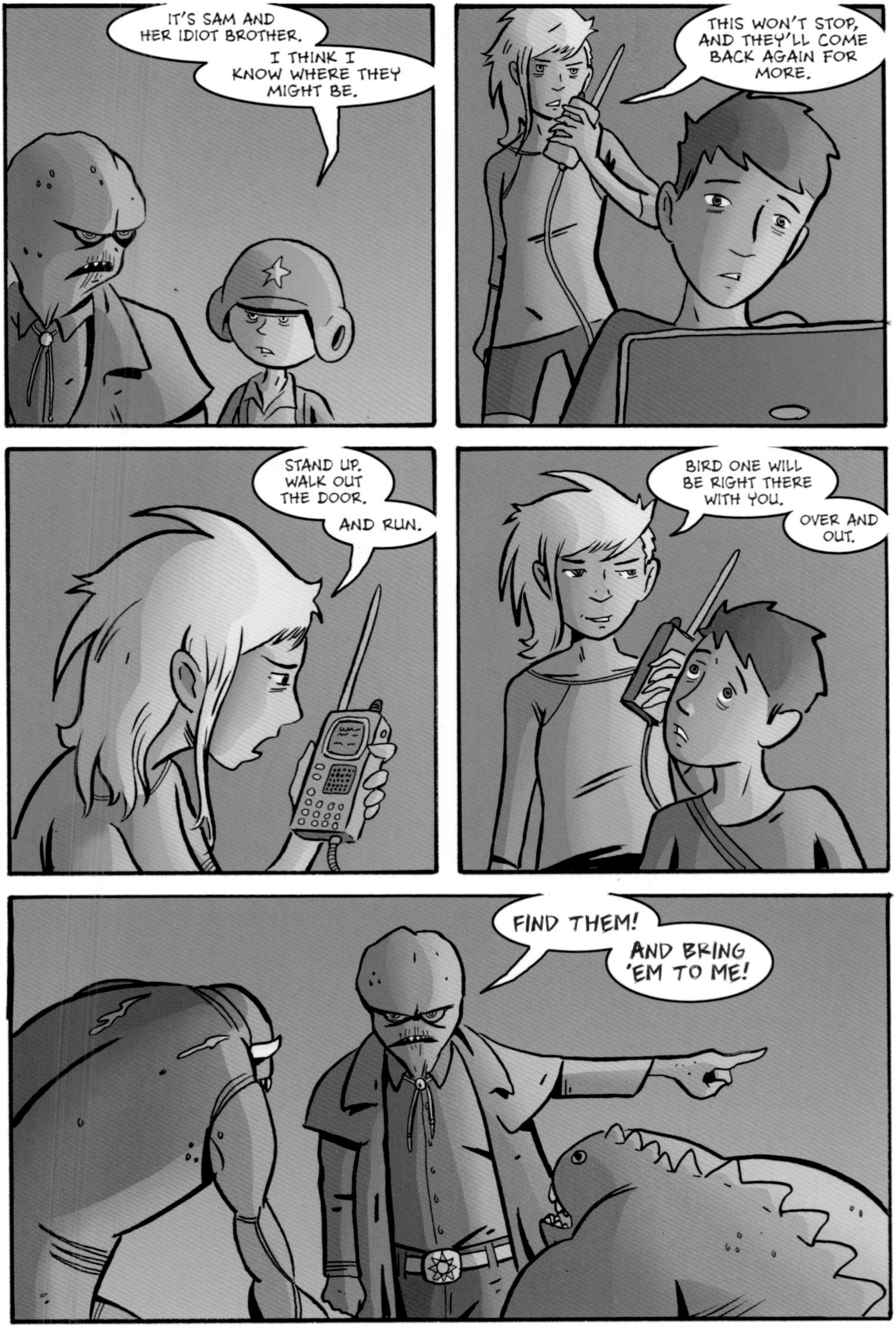
IT'S SAM AND HER IDIOT BROTHER.
I THINK I KNOW WHERE THEY MIGHT BE.
THIS WON'T STOP, AND THEY'LL COME BACK AGAIN FOR MORE.
STAND UP. WALK OUT THE DOOR.
AND RUN.
BIRD ONE WILL BE RIGHT THERE WITH YOU.
OVER AND OUT.
FIND THEM!
AND BRING 'EM TO ME!

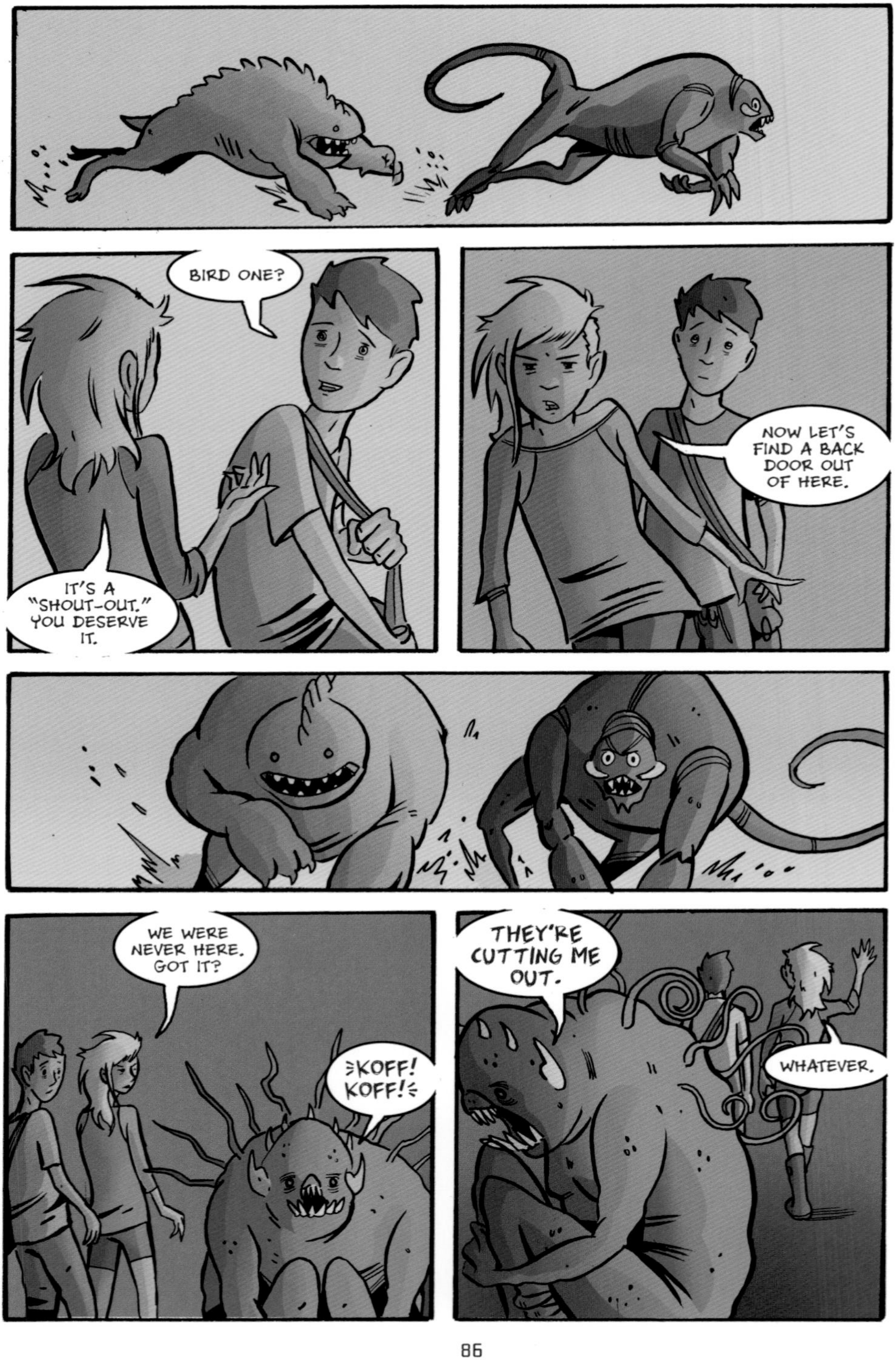
BIRD ONE?
IT'S A "SHOUT-OUT." YOU DESERVE IT.
NOW LET'S FIND A BACK DOOR OUT OF HERE.
WE WERE NEVER HERE. GOT IT?
KOFF! KOFF!
THEY'RE CUTTING ME OUT.
WHATEVER.

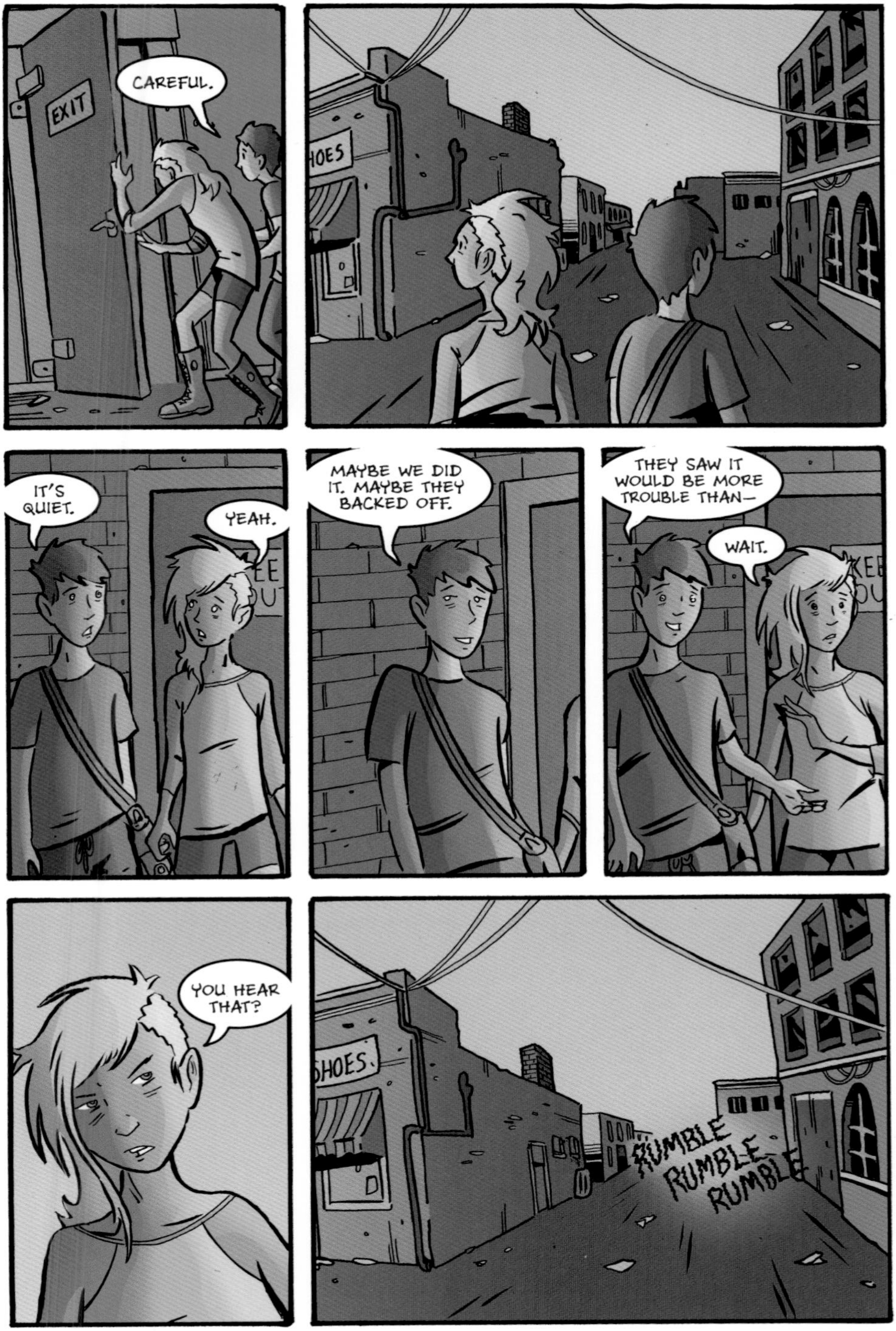
EXIT
CAREFUL.
SHOES
IT'S QUIET.
YEAH.
MAYBE WE DID IT. MAYBE THEY BACKED OFF.
THEY SAW IT WOULD BE MORE TROUBLE THAN—
WAIT.
YOU HEAR THAT?
SHOES.
RUMBLE
RUMBLE
RUMBLE

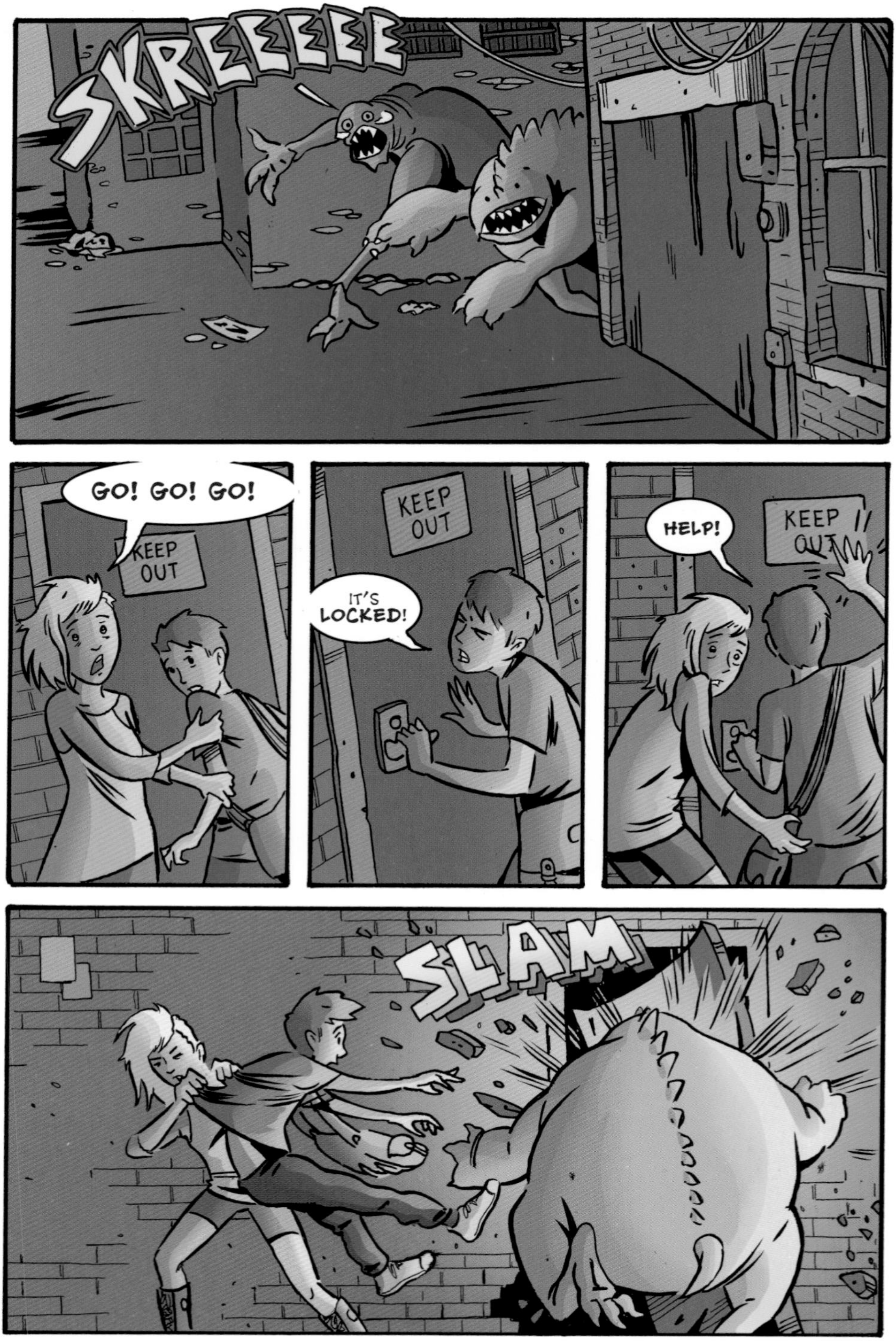
SKREEEEEE
GO! GO! GO!
KEEP OUT
KEEP OUT
IT'S LOCKED!
HELP!
KEEP OUT
SLAM

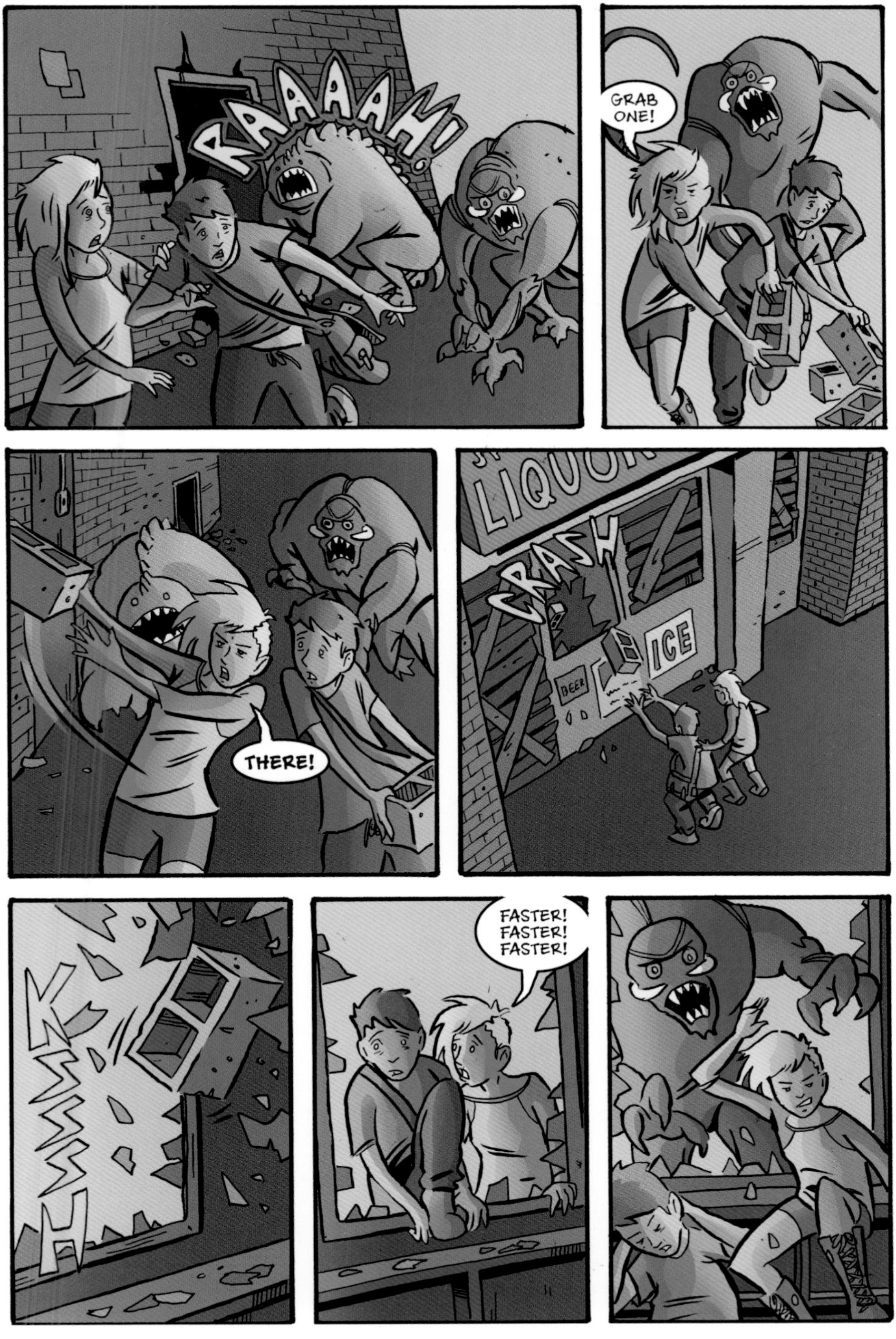
RAAAAH!
GRAB ONE!
THERE!
LIQUOR
CRASH
ICE
BEER
KSSSSH
FASTER! FASTER! FASTER!

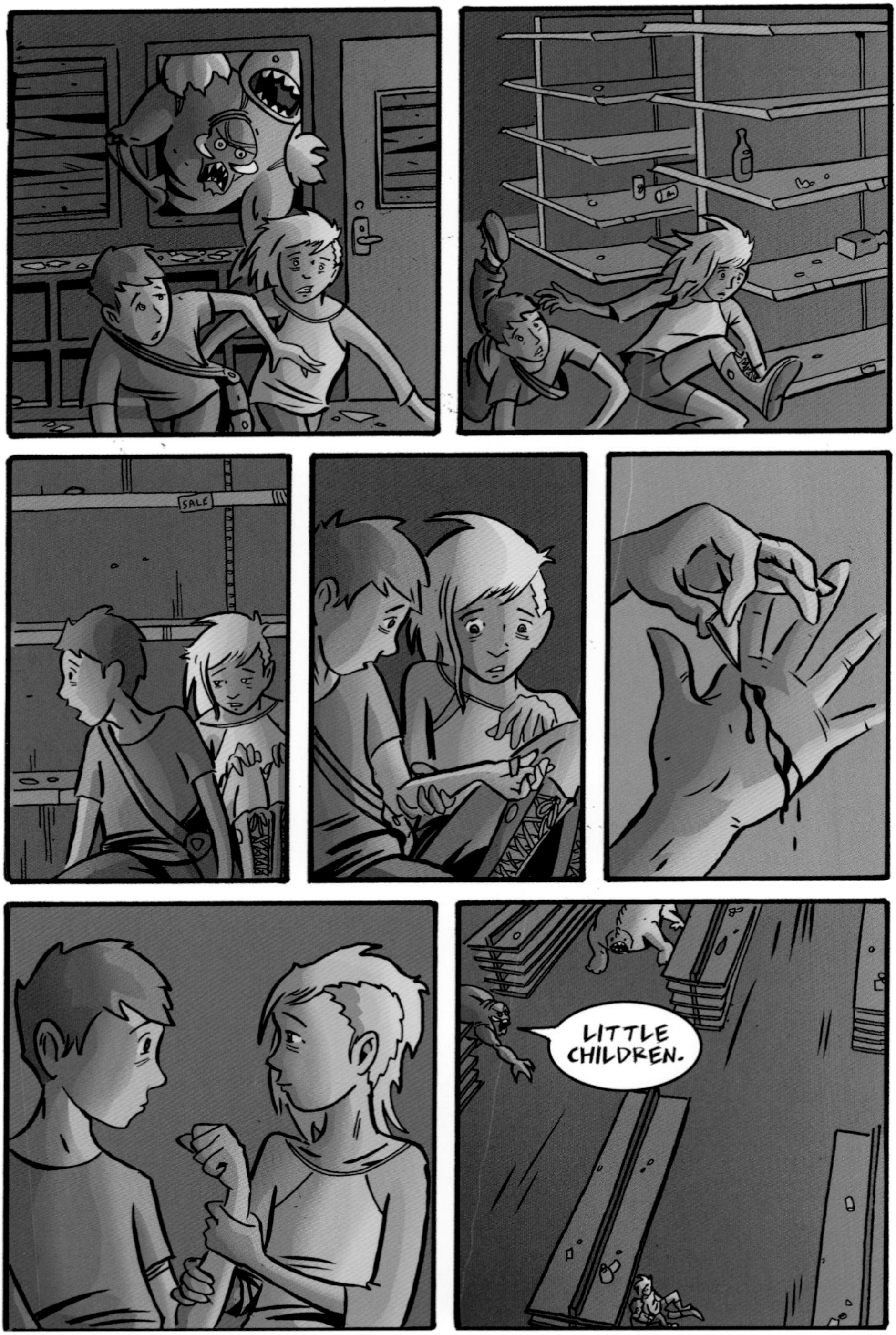
SALE
LITTLE CHILDREN.

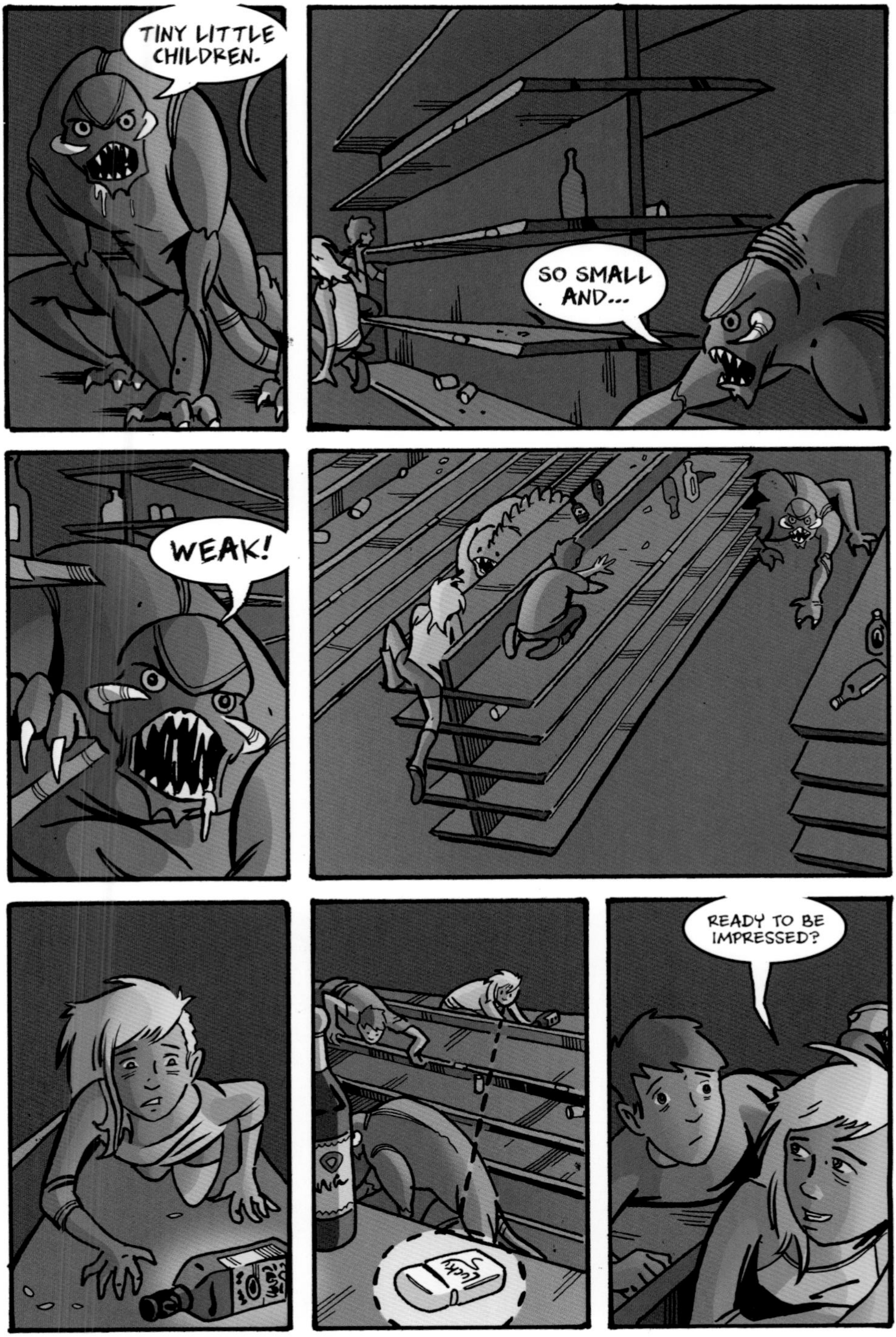
TINY LITTLE CHILDREN.
SO SMALL AND...
WEAK!
READY TO BE IMPRESSED?

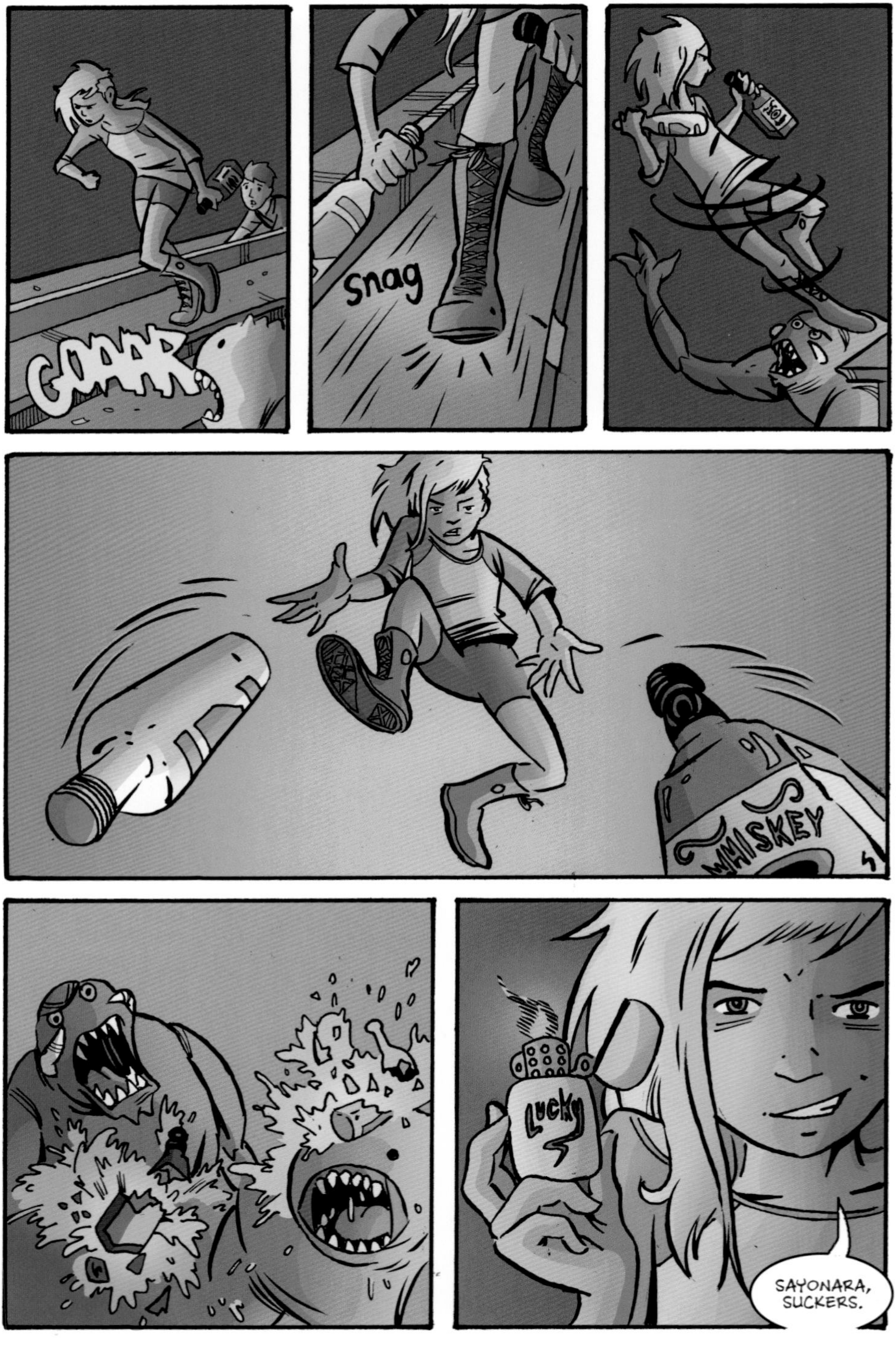
GOAR
Snag
WHISKEY
LUCKY
SAYONARA, SUCKERS.

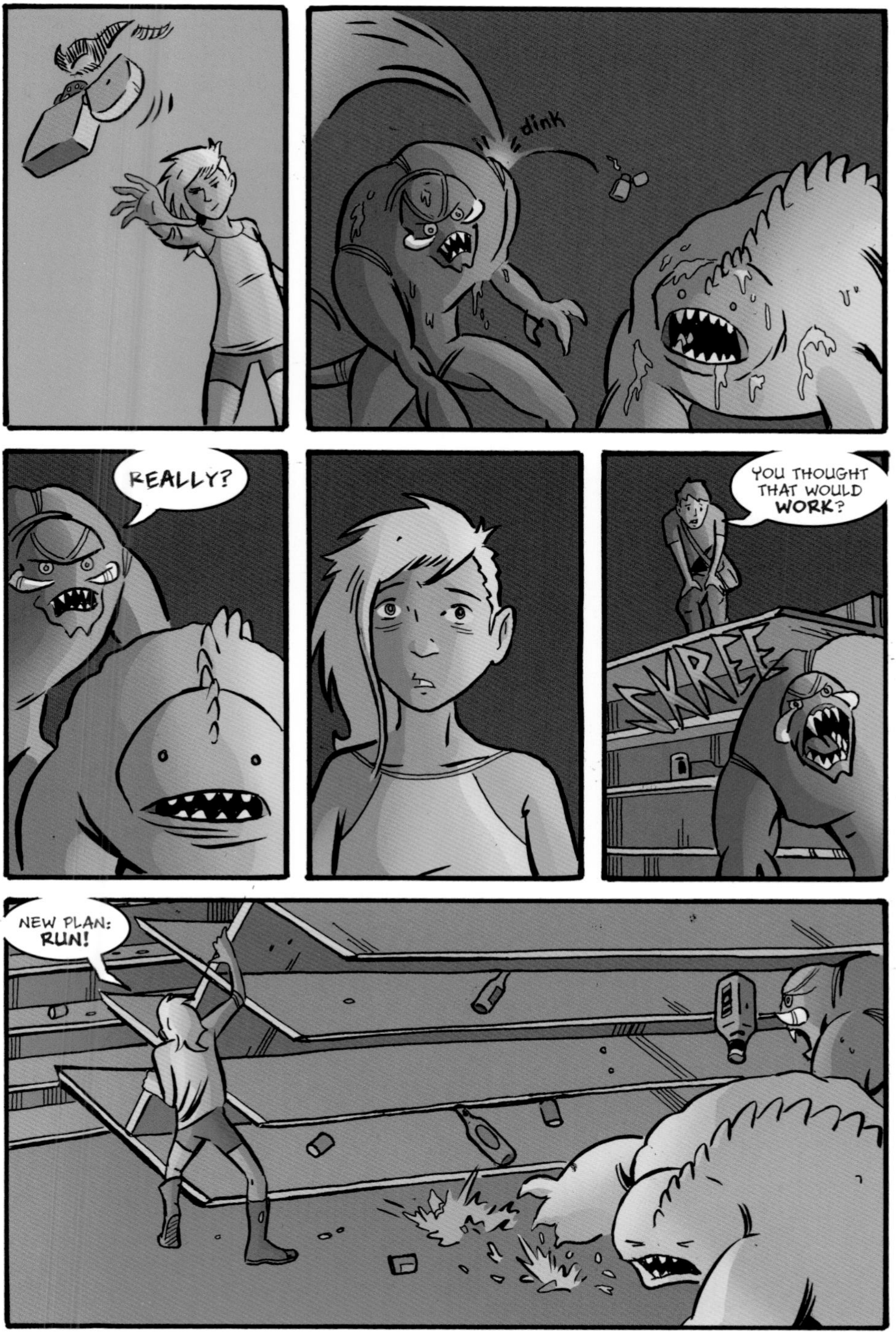
dink
REALLY?
YOU THOUGHT THAT WOULD WORK?
SKREE
NEW PLAN: RUN!

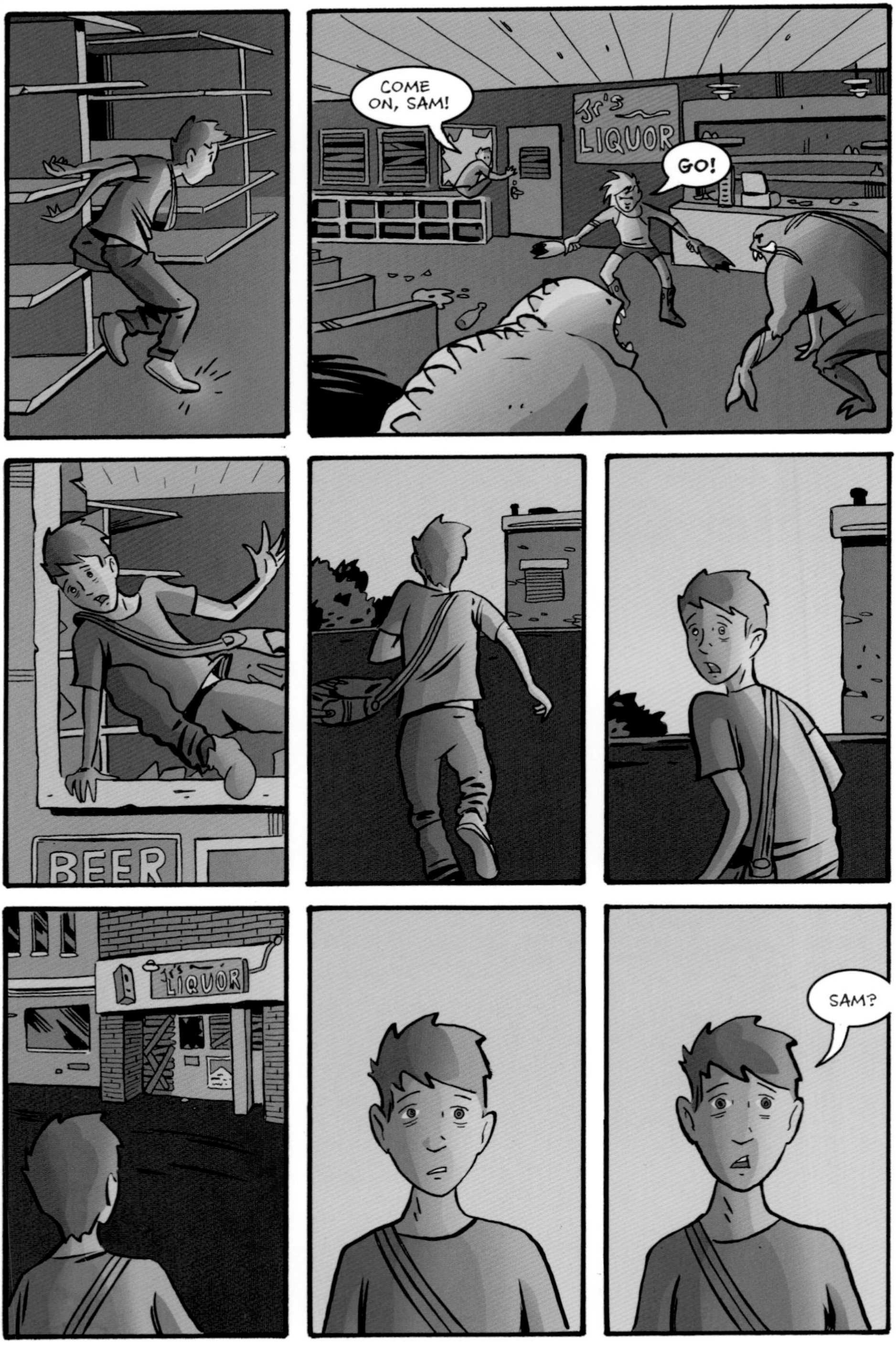
COME ON, SAM!
GO!
Jr's LIQUOR
BEER
Jr's LIQUOR
SAM?

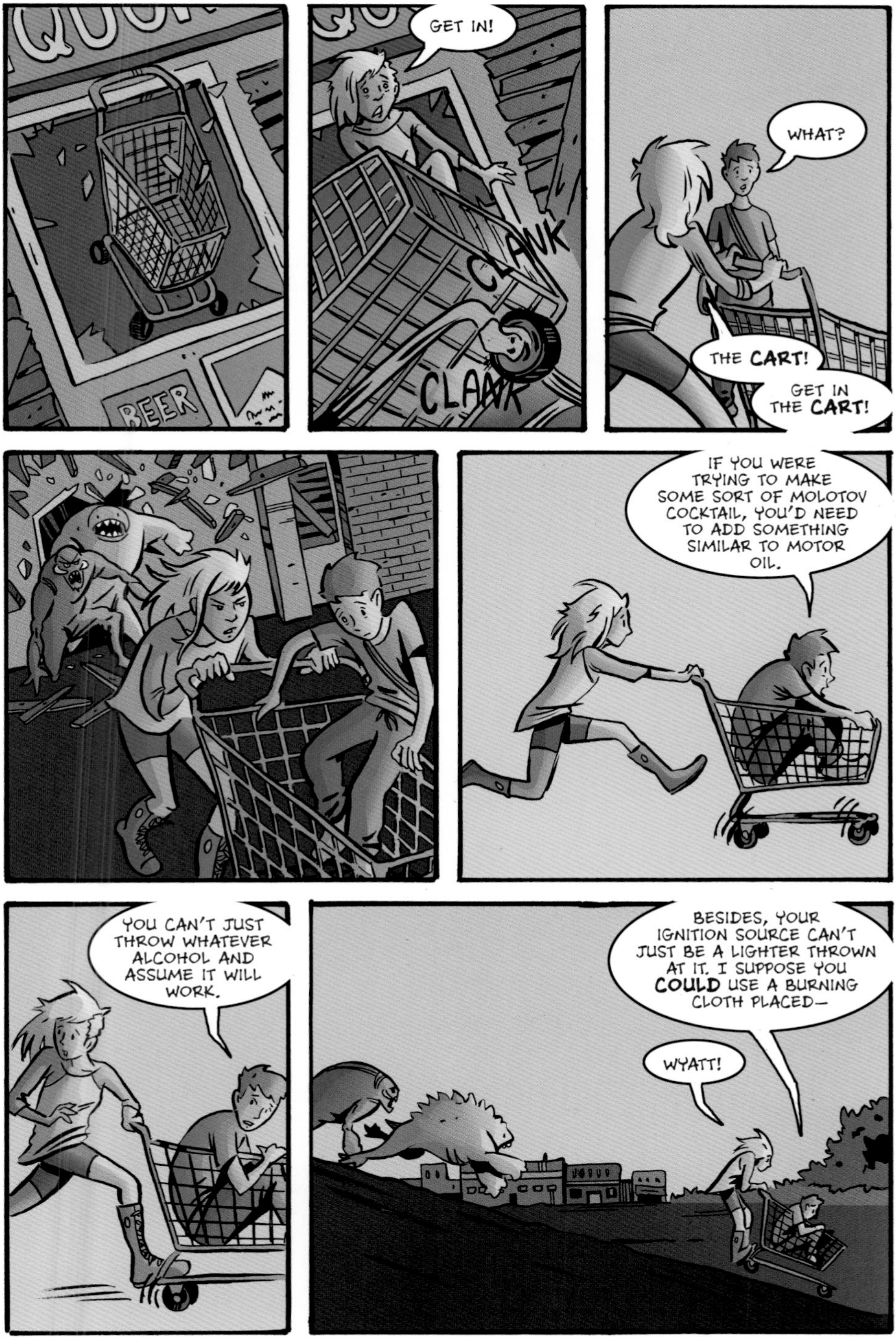
QUOR
BEER
GET IN!
CLANK
CLANK
WHAT?
THE **CART**!
GET IN THE **CART**!
IF YOU WERE TRYING TO MAKE SOME SORT OF MOLOTOV COCKTAIL, YOU'D NEED TO ADD SOMETHING SIMILAR TO MOTOR OIL.
YOU CAN'T JUST THROW WHATEVER ALCOHOL AND ASSUME IT WILL WORK.
BESIDES, YOUR IGNITION SOURCE CAN'T JUST BE A LIGHTER THROWN AT IT. I SUPPOSE YOU **COULD** USE A BURNING CLOTH PLACED—
WYATT!

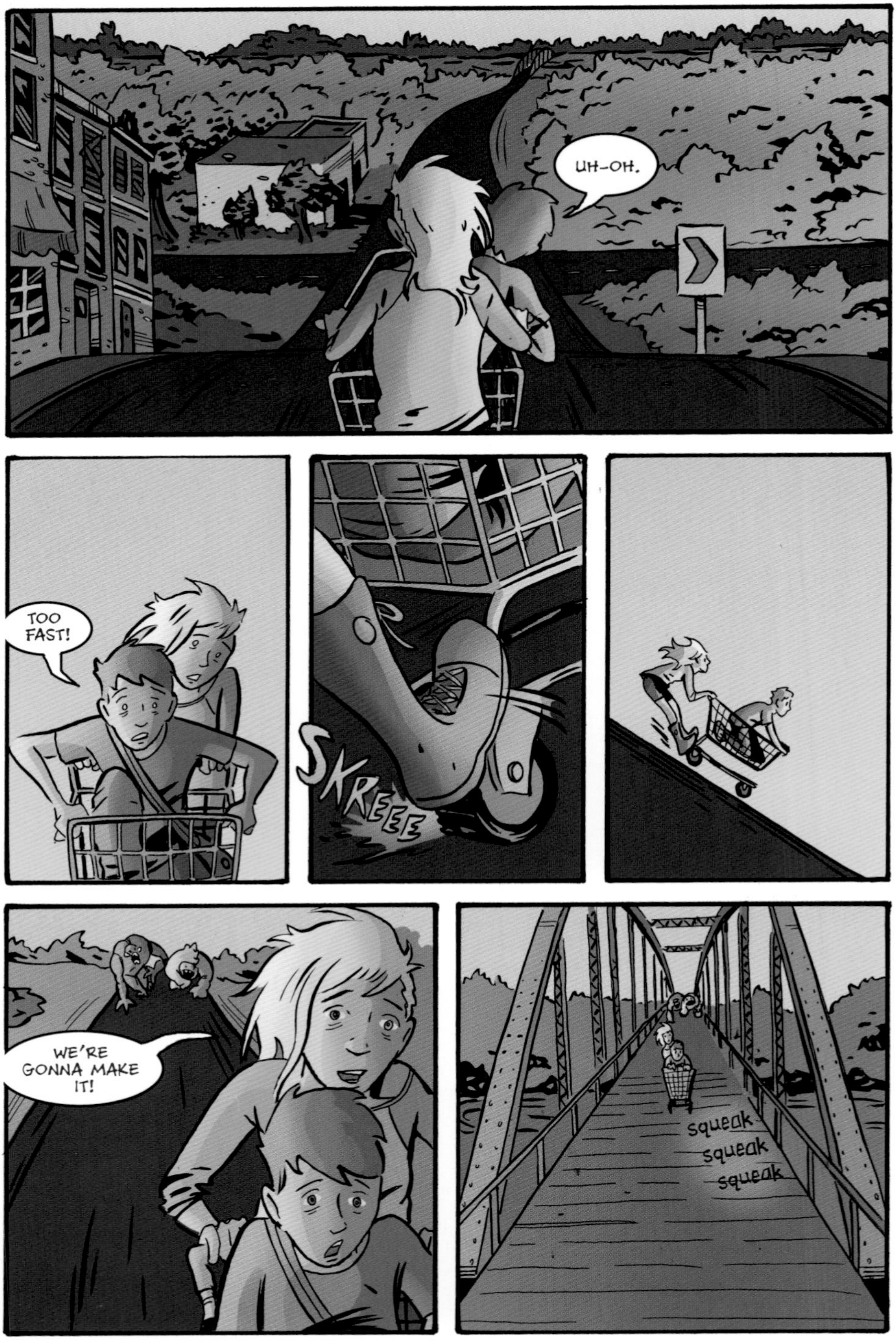
UH-OH.
TOO FAST!
SKREEEE
WE'RE GONNA MAKE IT!
squeak
squeak
squeak

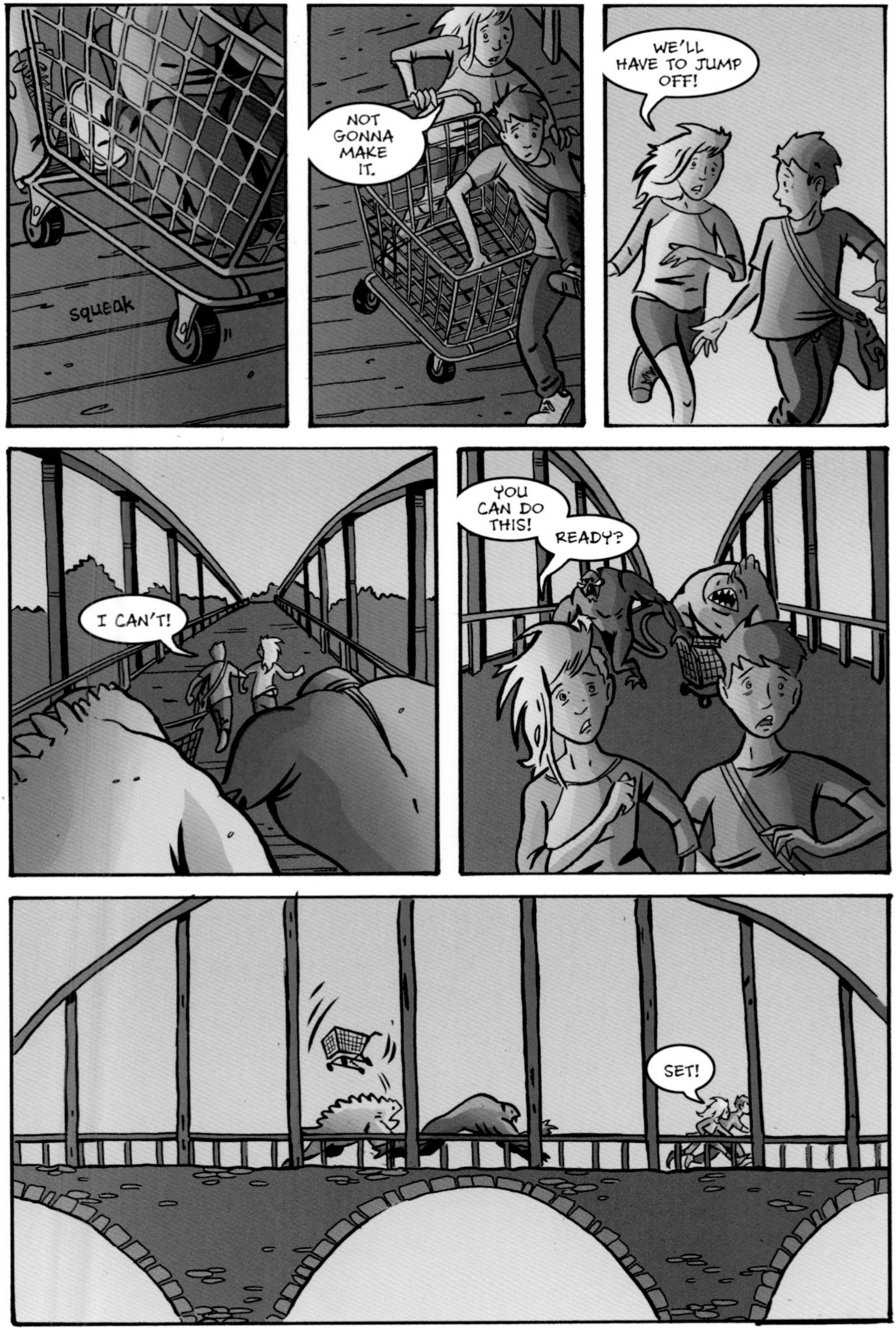
squeak
NOT GONNA MAKE IT.
WE'LL HAVE TO JUMP OFF!
I CAN'T!
YOU CAN DO THIS!
READY?
SET!

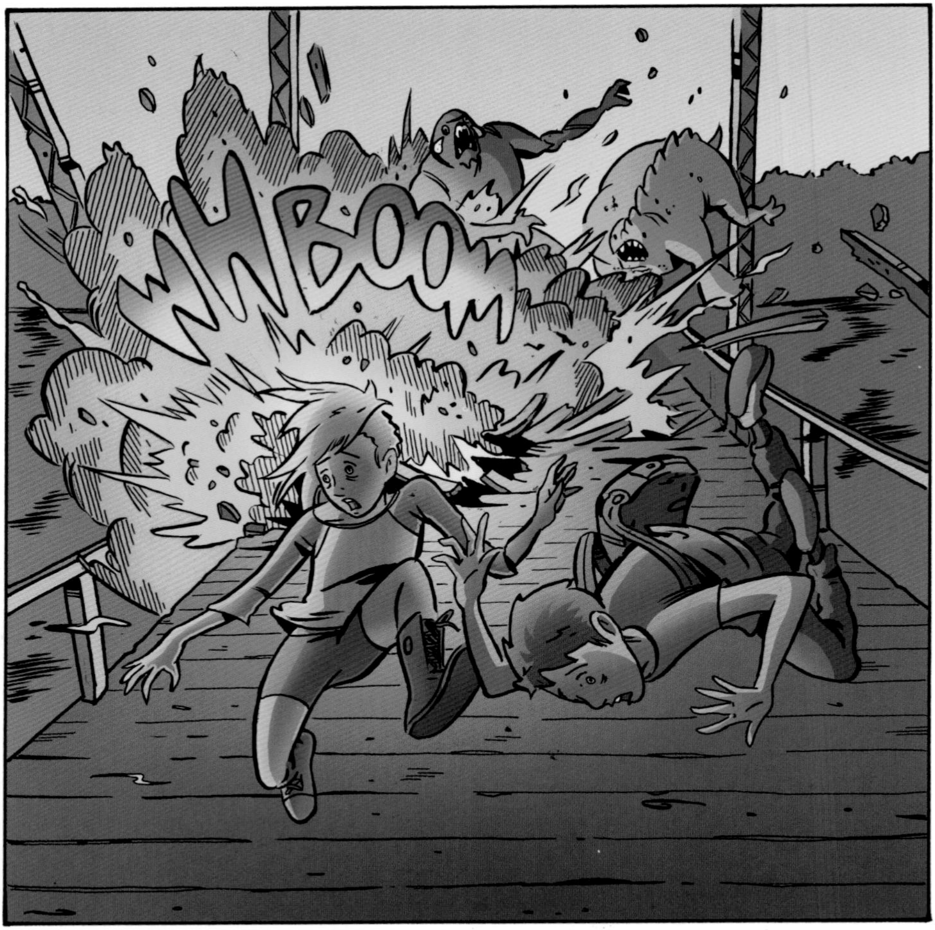
WHBOOM

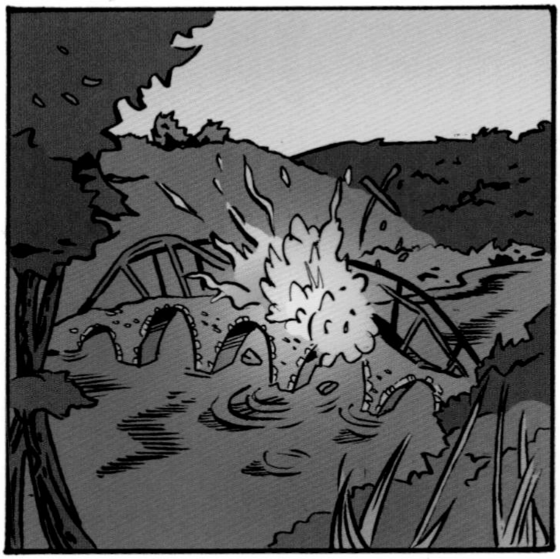

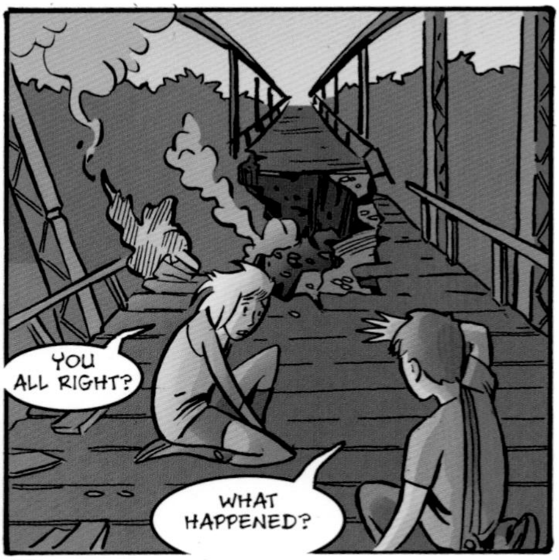
YOU ALL RIGHT?
WHAT HAPPENED?

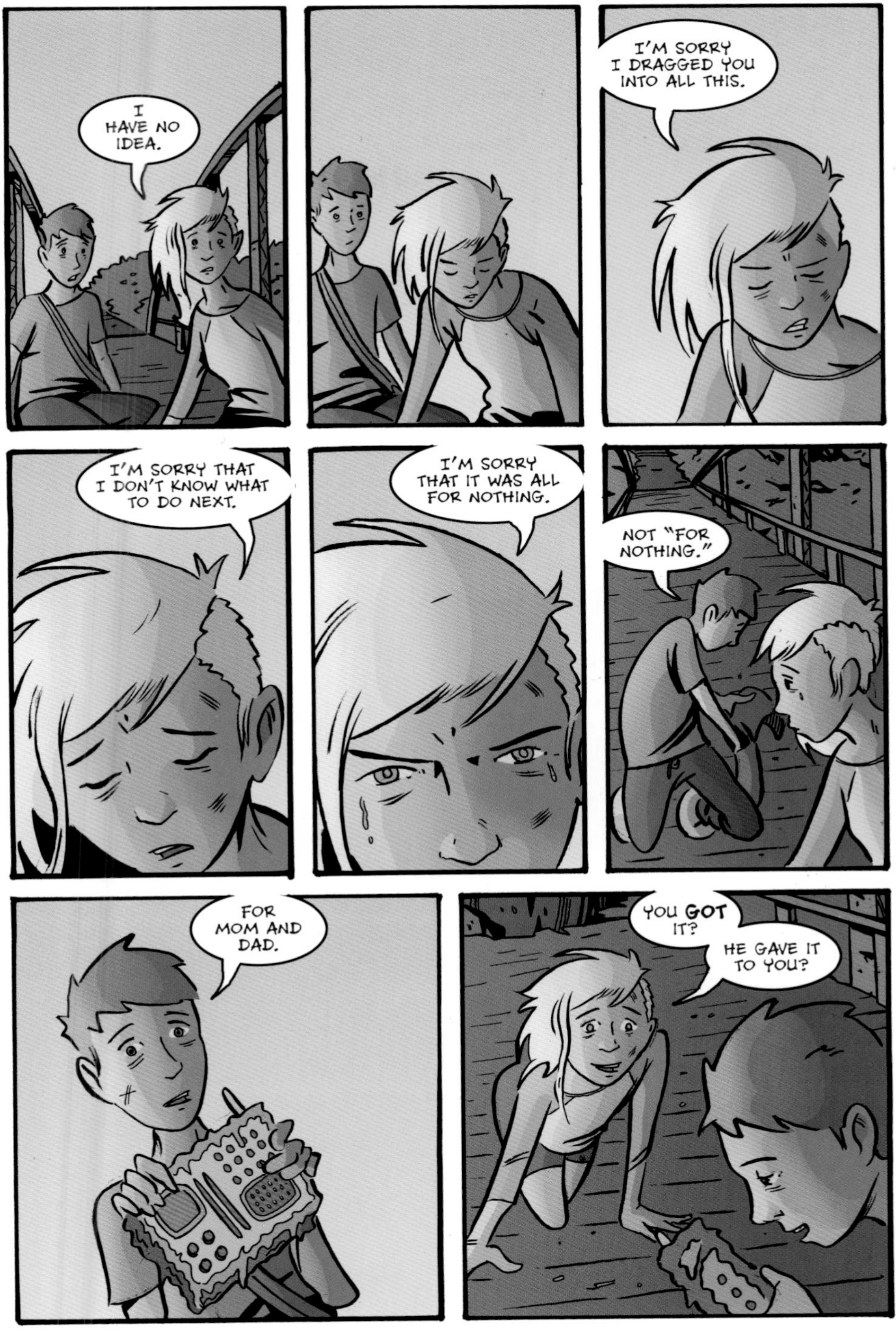
I HAVE NO IDEA.
I'M SORRY I DRAGGED YOU INTO ALL THIS.
I'M SORRY THAT I DON'T KNOW WHAT TO DO NEXT.
I'M SORRY THAT IT WAS ALL FOR NOTHING.
NOT "FOR NOTHING."
FOR MOM AND DAD.
YOU GOT IT?
HE GAVE IT TO YOU?

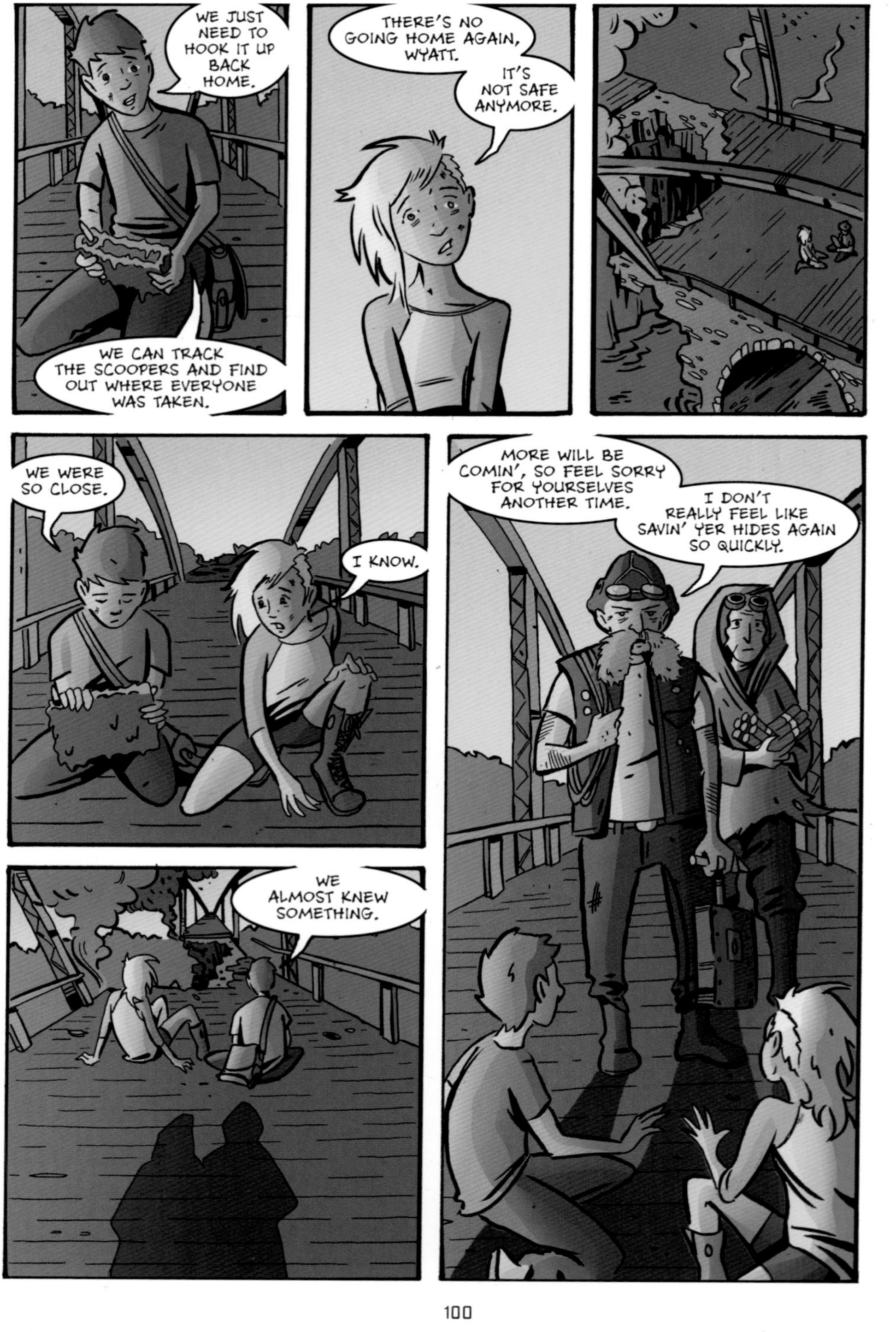
WE JUST NEED TO HOOK IT UP BACK HOME.
WE CAN TRACK THE SCOOPERS AND FIND OUT WHERE EVERYONE WAS TAKEN.
THERE'S NO GOING HOME AGAIN, WYATT.
IT'S NOT SAFE ANYMORE.
WE WERE SO CLOSE.
I KNOW.
WE ALMOST KNEW SOMETHING.
MORE WILL BE COMIN', SO FEEL SORRY FOR YOURSELVES ANOTHER TIME.
I DON'T REALLY FEEL LIKE SAVIN' YER HIDES AGAIN SO QUICKLY.

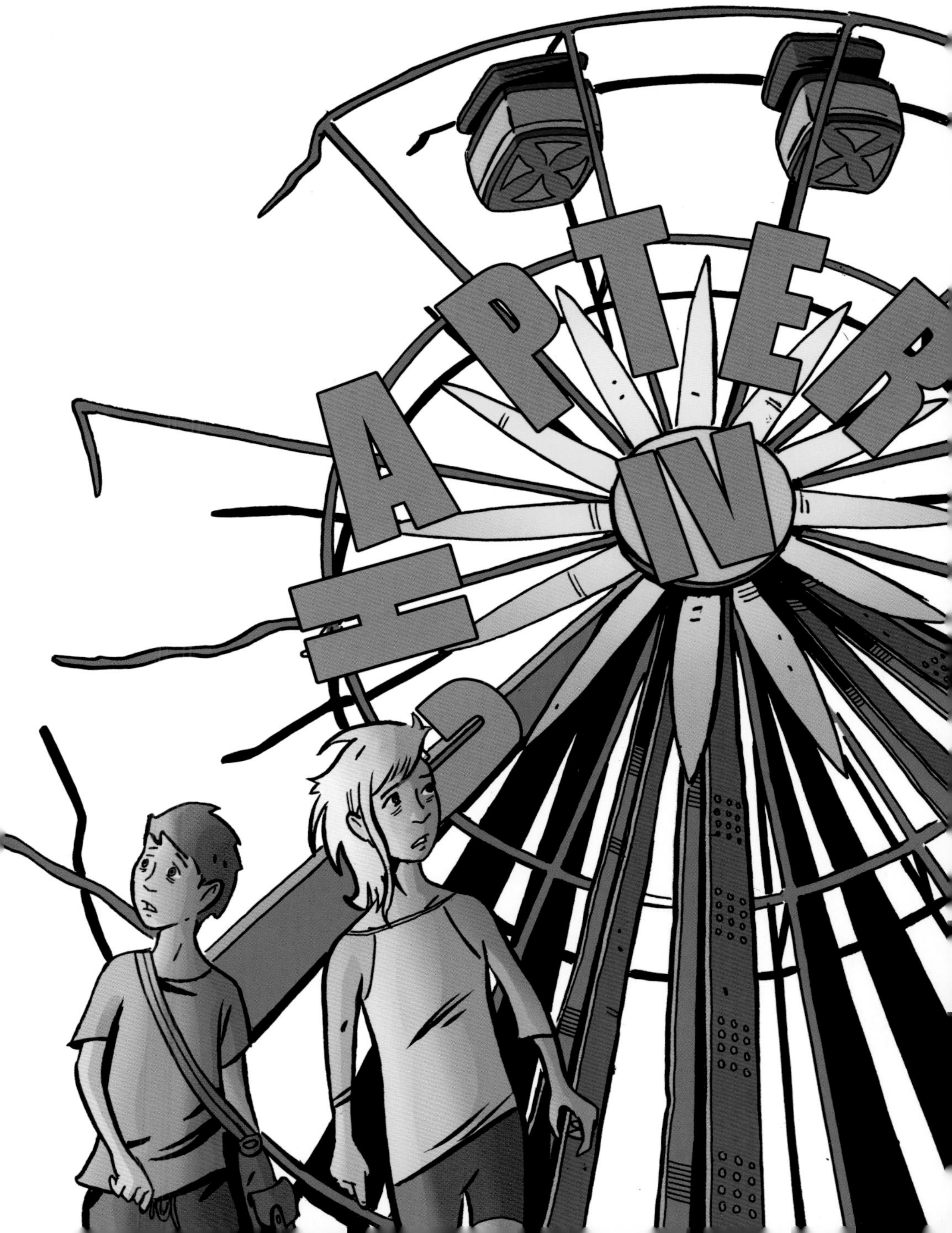
CHAPTER
IV

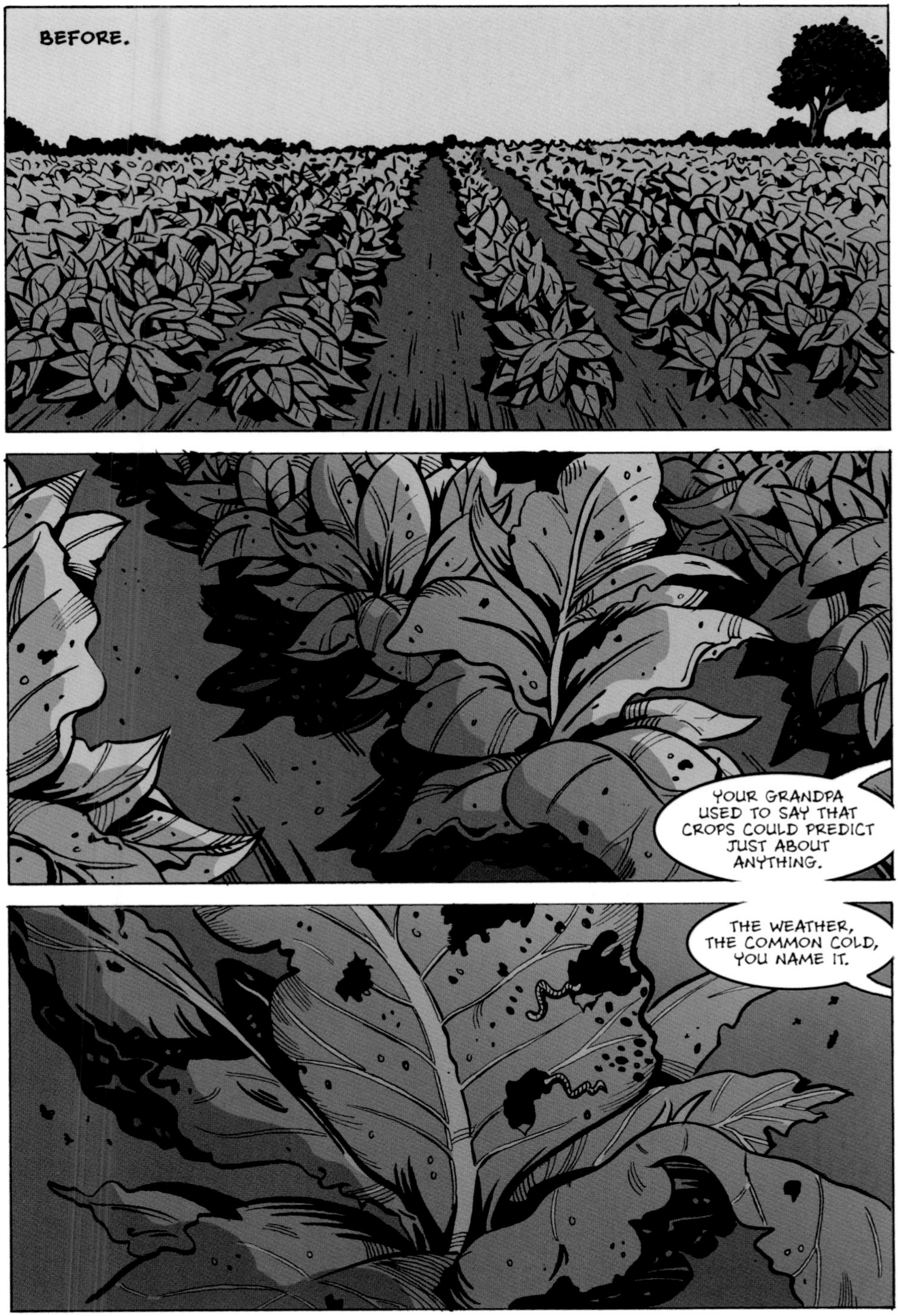
BEFORE.
YOUR GRANDPA USED TO SAY THAT CROPS COULD PREDICT JUST ABOUT ANYTHING.
THE WEATHER, THE COMMON COLD, YOU NAME IT.

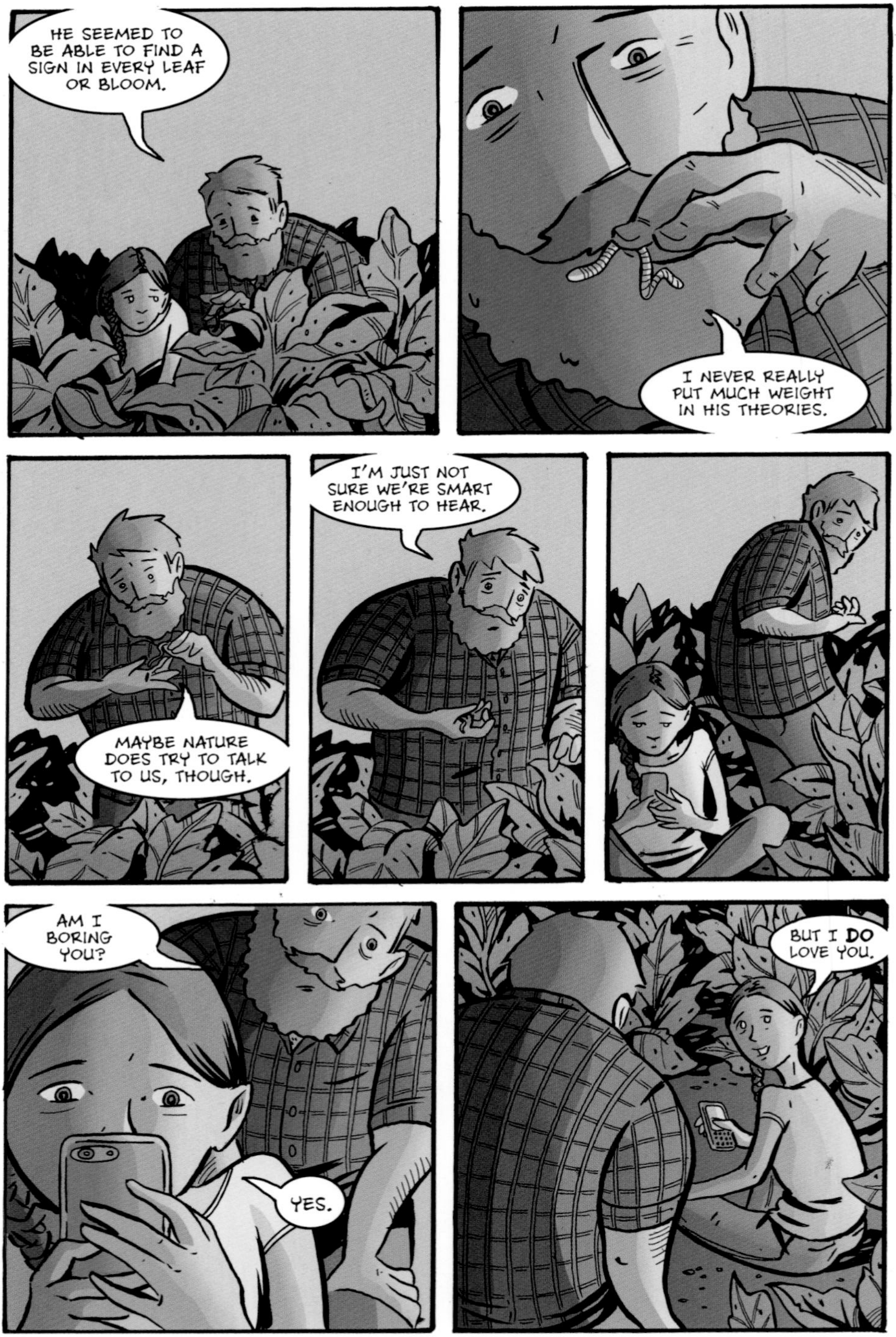
HE SEEMED TO BE ABLE TO FIND A SIGN IN EVERY LEAF OR BLOOM.
I NEVER REALLY PUT MUCH WEIGHT IN HIS THEORIES.
MAYBE NATURE DOES TRY TO TALK TO US, THOUGH.
I'M JUST NOT SURE WE'RE SMART ENOUGH TO HEAR.
AM I BORING YOU?
YES.
BUT I **DO** LOVE YOU.

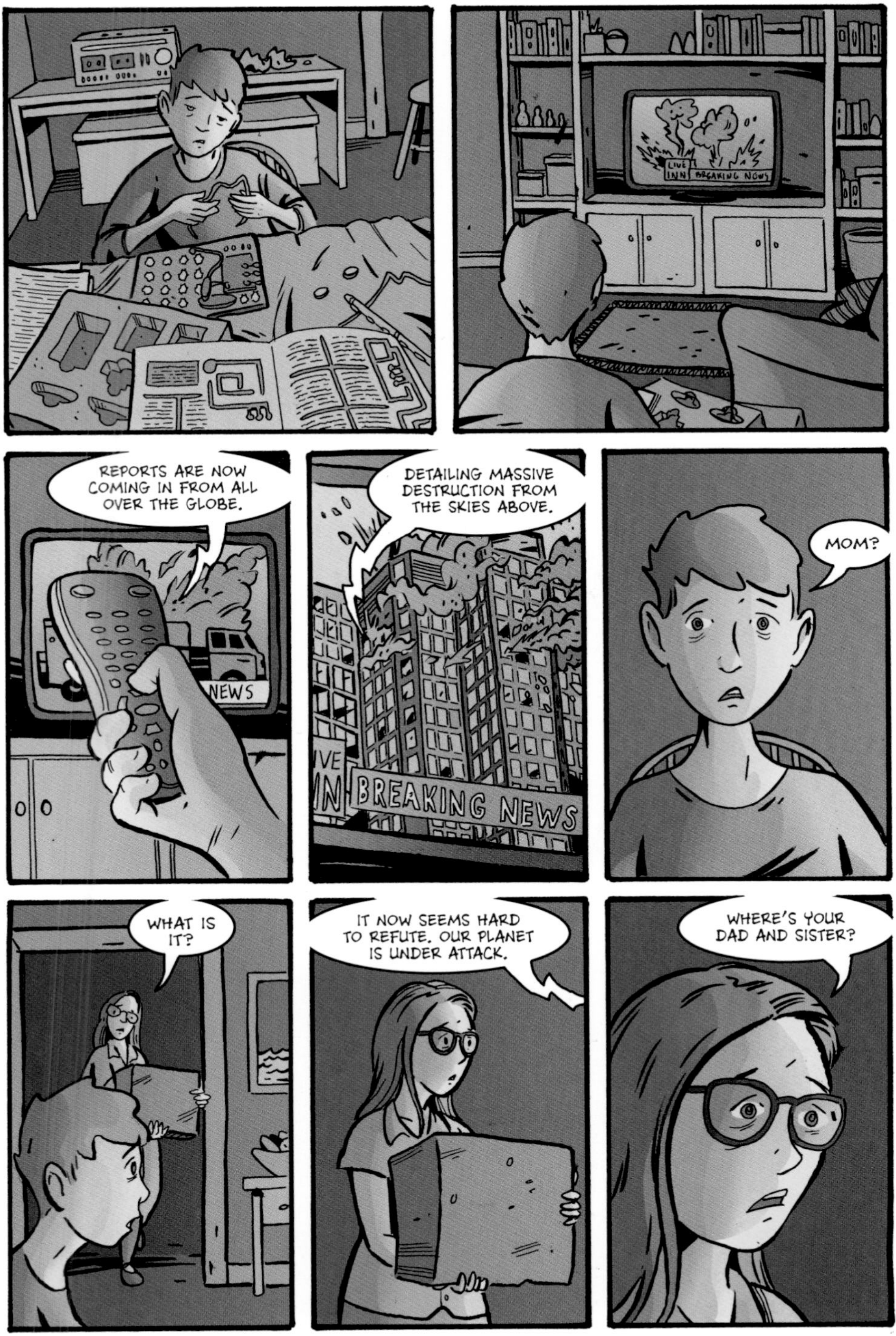
BREAKING NEWS
REPORTS ARE NOW COMING IN FROM ALL OVER THE GLOBE.
NEWS
DETAILING MASSIVE DESTRUCTION FROM THE SKIES ABOVE.
BREAKING NEWS
MOM?
WHAT IS IT?
IT NOW SEEMS HARD TO REFUTE. OUR PLANET IS UNDER ATTACK.
WHERE'S YOUR DAD AND SISTER?

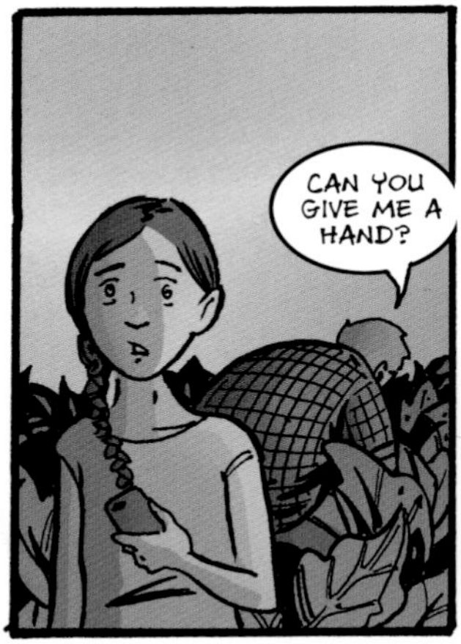
CAN YOU GIVE ME A HAND?
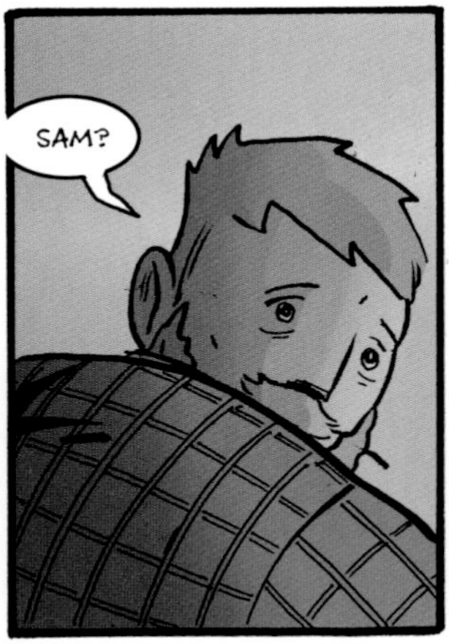
SAM?
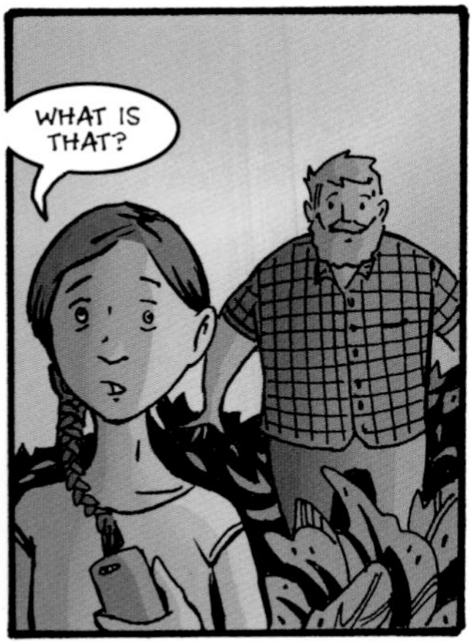
WHAT IS THAT?
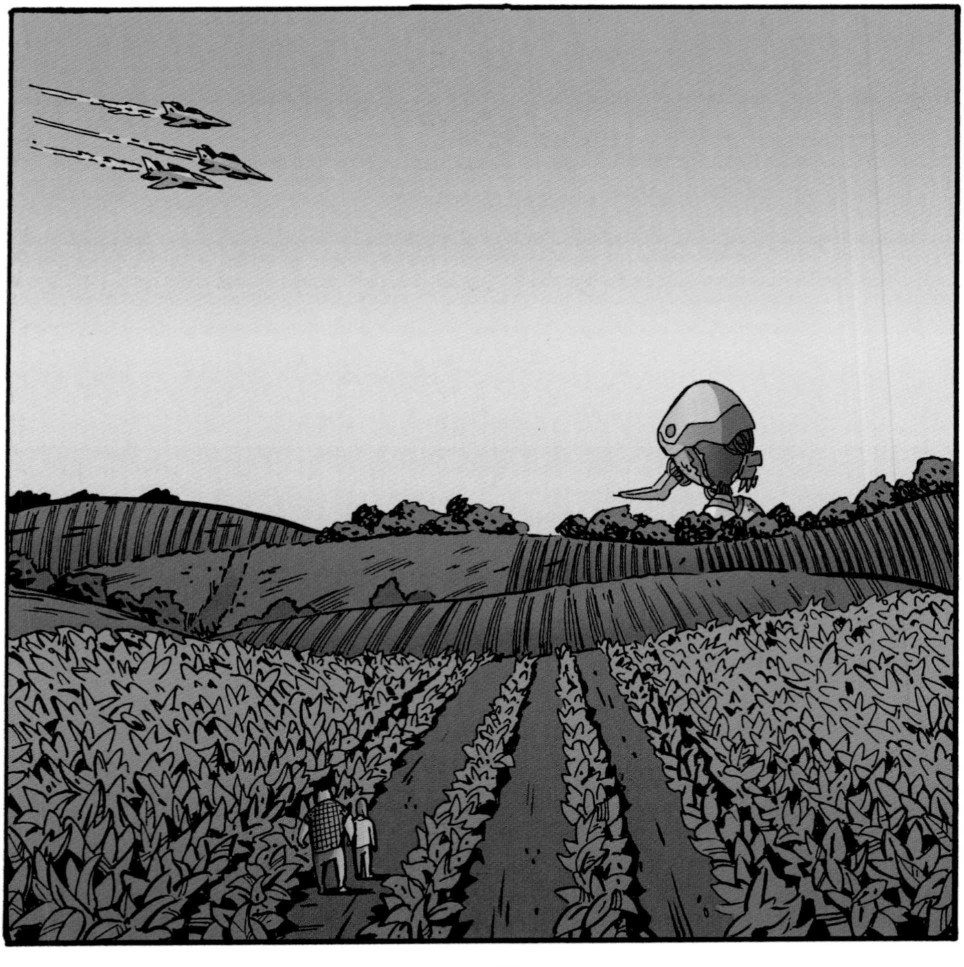

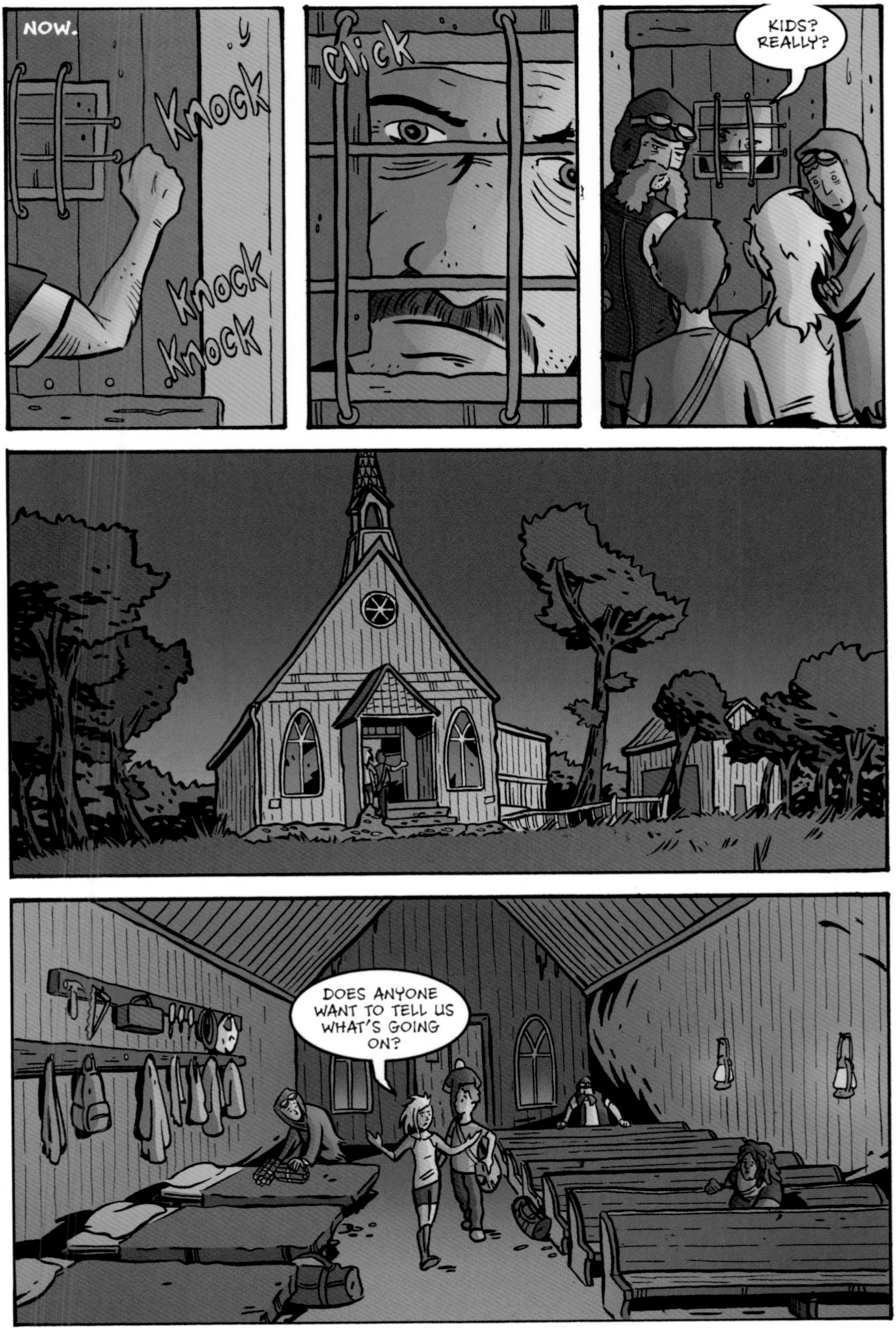
NOW.
Knock
Knock
Knock
click
KIDS? REALLY?
DOES ANYONE WANT TO TELL US WHAT'S GOING ON?

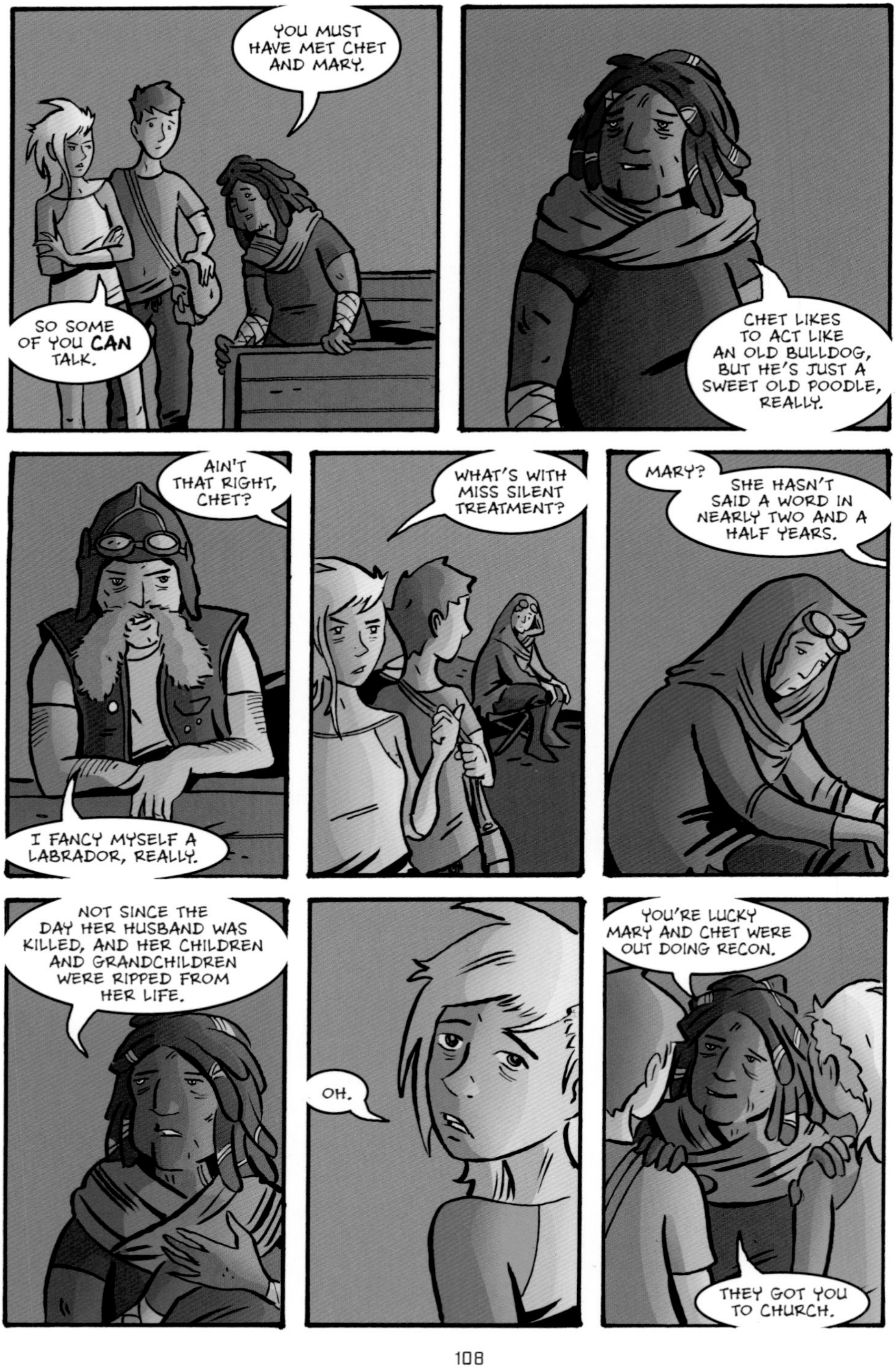
YOU MUST HAVE MET CHET AND MARY.
SO SOME OF YOU CAN TALK.
CHET LIKES TO ACT LIKE AN OLD BULLDOG, BUT HE'S JUST A SWEET OLD POODLE, REALLY.
AIN'T THAT RIGHT, CHET?
I FANCY MYSELF A LABRADOR, REALLY.
WHAT'S WITH MISS SILENT TREATMENT?
MARY?
SHE HASN'T SAID A WORD IN NEARLY TWO AND A HALF YEARS.
NOT SINCE THE DAY HER HUSBAND WAS KILLED, AND HER CHILDREN AND GRANDCHILDREN WERE RIPPED FROM HER LIFE.
OH.
YOU'RE LUCKY MARY AND CHET WERE OUT DOING RECON.
THEY GOT YOU TO CHURCH.

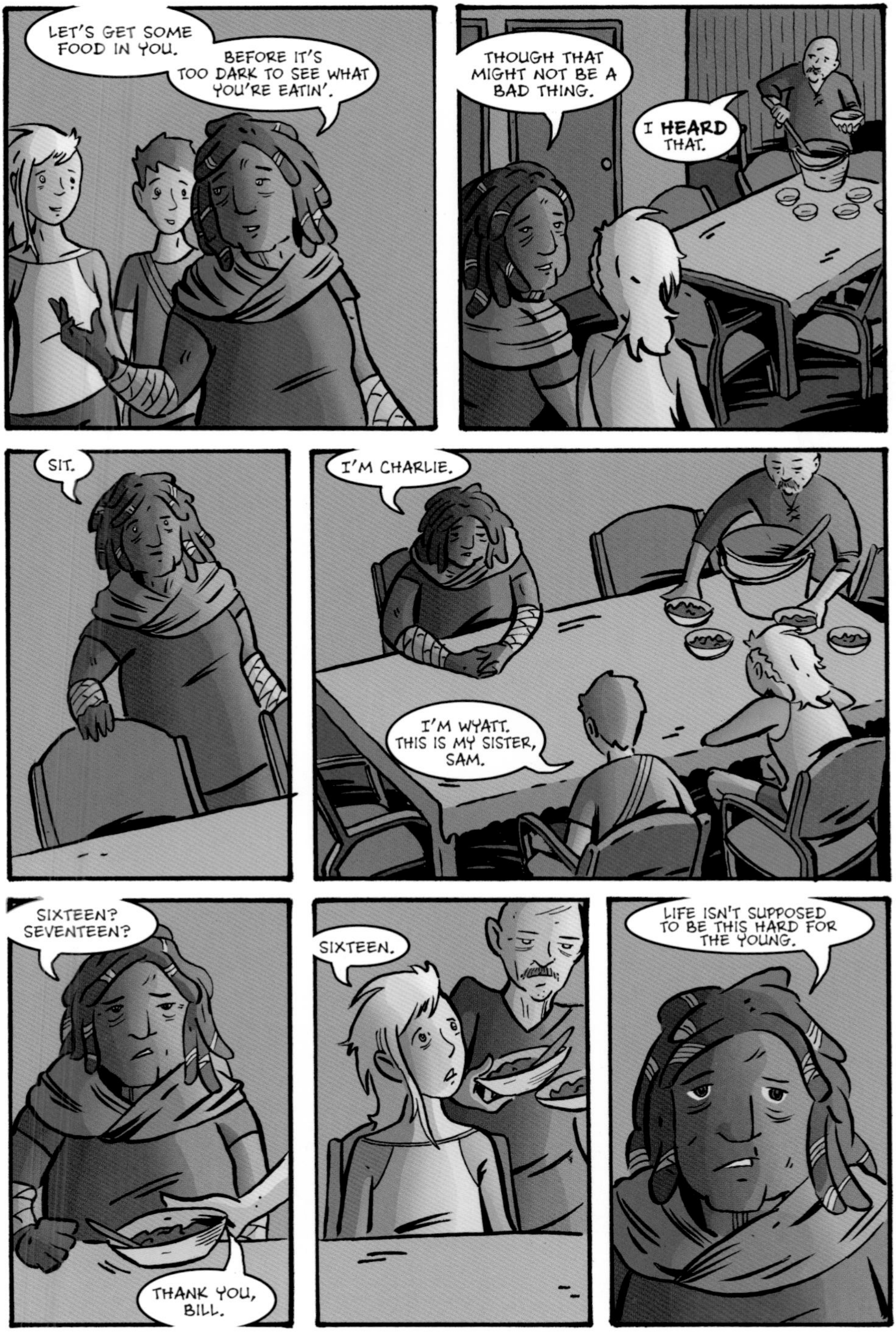
LET'S GET SOME FOOD IN YOU.
BEFORE IT'S TOO DARK TO SEE WHAT YOU'RE EATIN'.
THOUGH THAT MIGHT NOT BE A BAD THING.
I **HEARD** THAT.
SIT.
I'M CHARLIE.
I'M WYATT. THIS IS MY SISTER, SAM.
SIXTEEN? SEVENTEEN?
THANK YOU, BILL.
SIXTEEN.
LIFE ISN'T SUPPOSED TO BE THIS HARD FOR THE YOUNG.

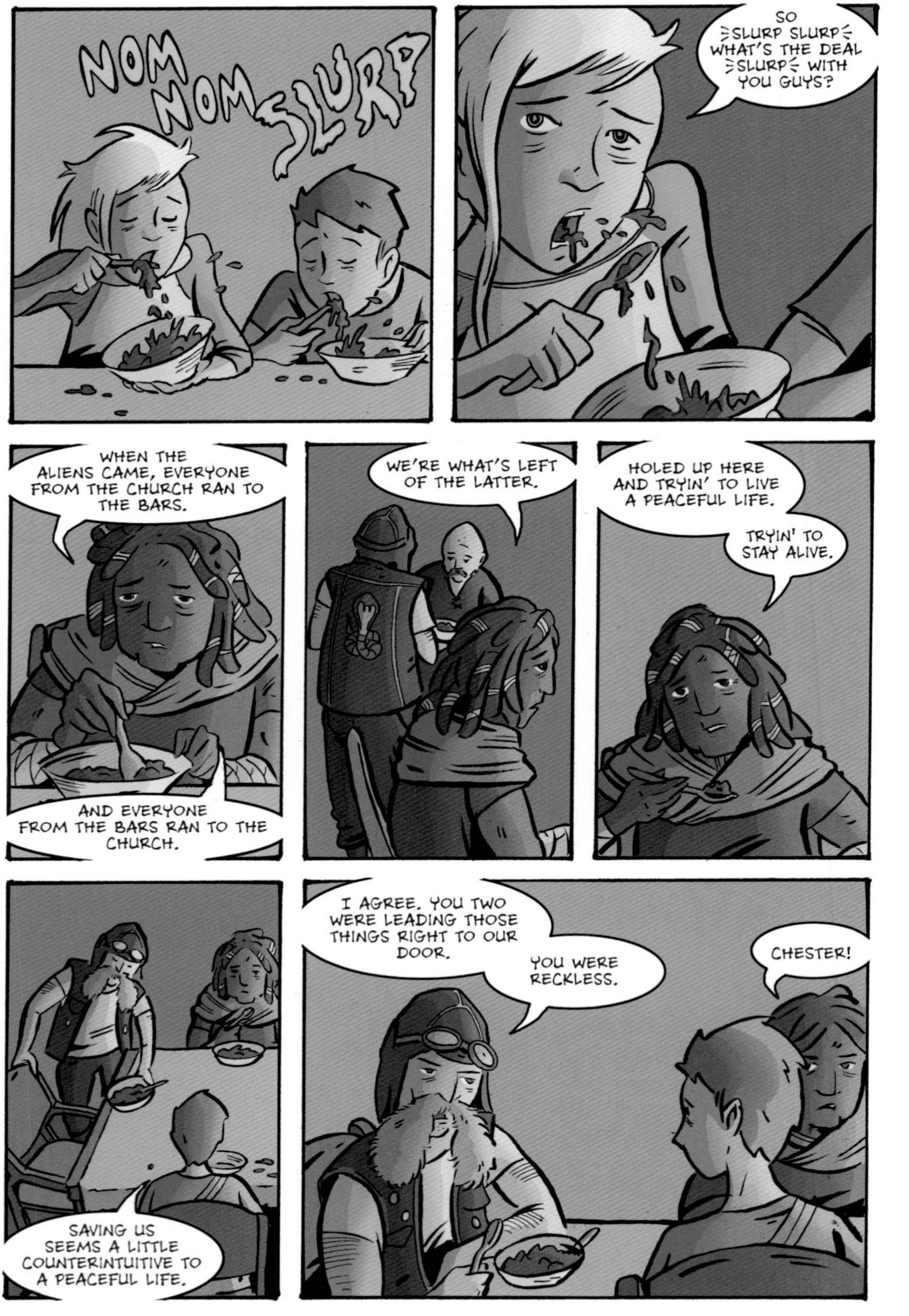
NOM NOM SLURP
SO SLURP SLURP WHAT'S THE DEAL SLURP WITH YOU GUYS?
WHEN THE ALIENS CAME, EVERYONE FROM THE CHURCH RAN TO THE BARS.
AND EVERYONE FROM THE BARS RAN TO THE CHURCH.
WE'RE WHAT'S LEFT OF THE LATTER.
HOLED UP HERE AND TRYIN' TO LIVE A PEACEFUL LIFE.
TRYIN' TO STAY ALIVE.
SAVING US SEEMS A LITTLE COUNTERINTUITIVE TO A PEACEFUL LIFE.
I AGREE. YOU TWO WERE LEADING THOSE THINGS RIGHT TO OUR DOOR.
YOU WERE RECKLESS.
CHESTER!

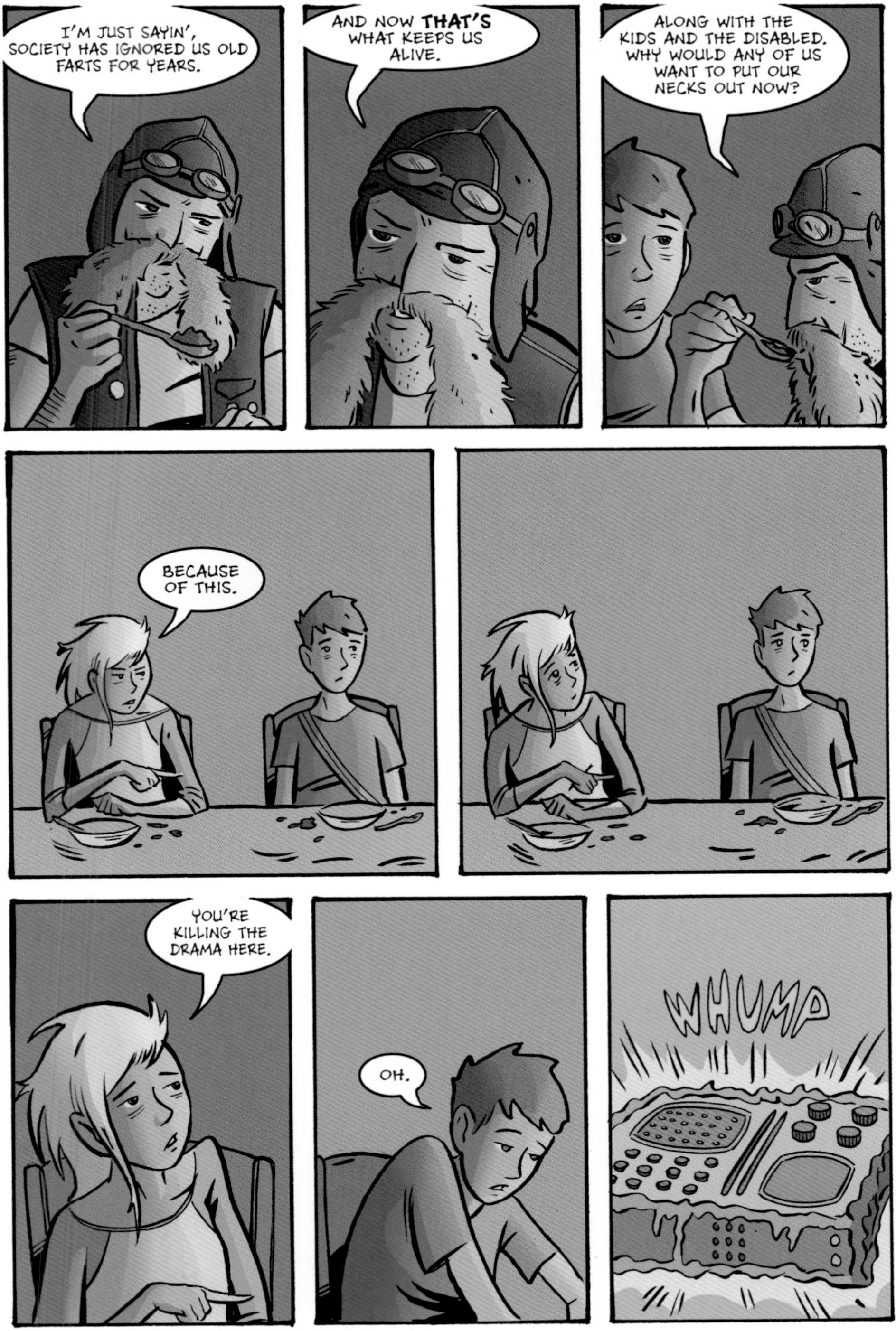
I'M JUST SAYIN', SOCIETY HAS IGNORED US OLD FARTS FOR YEARS.
AND NOW THAT'S WHAT KEEPS US ALIVE.
ALONG WITH THE KIDS AND THE DISABLED. WHY WOULD ANY OF US WANT TO PUT OUR NECKS OUT NOW?
BECAUSE OF THIS.
YOU'RE KILLING THE DRAMA HERE.
OH.
WHUMP

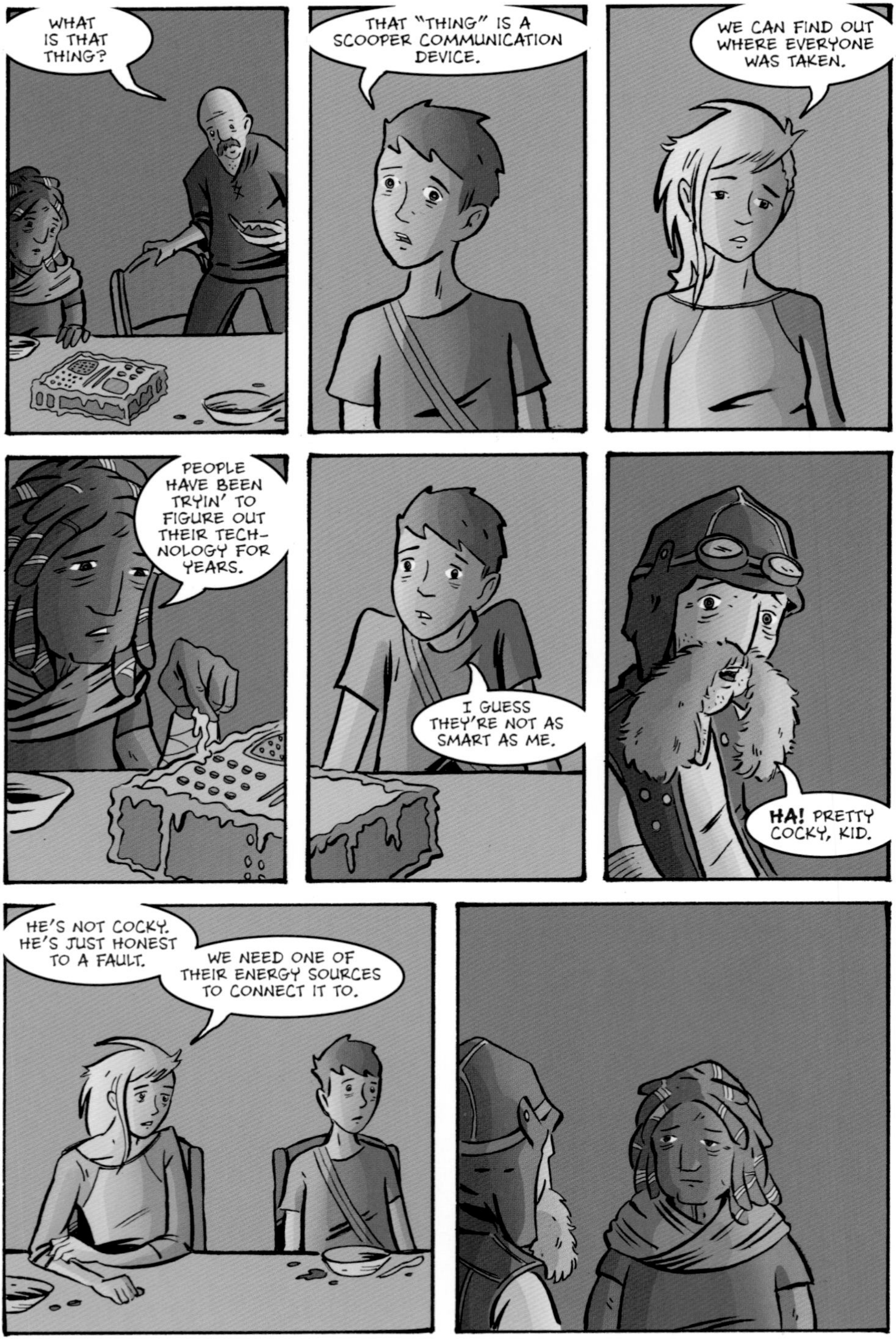
WHAT IS THAT THING?
THAT "THING" IS A SCOOPER COMMUNICATION DEVICE.
WE CAN FIND OUT WHERE EVERYONE WAS TAKEN.
PEOPLE HAVE BEEN TRYIN' TO FIGURE OUT THEIR TECH-NOLOGY FOR YEARS.
I GUESS THEY'RE NOT AS SMART AS ME.
HA! PRETTY COCKY, KID.
HE'S NOT COCKY. HE'S JUST HONEST TO A FAULT.
WE NEED ONE OF THEIR ENERGY SOURCES TO CONNECT IT TO.

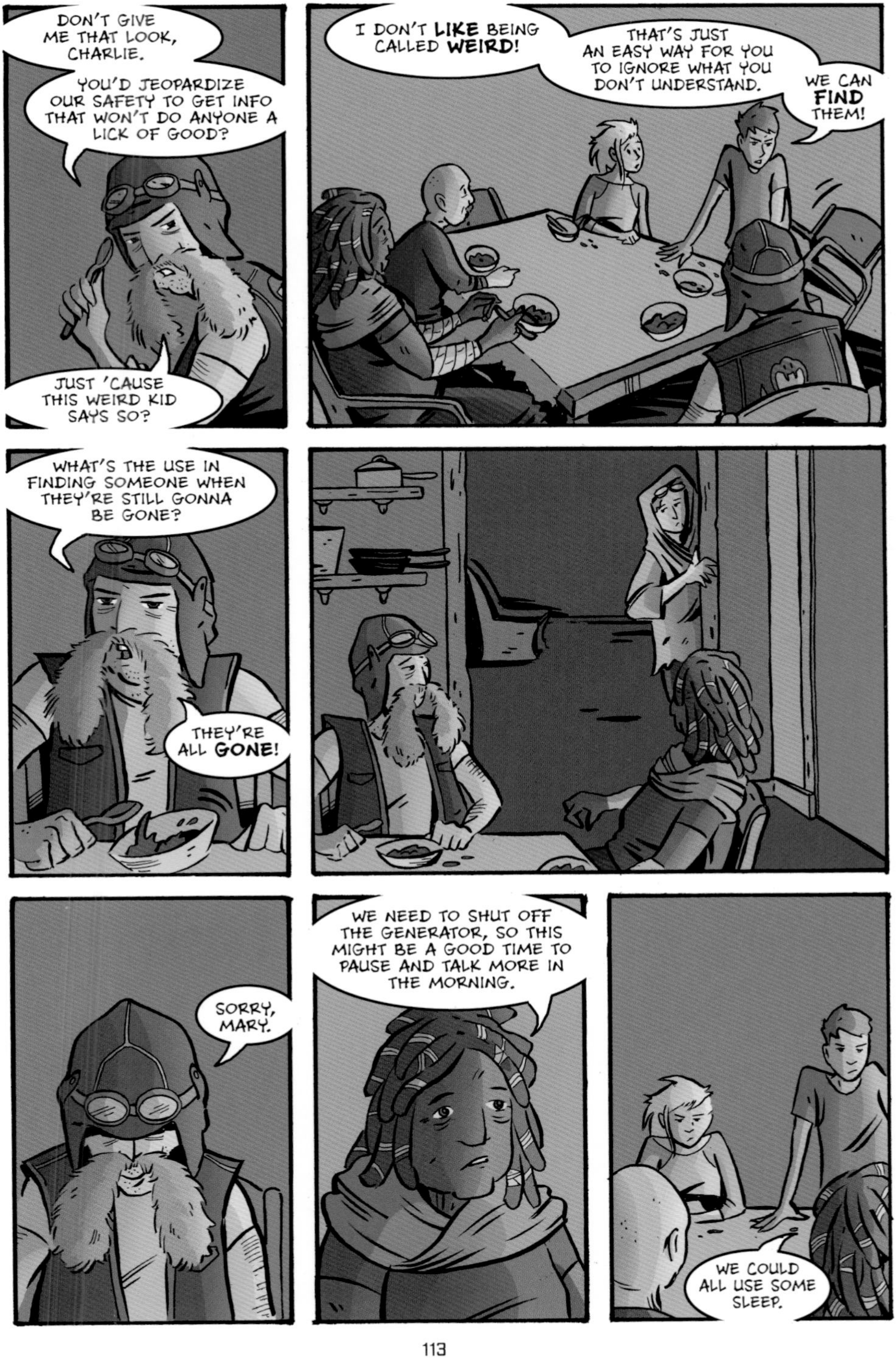
DON'T GIVE ME THAT LOOK, CHARLIE.
YOU'D JEOPARDIZE OUR SAFETY TO GET INFO THAT WON'T DO ANYONE A LICK OF GOOD?
JUST 'CAUSE THIS WEIRD KID SAYS SO?
I DON'T **LIKE** BEING CALLED **WEIRD**!
THAT'S JUST AN EASY WAY FOR YOU TO IGNORE WHAT YOU DON'T UNDERSTAND.
WE CAN **FIND** THEM!
WHAT'S THE USE IN FINDING SOMEONE WHEN THEY'RE STILL GONNA BE GONE?
THEY'RE ALL **GONE**!
SORRY, MARY.
WE NEED TO SHUT OFF THE GENERATOR, SO THIS MIGHT BE A GOOD TIME TO PAUSE AND TALK MORE IN THE MORNING.
WE COULD ALL USE SOME SLEEP.

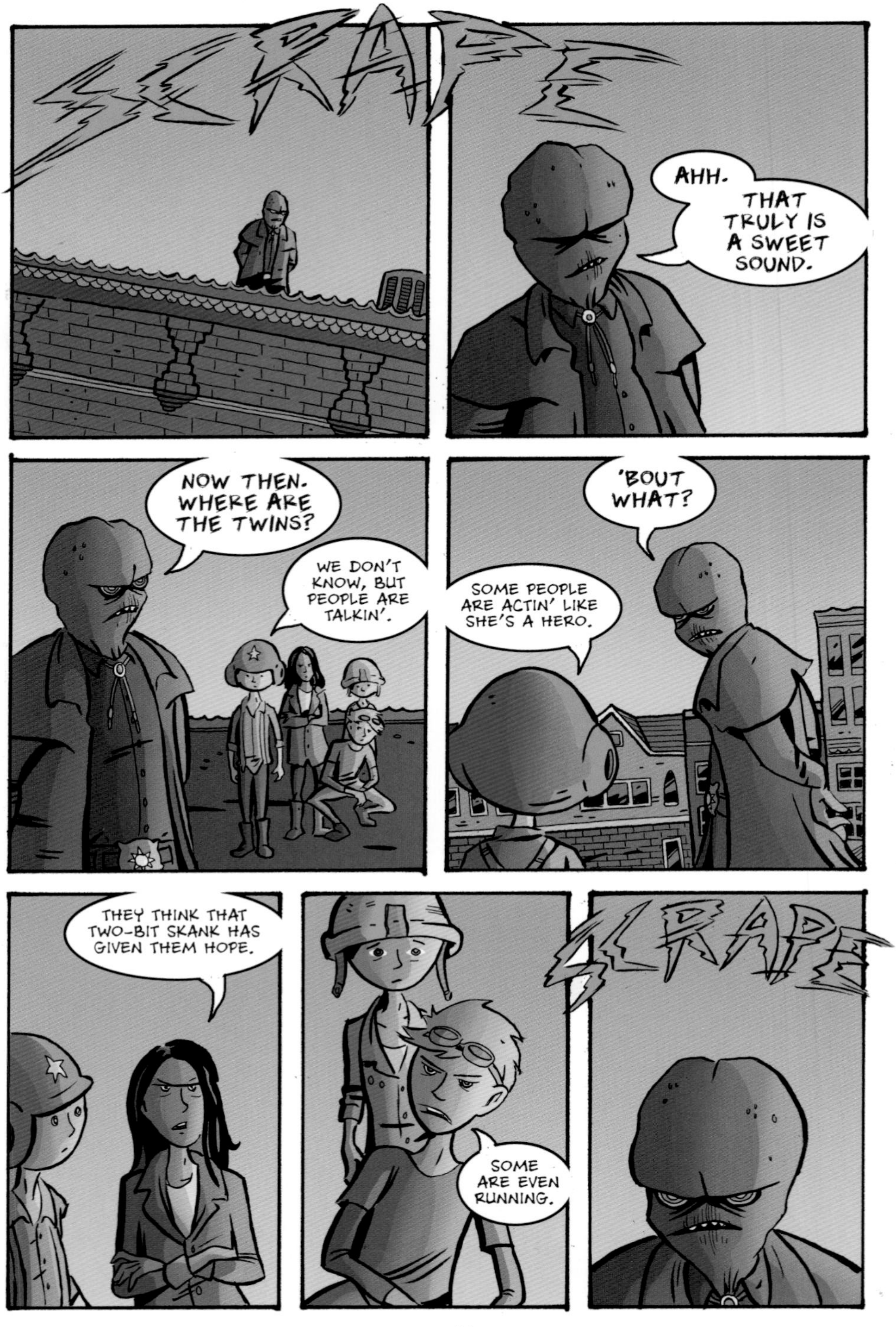
SCRAPE
AHH.
THAT TRULY IS A SWEET SOUND.
NOW THEN. WHERE ARE THE TWINS?
WE DON'T KNOW, BUT PEOPLE ARE TALKIN'.
'BOUT WHAT?
SOME PEOPLE ARE ACTIN' LIKE SHE'S A HERO.
THEY THINK THAT TWO-BIT SKANK HAS GIVEN THEM HOPE.
SOME ARE EVEN RUNNING.
SCRAPE

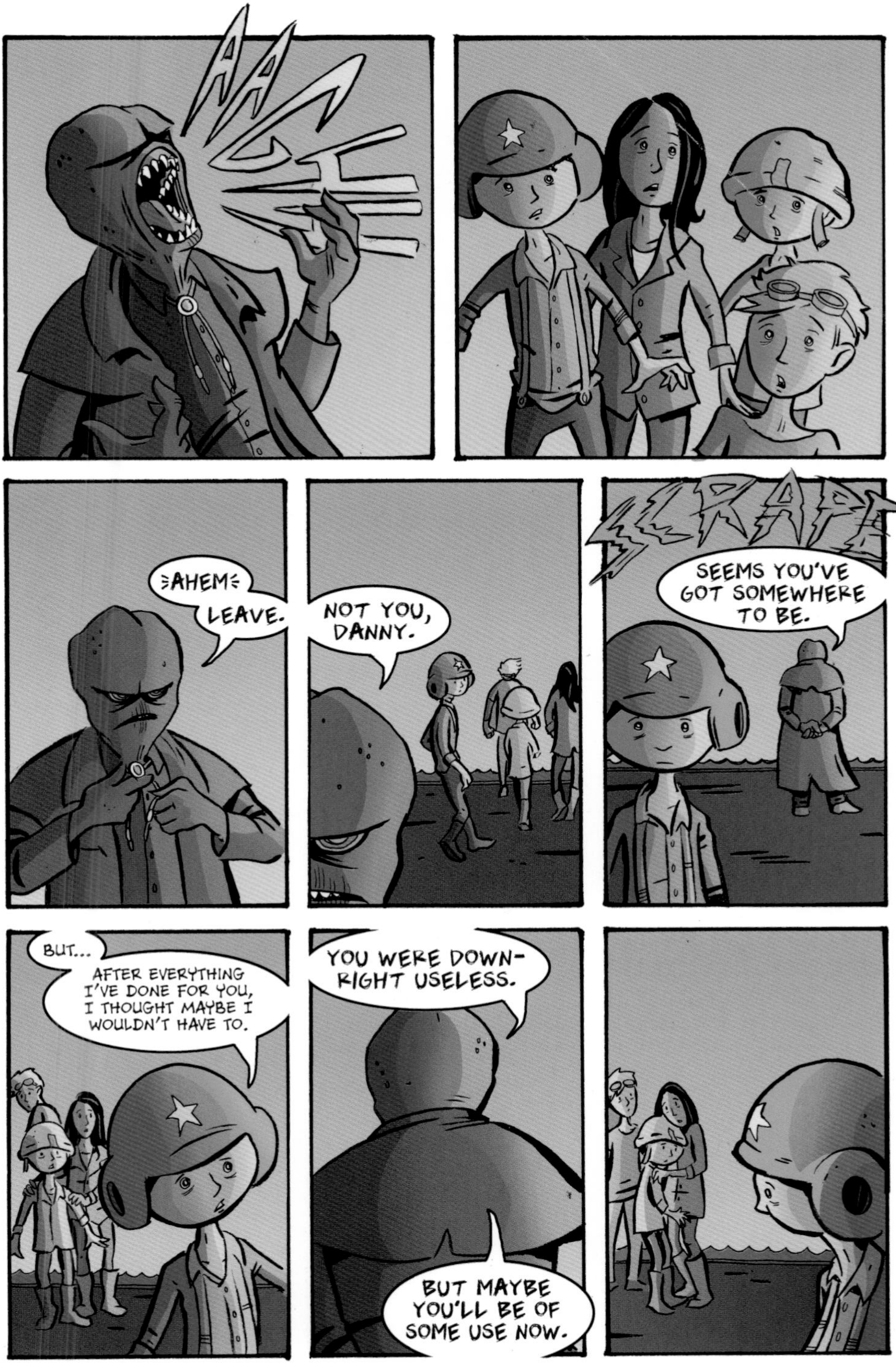
AAAGH
AHEM
LEAVE.
NOT YOU, DANNY.
SCRAPE
SEEMS YOU'VE GOT SOMEWHERE TO BE.
BUT...
AFTER EVERYTHING I'VE DONE FOR YOU, I THOUGHT MAYBE I WOULDN'T HAVE TO.
YOU WERE DOWN-RIGHT USELESS.
BUT MAYBE YOU'LL BE OF SOME USE NOW.

GET TO IT. THEY'RE WAITIN'.

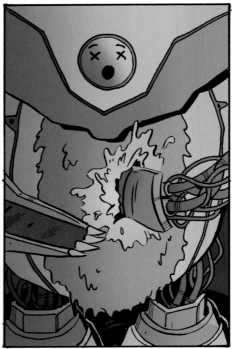

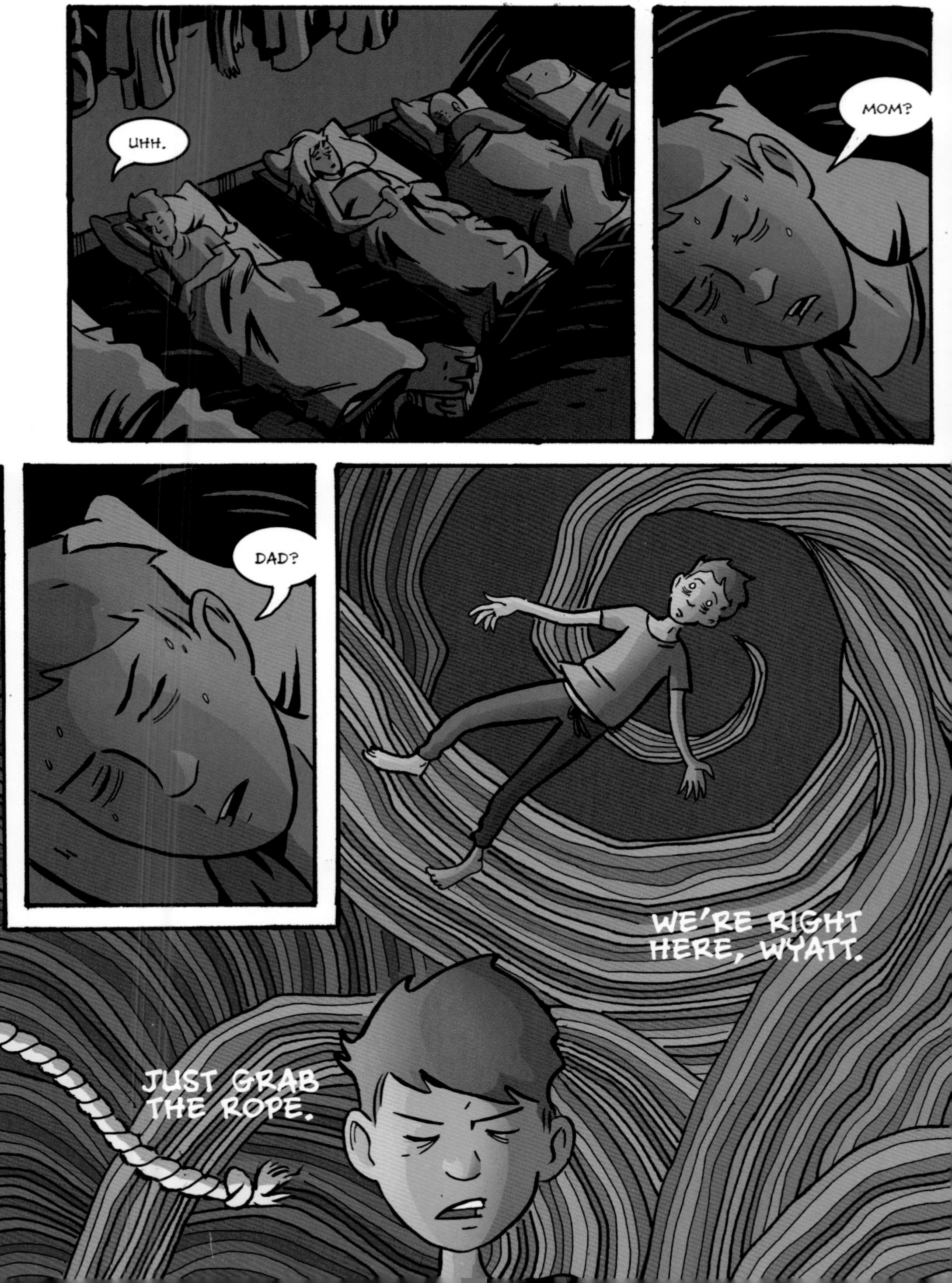
UHH.
MOM?
DAD?
WE'RE RIGHT HERE, WYATT.
JUST GRAB THE ROPE.

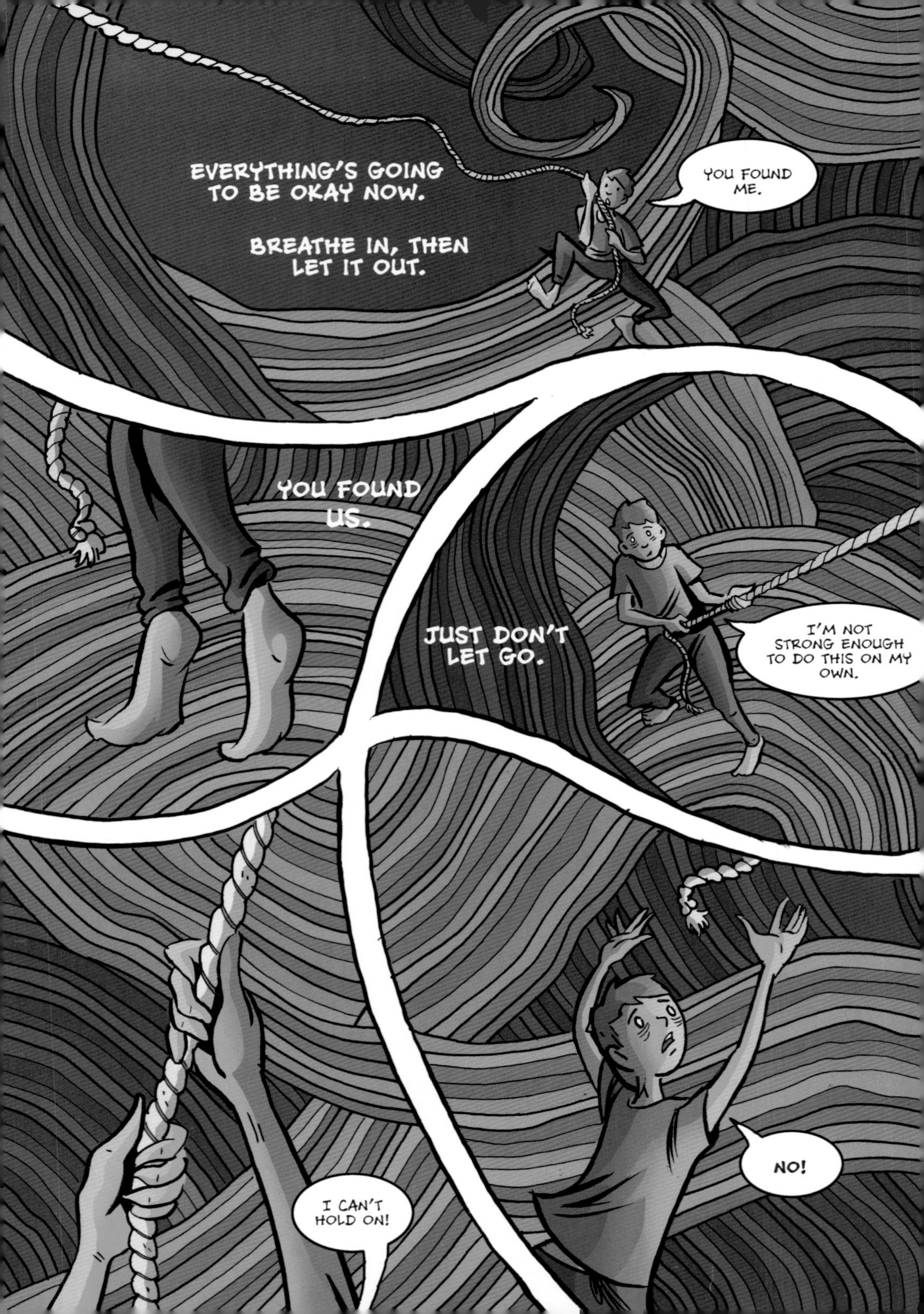
EVERYTHING'S GOING TO BE OKAY NOW.
BREATHE IN, THEN LET IT OUT.
YOU FOUND ME.
YOU FOUND US.
JUST DON'T LET GO.
I'M NOT STRONG ENOUGH TO DO THIS ON MY OWN.
I CAN'T HOLD ON!
NO!

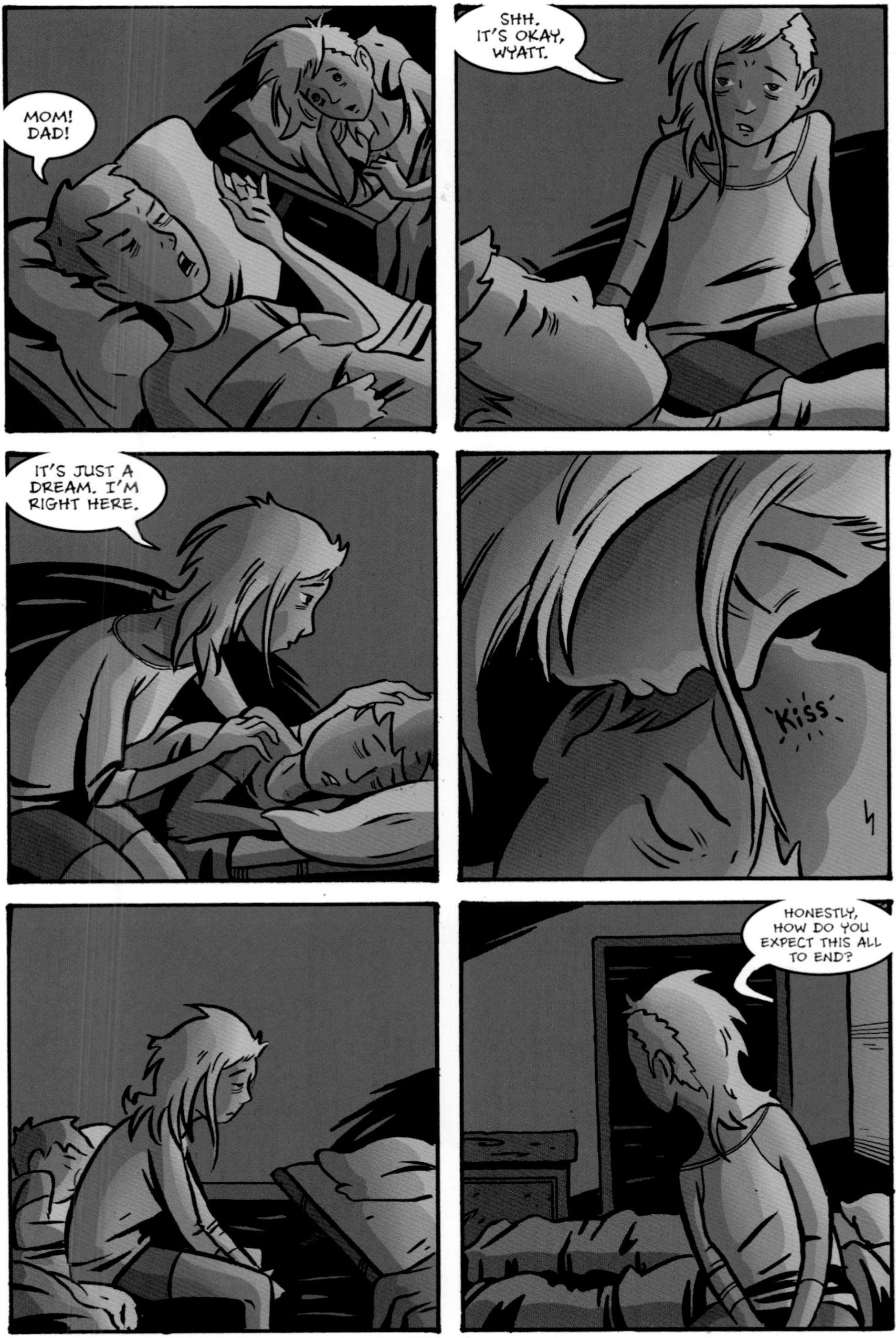
MOM! DAD!
SHH. IT'S OKAY, WYATT.
IT'S JUST A DREAM. I'M RIGHT HERE.
KISS
HONESTLY, HOW DO YOU EXPECT THIS ALL TO END?

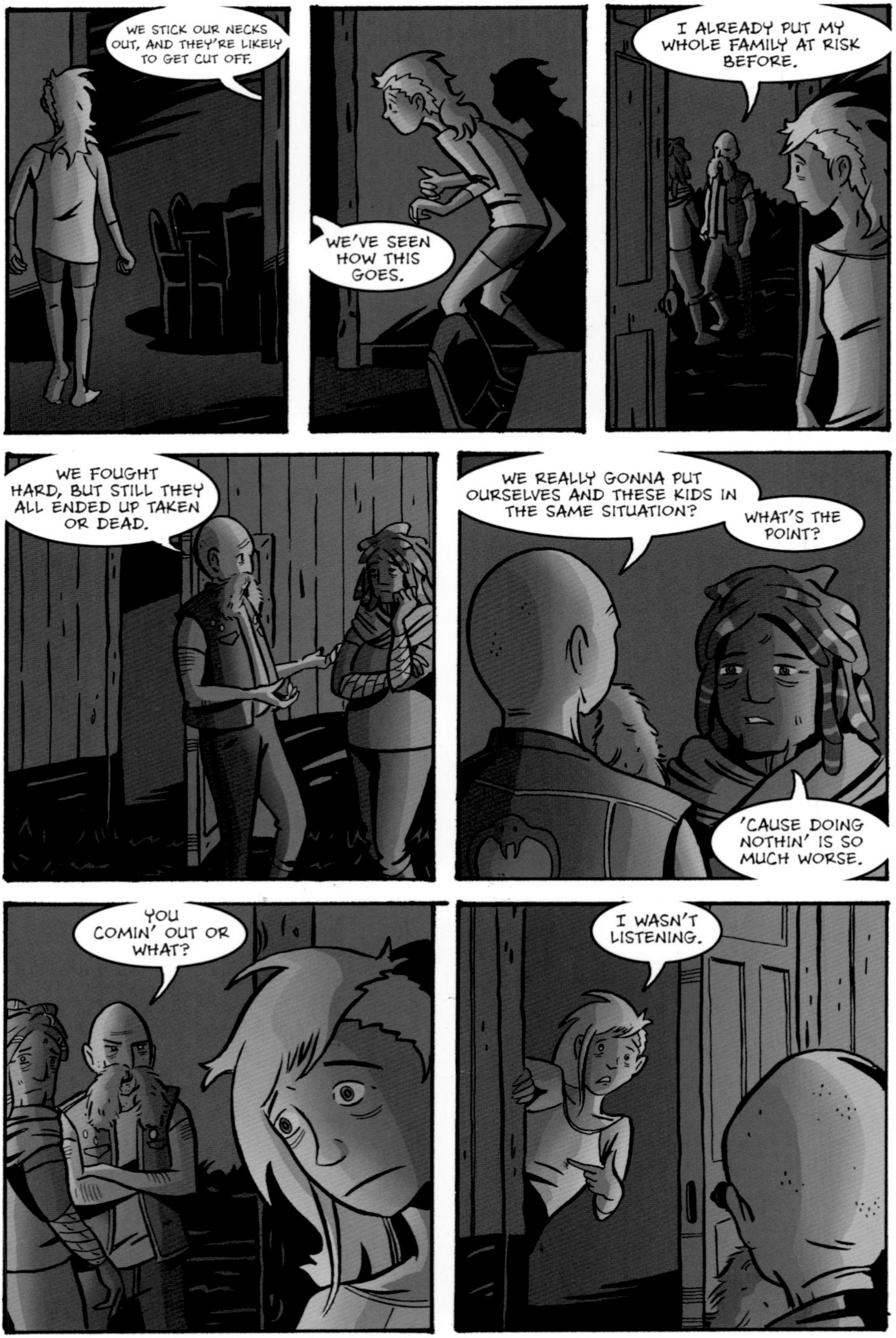
WE STICK OUR NECKS OUT, AND THEY'RE LIKELY TO GET CUT OFF.
WE'VE SEEN HOW THIS GOES.
I ALREADY PUT MY WHOLE FAMILY AT RISK BEFORE.
WE FOUGHT HARD, BUT STILL THEY ALL ENDED UP TAKEN OR DEAD.
WE REALLY GONNA PUT OURSELVES AND THESE KIDS IN THE SAME SITUATION?
WHAT'S THE POINT?
'CAUSE DOING NOTHIN' IS SO MUCH WORSE.
YOU COMIN' OUT OR WHAT?
I WASN'T LISTENING.

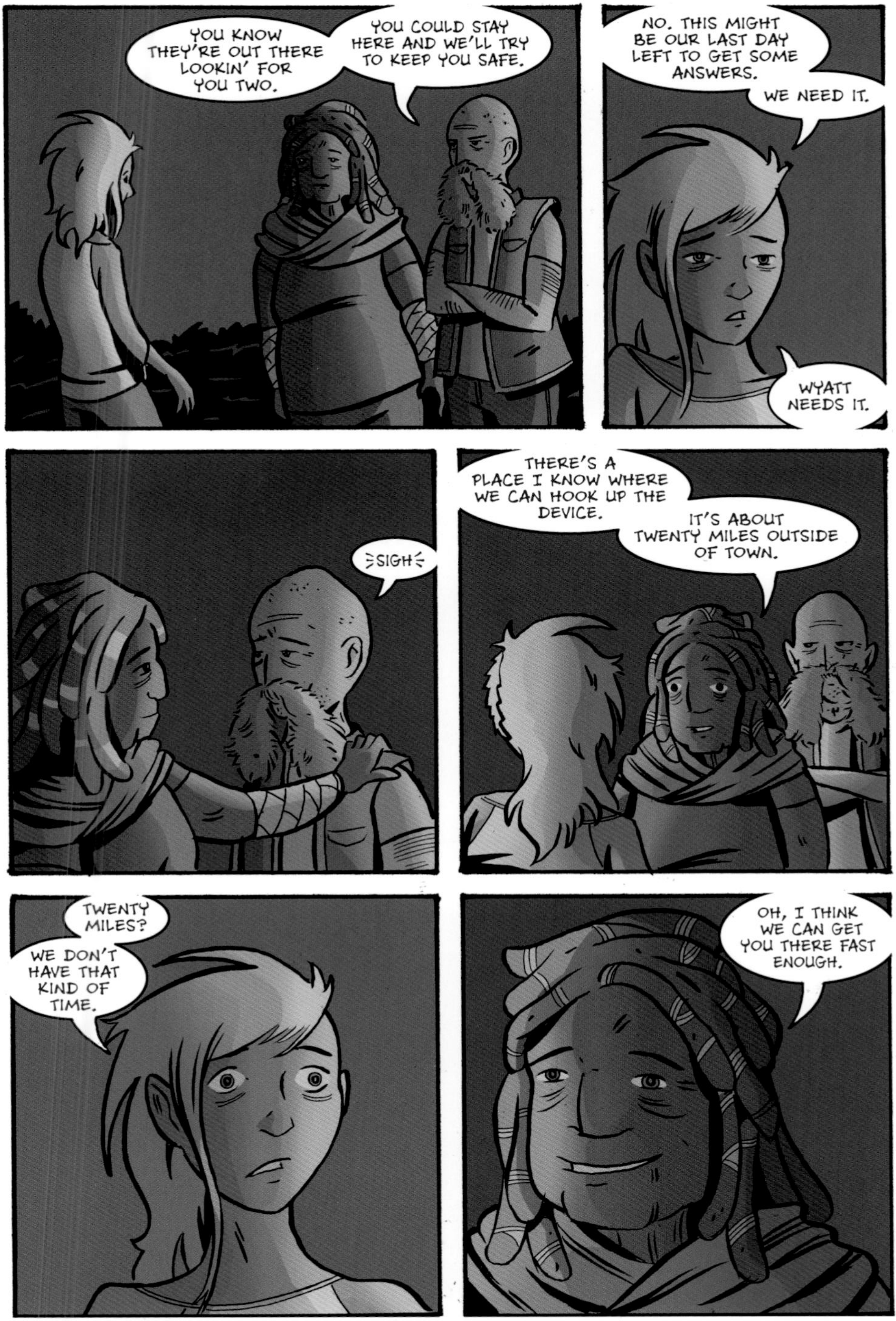

YOU KNOW THEY'RE OUT THERE LOOKIN' FOR YOU TWO.
YOU COULD STAY HERE AND WE'LL TRY TO KEEP YOU SAFE.
NO. THIS MIGHT BE OUR LAST DAY LEFT TO GET SOME ANSWERS.
WE NEED IT.
WYATT NEEDS IT.
SIGH
THERE'S A PLACE I KNOW WHERE WE CAN HOOK UP THE DEVICE.
IT'S ABOUT TWENTY MILES OUTSIDE OF TOWN.
TWENTY MILES?
WE DON'T HAVE THAT KIND OF TIME.
OH, I THINK WE CAN GET YOU THERE FAST ENOUGH.

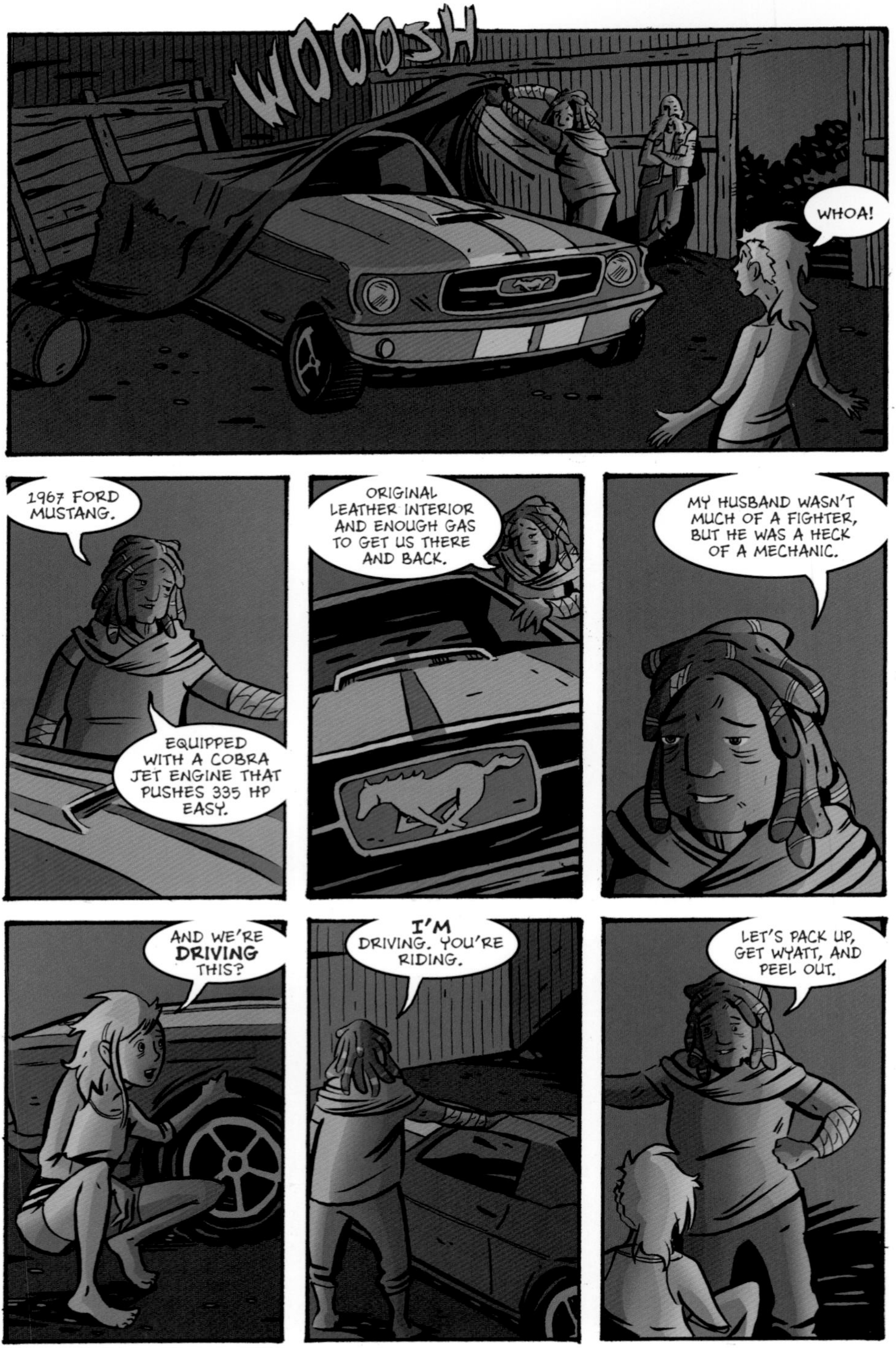
WOOOSH
WHOA!
1967 FORD MUSTANG.
EQUIPPED WITH A COBRA JET ENGINE THAT PUSHES 335 HP EASY.
ORIGINAL LEATHER INTERIOR AND ENOUGH GAS TO GET US THERE AND BACK.
MY HUSBAND WASN'T MUCH OF A FIGHTER, BUT HE WAS A HECK OF A MECHANIC.
AND WE'RE DRIVING THIS?
I'M DRIVING. YOU'RE RIDING.
LET'S PACK UP, GET WYATT, AND PEEL OUT.

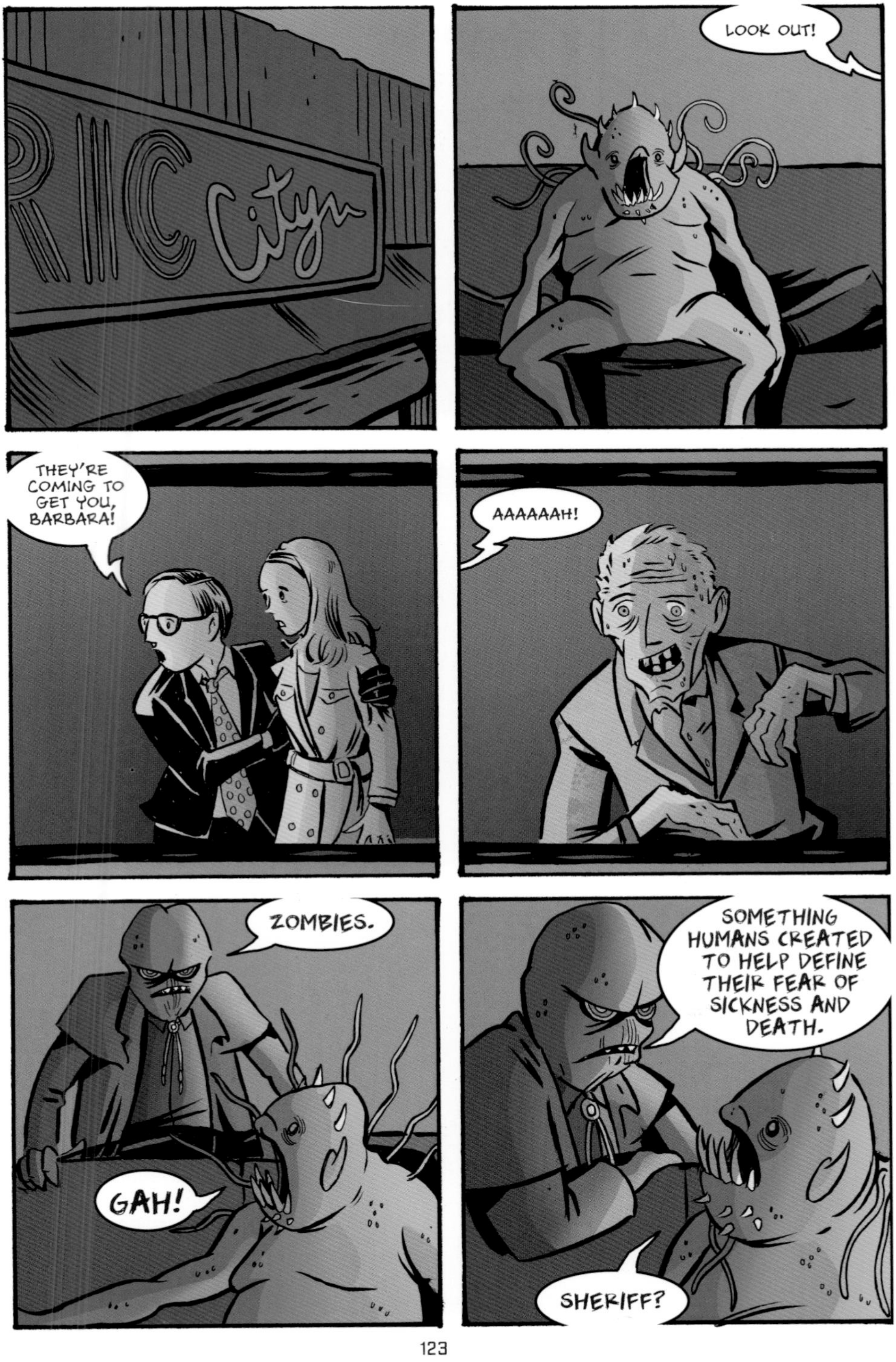
City
LOOK OUT!
THEY'RE COMING TO GET YOU, BARBARA!
AAAAAAH!
ZOMBIES.
GAH!
SOMETHING HUMANS CREATED TO HELP DEFINE THEIR FEAR OF SICKNESS AND DEATH.
SHERIFF?

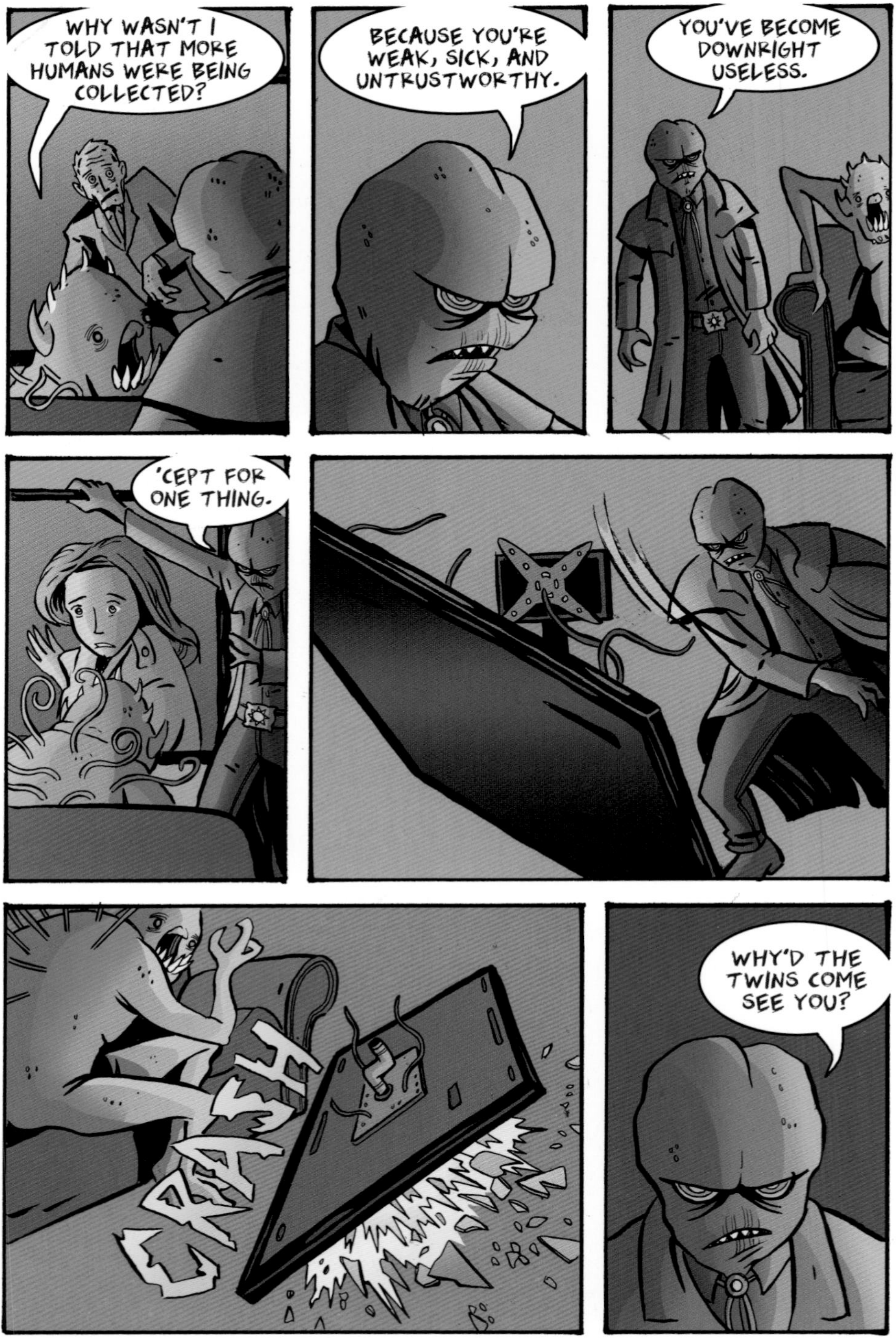
WHY WASN'T I TOLD THAT MORE HUMANS WERE BEING COLLECTED?
BECAUSE YOU'RE WEAK, SICK, AND UNTRUSTWORTHY.
YOU'VE BECOME DOWNRIGHT USELESS.
'CEPT FOR ONE THING.
CRASH
WHY'D THE TWINS COME SEE YOU?

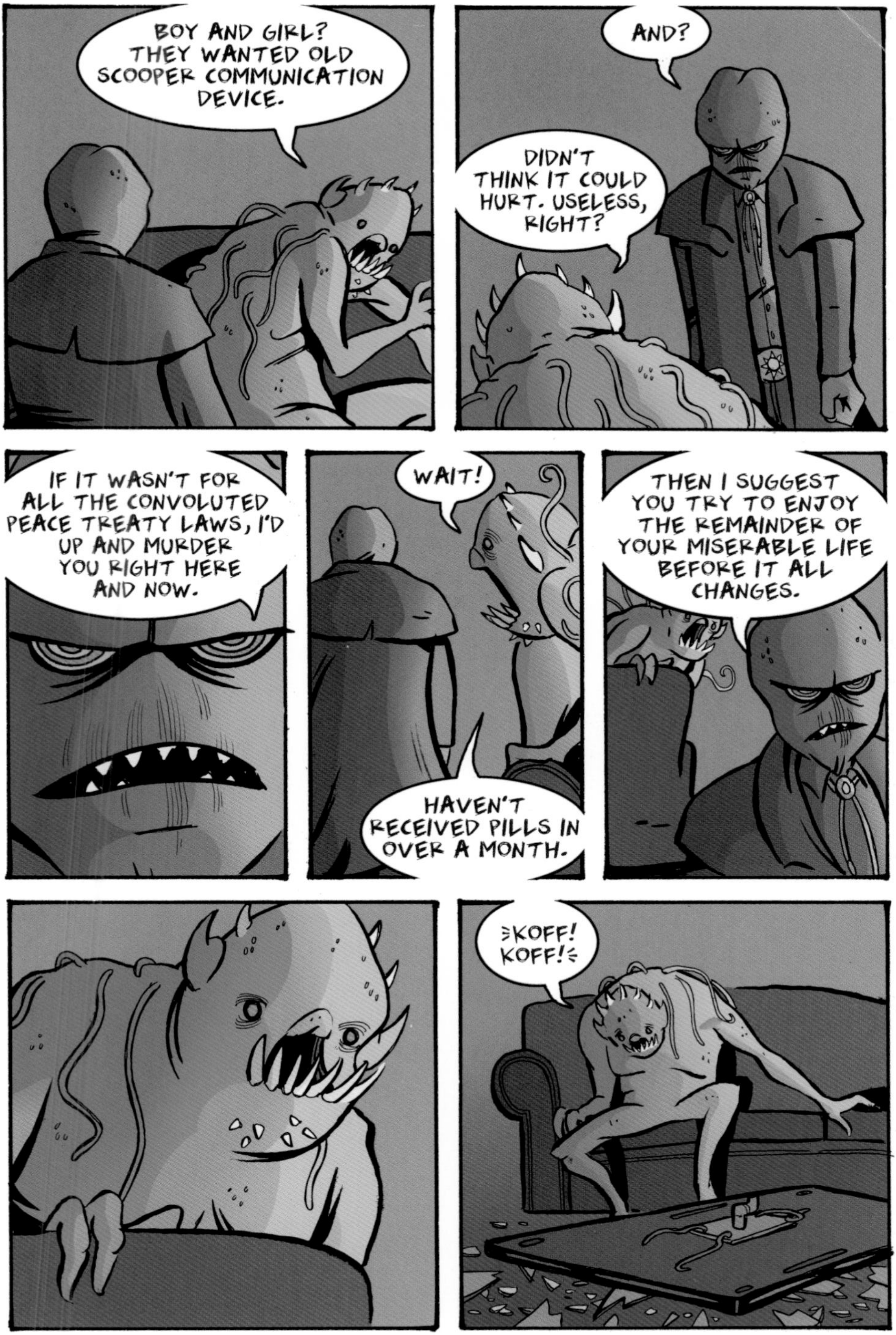
BOY AND GIRL? THEY WANTED OLD SCOOPER COMMUNICATION DEVICE.
AND?
DIDN'T THINK IT COULD HURT. USELESS, RIGHT?
IF IT WASN'T FOR ALL THE CONVOLUTED PEACE TREATY LAWS, I'D UP AND MURDER YOU RIGHT HERE AND NOW.
WAIT!
HAVEN'T RECEIVED PILLS IN OVER A MONTH.
THEN I SUGGEST YOU TRY TO ENJOY THE REMAINDER OF YOUR MISERABLE LIFE BEFORE IT ALL CHANGES.
KOFF! KOFF!

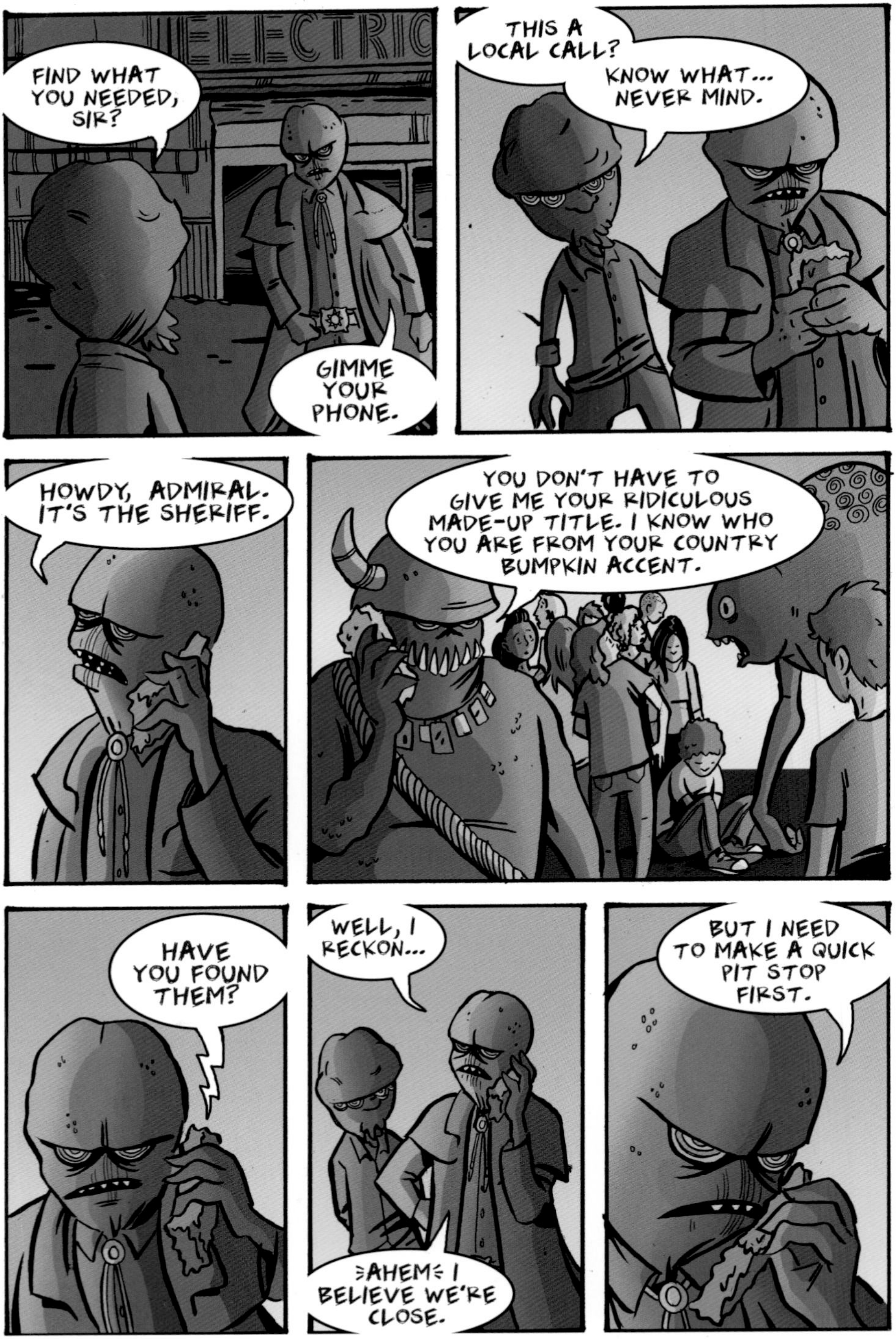
ELECTRIC
FIND WHAT YOU NEEDED, SIR?
GIMME YOUR PHONE.
THIS A LOCAL CALL?
KNOW WHAT... NEVER MIND.
HOWDY, ADMIRAL. IT'S THE SHERIFF.
YOU DON'T HAVE TO GIVE ME YOUR RIDICULOUS MADE-UP TITLE. I KNOW WHO YOU ARE FROM YOUR COUNTRY BUMPKIN ACCENT.
HAVE YOU FOUND THEM?
WELL, I RECKON...
≥AHEM≤ I BELIEVE WE'RE CLOSE.
BUT I NEED TO MAKE A QUICK PIT STOP FIRST.

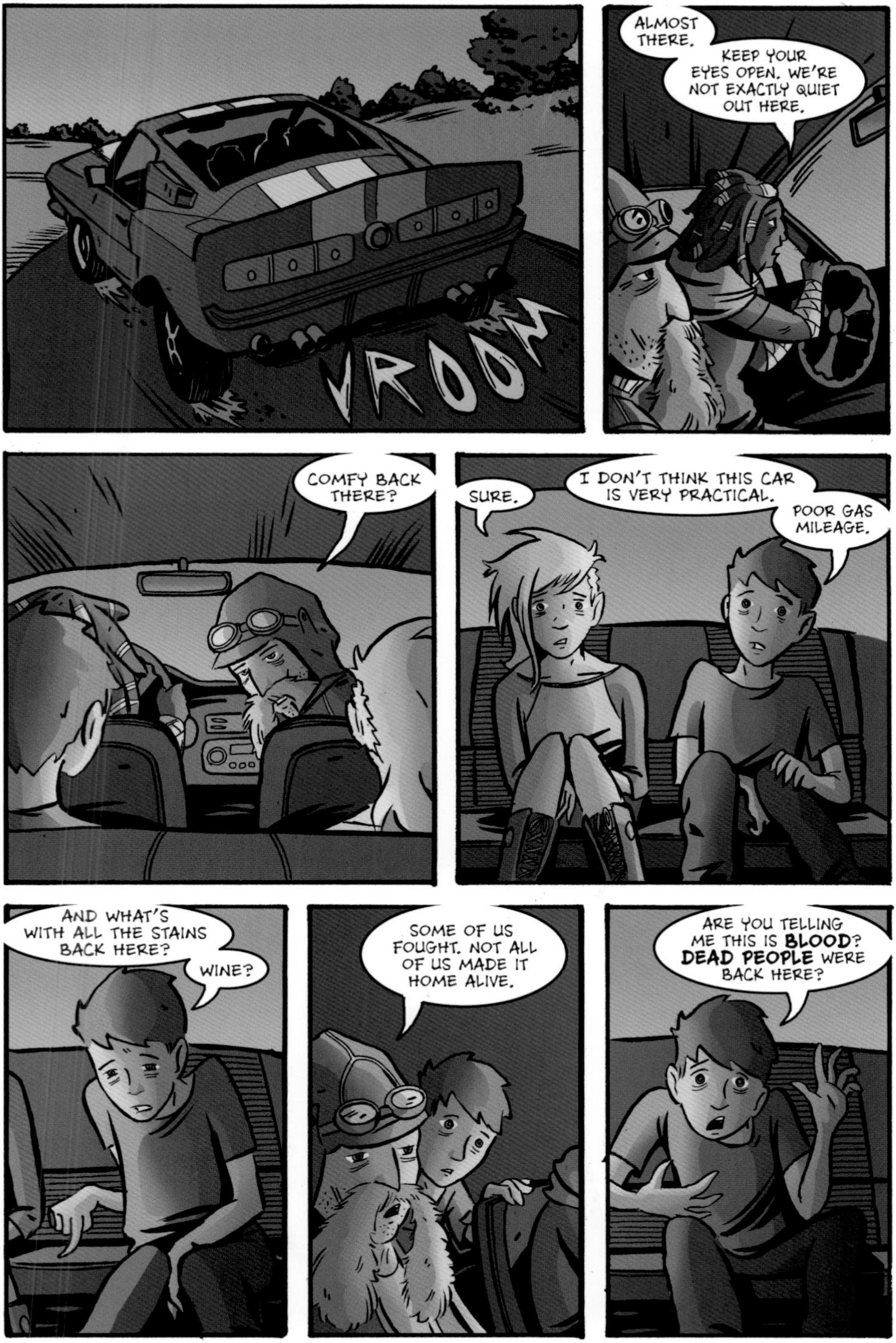
VROOM
ALMOST THERE.
KEEP YOUR EYES OPEN. WE'RE NOT EXACTLY QUIET OUT HERE.
COMFY BACK THERE?
SURE.
I DON'T THINK THIS CAR IS VERY PRACTICAL.
POOR GAS MILEAGE.
AND WHAT'S WITH ALL THE STAINS BACK HERE?
WINE?
SOME OF US FOUGHT. NOT ALL OF US MADE IT HOME ALIVE.
ARE YOU TELLING ME THIS IS **BLOOD**? **DEAD PEOPLE** WERE BACK HERE?

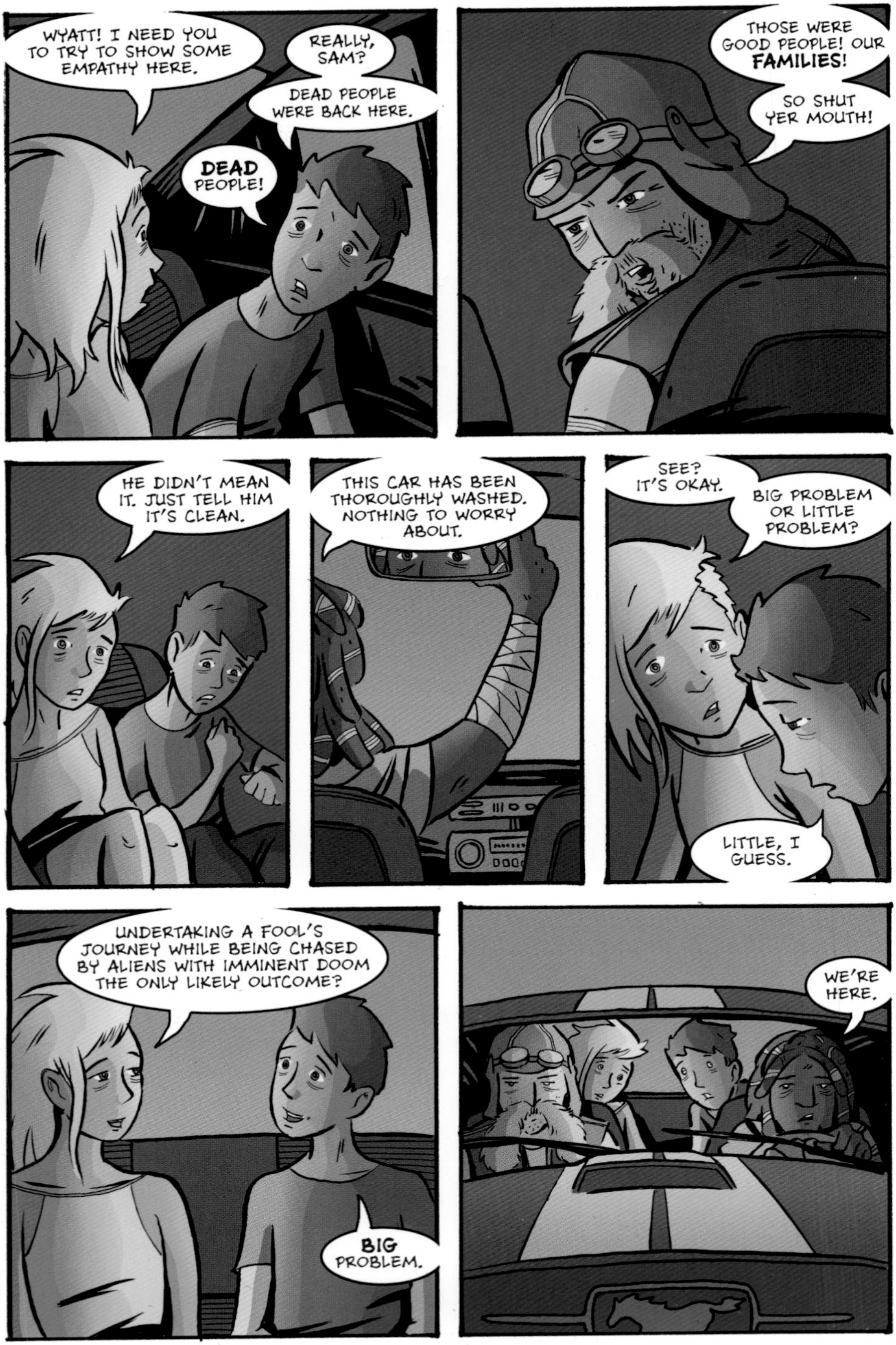
WYATT! I NEED YOU TO TRY TO SHOW SOME EMPATHY HERE.
REALLY, SAM?
DEAD PEOPLE WERE BACK HERE.
DEAD PEOPLE!
THOSE WERE GOOD PEOPLE! OUR FAMILIES!
SO SHUT YER MOUTH!
HE DIDN'T MEAN IT. JUST TELL HIM IT'S CLEAN.
THIS CAR HAS BEEN THOROUGHLY WASHED. NOTHING TO WORRY ABOUT.
SEE? IT'S OKAY.
BIG PROBLEM OR LITTLE PROBLEM?
LITTLE, I GUESS.
UNDERTAKING A FOOL'S JOURNEY WHILE BEING CHASED BY ALIENS WITH IMMINENT DOOM THE ONLY LIKELY OUTCOME?
BIG PROBLEM.
WE'RE HERE.

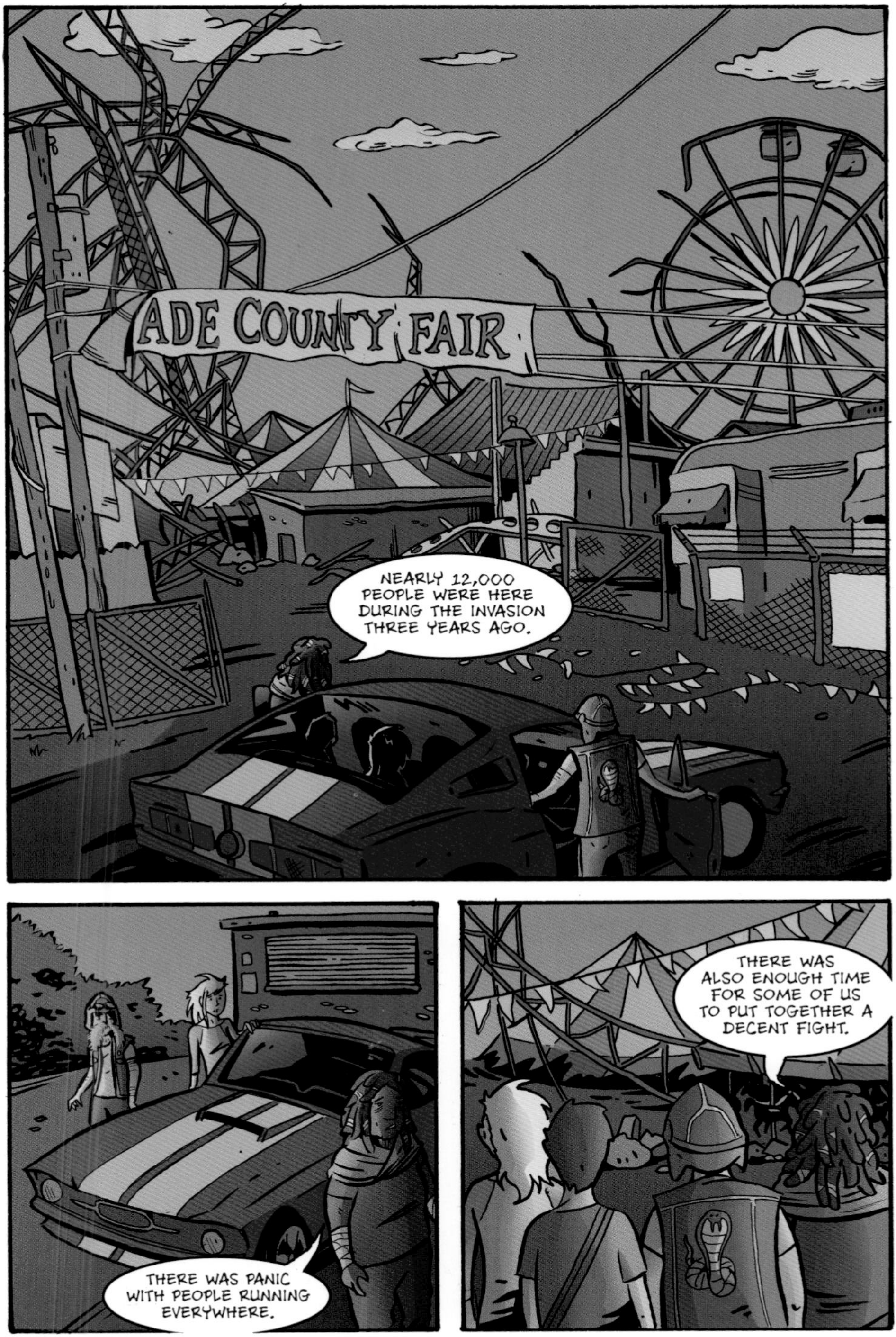
ADE COUNTY FAIR
NEARLY 12,000 PEOPLE WERE HERE DURING THE INVASION THREE YEARS AGO.
THERE WAS PANIC WITH PEOPLE RUNNING EVERYWHERE.
THERE WAS ALSO ENOUGH TIME FOR SOME OF US TO PUT TOGETHER A DECENT FIGHT.

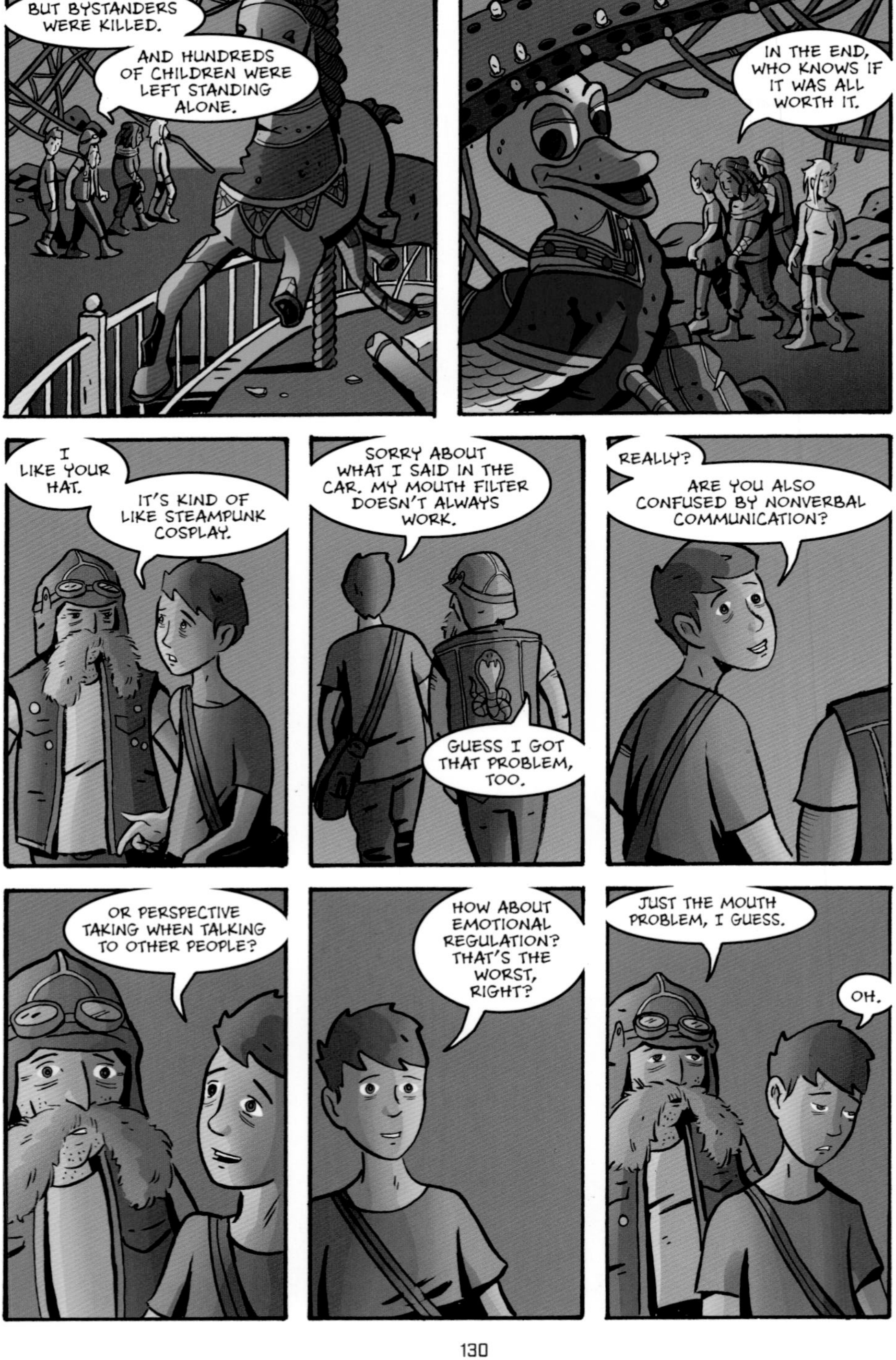
BUT BYSTANDERS WERE KILLED.
AND HUNDREDS OF CHILDREN WERE LEFT STANDING ALONE.
IN THE END, WHO KNOWS IF IT WAS ALL WORTH IT.
I LIKE YOUR HAT.
IT'S KIND OF LIKE STEAMPUNK COSPLAY.
SORRY ABOUT WHAT I SAID IN THE CAR. MY MOUTH FILTER DOESN'T ALWAYS WORK.
GUESS I GOT THAT PROBLEM, TOO.
REALLY?
ARE YOU ALSO CONFUSED BY NONVERBAL COMMUNICATION?
OR PERSPECTIVE TAKING WHEN TALKING TO OTHER PEOPLE?
HOW ABOUT EMOTIONAL REGULATION? THAT'S THE WORST, RIGHT?
JUST THE MOUTH PROBLEM, I GUESS.
OH.

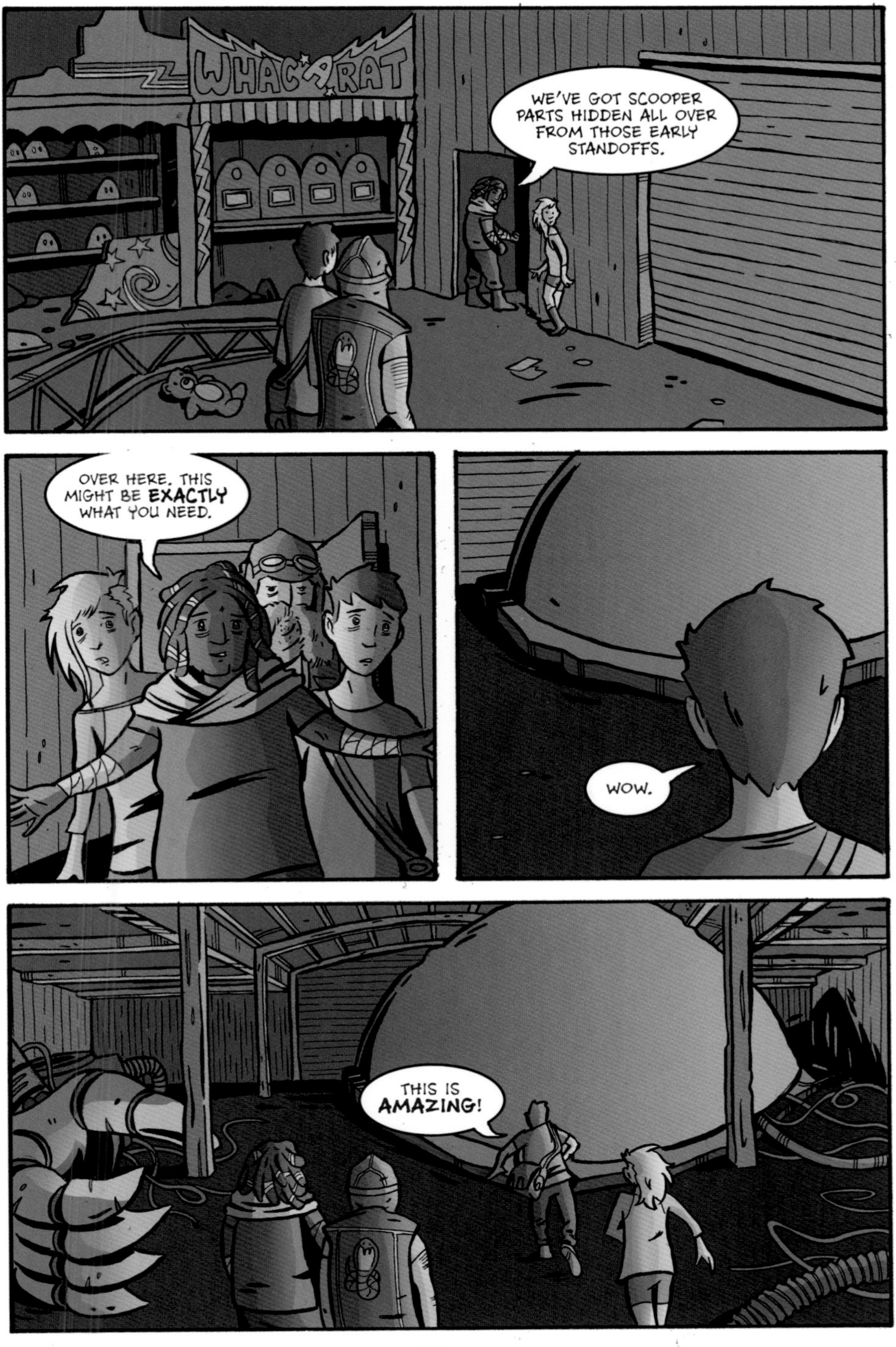
WHAC A RAT
WE'VE GOT SCOOPER PARTS HIDDEN ALL OVER FROM THOSE EARLY STANDOFFS.
OVER HERE. THIS MIGHT BE **EXACTLY** WHAT YOU NEED.
WOW.
THIS IS **AMAZING!**

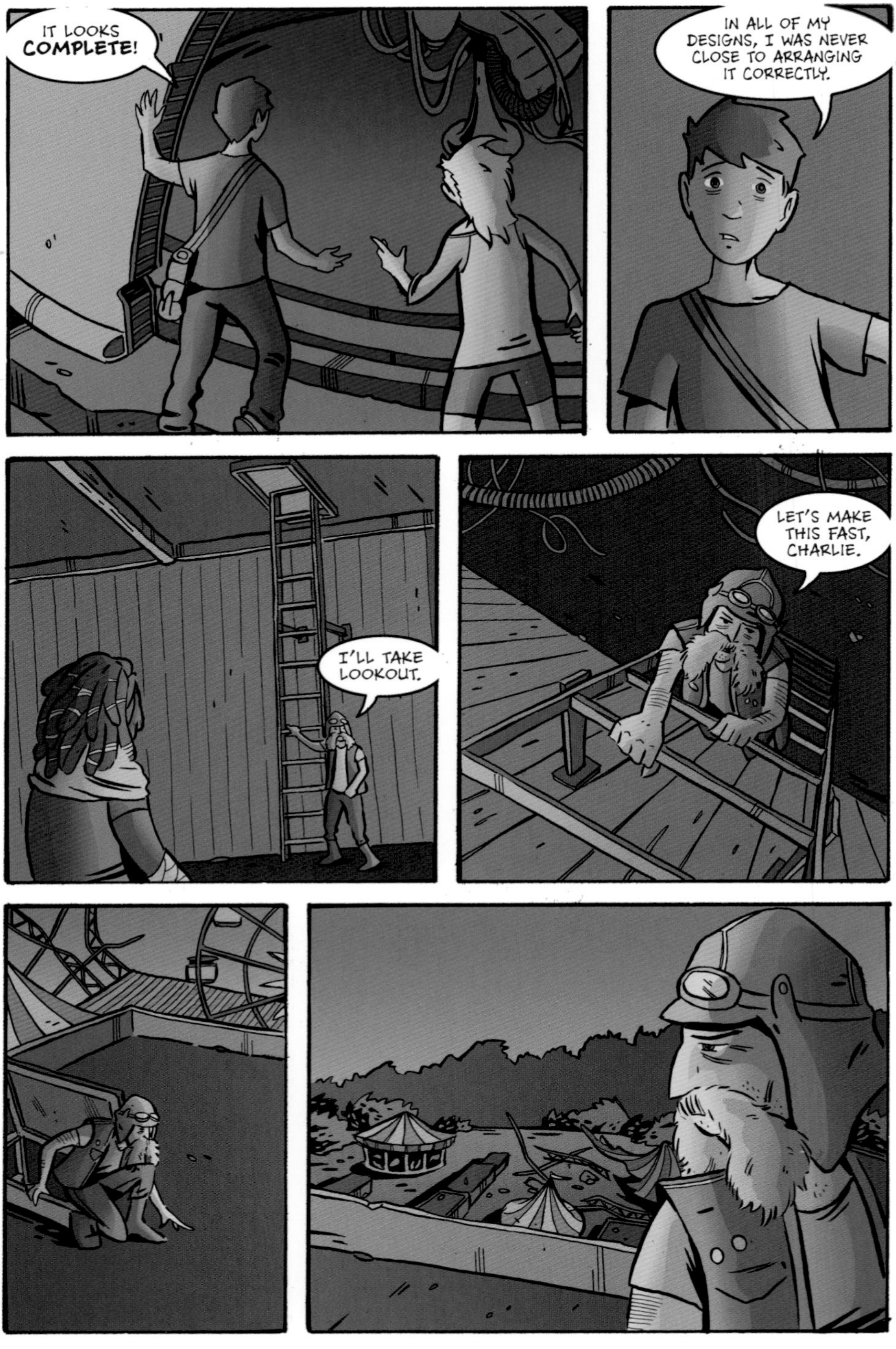
IT LOOKS COMPLETE!
IN ALL OF MY DESIGNS, I WAS NEVER CLOSE TO ARRANGING IT CORRECTLY.
I'LL TAKE LOOKOUT.
LET'S MAKE THIS FAST, CHARLIE.

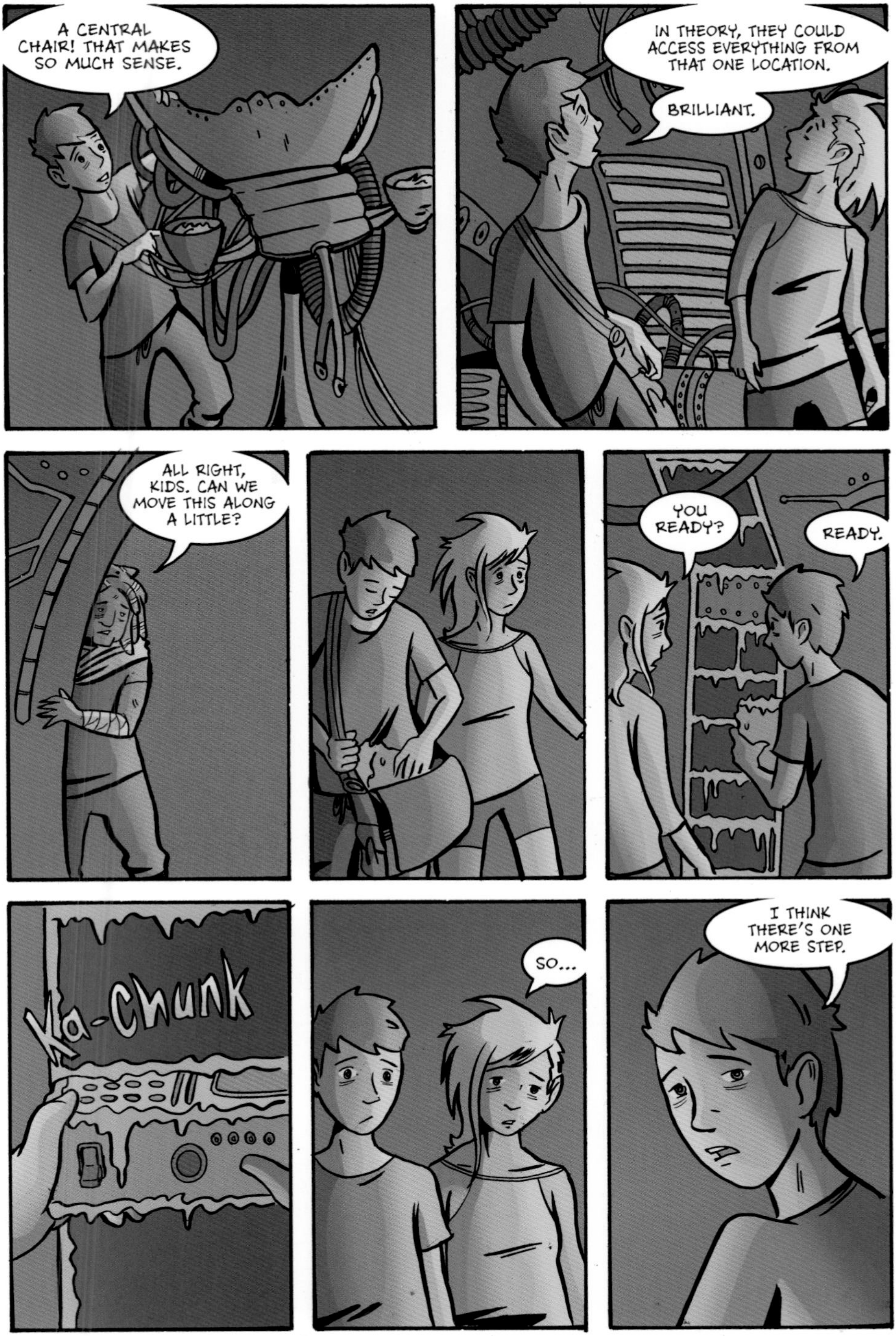
A CENTRAL CHAIR! THAT MAKES SO MUCH SENSE.
IN THEORY, THEY COULD ACCESS EVERYTHING FROM THAT ONE LOCATION.
BRILLIANT.
ALL RIGHT, KIDS. CAN WE MOVE THIS ALONG A LITTLE?
YOU READY?
READY.
KA-CHUNK
SO...
I THINK THERE'S ONE MORE STEP.

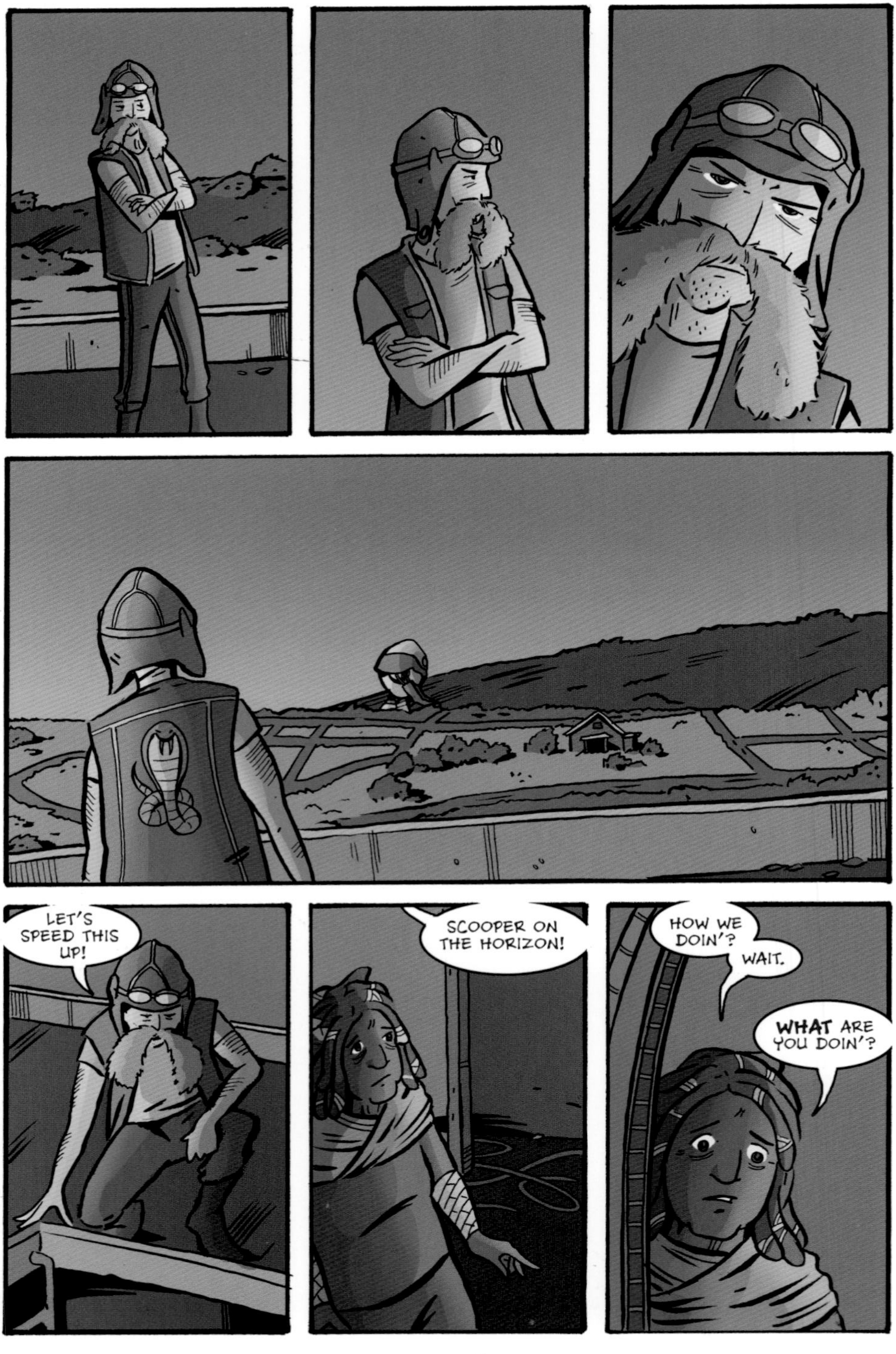
LET'S SPEED THIS UP!
SCOOPER ON THE HORIZON!
HOW WE DOIN'?
WAIT.
WHAT ARE YOU DOIN'?

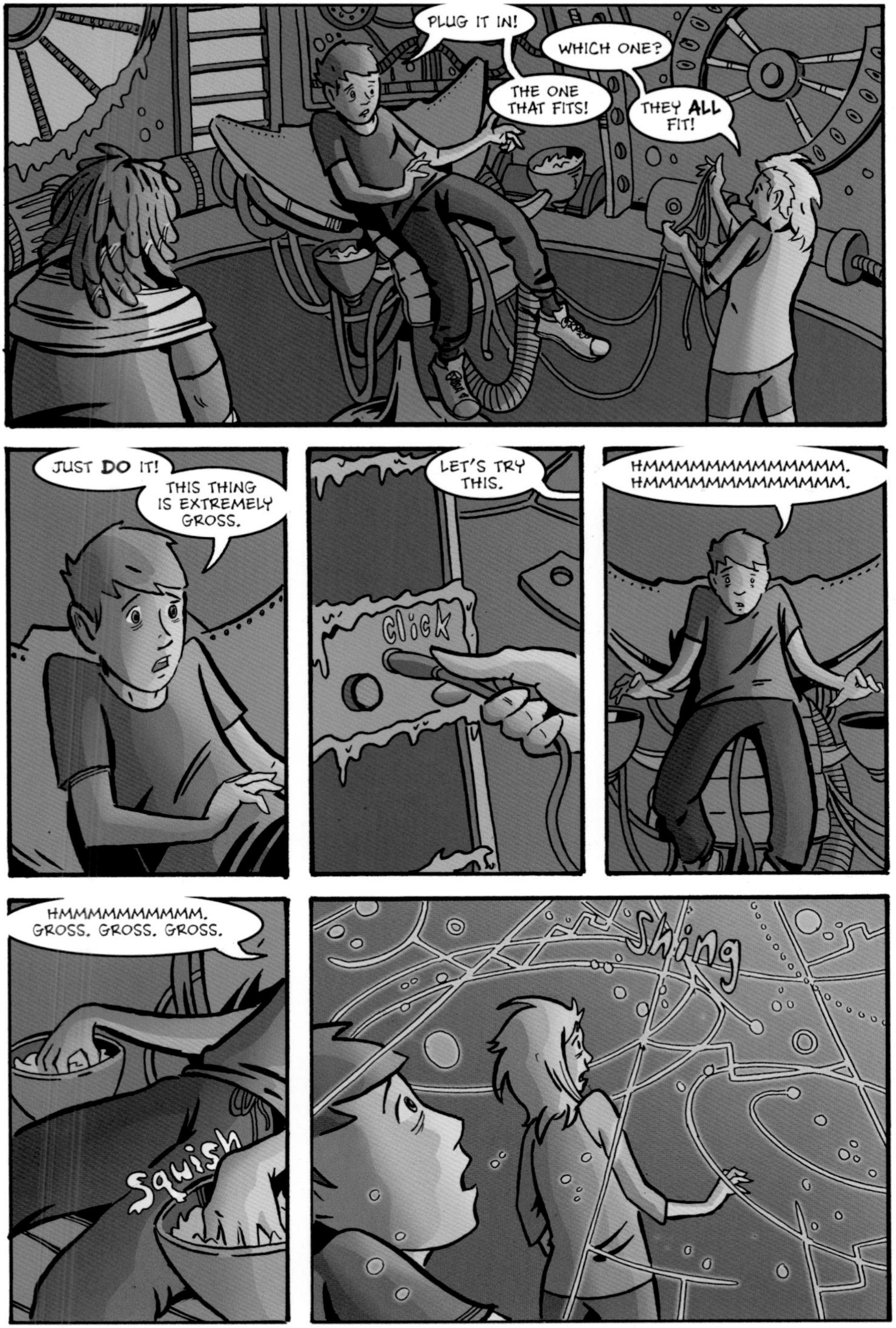
PLUG IT IN!
WHICH ONE?
THE ONE THAT FITS!
THEY ALL FIT!
JUST DO IT!
THIS THING IS EXTREMELY GROSS.
LET'S TRY THIS.
click
HMMMMMMMMMMMMMM. HMMMMMMMMMMMMMM.
HMMMMMMMMMM. GROSS. GROSS. GROSS.
squish
Shing

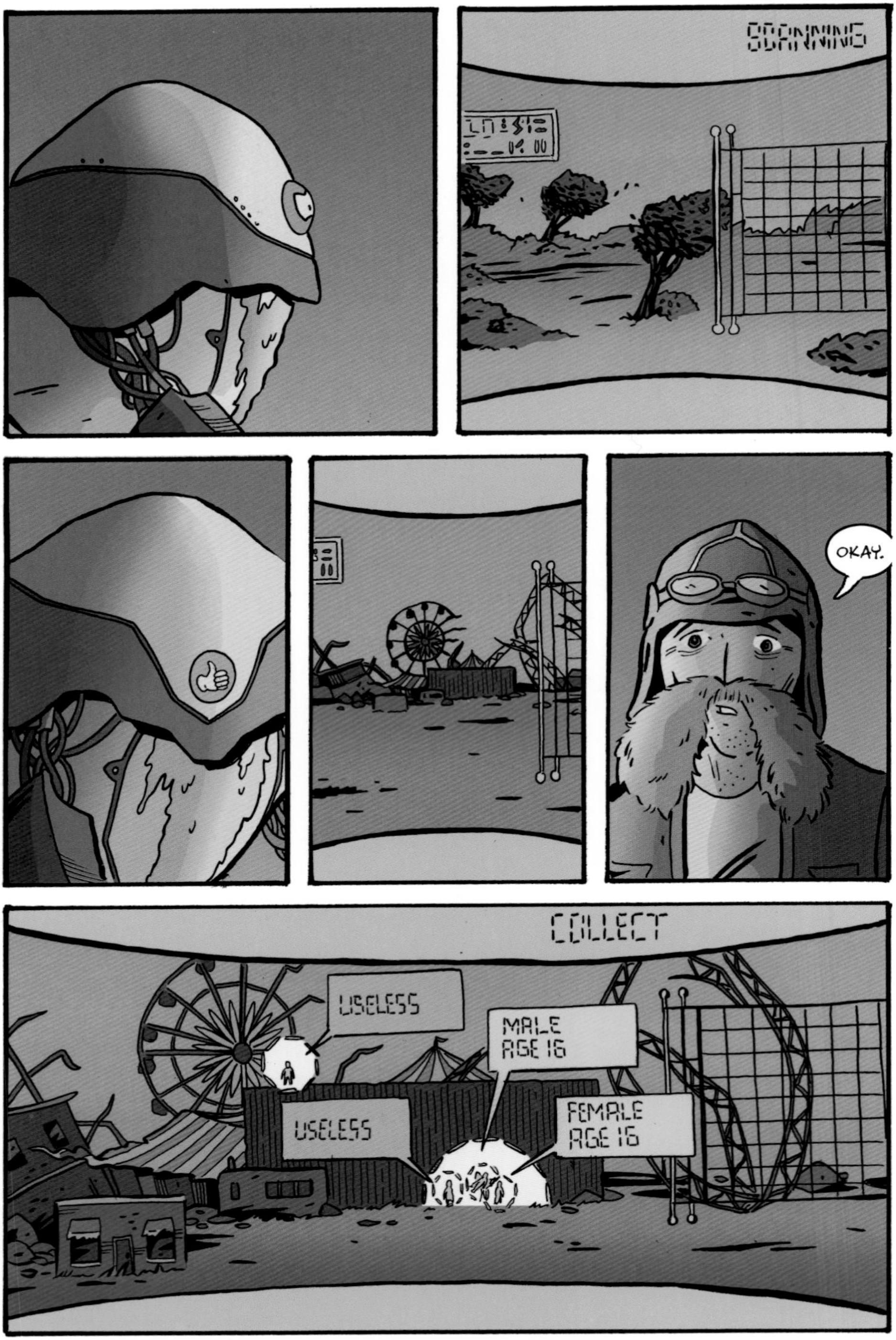
SCANNING
OKAY.
COLLECT
USELESS
MALE
AGE 16
USELESS
FEMALE
AGE 16

THESE THOUSANDS OF DOTS MUST BE THE SCOOPERS ON EARTH RIGHT NOW.

SO FIND SOMEWEHRE ELSE ON THE MAP WITH THOSE SAME DOTS.

HERE! THESE TWO PLANETS.

BUT...

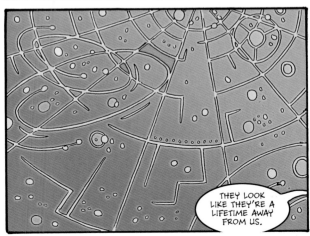

THEY LOOK LIKE THEY'RE A LIFETIME AWAY FROM US.

WE HAVE TO GO **NOW!**

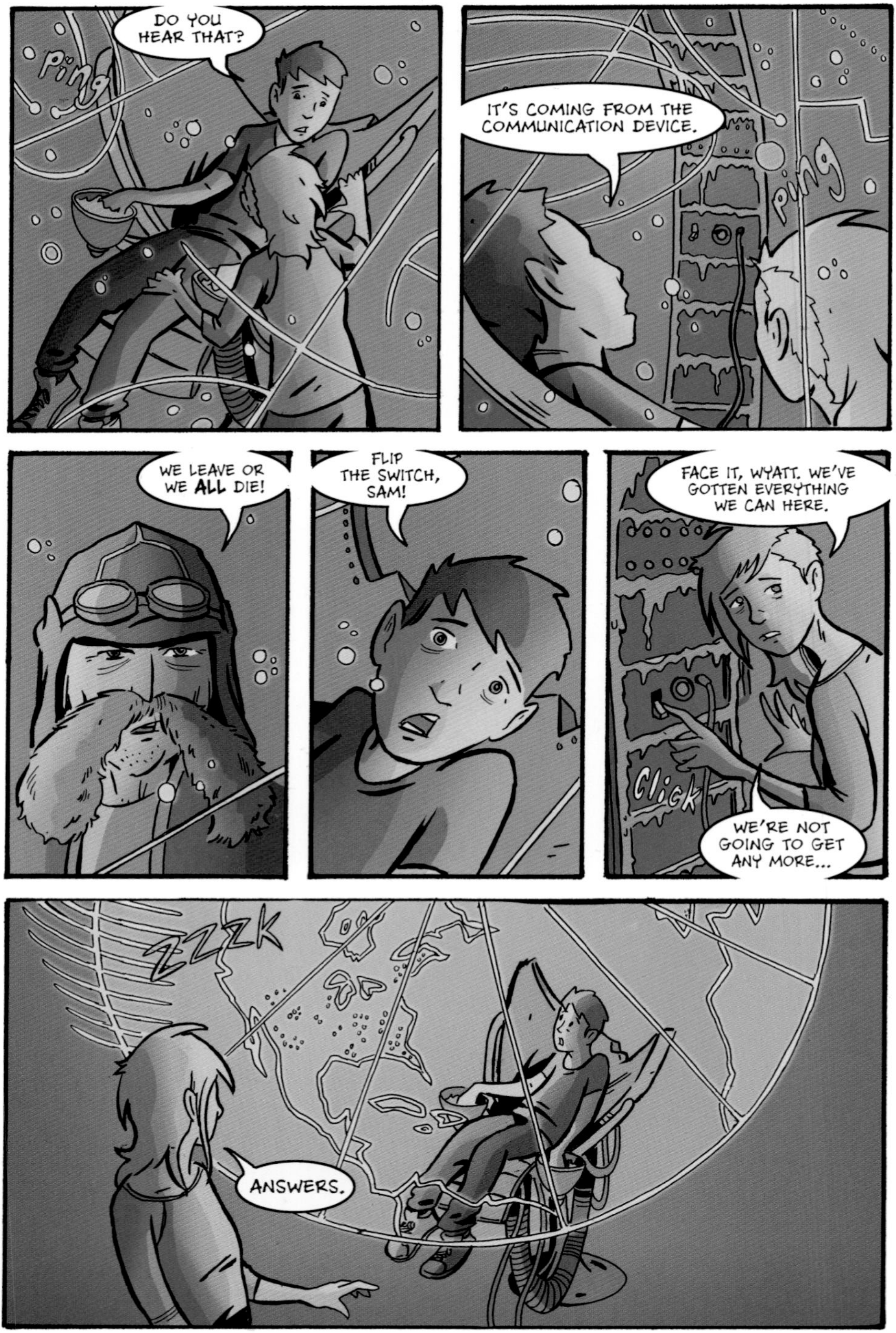

DO YOU HEAR THAT?
PING
IT'S COMING FROM THE COMMUNICATION DEVICE.
PING
WE LEAVE OR WE **ALL** DIE!
FLIP THE SWITCH, SAM!
FACE IT, WYATT. WE'VE GOTTEN EVERYTHING WE CAN HERE.
CLICK
WE'RE NOT GOING TO GET ANY MORE...
ZZZK
ANSWERS.

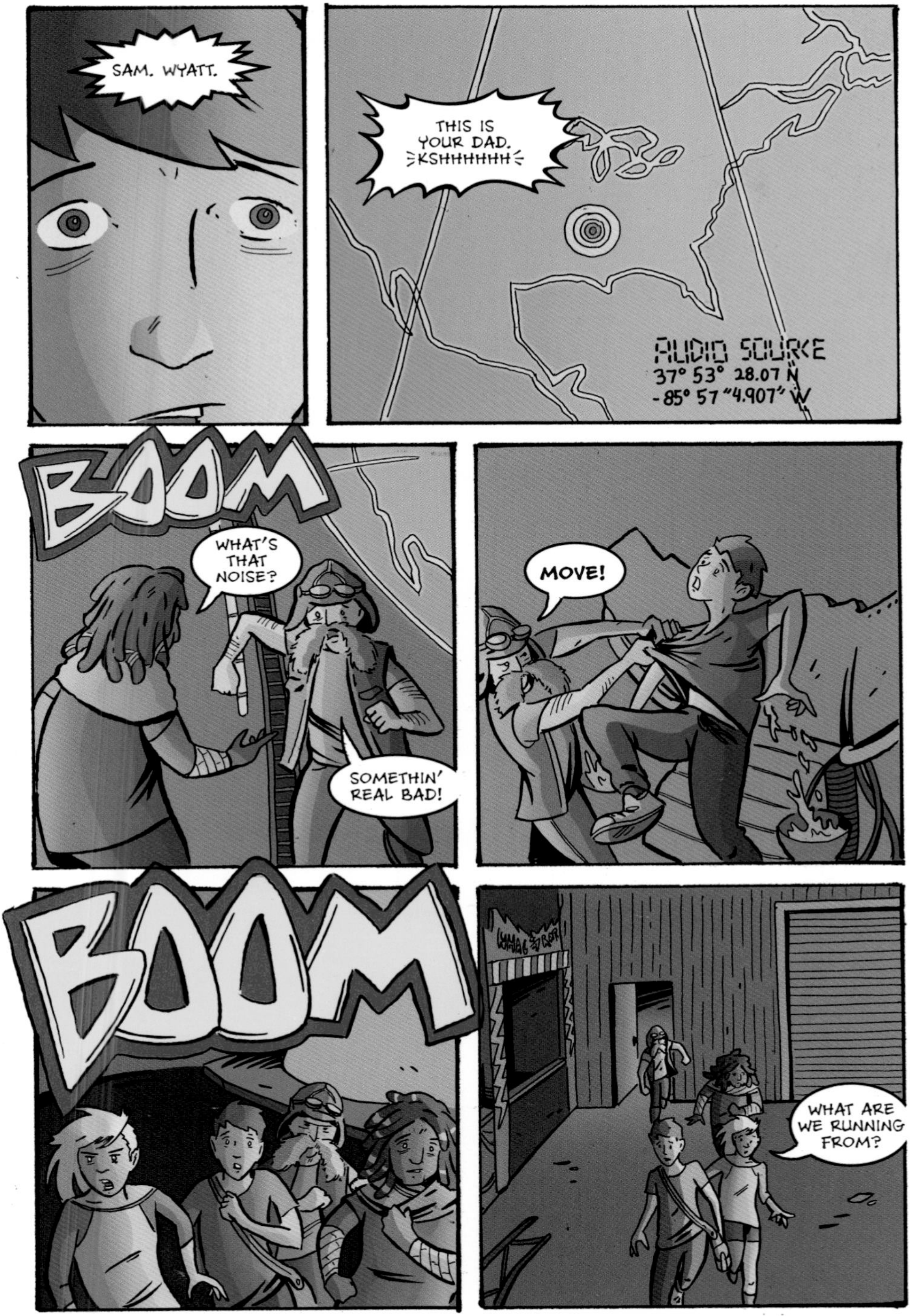

SAM. WYATT.
THIS IS YOUR DAD. ≡KSHHHHHH≡
AUDIO SOURCE
37° 53° 28.07 N
-85° 57 "4.907" W
BOOM
WHAT'S THAT NOISE?
SOMETHIN' REAL BAD!
MOVE!
BOOM
WHAT ARE WE RUNNING FROM?

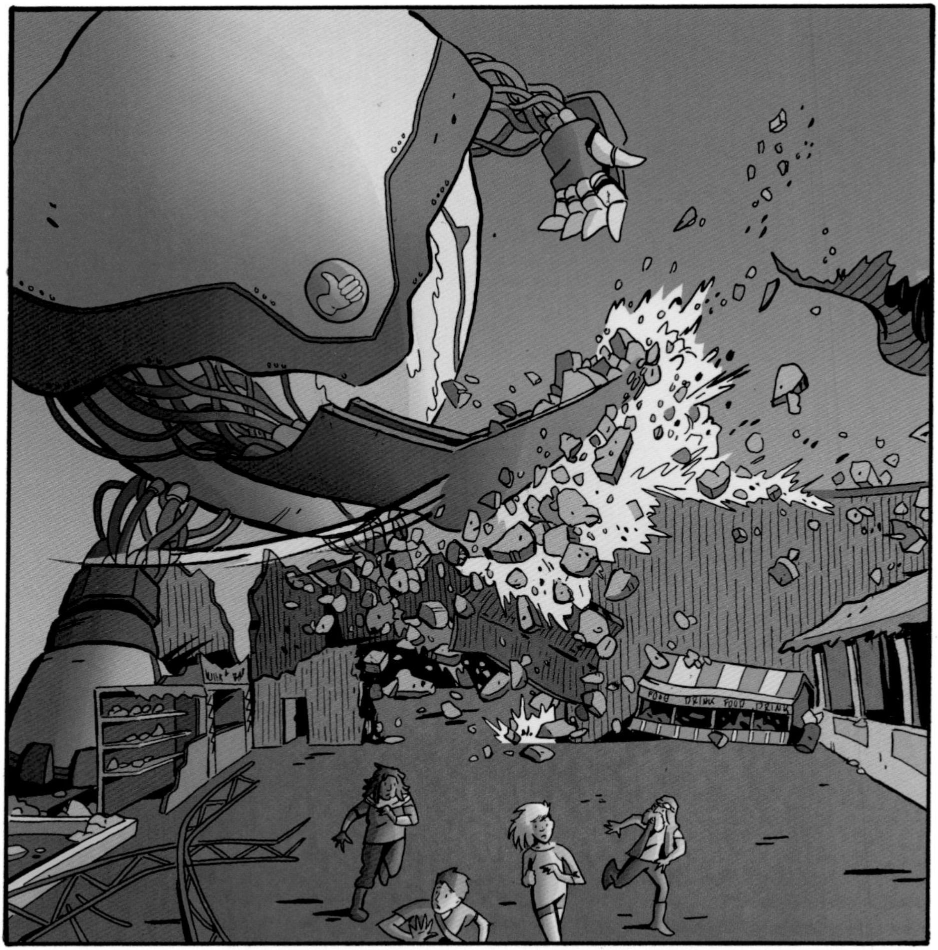

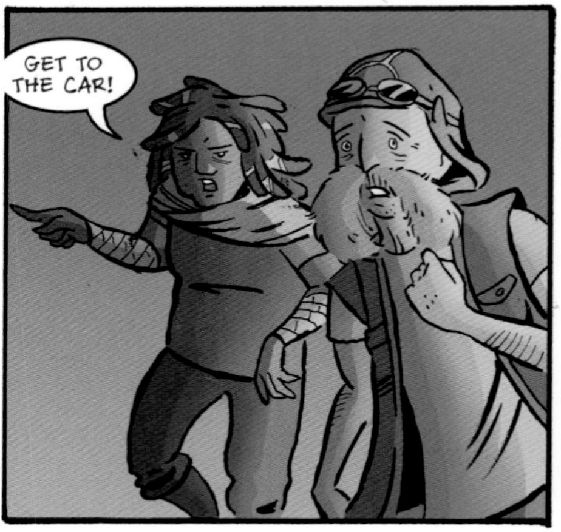
GET TO THE CAR!

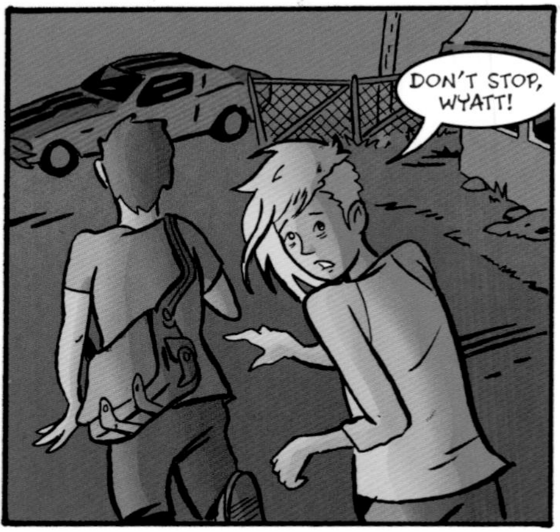
DON'T STOP, WYATT!

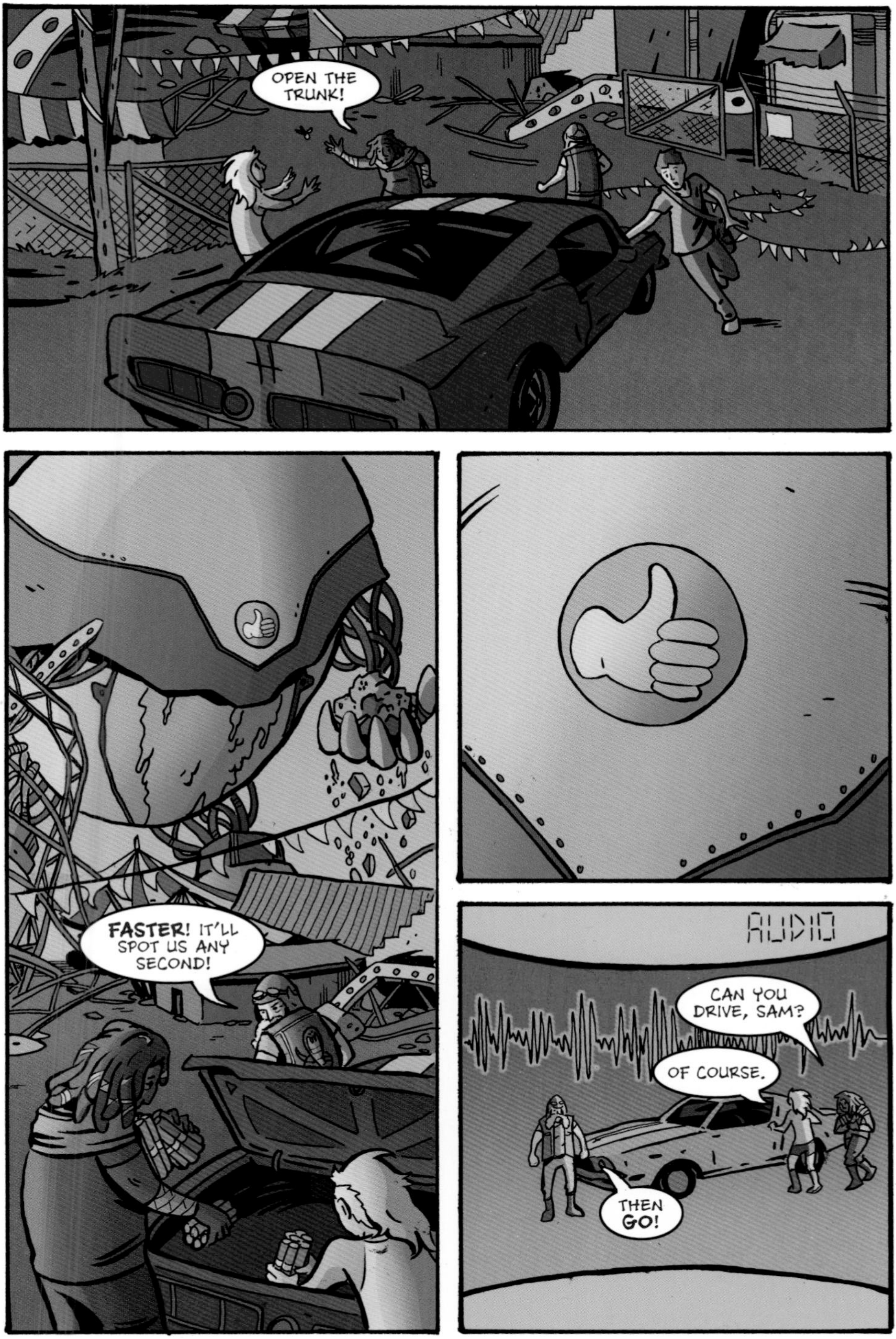
OPEN THE TRUNK!
FASTER! IT'LL SPOT US ANY SECOND!
AUDIO
CAN YOU DRIVE, SAM?
OF COURSE.
THEN GO!

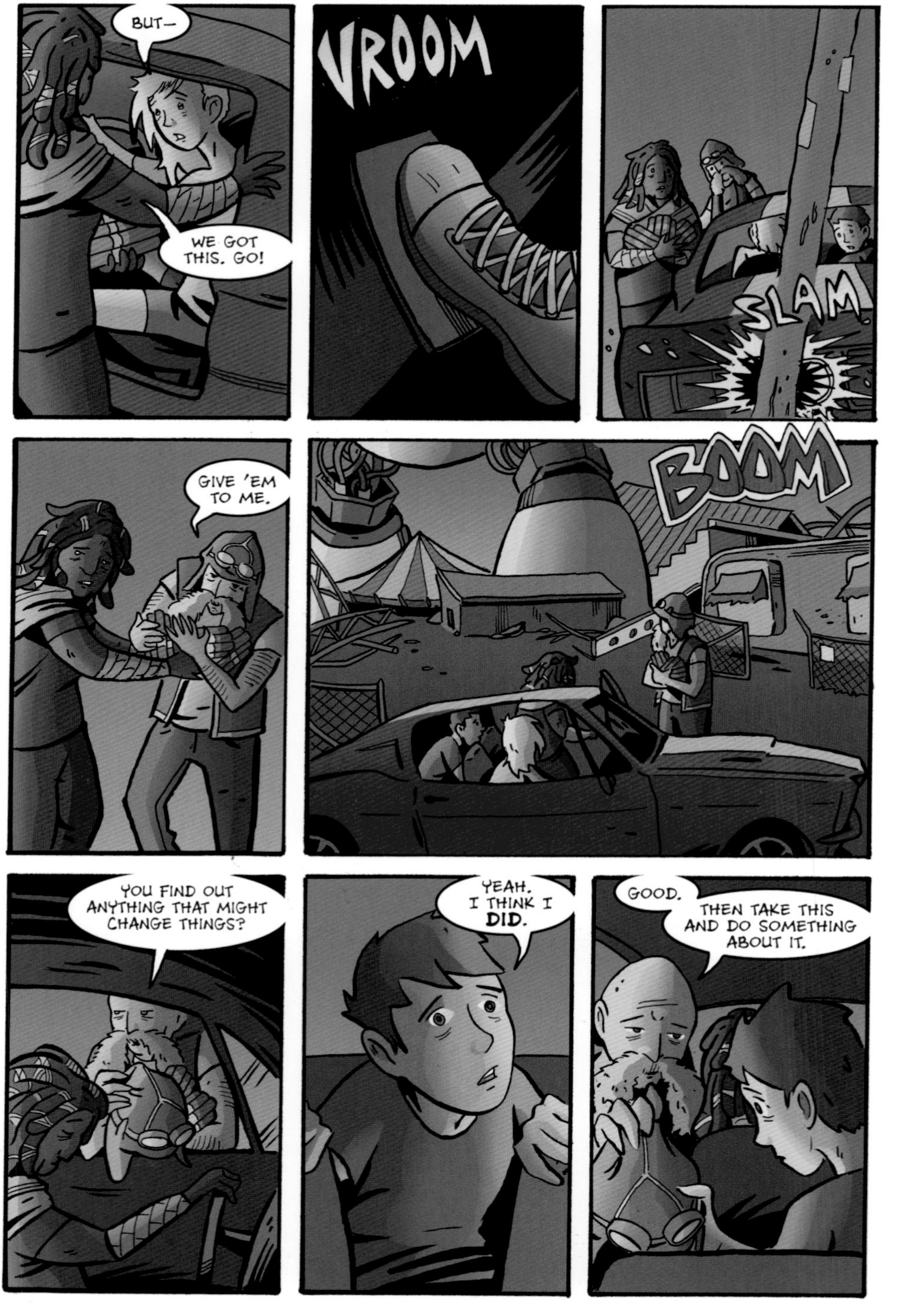
BUT—
WE GOT THIS. GO!
VROOM
SLAM
GIVE 'EM TO ME.
BOOM
YOU FIND OUT ANYTHING THAT MIGHT CHANGE THINGS?
YEAH. I THINK I DID.
GOOD.
THEN TAKE THIS AND DO SOMETHING ABOUT IT.

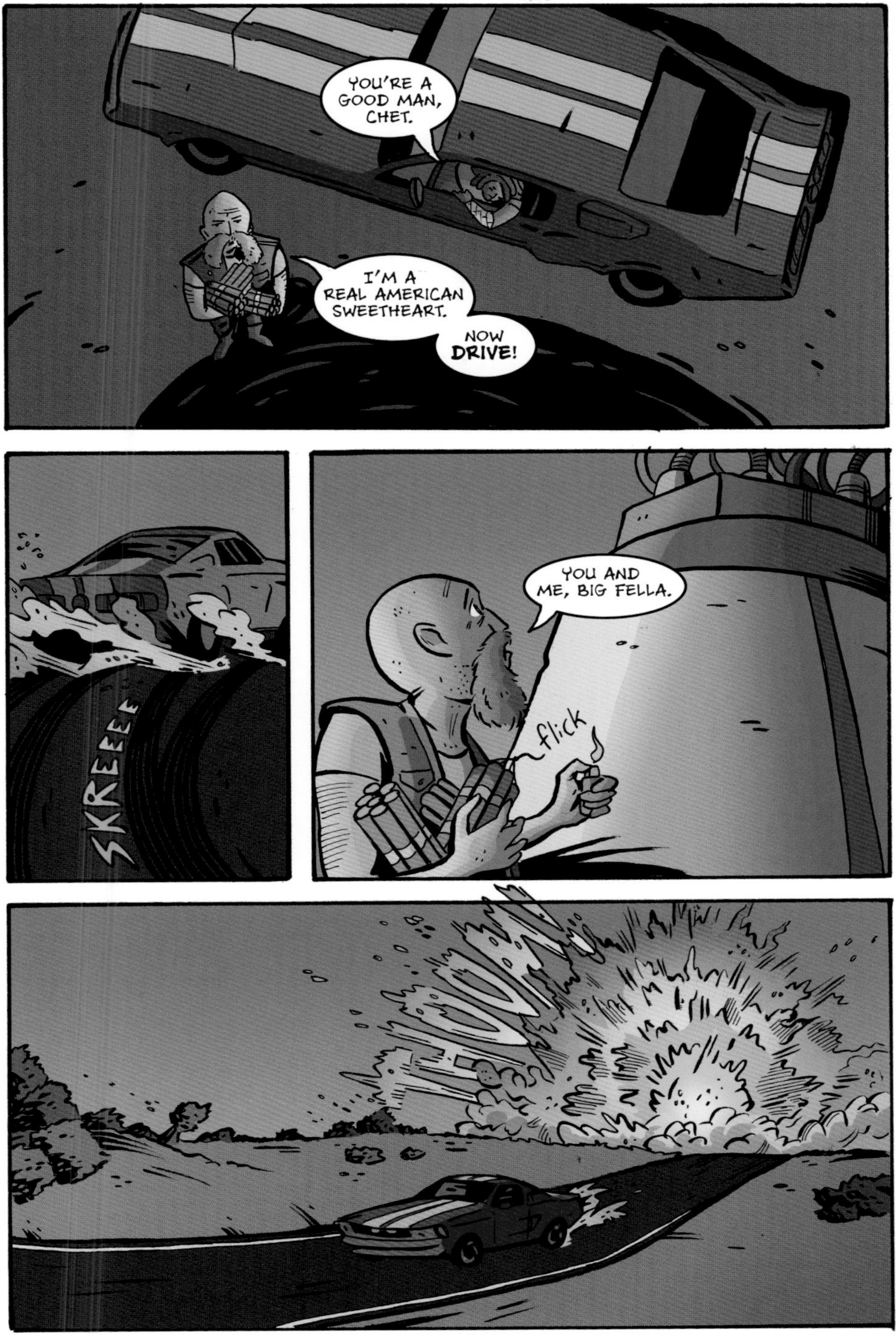
YOU'RE A GOOD MAN, CHET.
I'M A REAL AMERICAN SWEETHEART.
NOW **DRIVE!**
SKREEEE
YOU AND ME, BIG FELLA.
flick

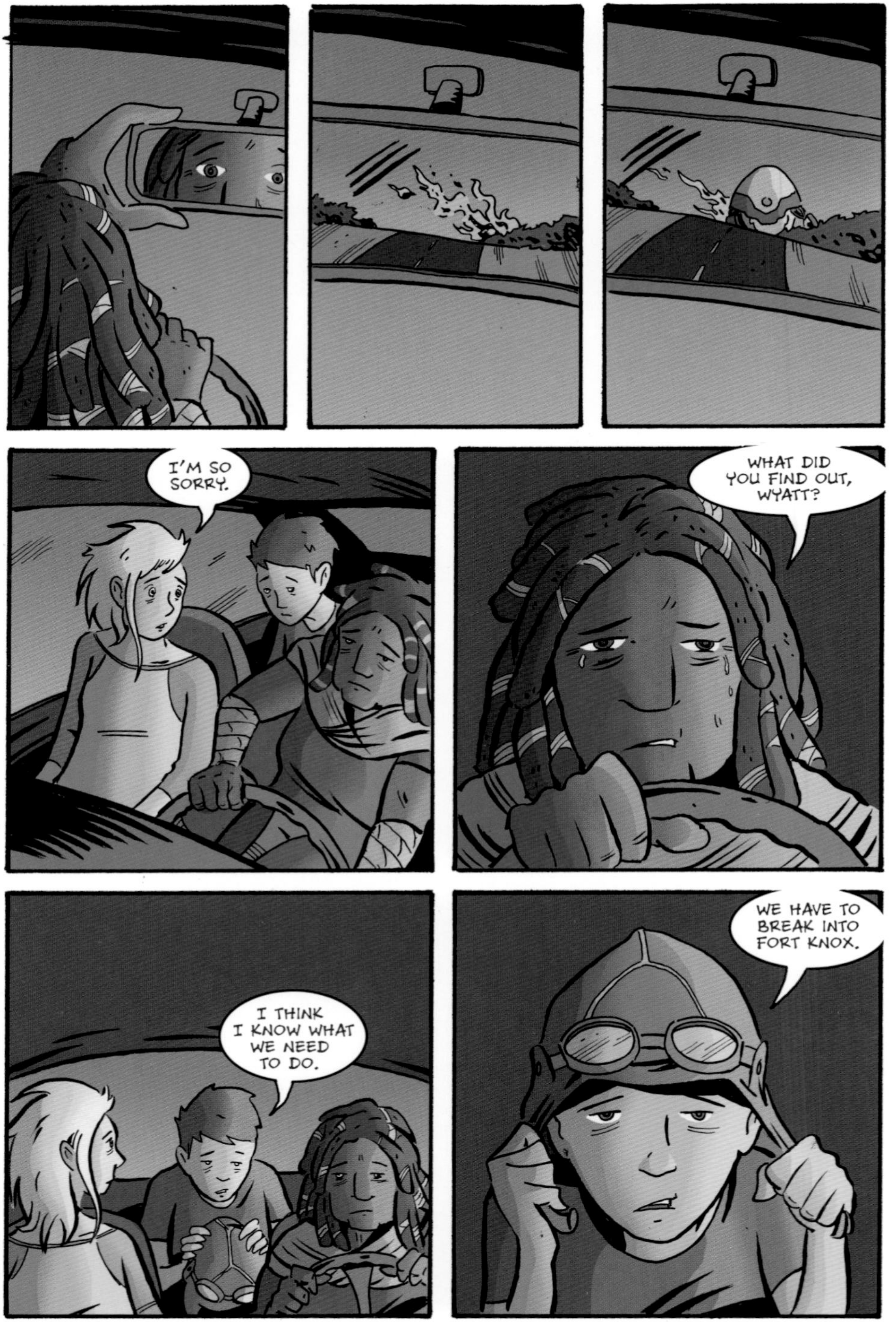
I'M SO SORRY.
WHAT DID YOU FIND OUT, WYATT?
I THINK I KNOW WHAT WE NEED TO DO.
WE HAVE TO BREAK INTO FORT KNOX.

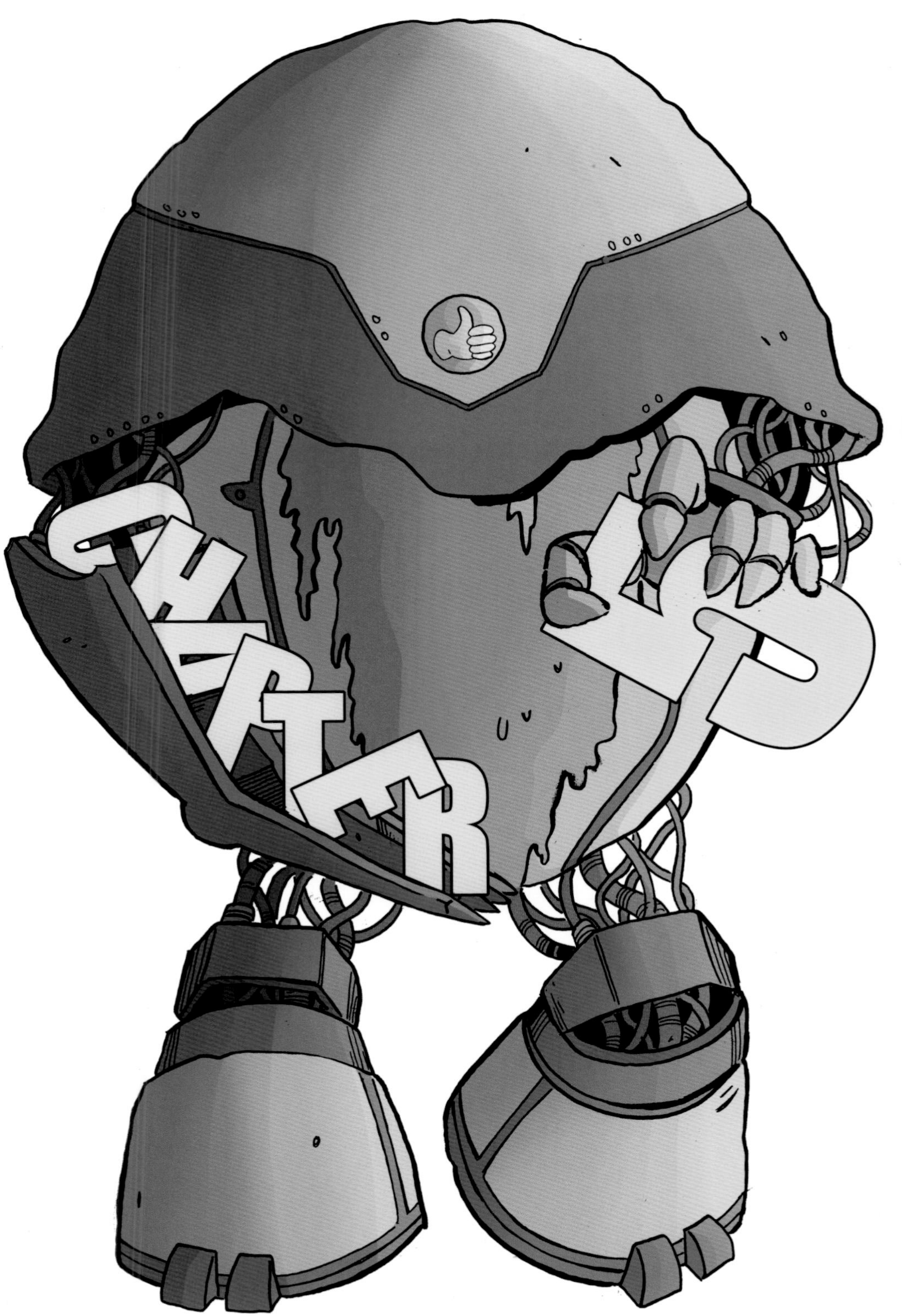
CHAPTER 5

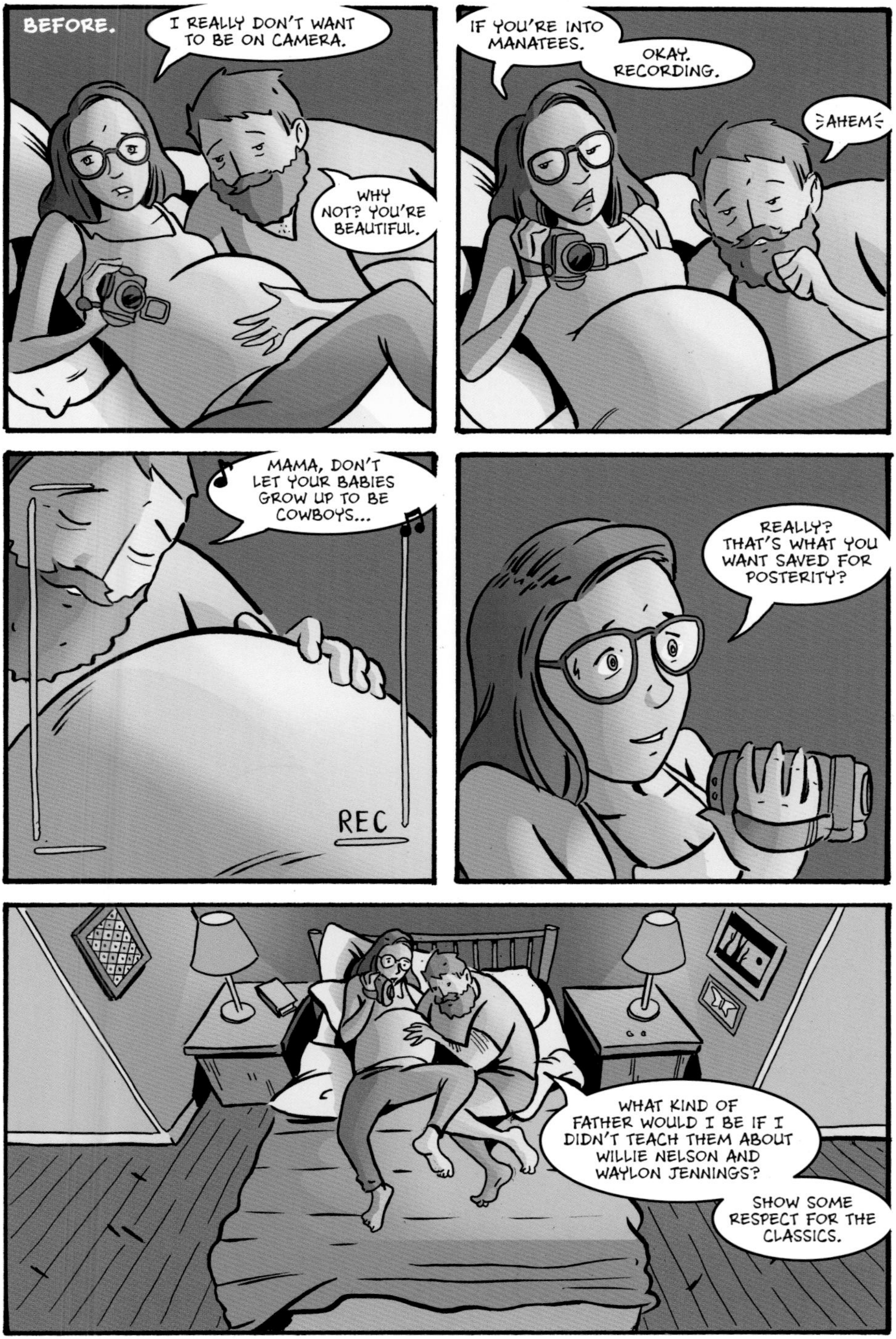
BEFORE.
I REALLY DON'T WANT TO BE ON CAMERA.
WHY NOT? YOU'RE BEAUTIFUL.
IF YOU'RE INTO MANATEES.
OKAY. RECORDING.
AHEM
MAMA, DON'T LET YOUR BABIES GROW UP TO BE COWBOYS...
REC
REALLY? THAT'S WHAT YOU WANT SAVED FOR POSTERITY?
WHAT KIND OF FATHER WOULD I BE IF I DIDN'T TEACH THEM ABOUT WILLIE NELSON AND WAYLON JENNINGS?
SHOW SOME RESPECT FOR THE CLASSICS.

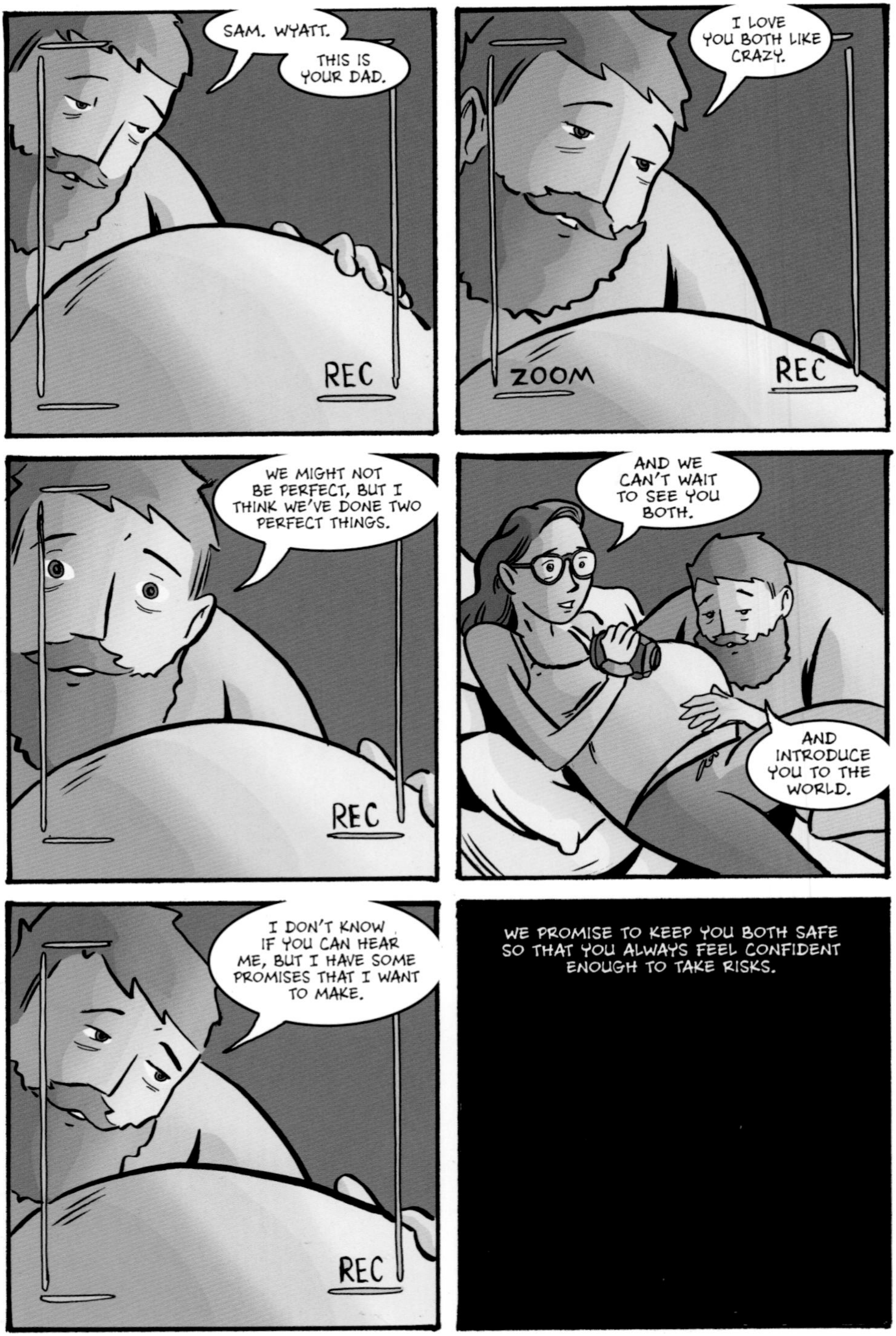
SAM. WYATT.
THIS IS YOUR DAD.
REC
I LOVE YOU BOTH LIKE CRAZY.
ZOOM
REC
WE MIGHT NOT BE PERFECT, BUT I THINK WE'VE DONE TWO PERFECT THINGS.
REC
AND WE CAN'T WAIT TO SEE YOU BOTH.
AND INTRODUCE YOU TO THE WORLD.
I DON'T KNOW IF YOU CAN HEAR ME, BUT I HAVE SOME PROMISES THAT I WANT TO MAKE.
REC
WE PROMISE TO KEEP YOU BOTH SAFE SO THAT YOU ALWAYS FEEL CONFIDENT ENOUGH TO TAKE RISKS.

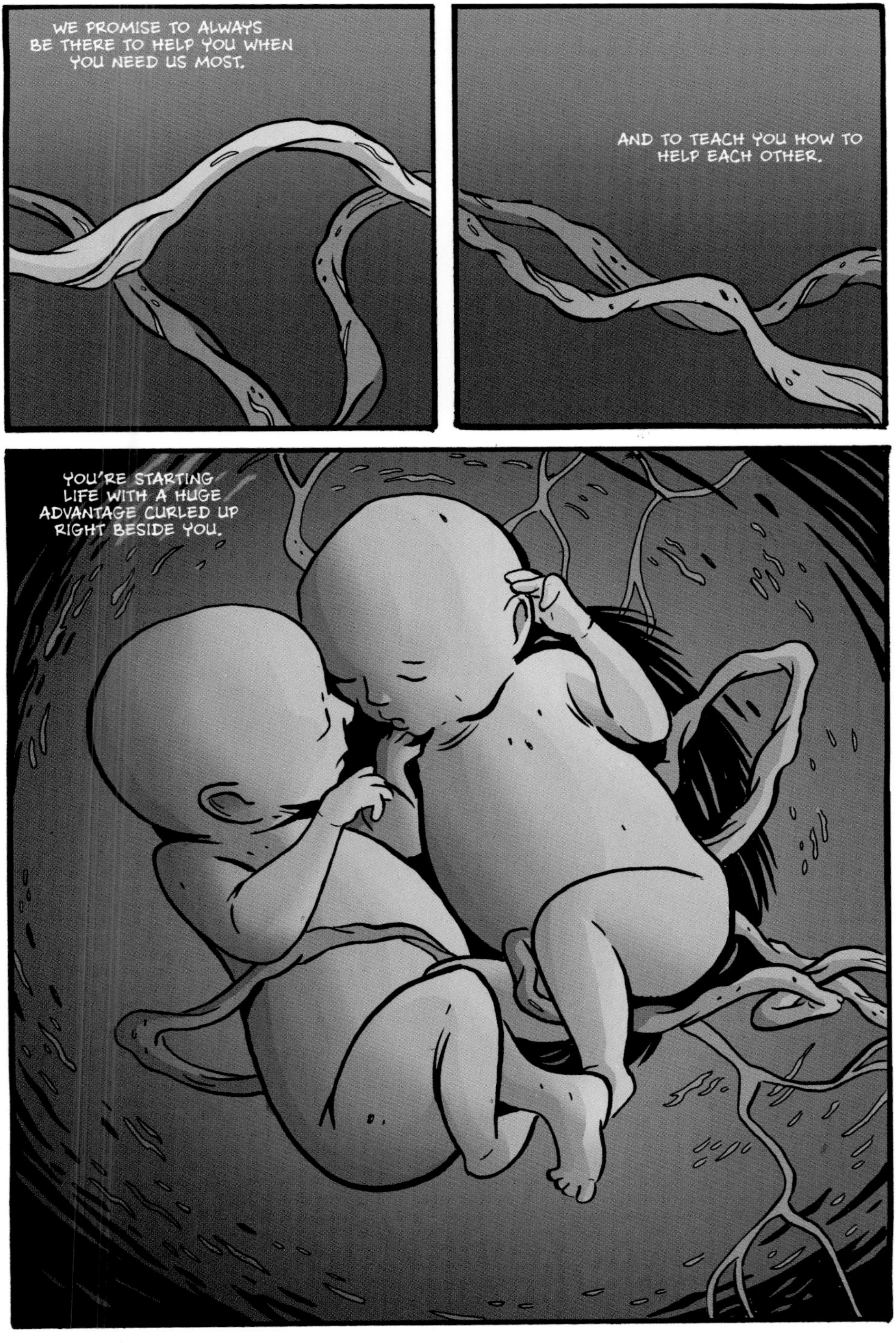
WE PROMISE TO ALWAYS BE THERE TO HELP YOU WHEN YOU NEED US MOST.
AND TO TEACH YOU HOW TO HELP EACH OTHER.
YOU'RE STARTING LIFE WITH A HUGE ADVANTAGE CURLED UP RIGHT BESIDE YOU.

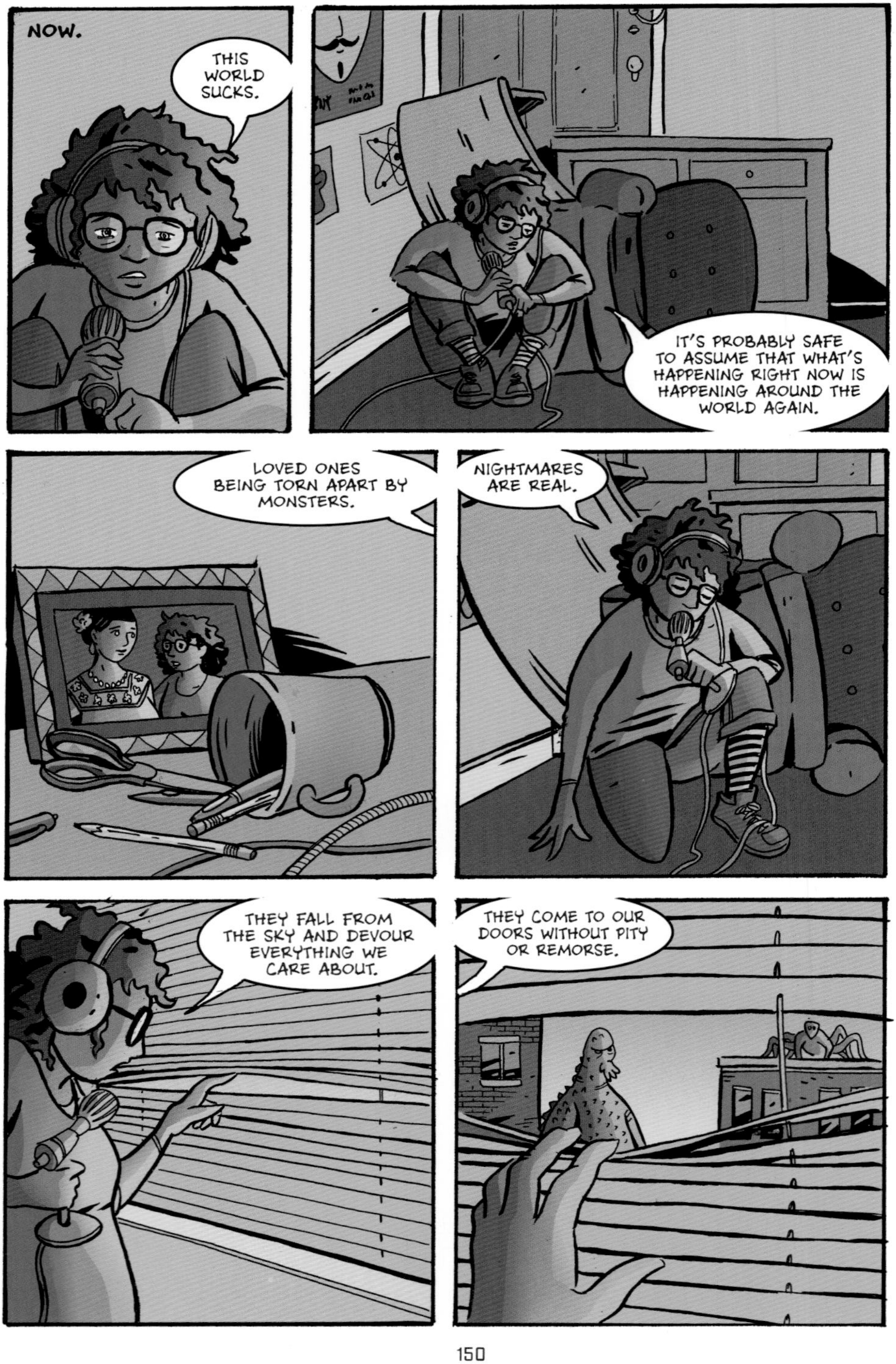
NOW.
THIS WORLD SUCKS.
IT'S PROBABLY SAFE TO ASSUME THAT WHAT'S HAPPENING RIGHT NOW IS HAPPENING AROUND THE WORLD AGAIN.
LOVED ONES BEING TORN APART BY MONSTERS.
NIGHTMARES ARE REAL.
THEY FALL FROM THE SKY AND DEVOUR EVERYTHING WE CARE ABOUT.
THEY COME TO OUR DOORS WITHOUT PITY OR REMORSE.

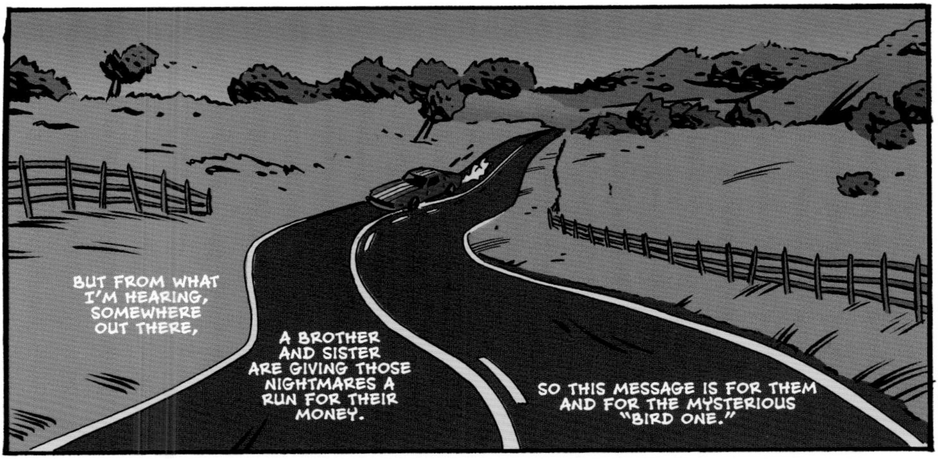
BUT FROM WHAT I'M HEARING, SOMEWHERE OUT THERE,
A BROTHER AND SISTER ARE GIVING THOSE NIGHTMARES A RUN FOR THEIR MONEY.
SO THIS MESSAGE IS FOR THEM AND FOR THE MYSTERIOUS "BIRD ONE."

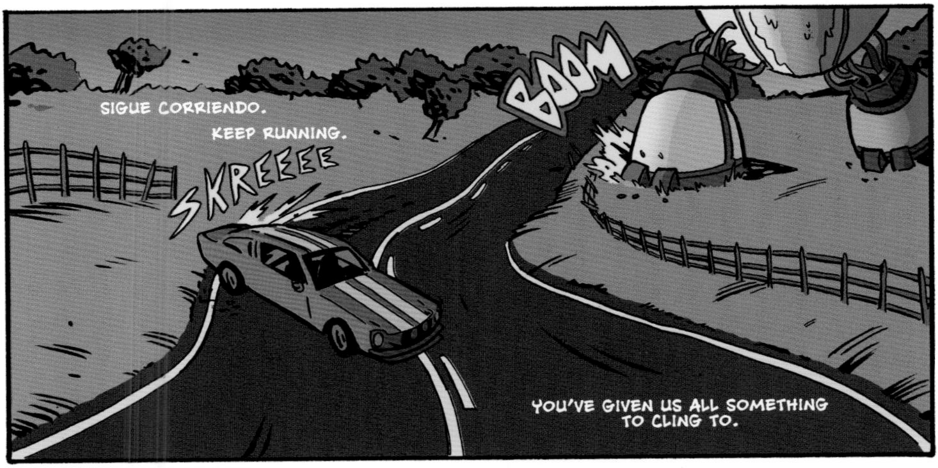
SIGUE CORRIENDO.
KEEP RUNNING.
BOOM
SKREEEE
YOU'VE GIVEN US ALL SOMETHING TO CLING TO.

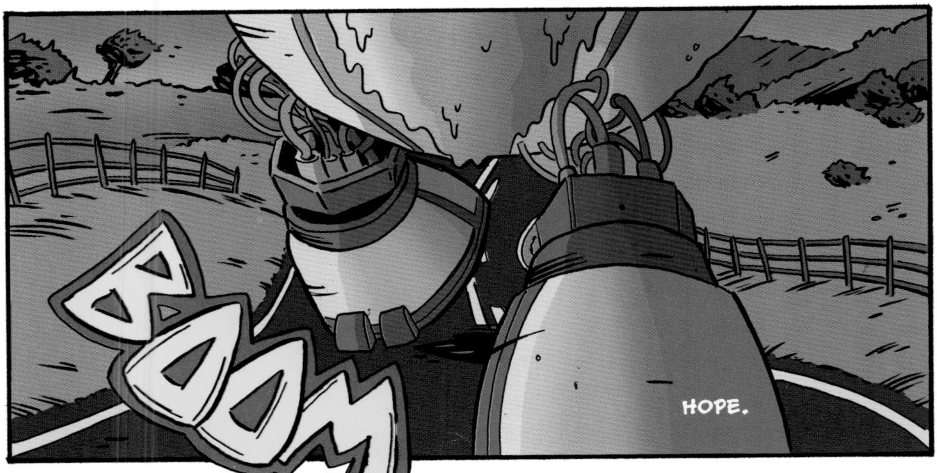
BOOM
HOPE.

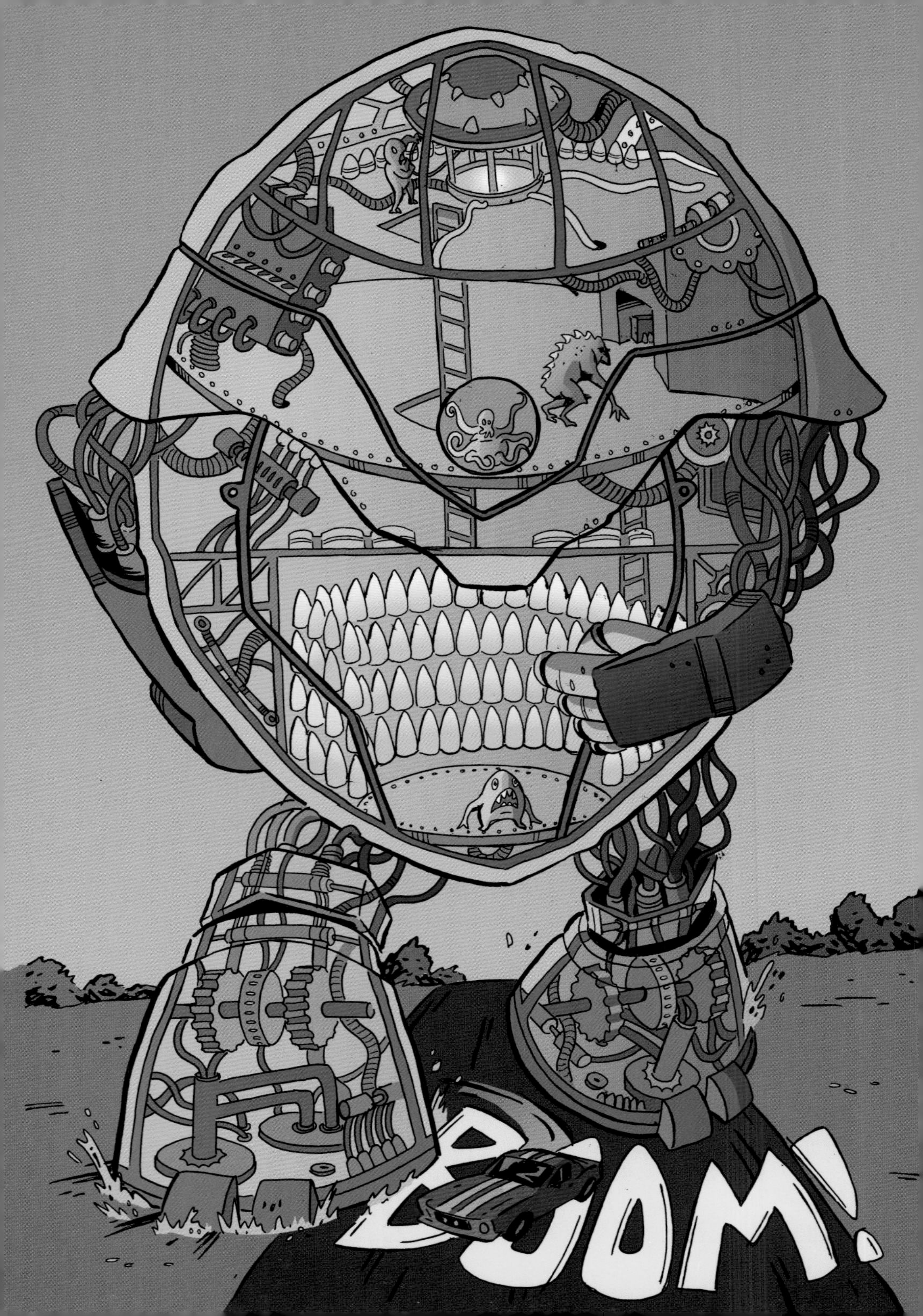
BOOM!

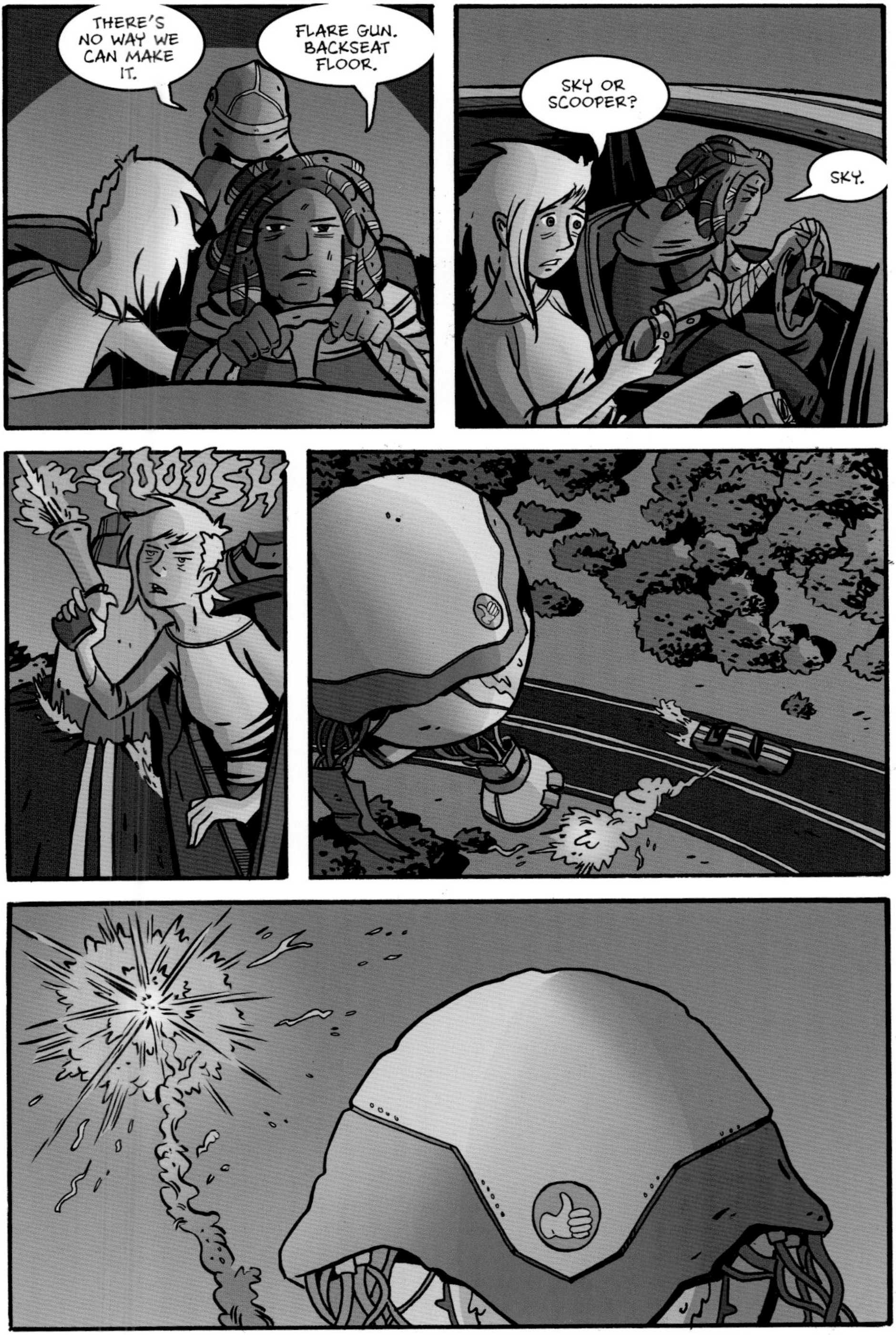
THERE'S NO WAY WE CAN MAKE IT.
FLARE GUN. BACKSEAT FLOOR.
SKY OR SCOOPER?
SKY.
FOOOSH

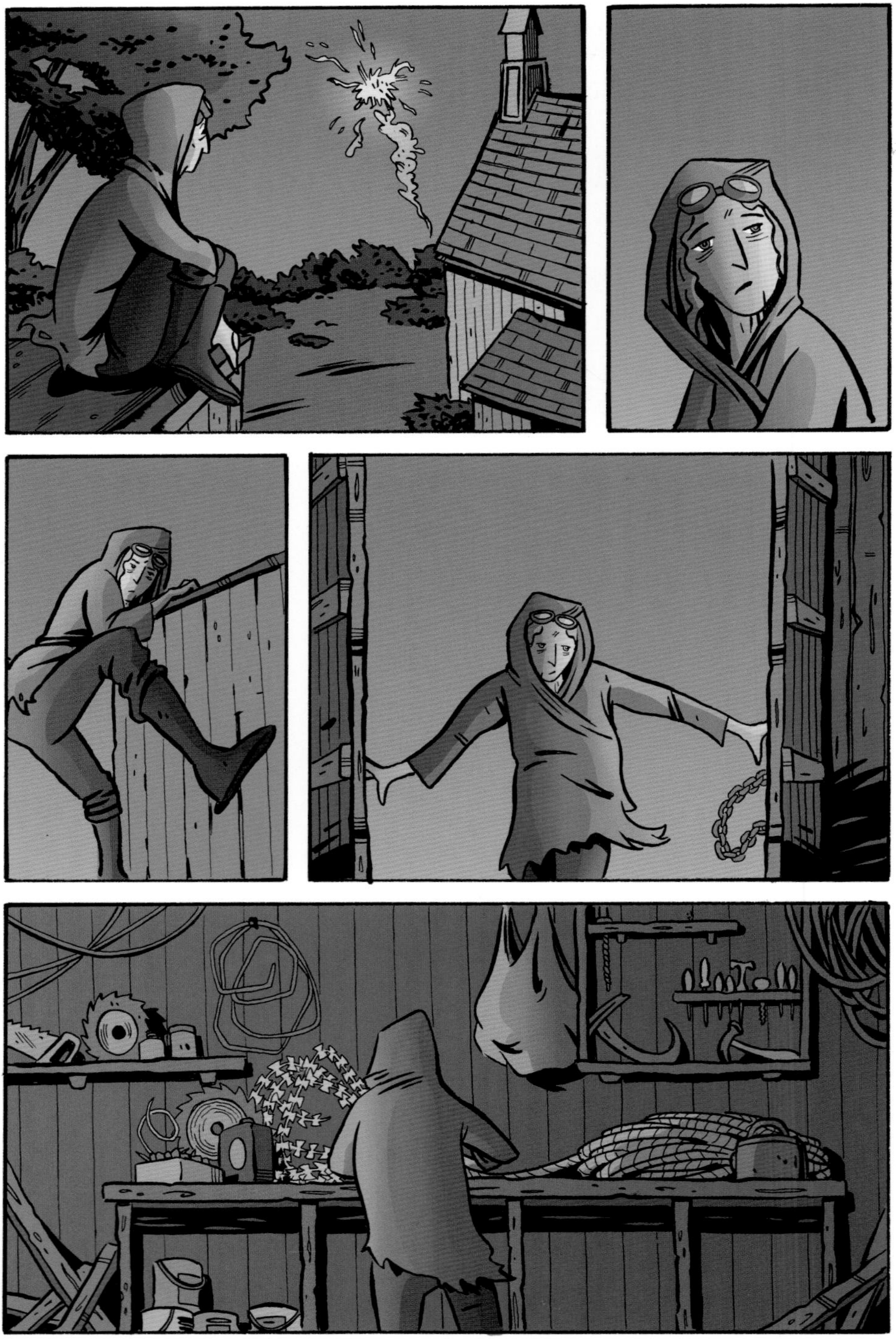

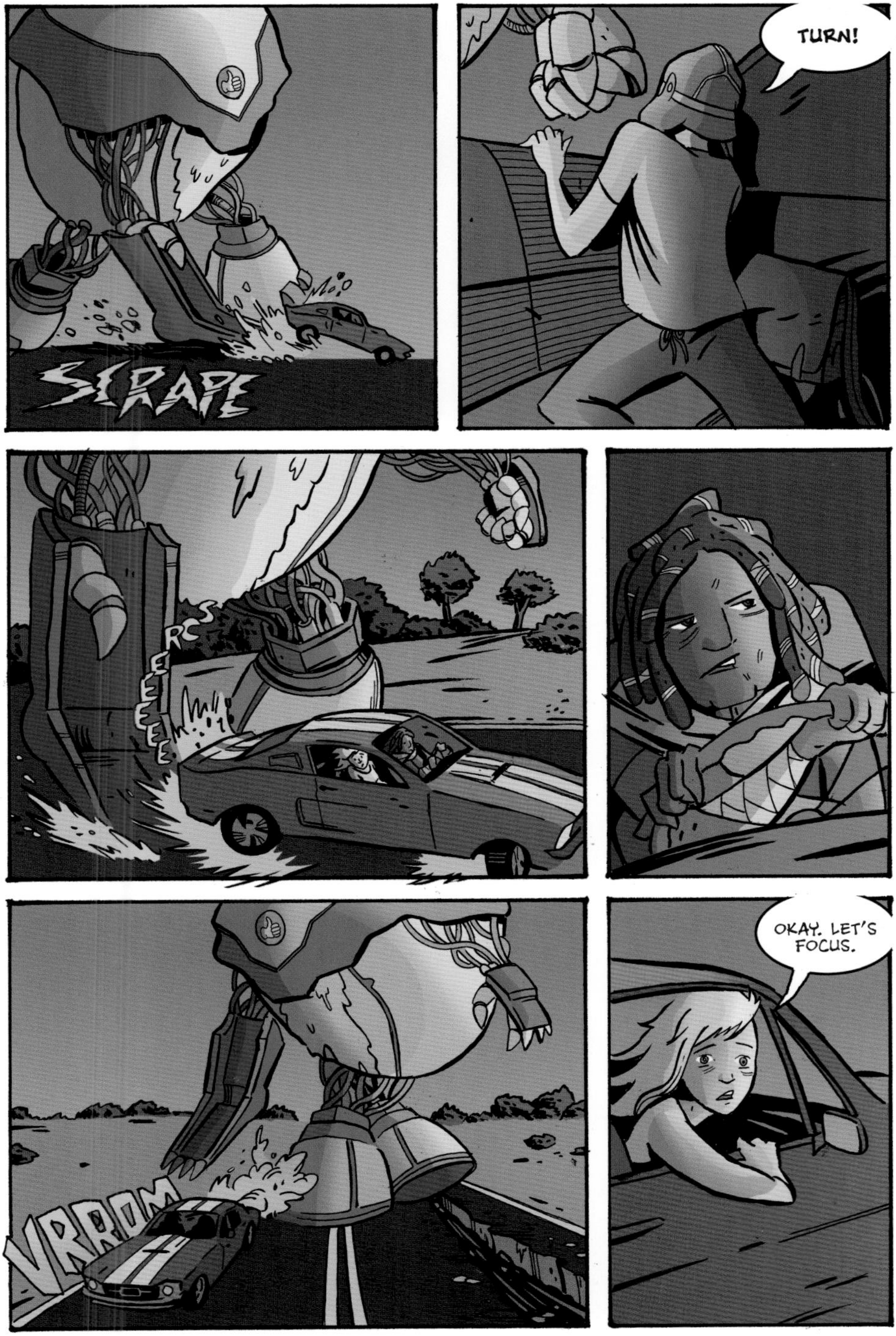
SCRAPE
TURN!
SCREEEEEE
OKAY. LET'S FOCUS.
VRROOM

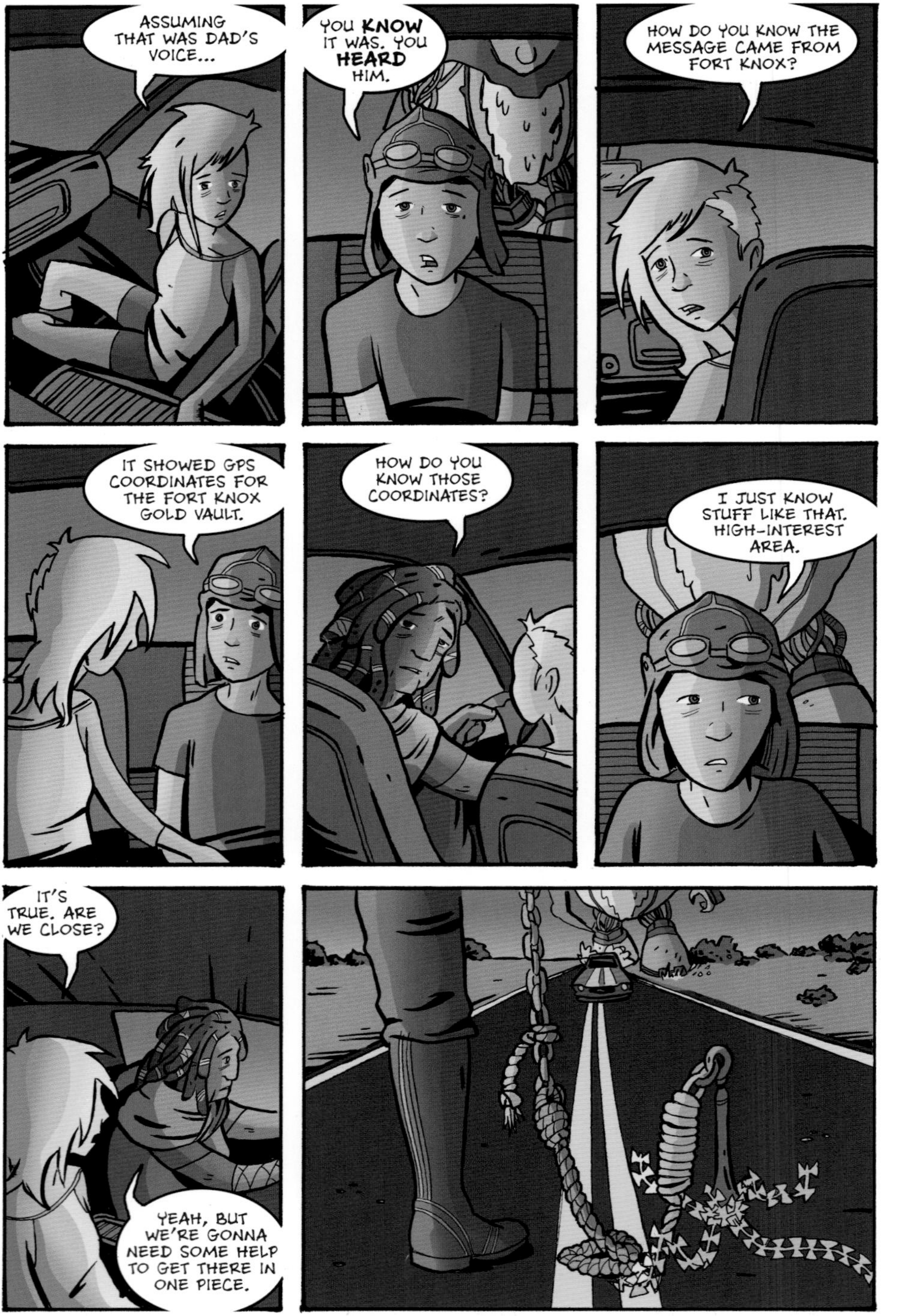
ASSUMING THAT WAS DAD'S VOICE...
YOU **KNOW** IT WAS. YOU **HEARD** HIM.
HOW DO YOU KNOW THE MESSAGE CAME FROM FORT KNOX?
IT SHOWED GPS COORDINATES FOR THE FORT KNOX GOLD VAULT.
HOW DO YOU KNOW THOSE COORDINATES?
I JUST KNOW STUFF LIKE THAT. HIGH-INTEREST AREA.
IT'S TRUE. ARE WE CLOSE?
YEAH, BUT WE'RE GONNA NEED SOME HELP TO GET THERE IN ONE PIECE.

IS THAT...?

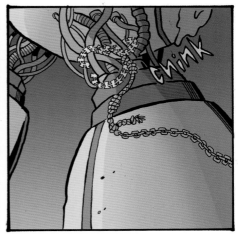

chink

CITY OF ELIZAB

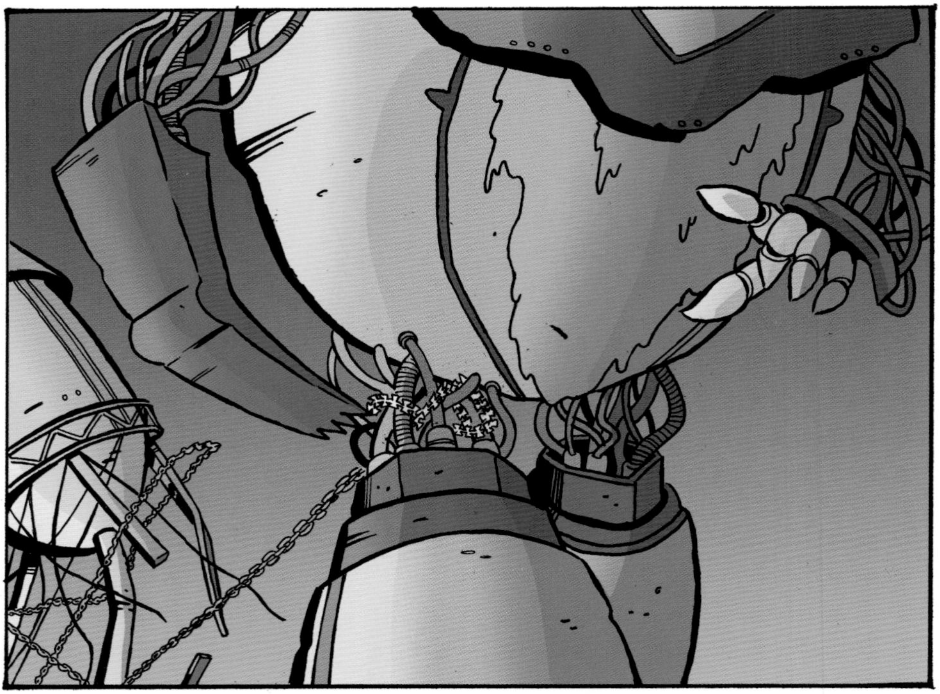
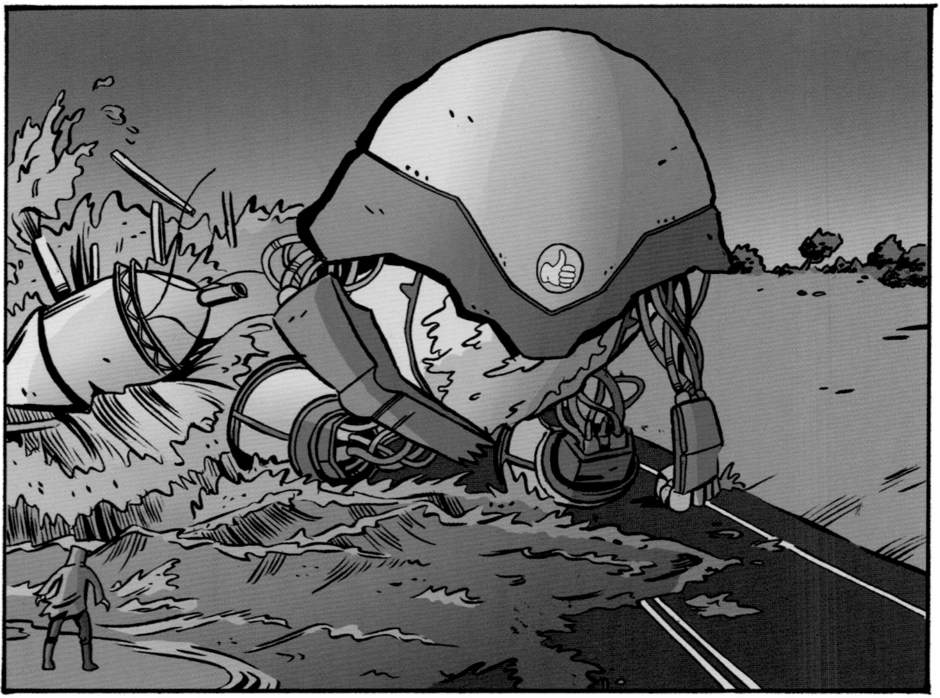

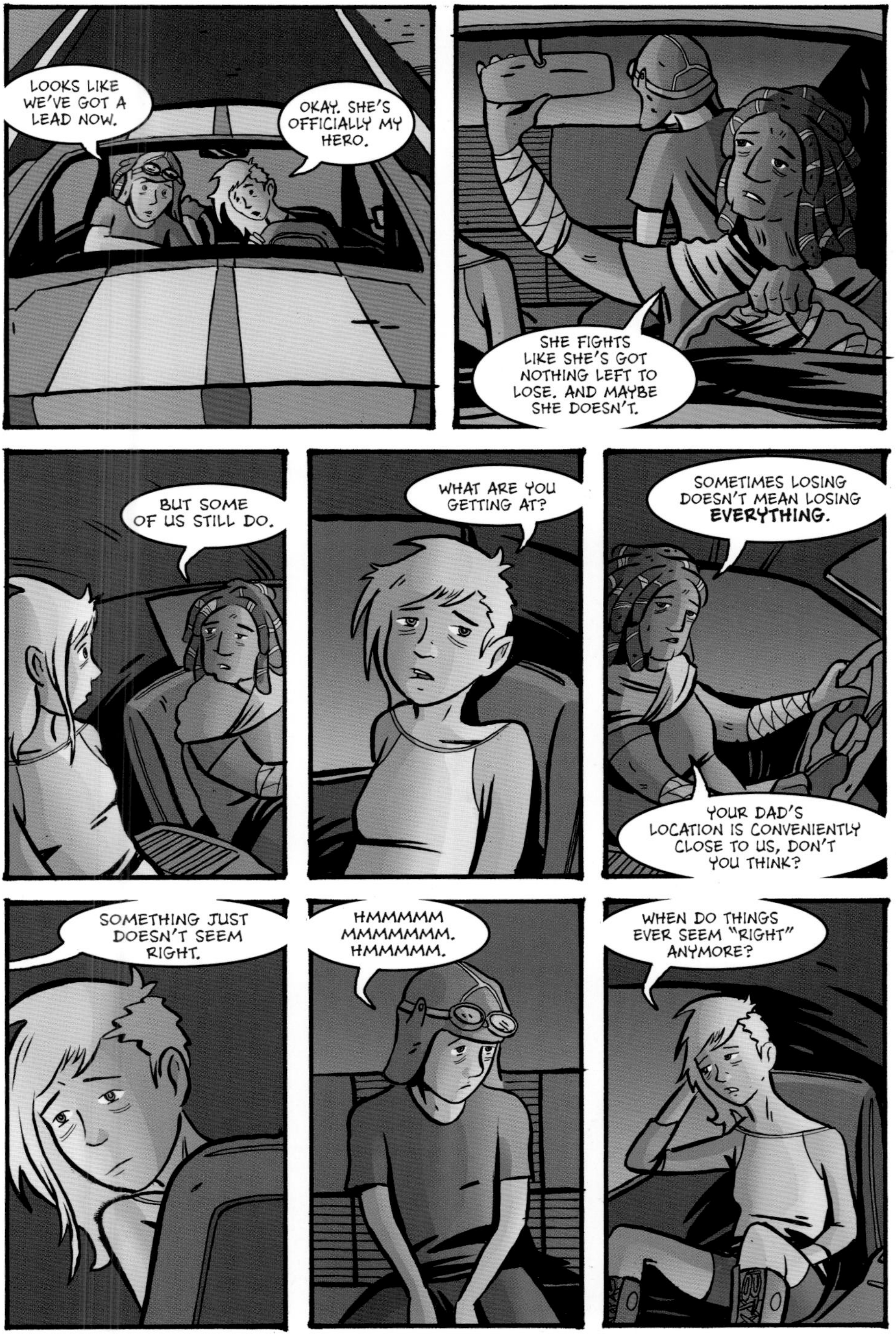
LOOKS LIKE WE'VE GOT A LEAD NOW.
OKAY. SHE'S OFFICIALLY MY HERO.
SHE FIGHTS LIKE SHE'S GOT NOTHING LEFT TO LOSE. AND MAYBE SHE DOESN'T.
BUT SOME OF US STILL DO.
WHAT ARE YOU GETTING AT?
SOMETIMES LOSING DOESN'T MEAN LOSING **EVERYTHING.**
YOUR DAD'S LOCATION IS CONVENIENTLY CLOSE TO US, DON'T YOU THINK?
SOMETHING JUST DOESN'T SEEM RIGHT.
HMMMMM MMMMMMM. HMMMMM.
WHEN DO THINGS EVER SEEM "RIGHT" ANYMORE?

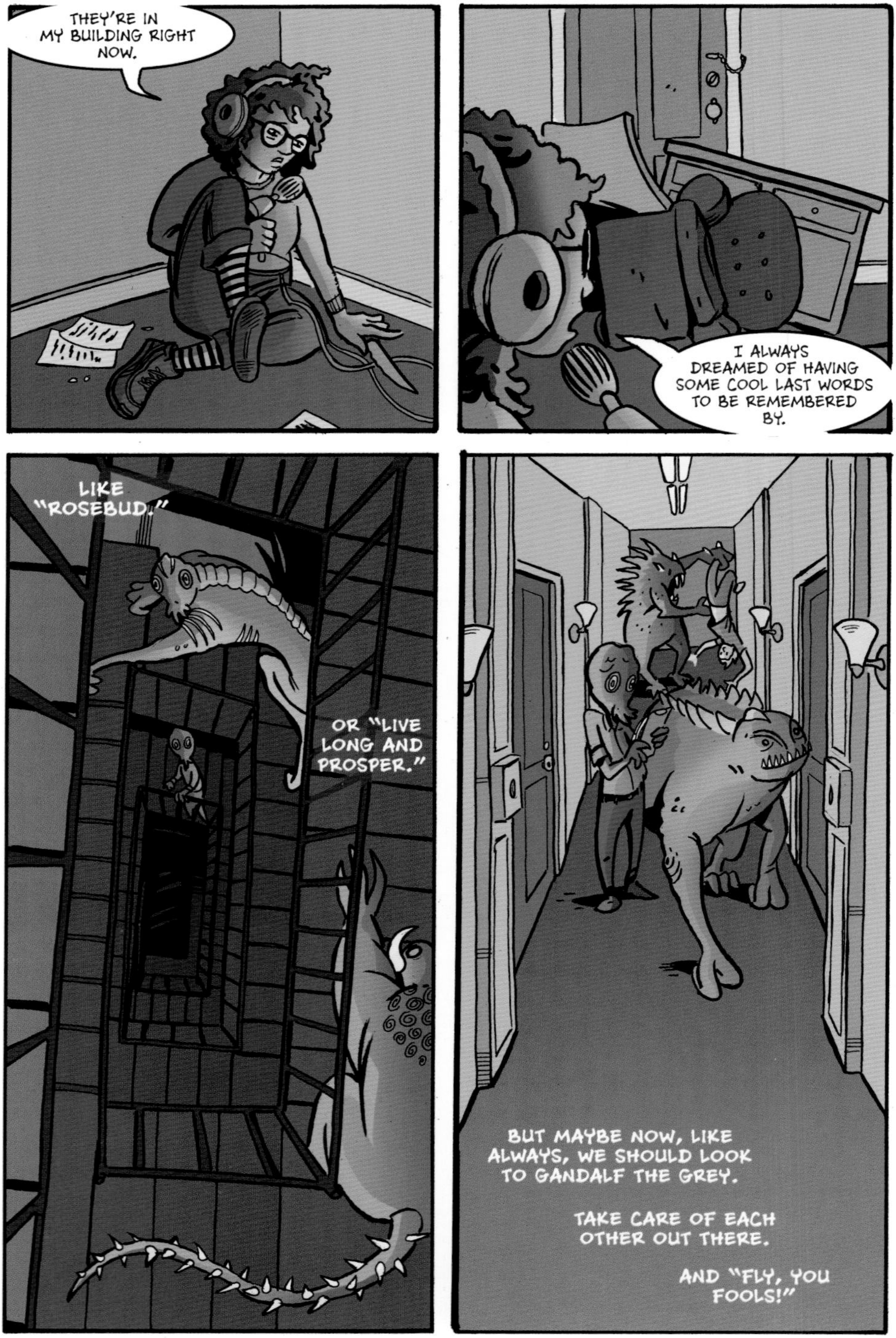
THEY'RE IN MY BUILDING RIGHT NOW.
I ALWAYS DREAMED OF HAVING SOME COOL LAST WORDS TO BE REMEMBERED BY.
LIKE "ROSEBUD."
OR "LIVE LONG AND PROSPER."
BUT MAYBE NOW, LIKE ALWAYS, WE SHOULD LOOK TO GANDALF THE GREY.
TAKE CARE OF EACH OTHER OUT THERE.
AND "FLY, YOU FOOLS!"

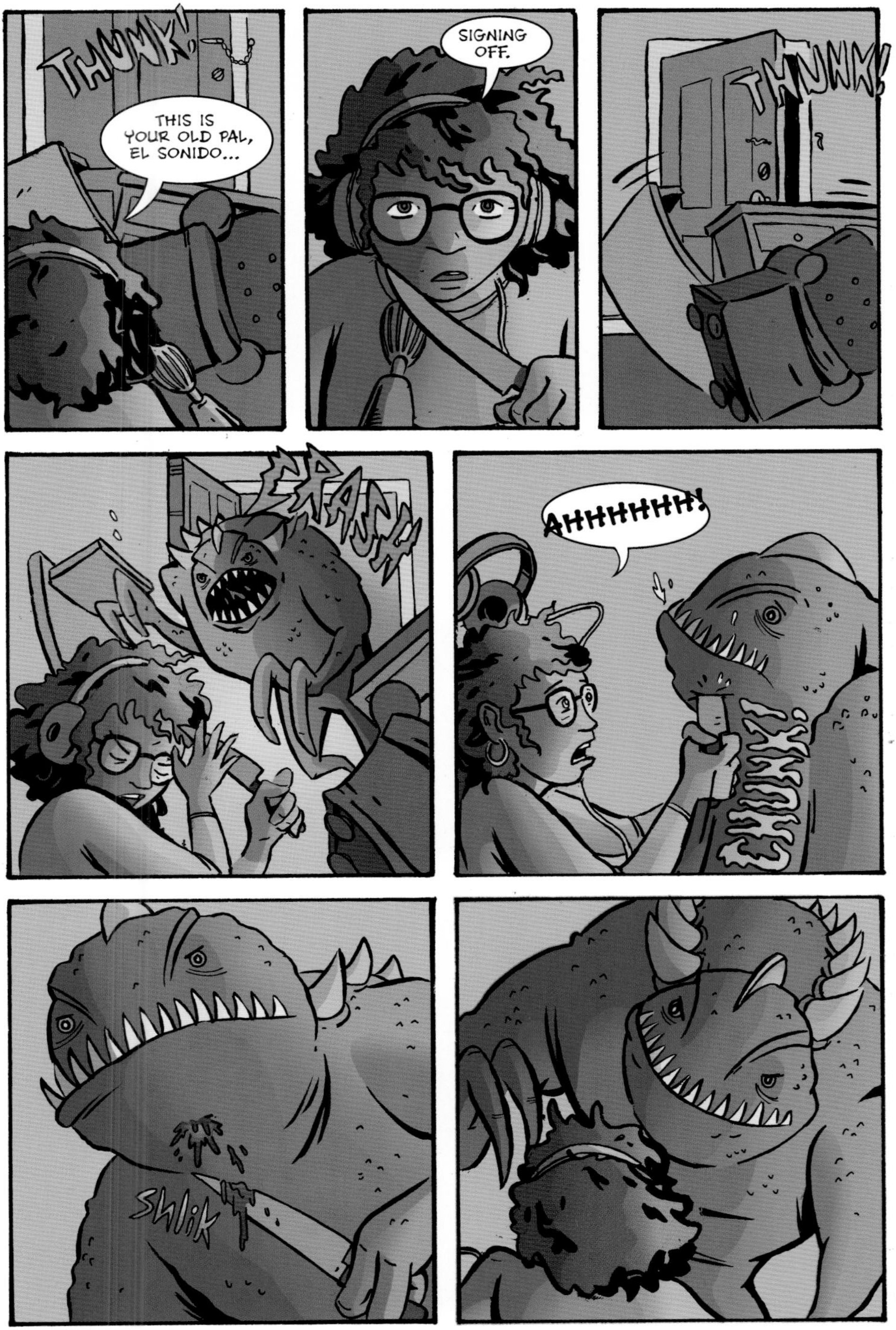
THUNK!
THIS IS YOUR OLD PAL, EL SONIDO...
SIGNING OFF.
THUNK!
CRASH
AHHHHHH!
CHUNK!
SHLIK

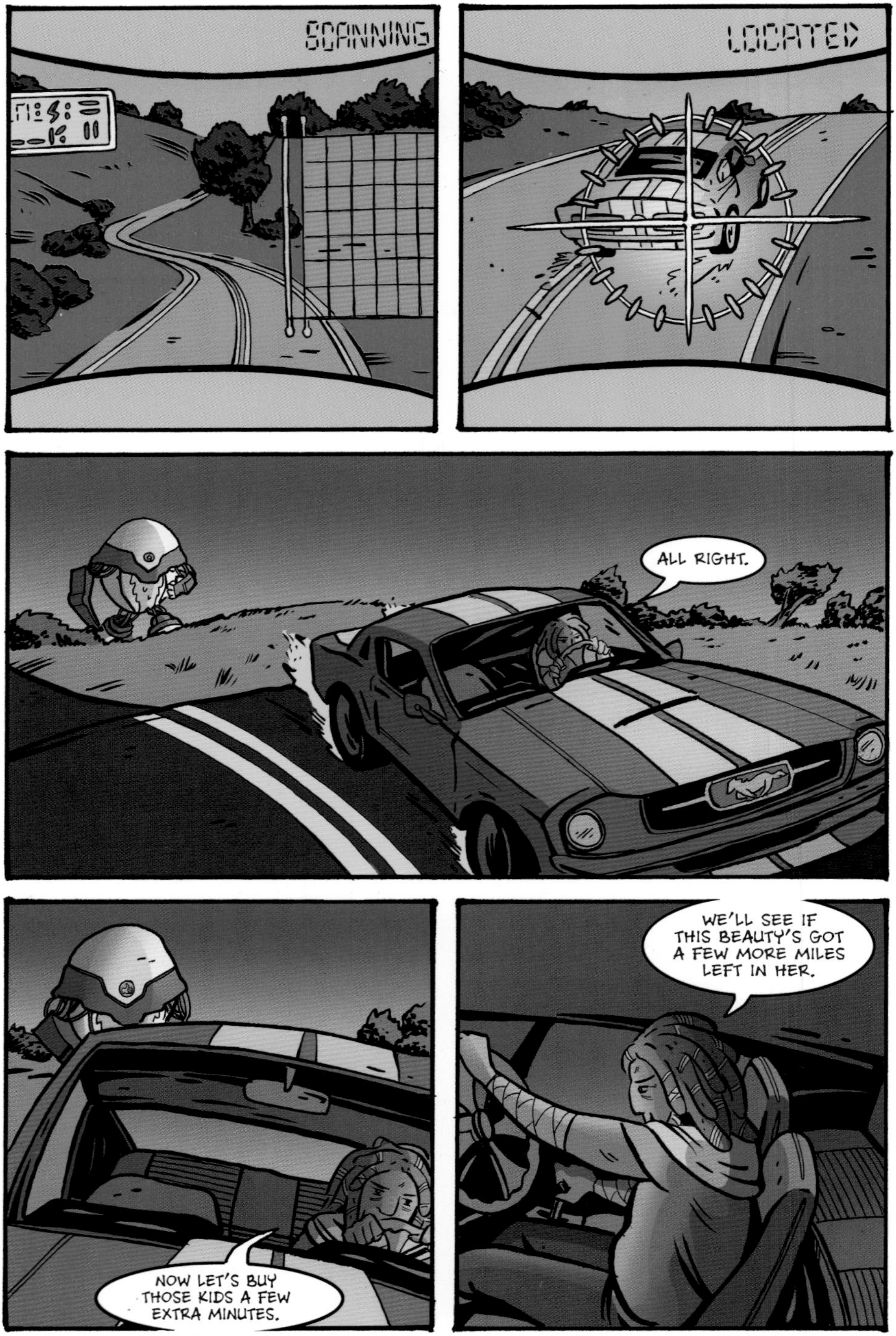
SCANNING
LOCATED
ALL RIGHT.
NOW LET'S BUY THOSE KIDS A FEW EXTRA MINUTES.
WE'LL SEE IF THIS BEAUTY'S GOT A FEW MORE MILES LEFT IN HER.

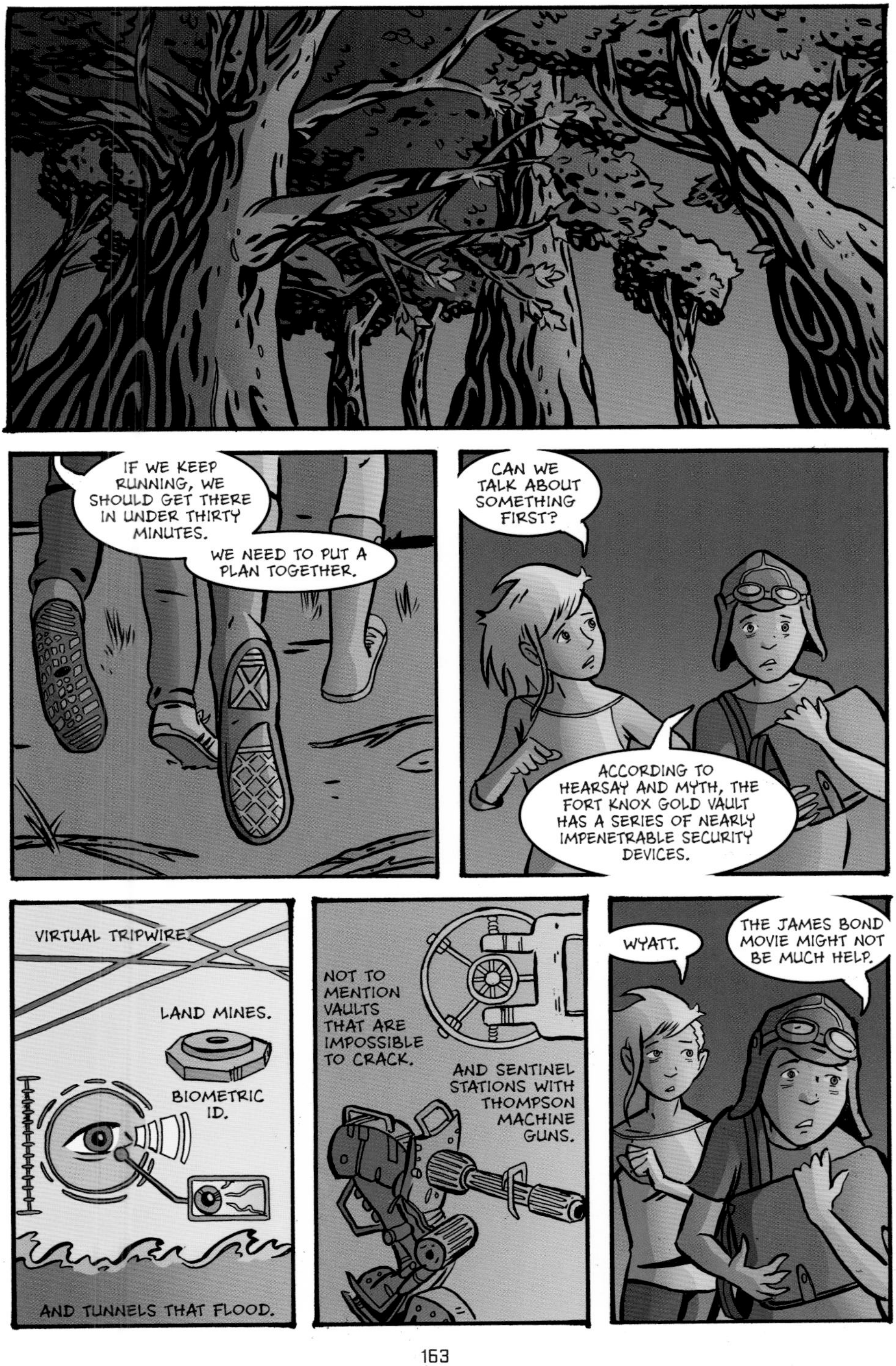
IF WE KEEP RUNNING, WE SHOULD GET THERE IN UNDER THIRTY MINUTES.
WE NEED TO PUT A PLAN TOGETHER.
CAN WE TALK ABOUT SOMETHING FIRST?
ACCORDING TO HEARSAY AND MYTH, THE FORT KNOX GOLD VAULT HAS A SERIES OF NEARLY IMPENETRABLE SECURITY DEVICES.
VIRTUAL TRIPWIRE.
LAND MINES.
BIOMETRIC ID.
AND TUNNELS THAT FLOOD.
NOT TO MENTION VAULTS THAT ARE IMPOSSIBLE TO CRACK.
AND SENTINEL STATIONS WITH THOMPSON MACHINE GUNS.
WYATT.
THE JAMES BOND MOVIE MIGHT NOT BE MUCH HELP.

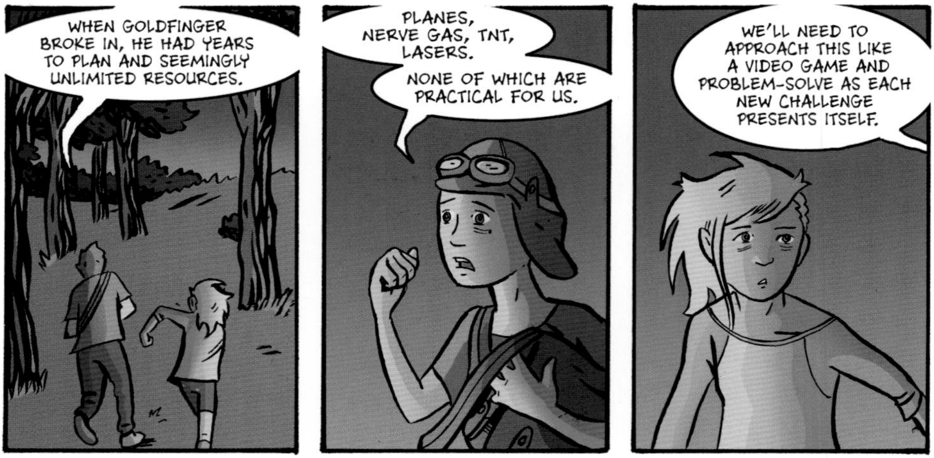
WHEN GOLDFINGER BROKE IN, HE HAD YEARS TO PLAN AND SEEMINGLY UNLIMITED RESOURCES.
PLANES, NERVE GAS, TNT, LASERS.
NONE OF WHICH ARE PRACTICAL FOR US.
WE'LL NEED TO APPROACH THIS LIKE A VIDEO GAME AND PROBLEM-SOLVE AS EACH NEW CHALLENGE PRESENTS ITSELF.

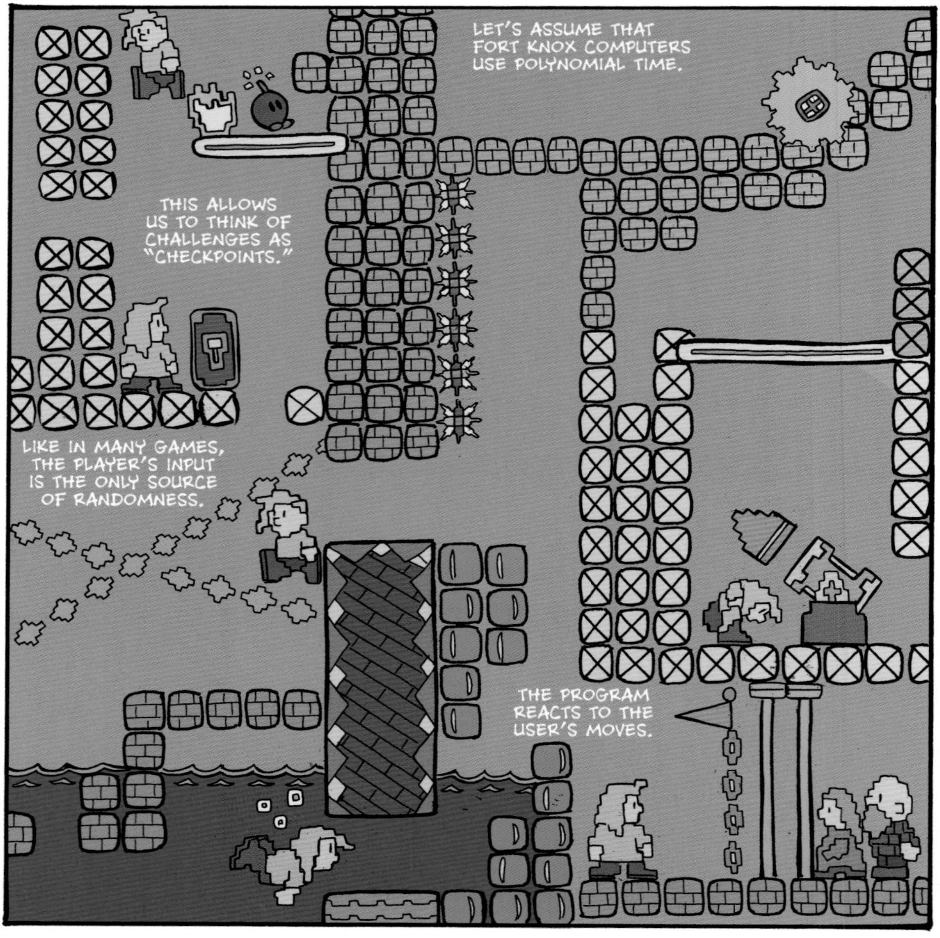
LET'S ASSUME THAT FORT KNOX COMPUTERS USE POLYNOMIAL TIME.
THIS ALLOWS US TO THINK OF CHALLENGES AS "CHECKPOINTS."
LIKE IN MANY GAMES, THE PLAYER'S INPUT IS THE ONLY SOURCE OF RANDOMNESS.
THE PROGRAM REACTS TO THE USER'S MOVES.

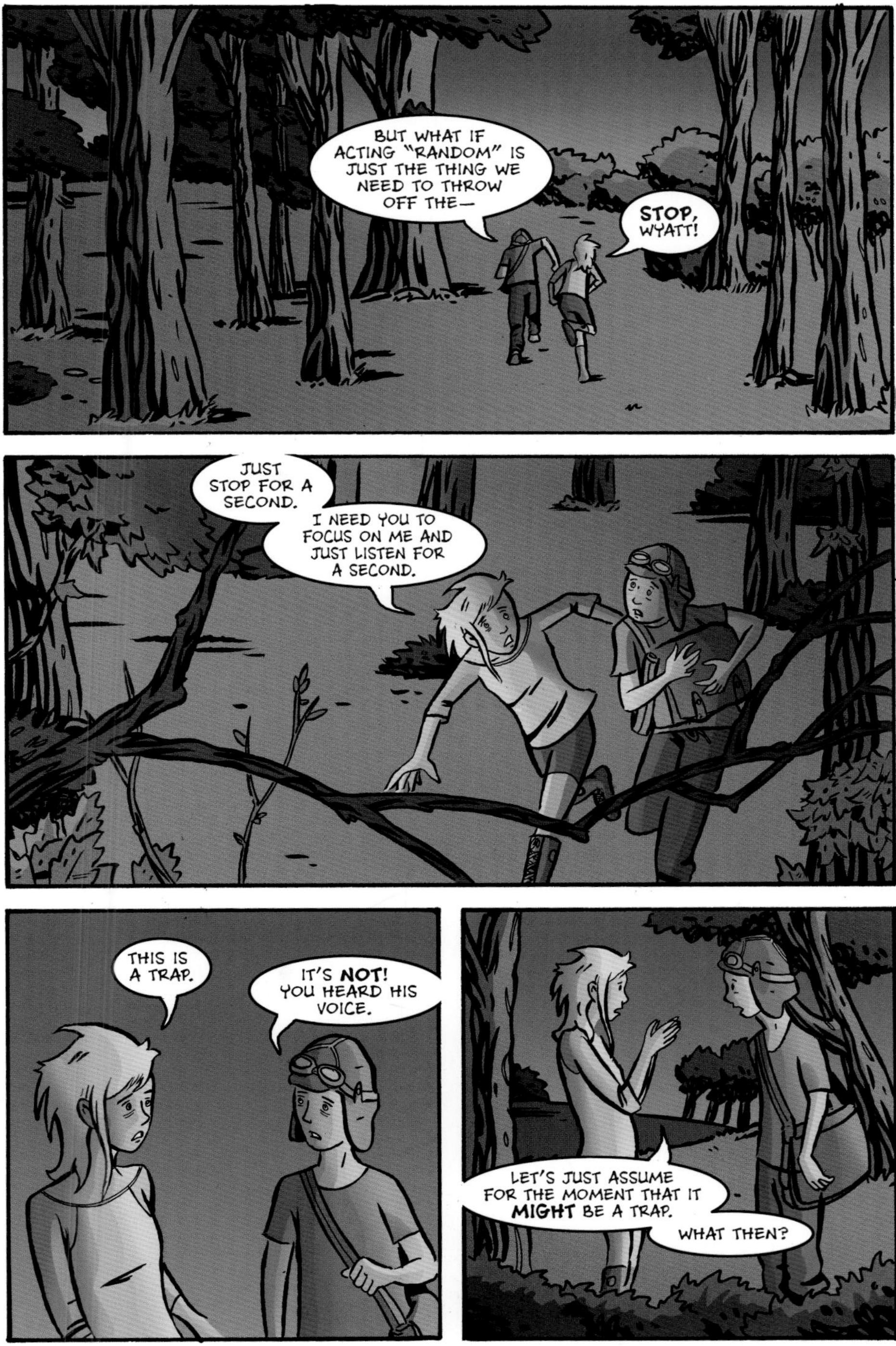

BUT WHAT IF ACTING "RANDOM" IS JUST THE THING WE NEED TO THROW OFF THE—
STOP, WYATT!
JUST STOP FOR A SECOND.
I NEED YOU TO FOCUS ON ME AND JUST LISTEN FOR A SECOND.
THIS IS A TRAP.
IT'S NOT! YOU HEARD HIS VOICE.
LET'S JUST ASSUME FOR THE MOMENT THAT IT MIGHT BE A TRAP.
WHAT THEN?

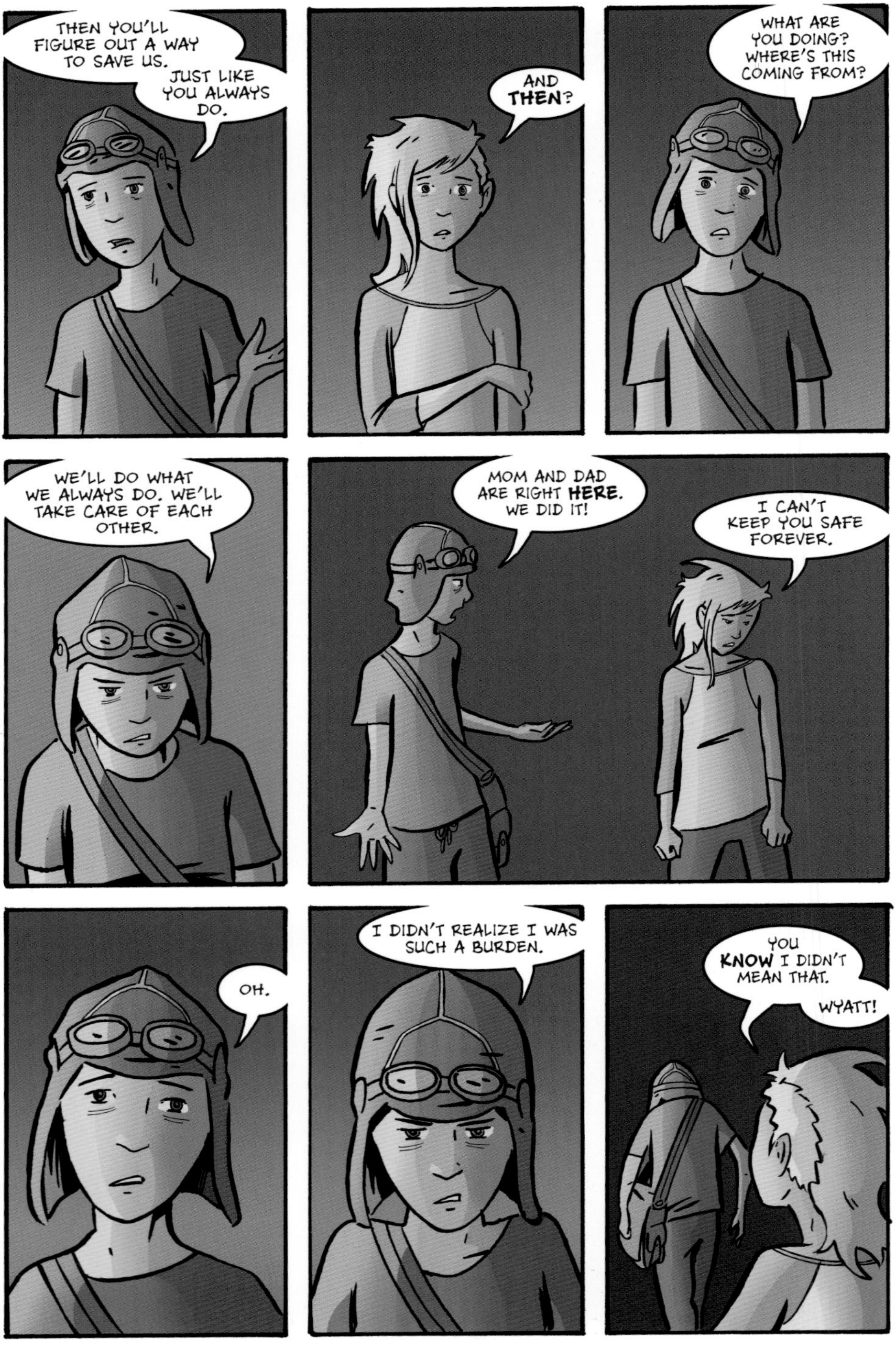
THEN YOU'LL FIGURE OUT A WAY TO SAVE US.
JUST LIKE YOU ALWAYS DO.
AND **THEN**?
WHAT ARE YOU DOING? WHERE'S THIS COMING FROM?
WE'LL DO WHAT WE ALWAYS DO. WE'LL TAKE CARE OF EACH OTHER.
MOM AND DAD ARE RIGHT **HERE**. WE DID IT!
I CAN'T KEEP YOU SAFE FOREVER.
OH.
I DIDN'T REALIZE I WAS SUCH A BURDEN.
YOU **KNOW** I DIDN'T MEAN THAT.
WYATT!

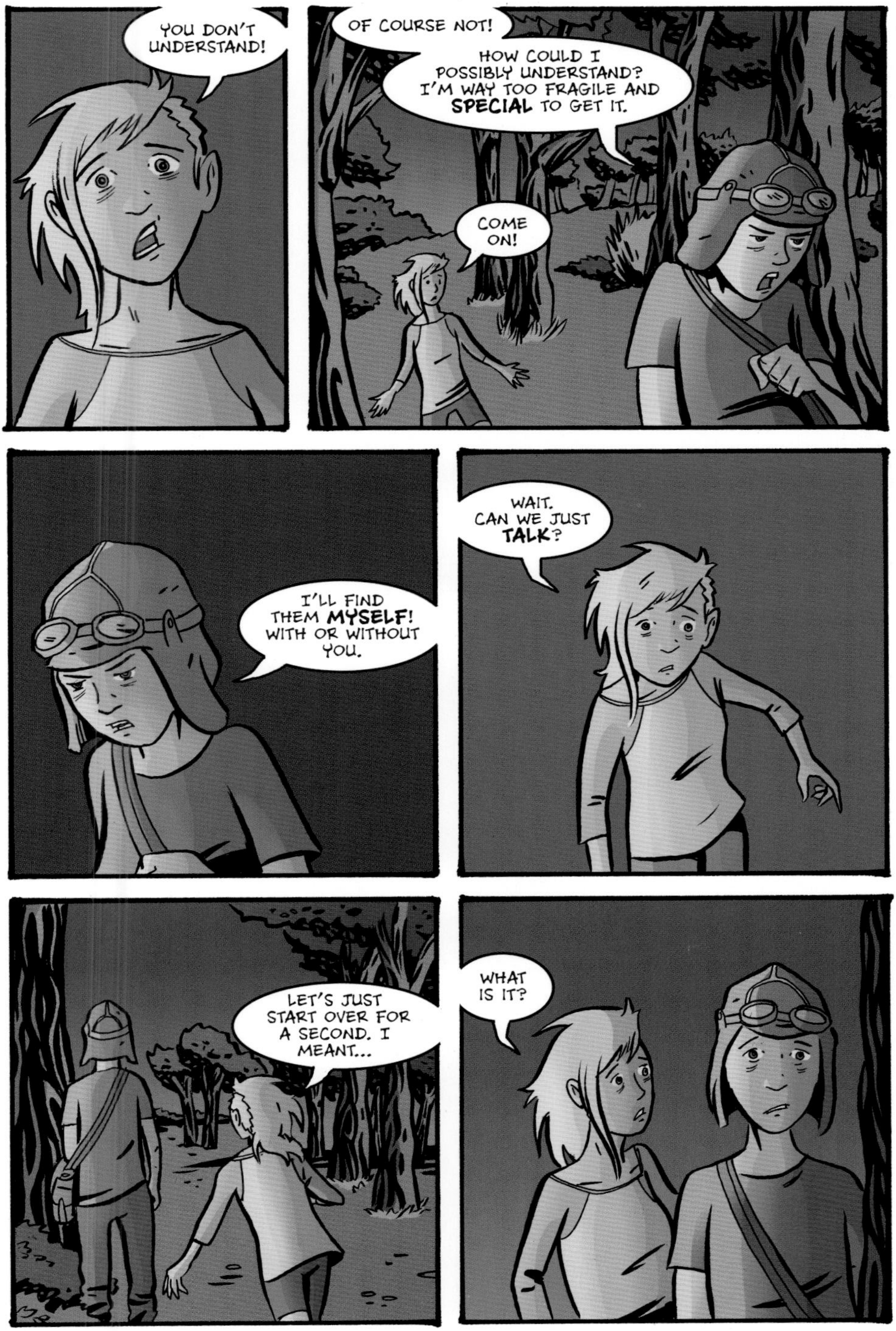
YOU DON'T UNDERSTAND!
OF COURSE NOT!
HOW COULD I POSSIBLY UNDERSTAND? I'M WAY TOO FRAGILE AND SPECIAL TO GET IT.
COME ON!
I'LL FIND THEM MYSELF! WITH OR WITHOUT YOU.
WAIT. CAN WE JUST TALK?
LET'S JUST START OVER FOR A SECOND. I MEANT...
WHAT IS IT?

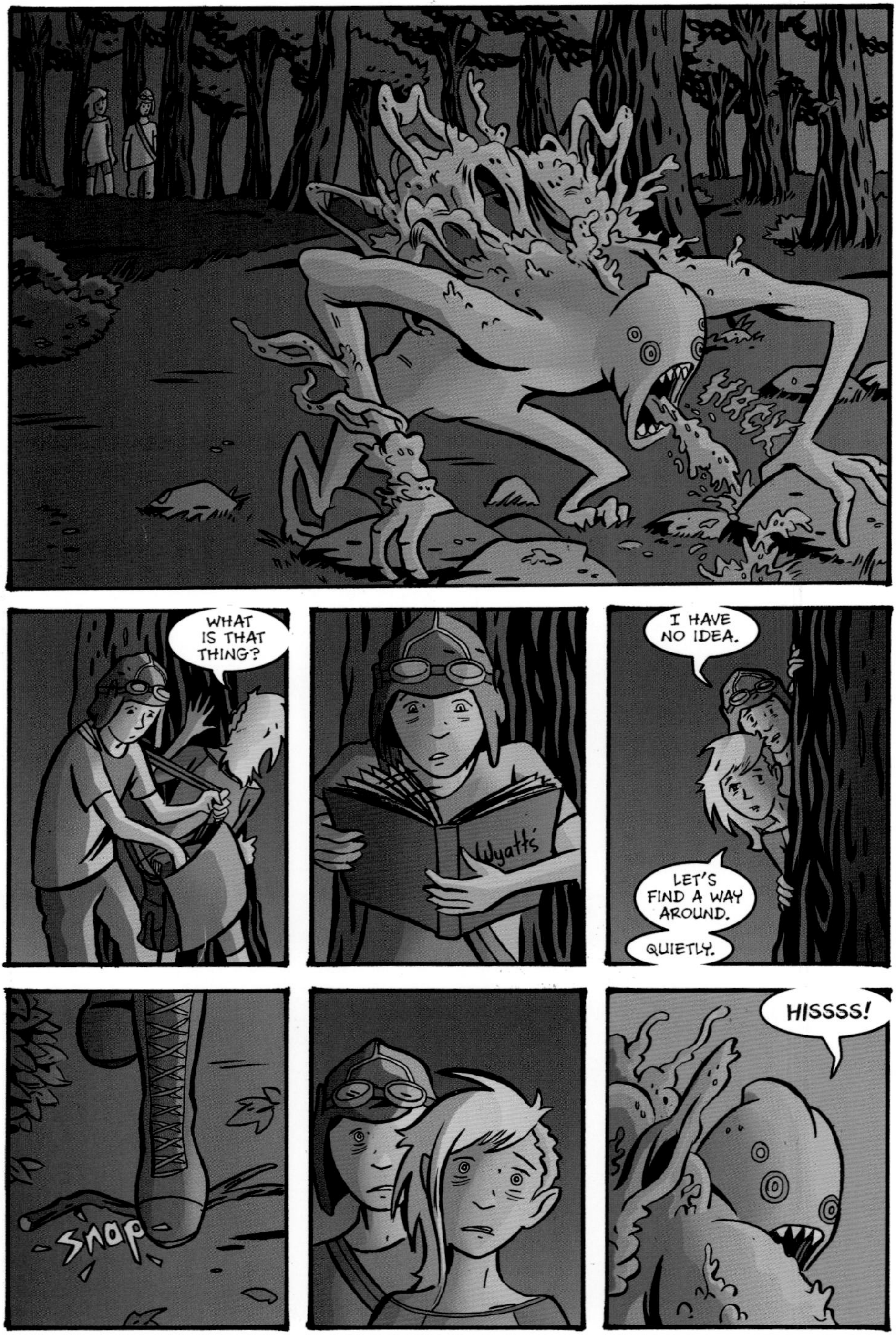
HACK
WHAT IS THAT THING?
Wyatt's
I HAVE NO IDEA.
LET'S FIND A WAY AROUND.
QUIETLY.
SNAP
HISSSS!

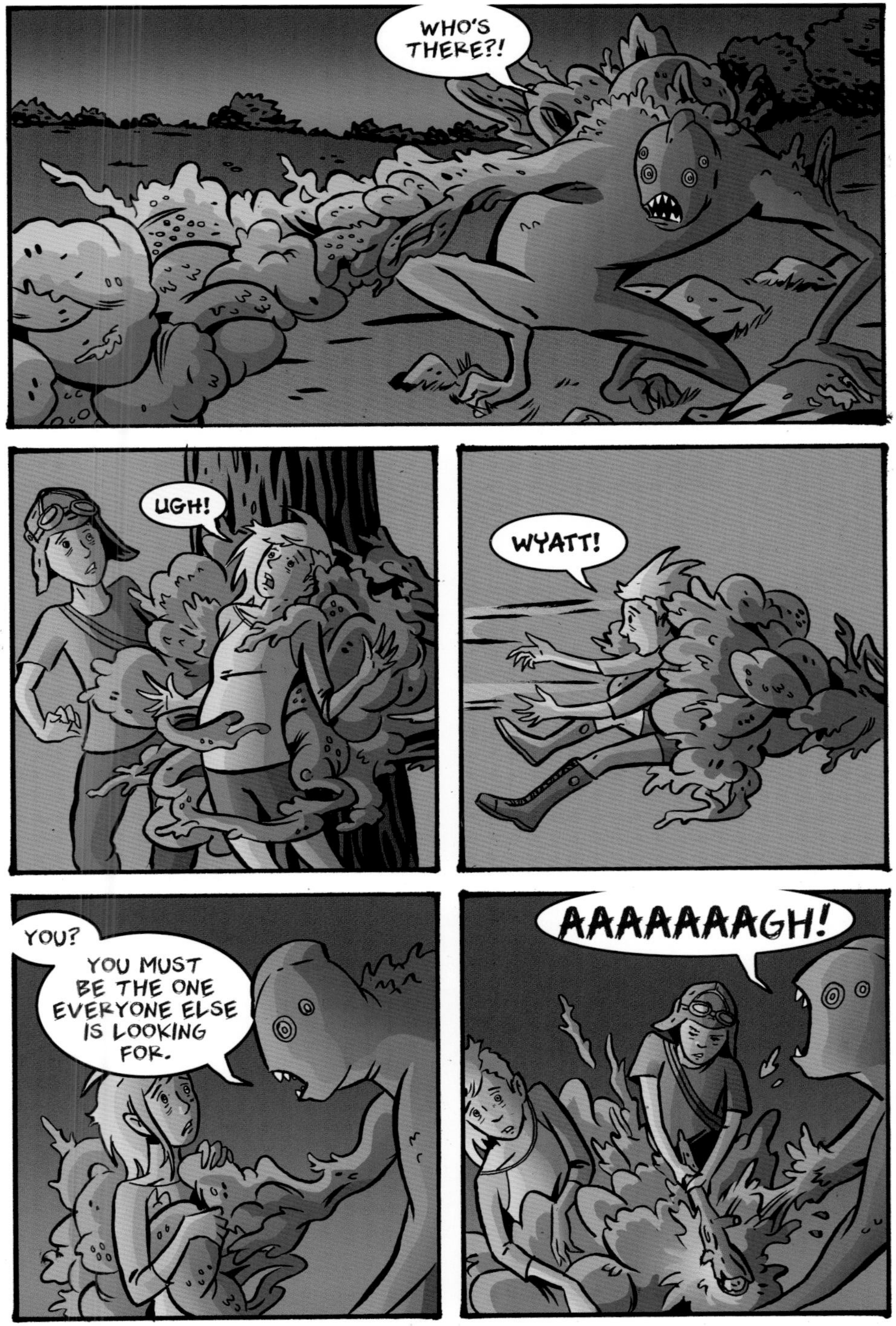
WHO'S THERE?!
UGH!
WYATT!
YOU?
YOU MUST BE THE ONE EVERYONE ELSE IS LOOKING FOR.
AAAAAAAGH!

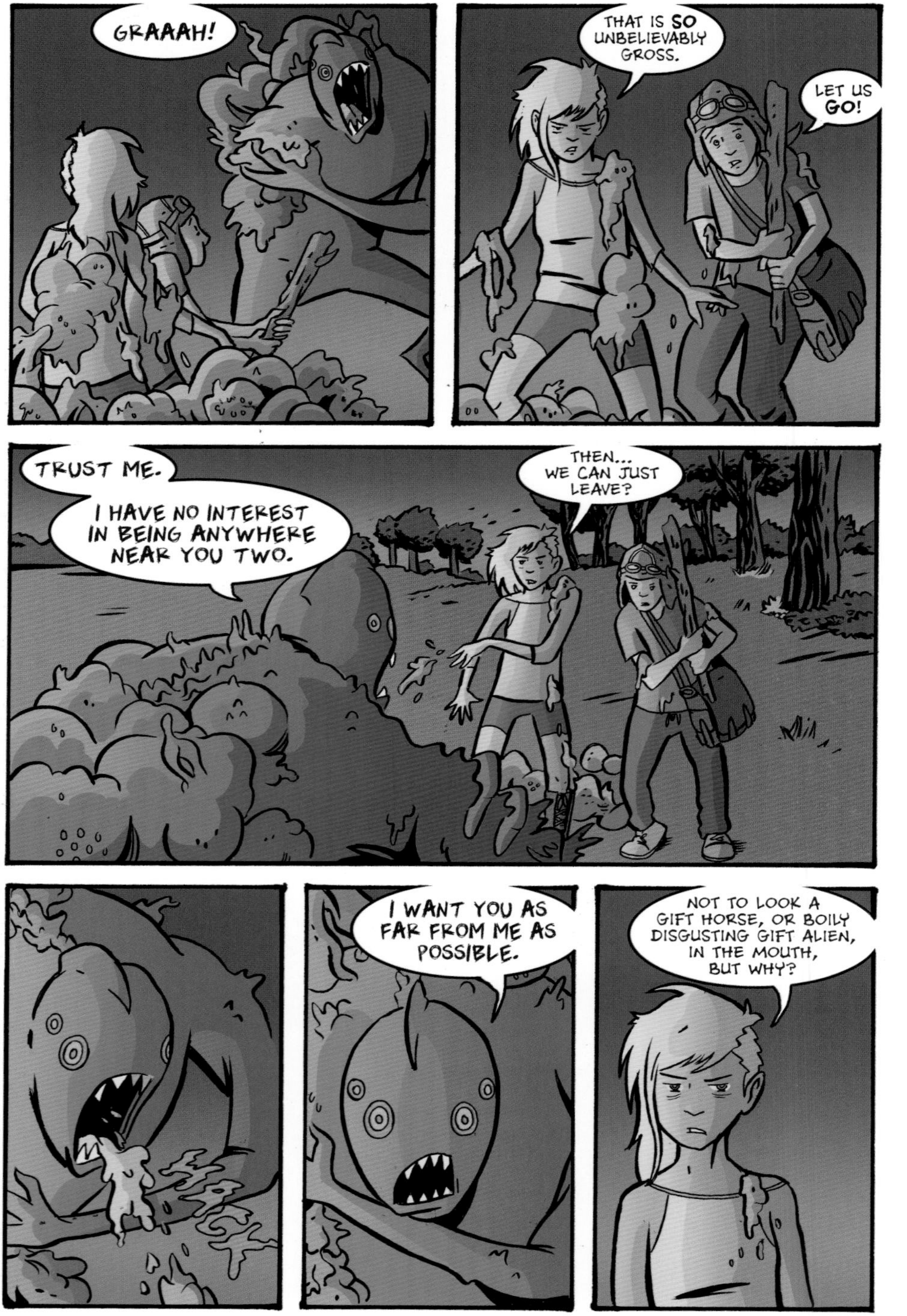
GRAAAH!
THAT IS SO UNBELIEVABLY GROSS.
LET US GO!
TRUST ME.
I HAVE NO INTEREST IN BEING ANYWHERE NEAR YOU TWO.
THEN... WE CAN JUST LEAVE?
I WANT YOU AS FAR FROM ME AS POSSIBLE.
NOT TO LOOK A GIFT HORSE, OR BOILY DISGUSTING GIFT ALIEN, IN THE MOUTH, BUT WHY?

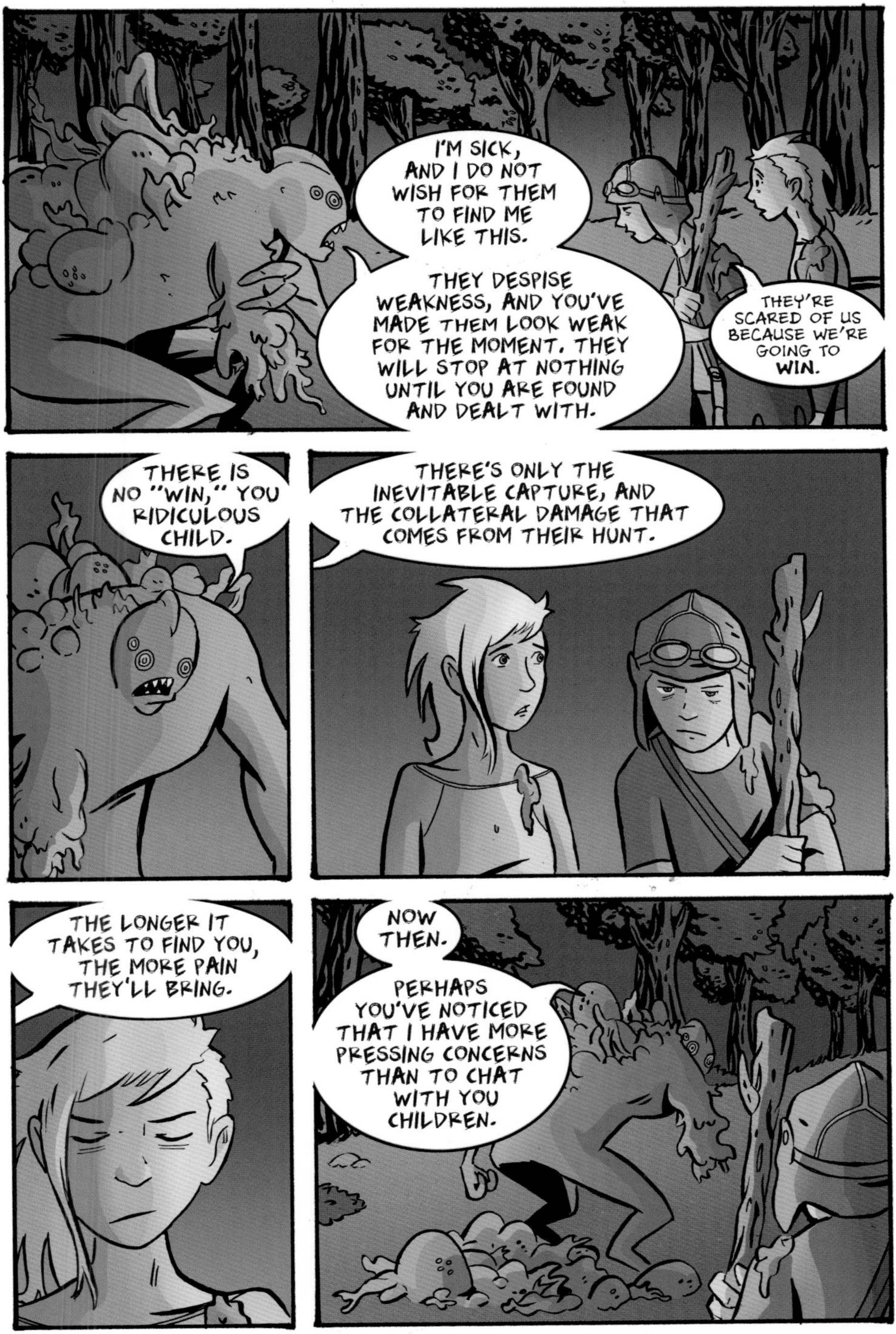
I'M SICK, AND I DO NOT WISH FOR THEM TO FIND ME LIKE THIS.
THEY DESPISE WEAKNESS, AND YOU'VE MADE THEM LOOK WEAK FOR THE MOMENT. THEY WILL STOP AT NOTHING UNTIL YOU ARE FOUND AND DEALT WITH.
THEY'RE SCARED OF US BECAUSE WE'RE GOING TO WIN.
THERE IS NO "WIN," YOU RIDICULOUS CHILD.
THERE'S ONLY THE INEVITABLE CAPTURE, AND THE COLLATERAL DAMAGE THAT COMES FROM THEIR HUNT.
THE LONGER IT TAKES TO FIND YOU, THE MORE PAIN THEY'LL BRING.
NOW THEN.
PERHAPS YOU'VE NOTICED THAT I HAVE MORE PRESSING CONCERNS THAN TO CHAT WITH YOU CHILDREN.

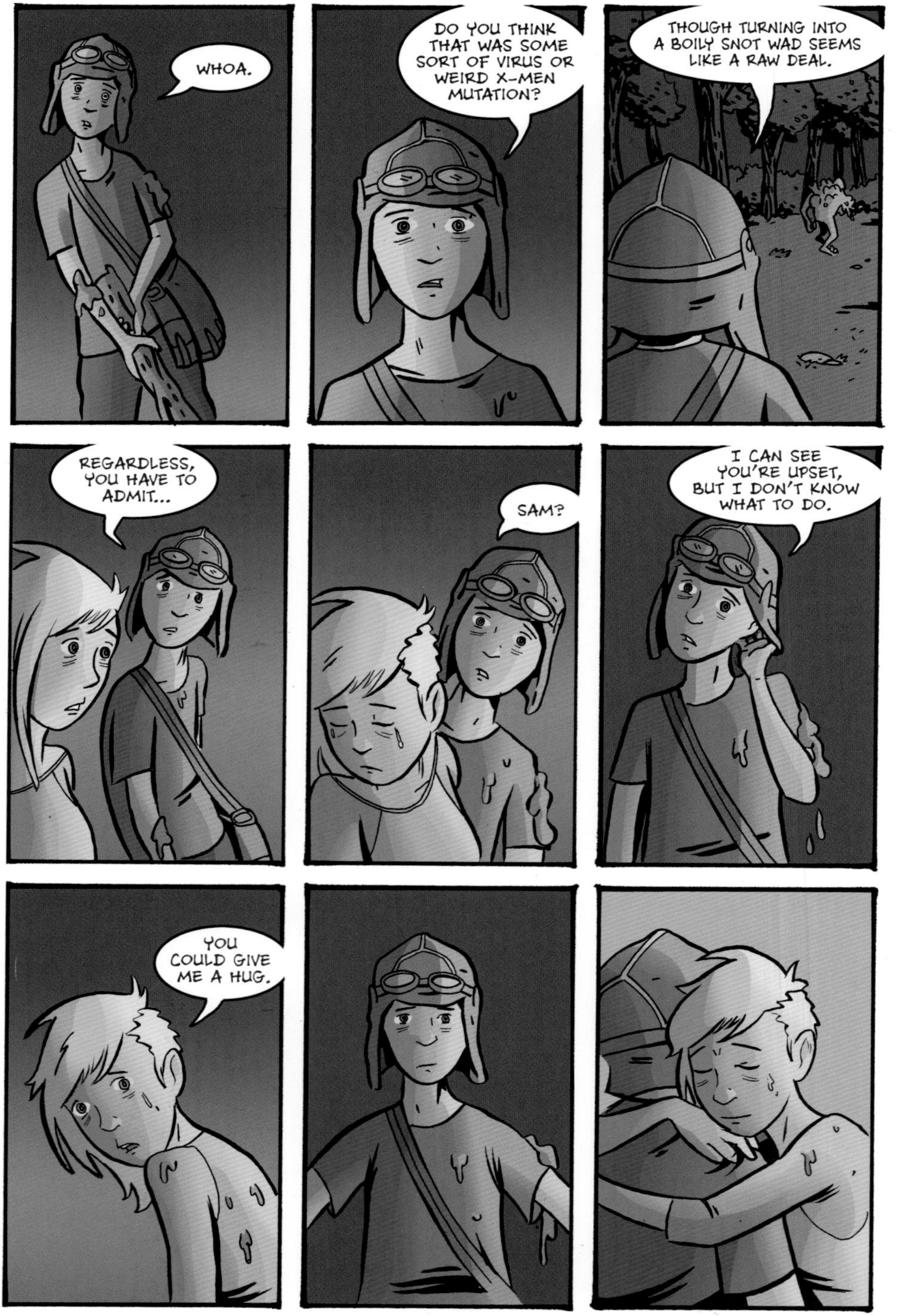
WHOA.
DO YOU THINK THAT WAS SOME SORT OF VIRUS OR WEIRD X-MEN MUTATION?
THOUGH TURNING INTO A BOILY SNOT WAD SEEMS LIKE A RAW DEAL.
REGARDLESS, YOU HAVE TO ADMIT...
SAM?
I CAN SEE YOU'RE UPSET, BUT I DON'T KNOW WHAT TO DO.
YOU COULD GIVE ME A HUG.

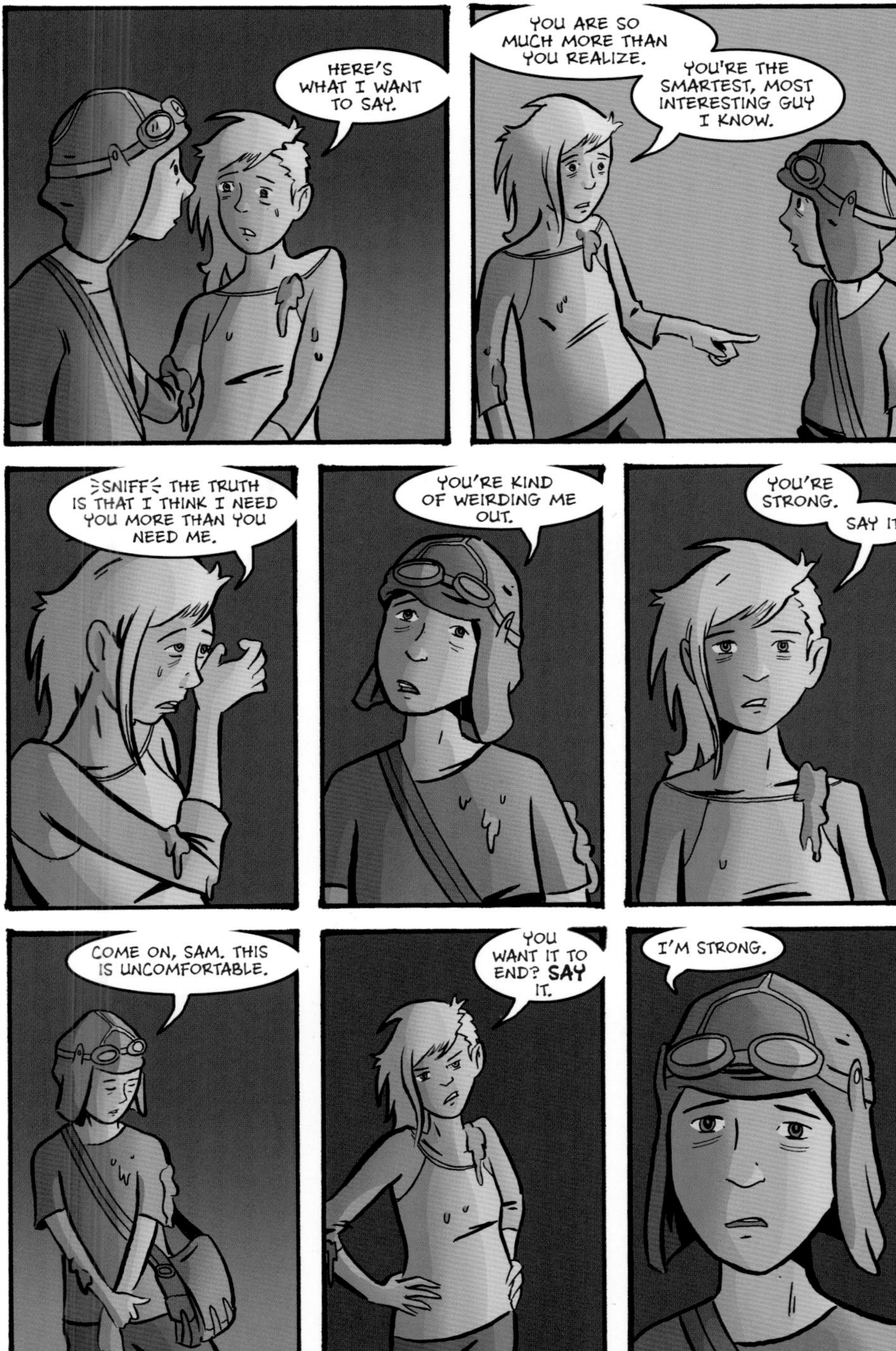
HERE'S WHAT I WANT TO SAY.
YOU ARE SO MUCH MORE THAN YOU REALIZE.
YOU'RE THE SMARTEST, MOST INTERESTING GUY I KNOW.
SNIFF THE TRUTH IS THAT I THINK I NEED YOU MORE THAN YOU NEED ME.
YOU'RE KIND OF WEIRDING ME OUT.
YOU'RE STRONG.
SAY IT.
COME ON, SAM. THIS IS UNCOMFORTABLE.
YOU WANT IT TO END? **SAY** IT.
I'M STRONG.

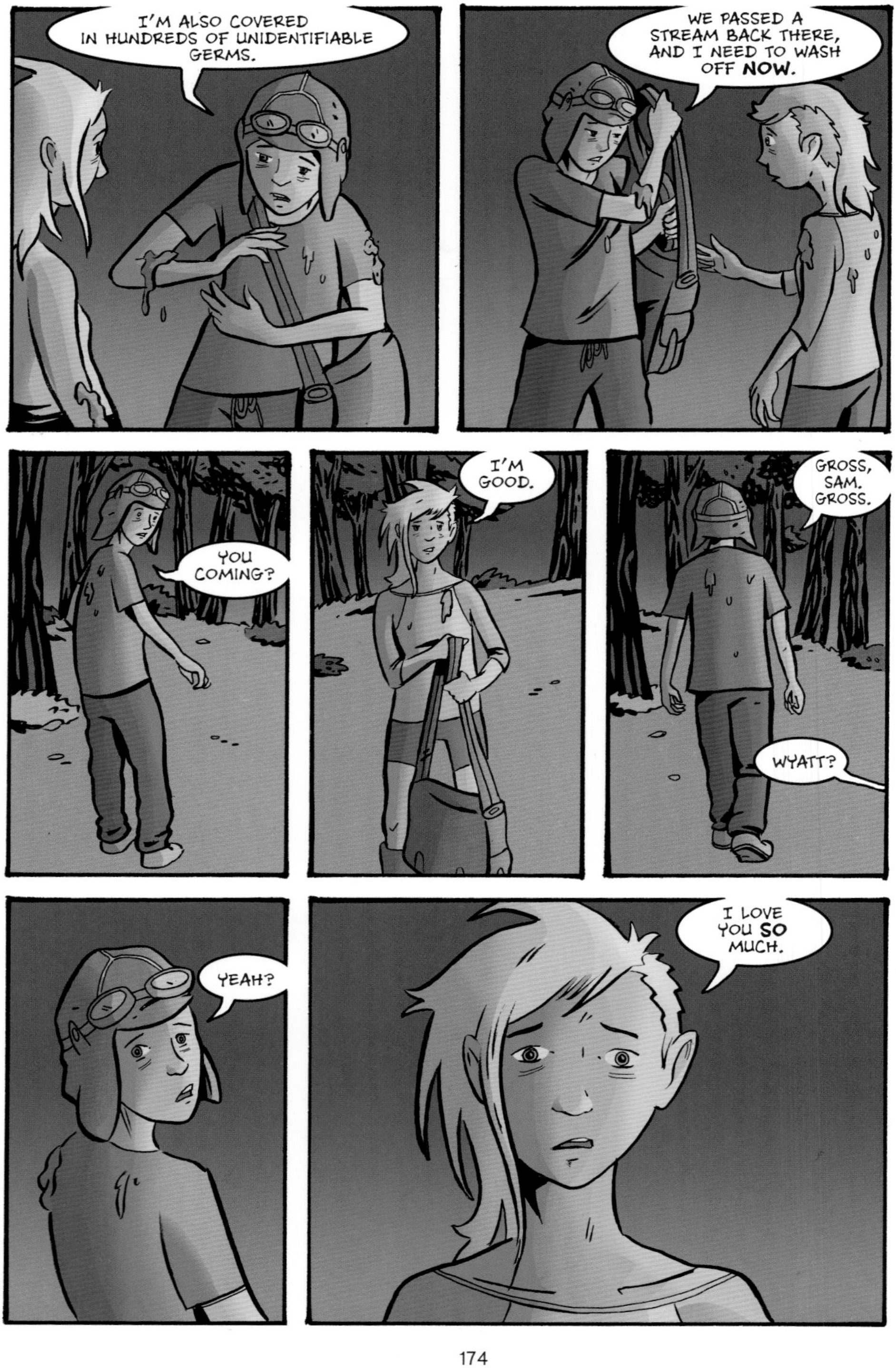
I'M ALSO COVERED IN HUNDREDS OF UNIDENTIFIABLE GERMS.
WE PASSED A STREAM BACK THERE, AND I NEED TO WASH OFF **NOW**.
YOU COMING?
I'M GOOD.
GROSS, SAM. GROSS.
WYATT?
YEAH?
I LOVE YOU **SO** MUCH.

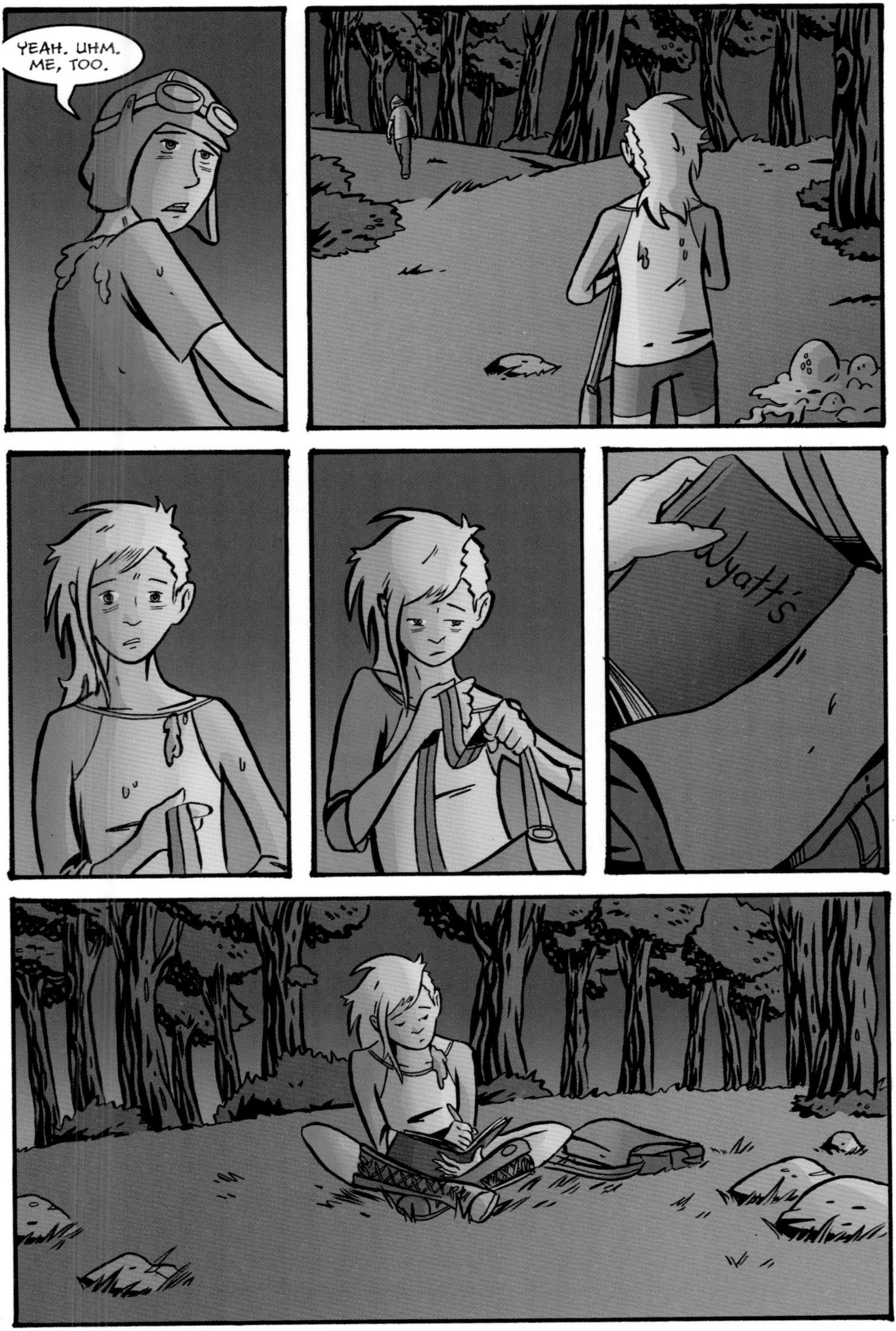
YEAH. UHM. ME, TOO.
Wyatt's

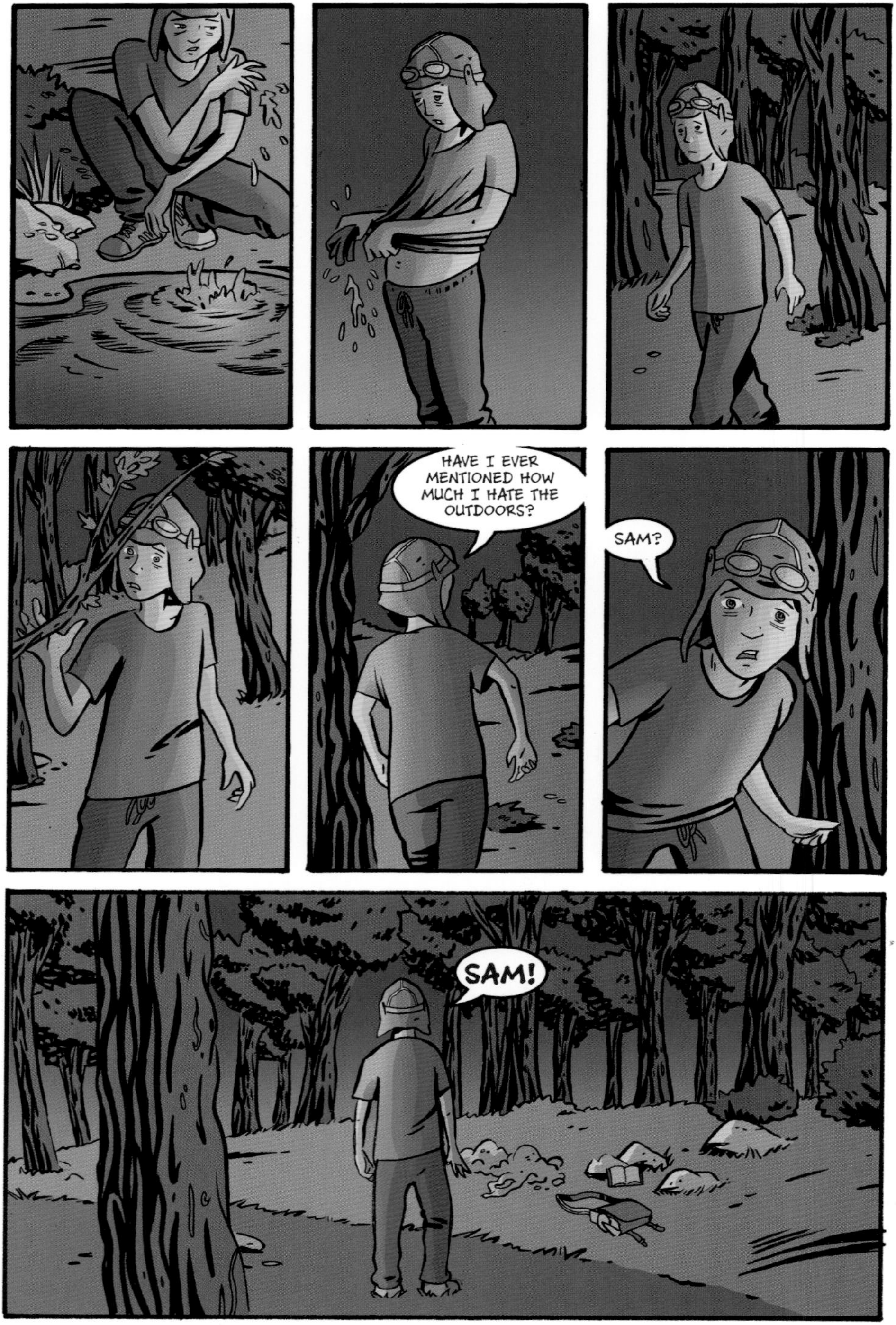
HAVE I EVER MENTIONED HOW MUCH I HATE THE OUTDOORS?
SAM?
SAM!

CHAPTER SIX

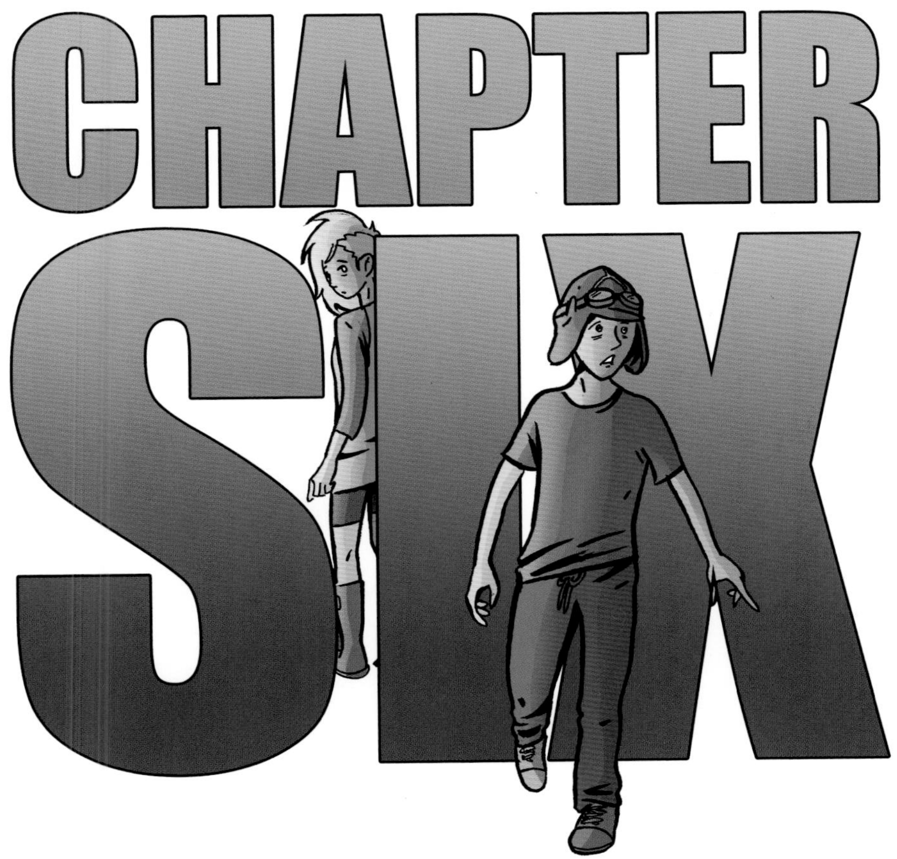

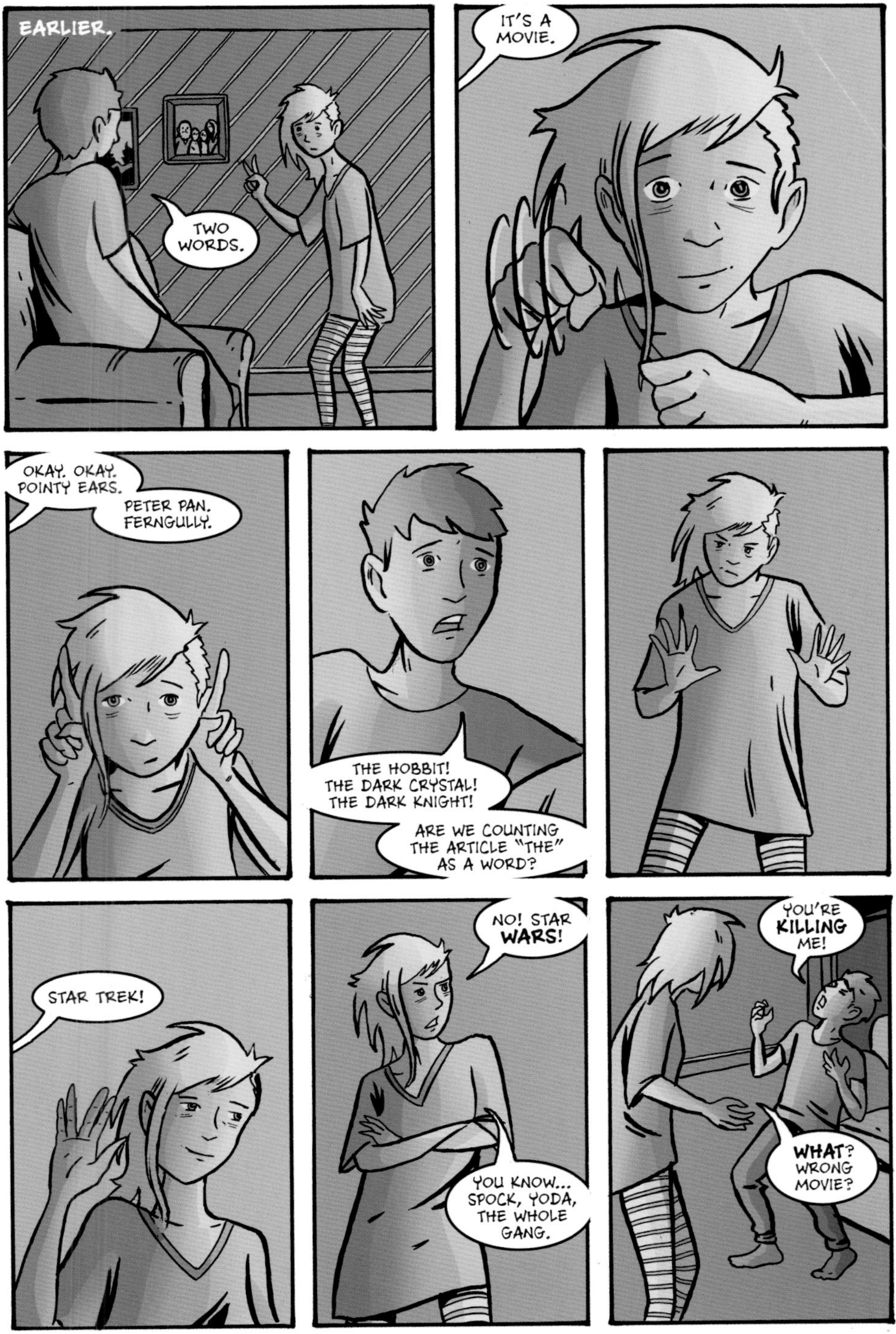
EARLIER.
TWO WORDS.
IT'S A MOVIE.
OKAY. OKAY. POINTY EARS.
PETER PAN. FERNGULLY.
THE HOBBIT! THE DARK CRYSTAL! THE DARK KNIGHT!
ARE WE COUNTING THE ARTICLE "THE" AS A WORD?
STAR TREK!
NO! STAR WARS!
YOU KNOW... SPOCK, YODA, THE WHOLE GANG.
YOU'RE KILLING ME!
WHAT? WRONG MOVIE?

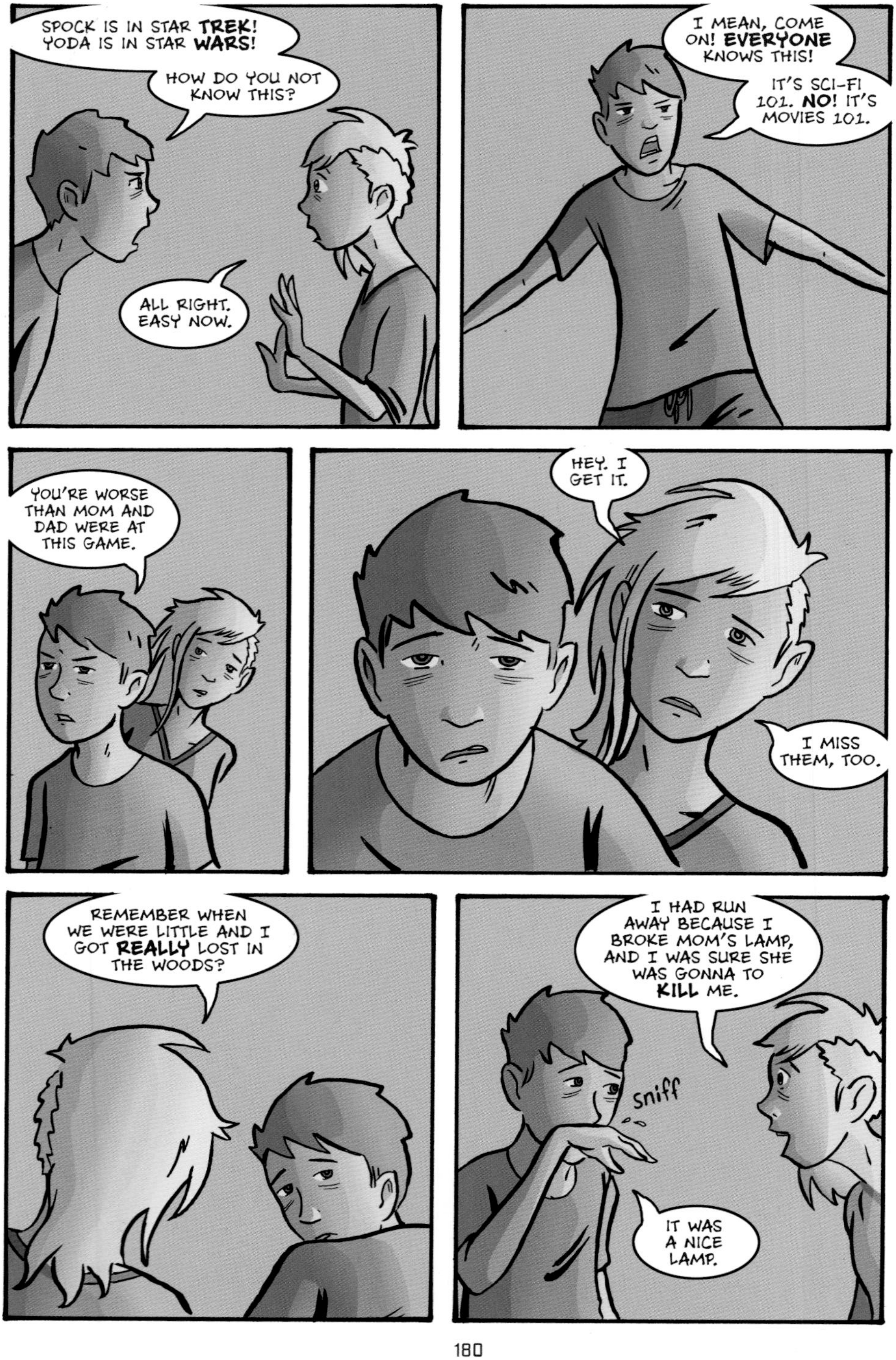
SPOCK IS IN STAR TREK! YODA IS IN STAR WARS!
HOW DO YOU NOT KNOW THIS?
ALL RIGHT. EASY NOW.
I MEAN, COME ON! EVERYONE KNOWS THIS!
IT'S SCI-FI 101. NO! IT'S MOVIES 101.
YOU'RE WORSE THAN MOM AND DAD WERE AT THIS GAME.
HEY. I GET IT.
I MISS THEM, TOO.
REMEMBER WHEN WE WERE LITTLE AND I GOT REALLY LOST IN THE WOODS?
I HAD RUN AWAY BECAUSE I BROKE MOM'S LAMP, AND I WAS SURE SHE WAS GONNA TO KILL ME.
sniff
IT WAS A NICE LAMP.

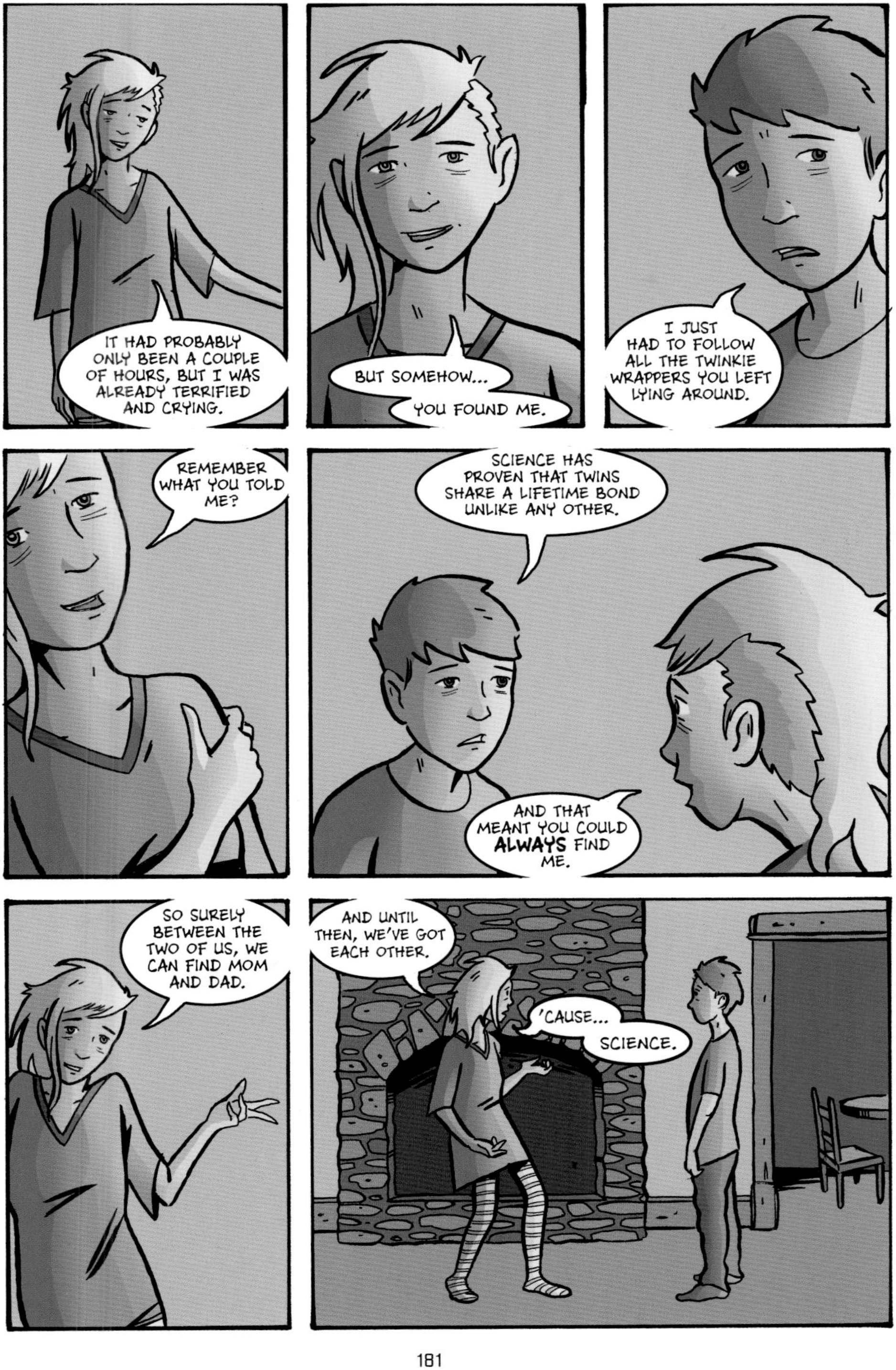
IT HAD PROBABLY ONLY BEEN A COUPLE OF HOURS, BUT I WAS ALREADY TERRIFIED AND CRYING.
BUT SOMEHOW...
YOU FOUND ME.
I JUST HAD TO FOLLOW ALL THE TWINKIE WRAPPERS YOU LEFT LYING AROUND.
REMEMBER WHAT YOU TOLD ME?
SCIENCE HAS PROVEN THAT TWINS SHARE A LIFETIME BOND UNLIKE ANY OTHER.
AND THAT MEANT YOU COULD **ALWAYS** FIND ME.
SO SURELY BETWEEN THE TWO OF US, WE CAN FIND MOM AND DAD.
AND UNTIL THEN, WE'VE GOT EACH OTHER.
'CAUSE...
SCIENCE.

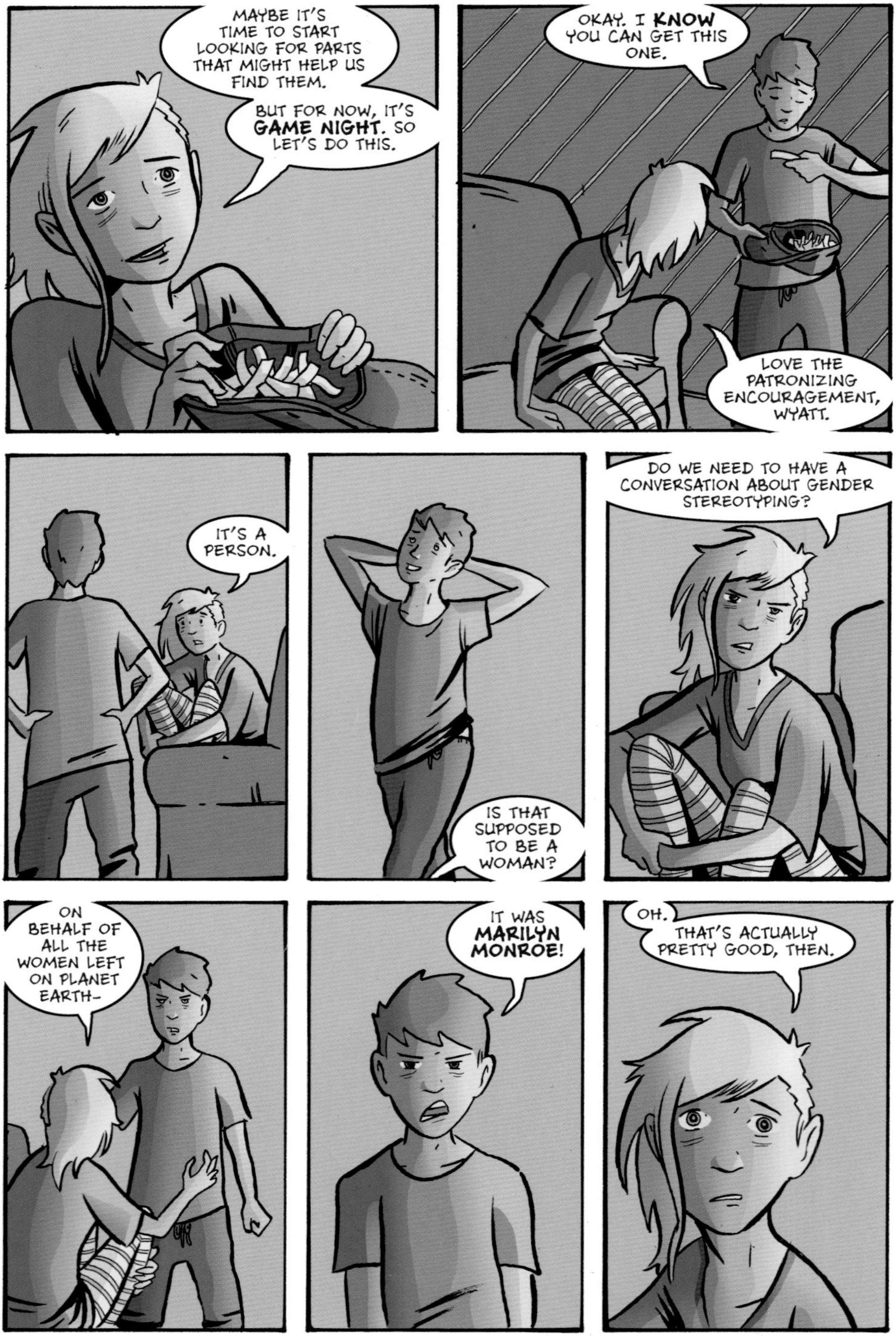
MAYBE IT'S TIME TO START LOOKING FOR PARTS THAT MIGHT HELP US FIND THEM.
BUT FOR NOW, IT'S GAME NIGHT. SO LET'S DO THIS.
OKAY. I KNOW YOU CAN GET THIS ONE.
LOVE THE PATRONIZING ENCOURAGEMENT, WYATT.
IT'S A PERSON.
IS THAT SUPPOSED TO BE A WOMAN?
DO WE NEED TO HAVE A CONVERSATION ABOUT GENDER STEREOTYPING?
ON BEHALF OF ALL THE WOMEN LEFT ON PLANET EARTH-
IT WAS MARILYN MONROE!
OH.
THAT'S ACTUALLY PRETTY GOOD, THEN.

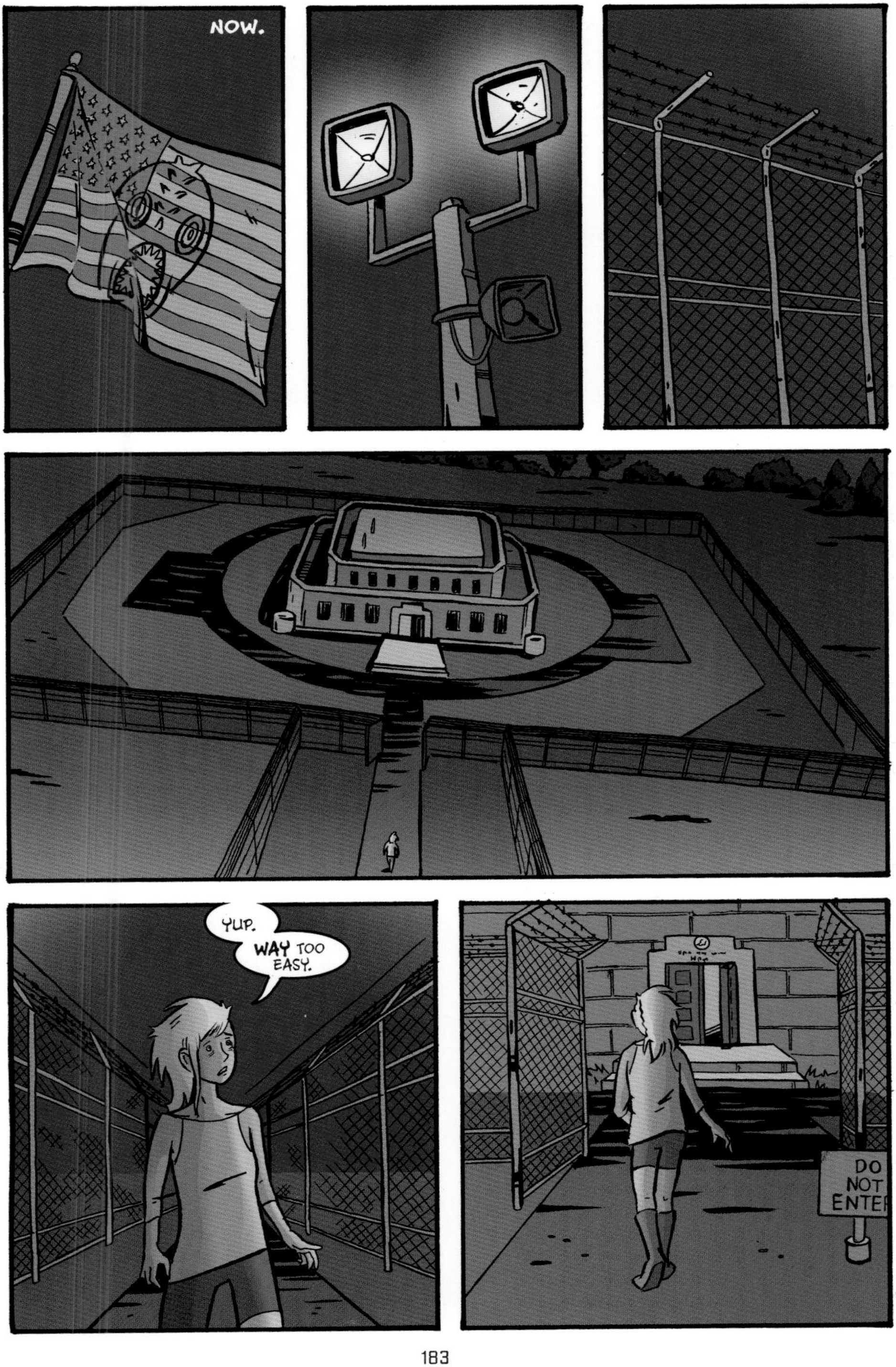
NOW.
YUP.
WAY TOO EASY.
DO NOT ENTER

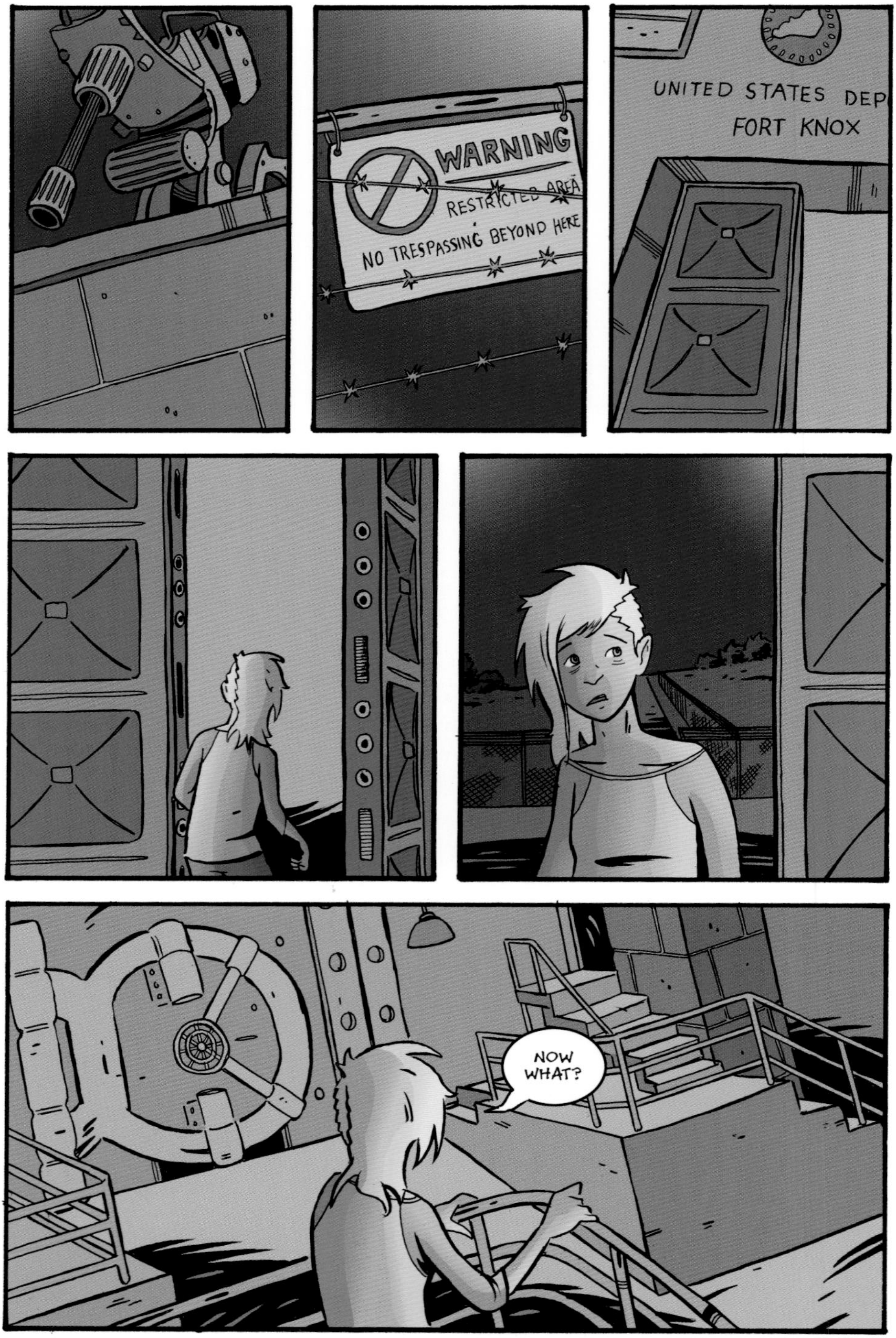
WARNING
RESTRICTED AREA
NO TRESPASSING BEYOND HERE
UNITED STATES DEP
FORT KNOX
NOW WHAT?

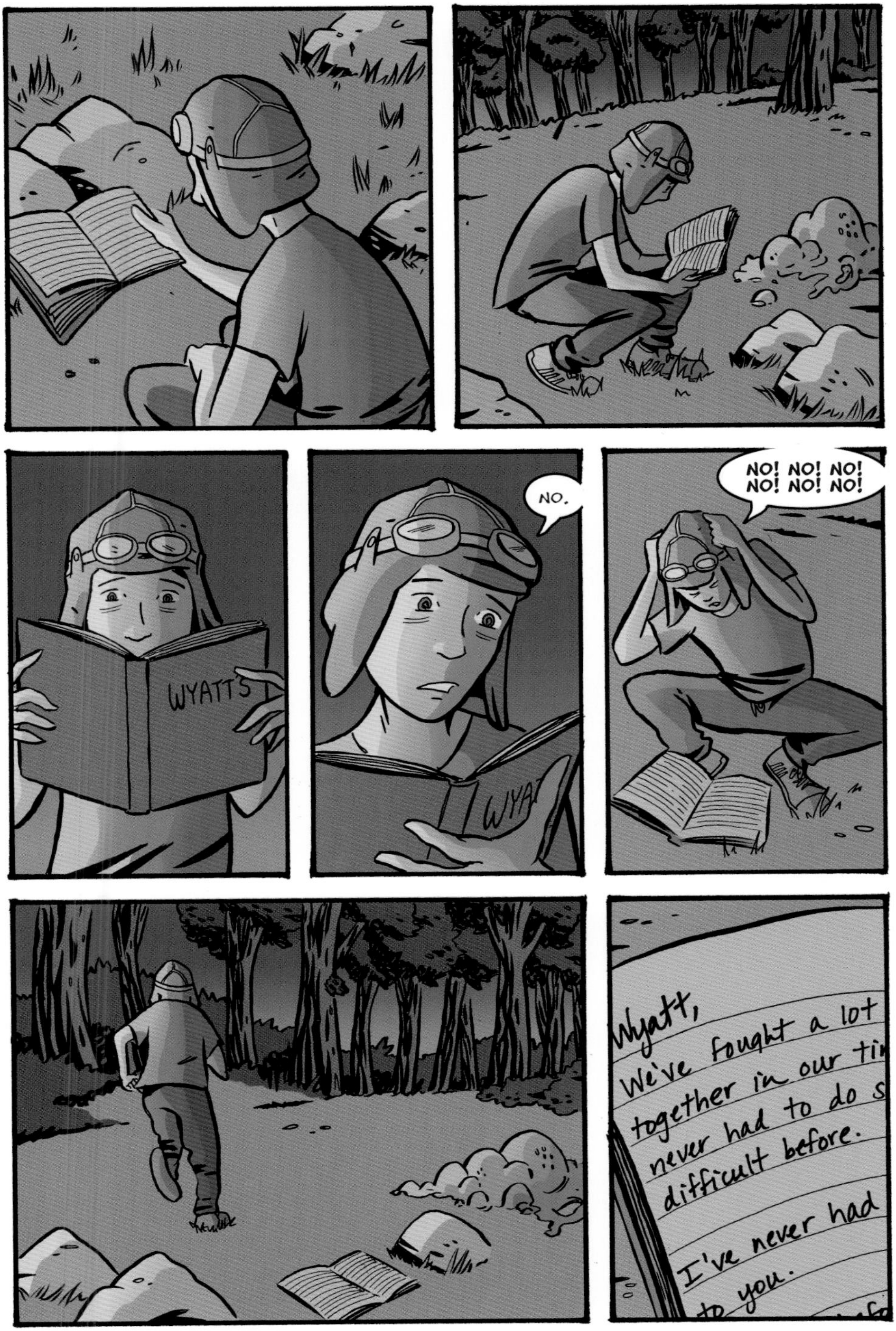
WYATT'S
NO.
NO! NO! NO!
NO! NO! NO!
Wyatt,
We've fought a lot
together in our ti
never had to do s
difficult before.
I've never had
to you.

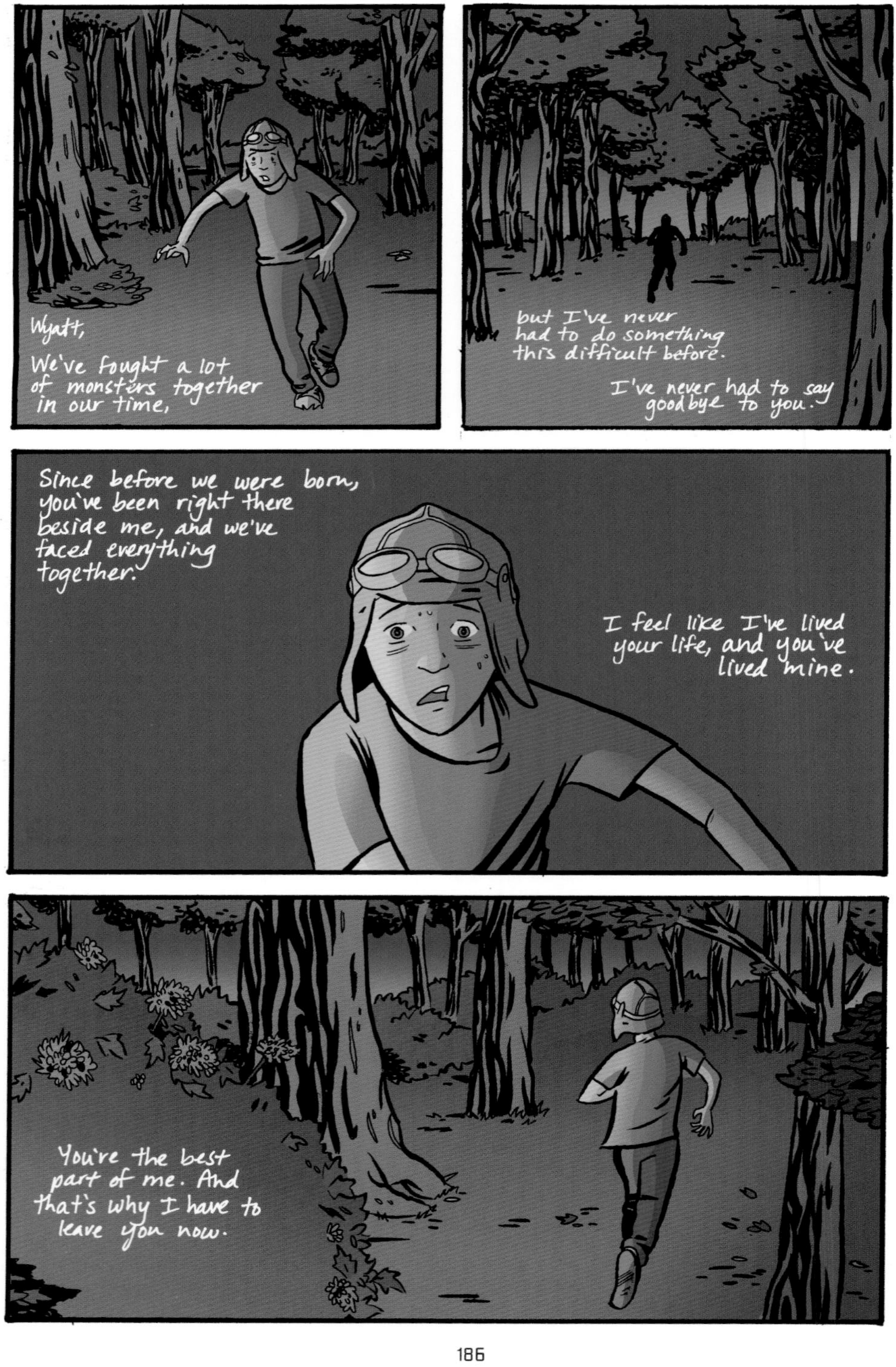
Wyatt,
We've fought a lot of monsters together in our time,
but I've never had to do something this difficult before.
I've never had to say goodbye to you.
Since before we were born, you've been right there beside me, and we've faced everything together.
I feel like I've lived your life, and you've lived mine.
You're the best part of me. And that's why I have to leave you now.

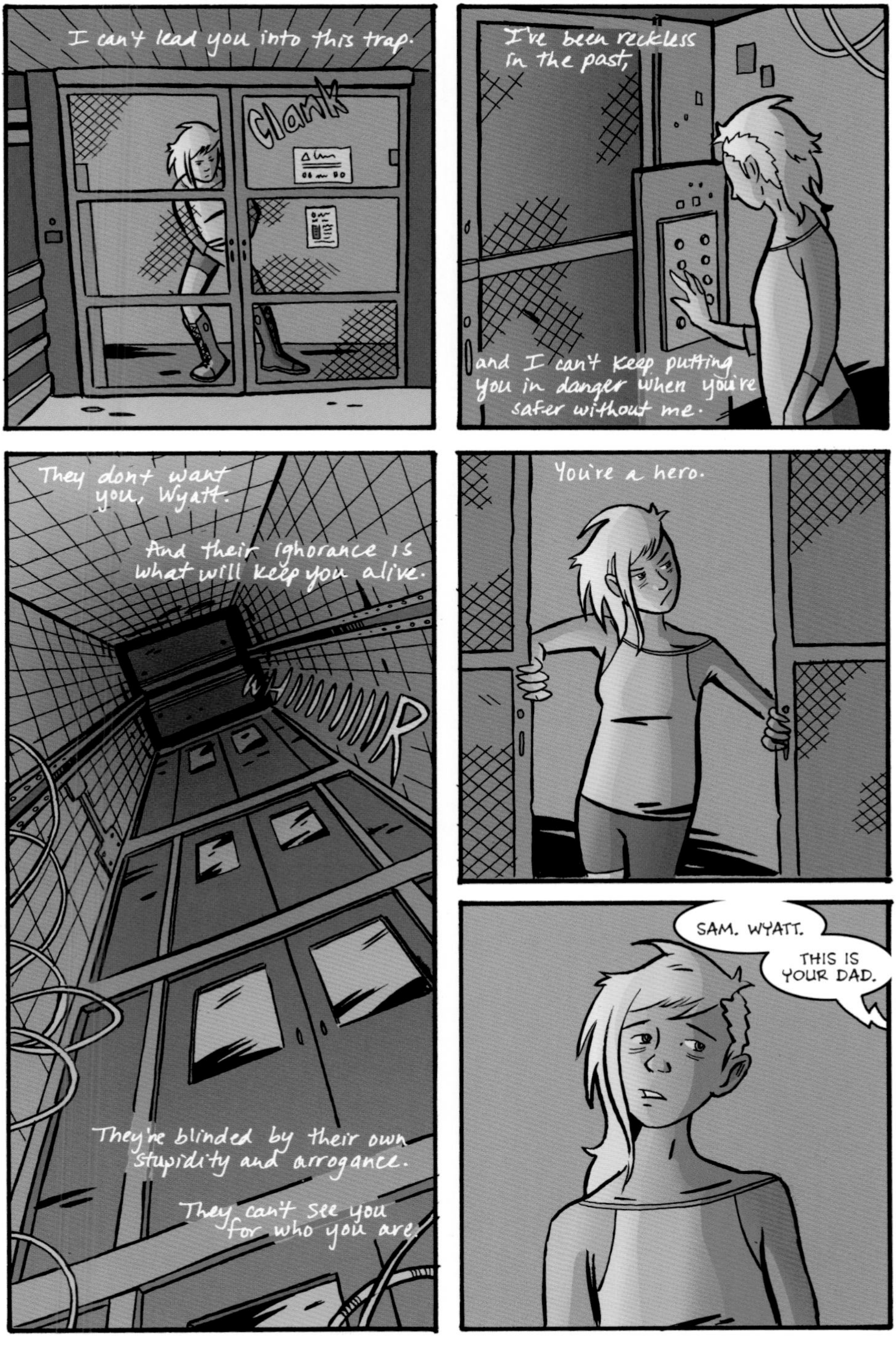
I can't lead you into this trap.
CLANK
I've been reckless in the past,
and I can't keep putting you in danger when you're safer without me.
They don't want you, Wyatt.
And their ignorance is what will keep you alive.
WHIIIIIIR
They're blinded by their own stupidity and arrogance.
They can't see you for who you are.
You're a hero.
SAM. WYATT.
THIS IS YOUR DAD.

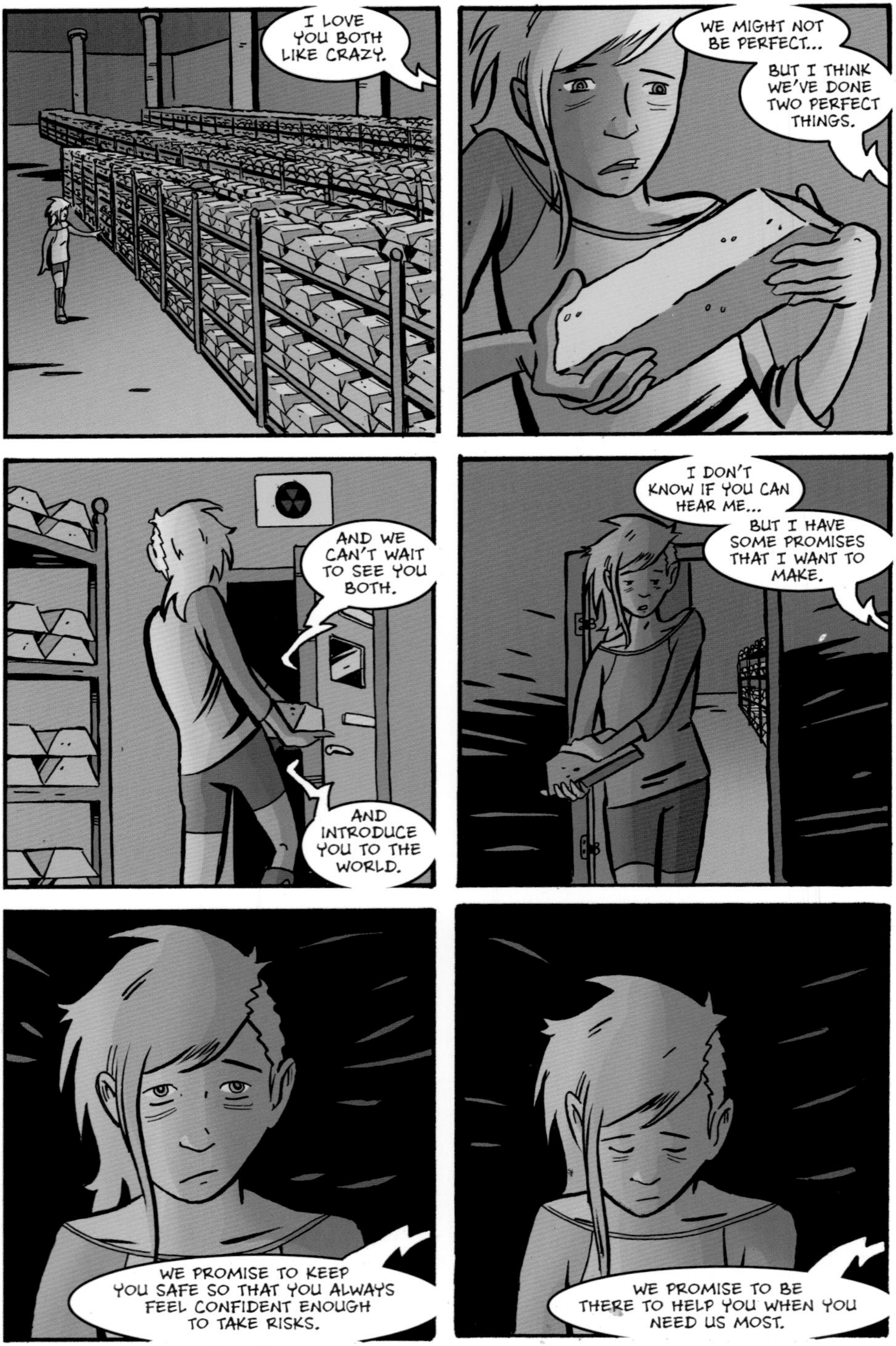
I LOVE YOU BOTH LIKE CRAZY.
WE MIGHT NOT BE PERFECT...
BUT I THINK WE'VE DONE TWO PERFECT THINGS.
AND WE CAN'T WAIT TO SEE YOU BOTH.
AND INTRODUCE YOU TO THE WORLD.
I DON'T KNOW IF YOU CAN HEAR ME...
BUT I HAVE SOME PROMISES THAT I WANT TO MAKE.
WE PROMISE TO KEEP YOU SAFE SO THAT YOU ALWAYS FEEL CONFIDENT ENOUGH TO TAKE RISKS.
WE PROMISE TO BE THERE TO HELP YOU WHEN YOU NEED US MOST.

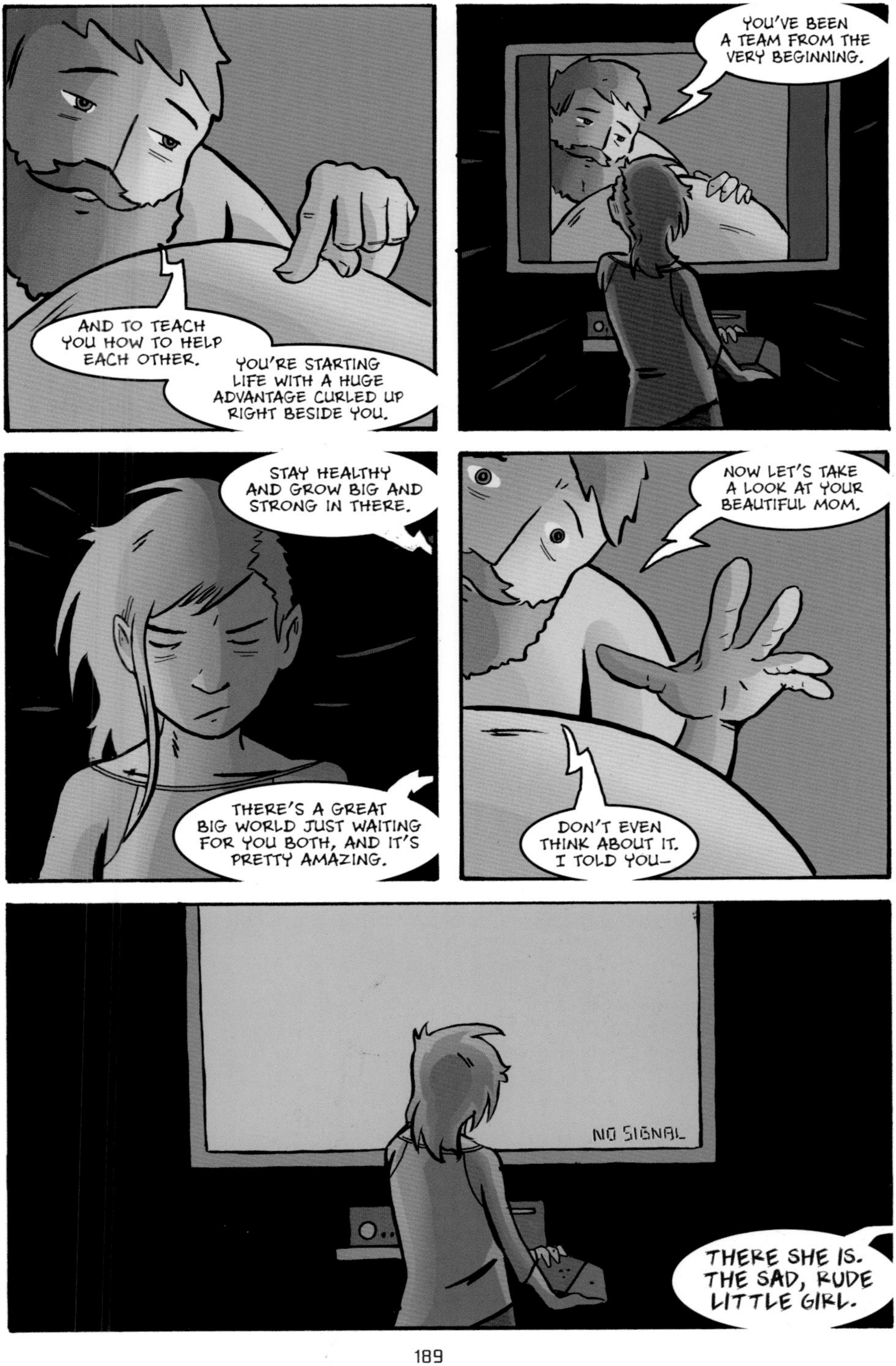
AND TO TEACH YOU HOW TO HELP EACH OTHER.
YOU'RE STARTING LIFE WITH A HUGE ADVANTAGE CURLED UP RIGHT BESIDE YOU.
YOU'VE BEEN A TEAM FROM THE VERY BEGINNING.
STAY HEALTHY AND GROW BIG AND STRONG IN THERE.
THERE'S A GREAT BIG WORLD JUST WAITING FOR YOU BOTH, AND IT'S PRETTY AMAZING.
NOW LET'S TAKE A LOOK AT YOUR BEAUTIFUL MOM.
DON'T EVEN THINK ABOUT IT. I TOLD YOU–
NO SIGNAL
THERE SHE IS. THE SAD, RUDE LITTLE GIRL.

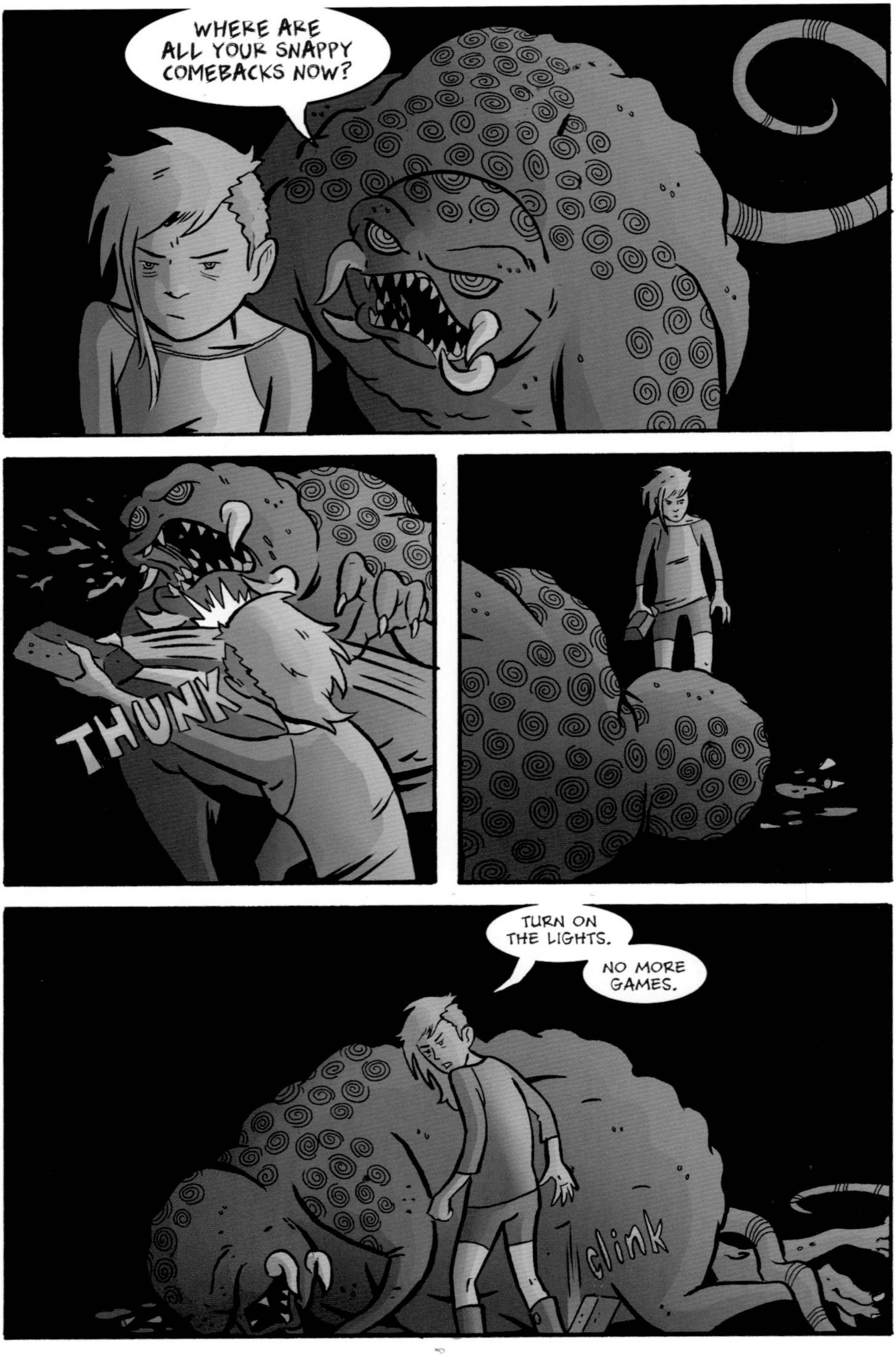
WHERE ARE ALL YOUR SNAPPY COMEBACKS NOW?
THUNK
TURN ON THE LIGHTS.
NO MORE GAMES.
clink

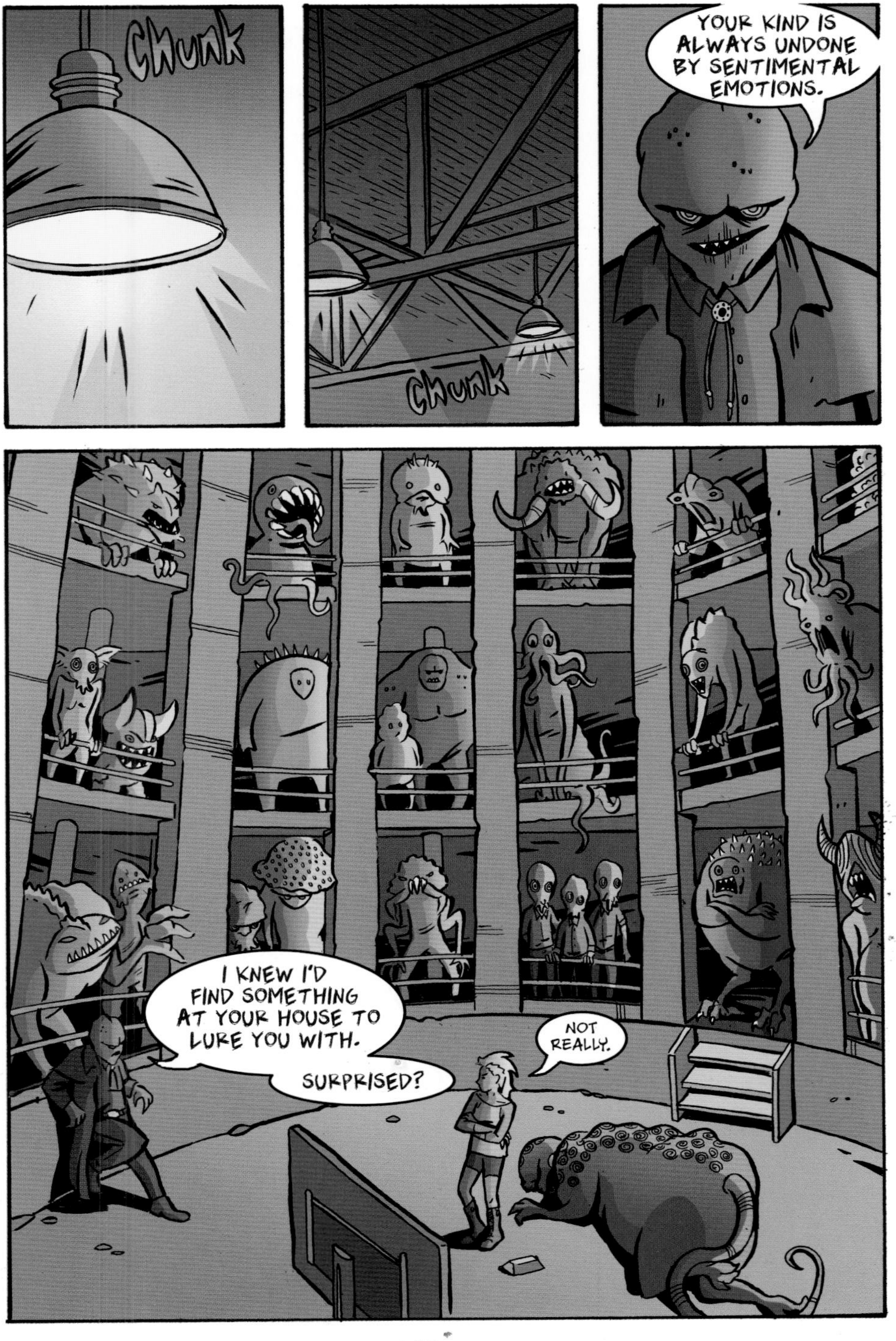
Chunk
Chunk
YOUR KIND IS ALWAYS UNDONE BY SENTIMENTAL EMOTIONS.
I KNEW I'D FIND SOMETHING AT YOUR HOUSE TO LURE YOU WITH.
SURPRISED?
NOT REALLY.

PRETTY MUCH SAW THIS COMING.
YOU KNEW THIS WAS A SETUP?
WE HAD TO WATCH THAT VIDEO LIKE A HUNDRED TIMES GROWING UP.
I KNOW IT BY HEART.
SO, YEAH.
YOU'RE NOT THAT CLEVER.
AND YOUR BROTHER?
WHERE IS HE?
NO MORE GAMES. REMEMBER?
YOU NEVER REALLY WANTED HIM, SO LET'S KEEP HIM OUT OF THIS.
Nudge
ALMOST FEEL SORRY FOR THE LITTLE FELLA.
HA HA HA HAHA
HA HA HA HAHA
HA HA HA HAHA
WHAT WITH HIS KIN JUST UP AND LEAVIN' HIM.

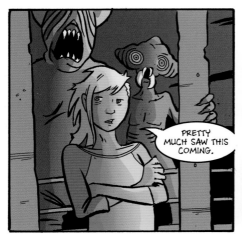

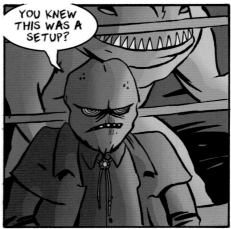

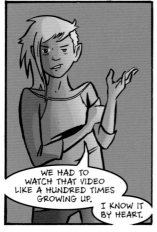

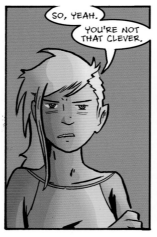

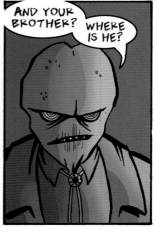

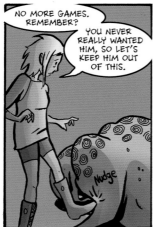

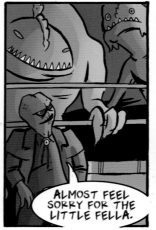

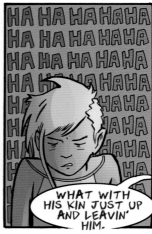

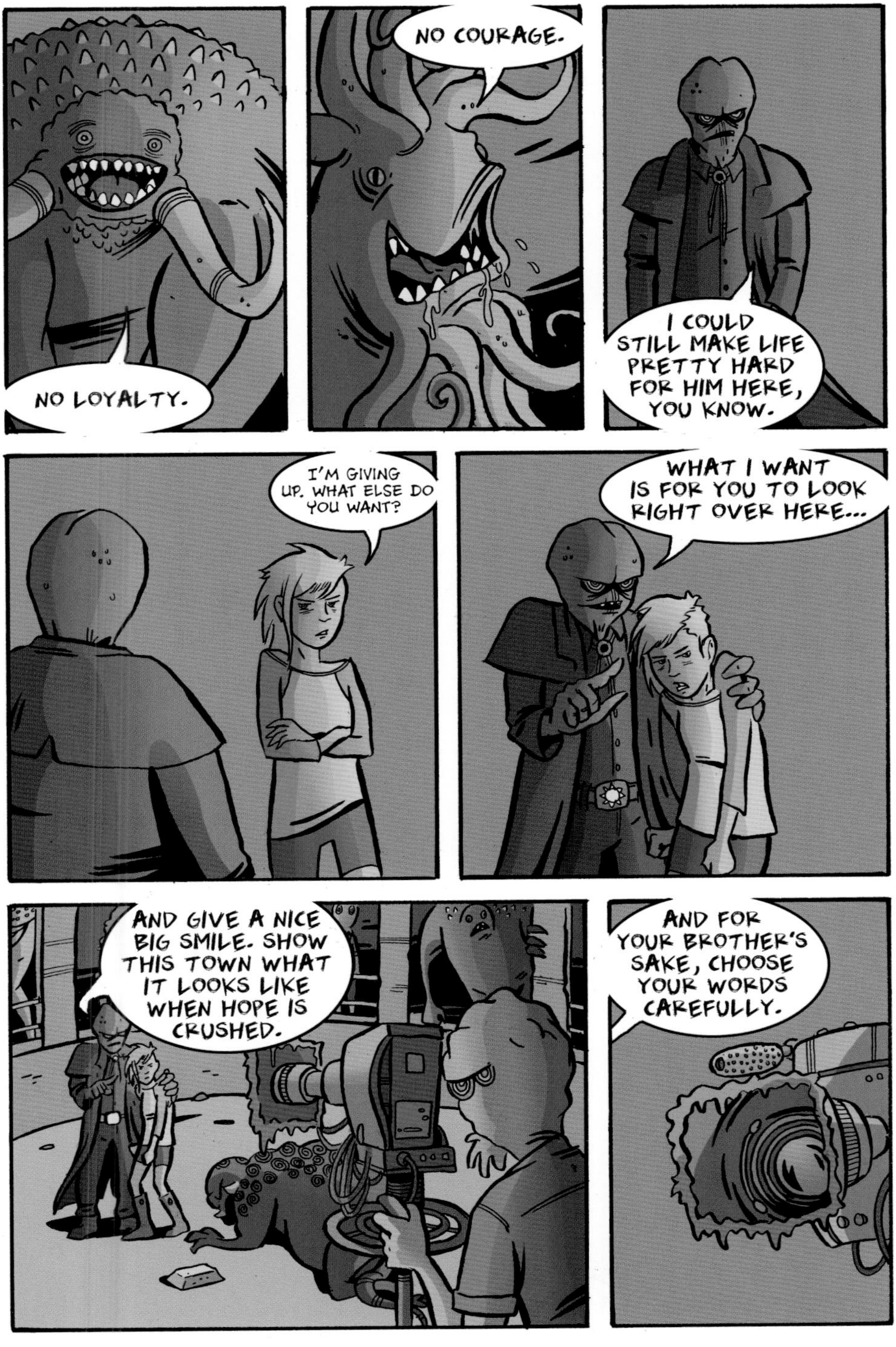
NO LOYALTY.
NO COURAGE.
I COULD STILL MAKE LIFE PRETTY HARD FOR HIM HERE, YOU KNOW.
I'M GIVING UP. WHAT ELSE DO YOU WANT?
WHAT I WANT IS FOR YOU TO LOOK RIGHT OVER HERE...
AND GIVE A NICE BIG SMILE. SHOW THIS TOWN WHAT IT LOOKS LIKE WHEN HOPE IS CRUSHED.
AND FOR YOUR BROTHER'S SAKE, CHOOSE YOUR WORDS CAREFULLY.

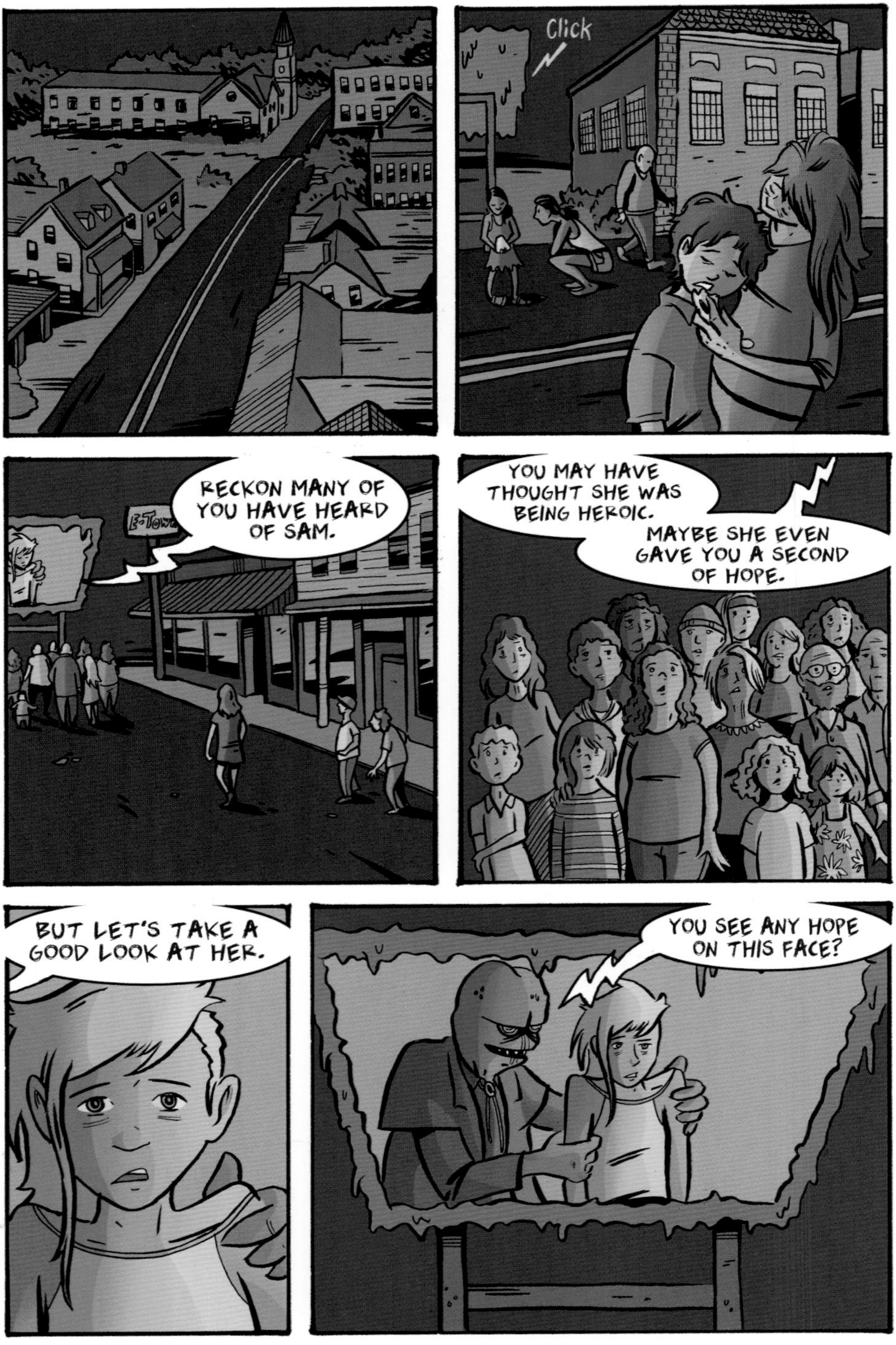
Click
RECKON MANY OF YOU HAVE HEARD OF SAM.
E-Town
YOU MAY HAVE THOUGHT SHE WAS BEING HEROIC.
MAYBE SHE EVEN GAVE YOU A SECOND OF HOPE.
BUT LET'S TAKE A GOOD LOOK AT HER.
YOU SEE ANY HOPE ON THIS FACE?

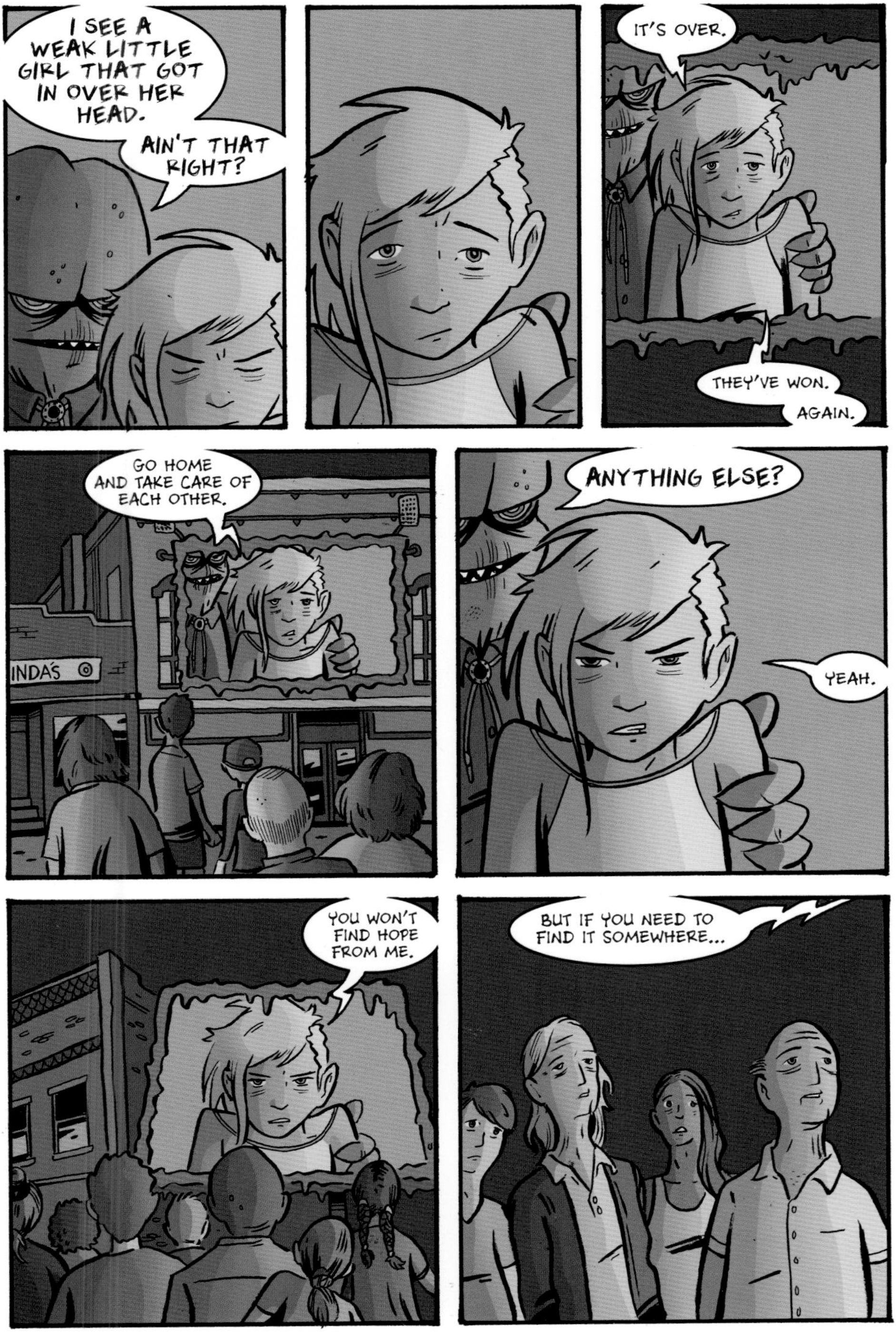

I SEE A WEAK LITTLE GIRL THAT GOT IN OVER HER HEAD.
AIN'T THAT RIGHT?
IT'S OVER.
THEY'VE WON.
AGAIN.
GO HOME AND TAKE CARE OF EACH OTHER.
INDA'S
ANYTHING ELSE?
YEAH.
YOU WON'T FIND HOPE FROM ME.
BUT IF YOU NEED TO FIND IT SOMEWHERE...

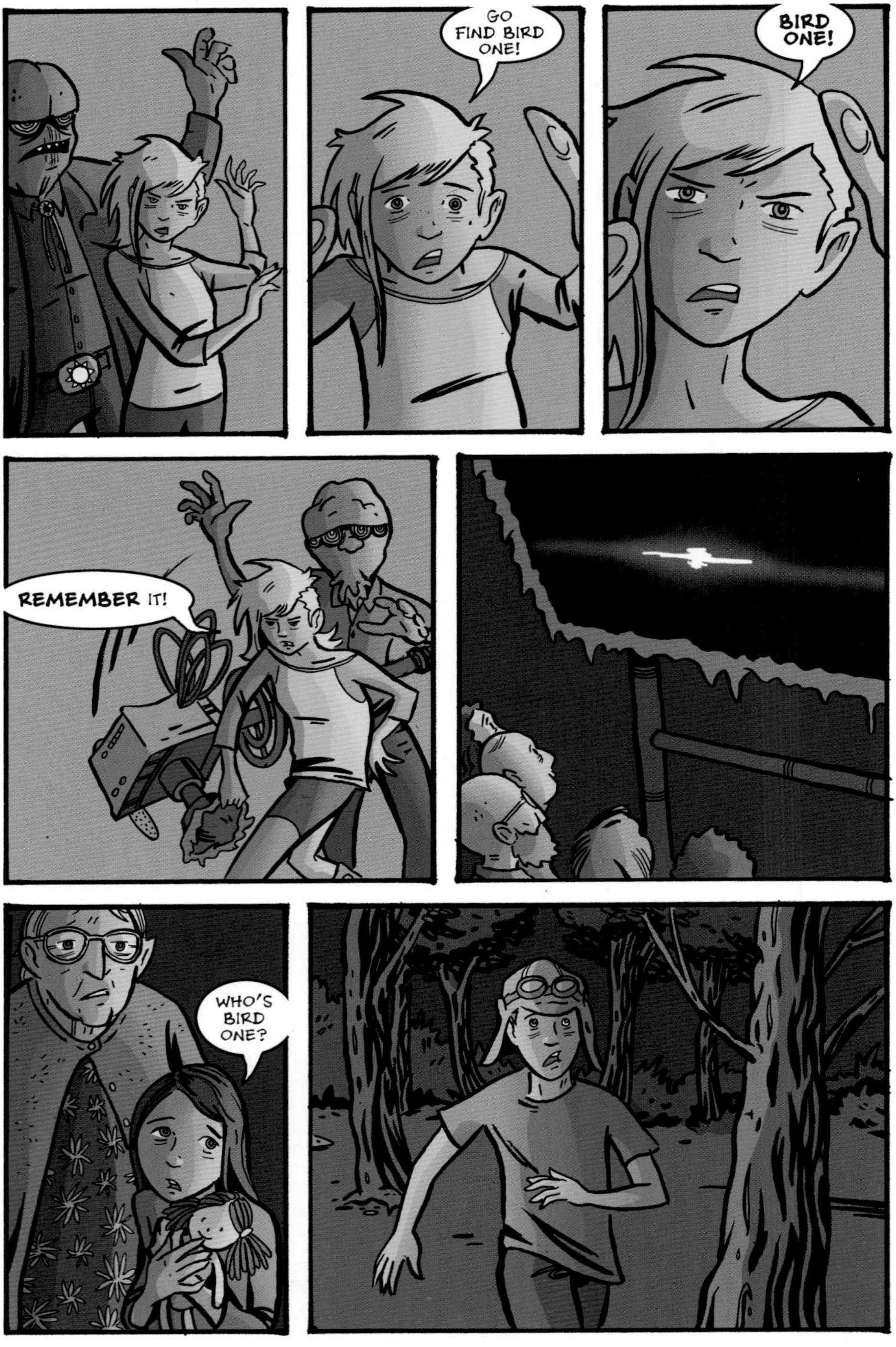
GO FIND BIRD ONE!
BIRD ONE!
REMEMBER IT!
WHO'S BIRD ONE?

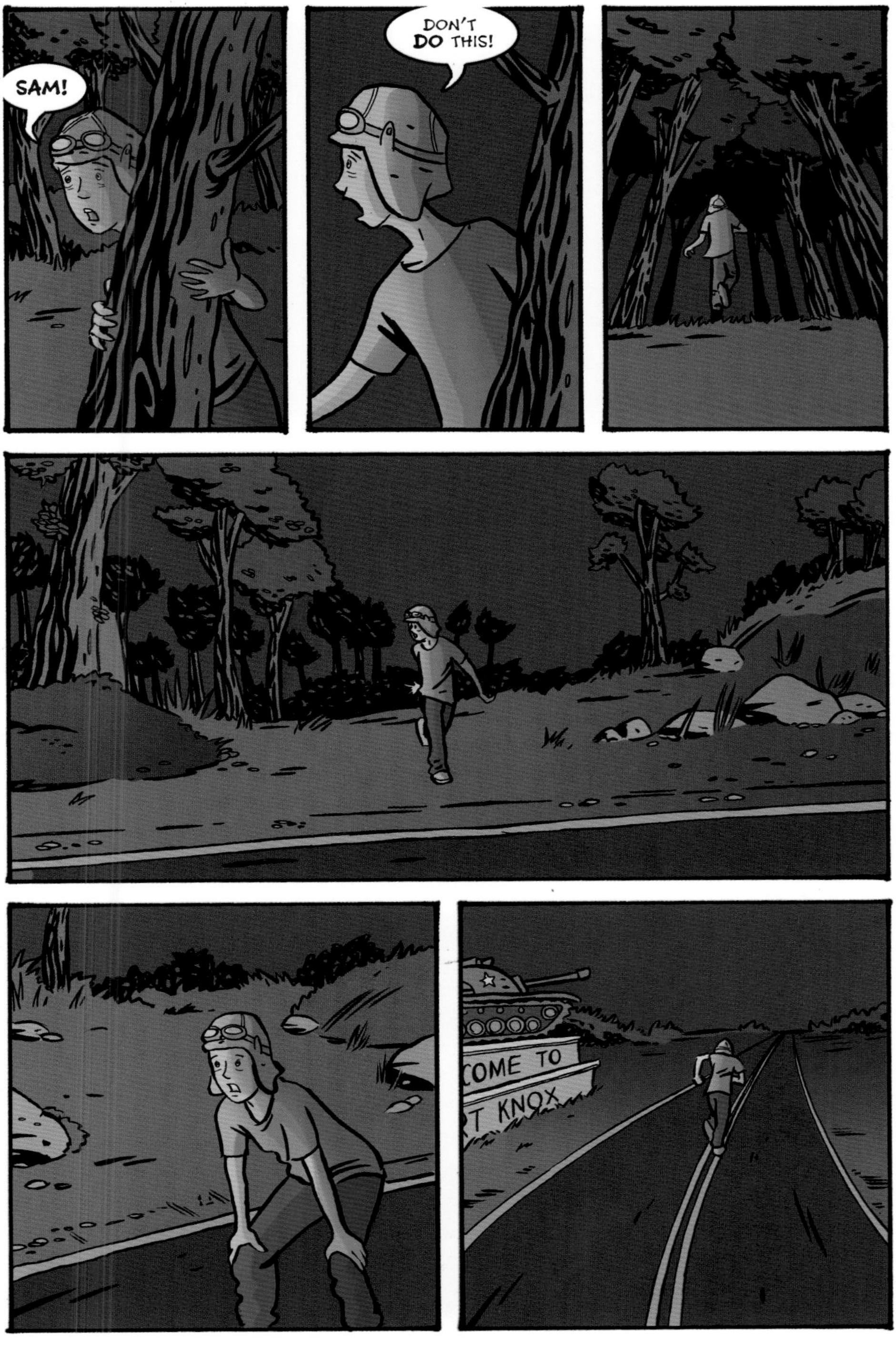
SAM!
DON'T DO THIS!
COME TO
T KNOX

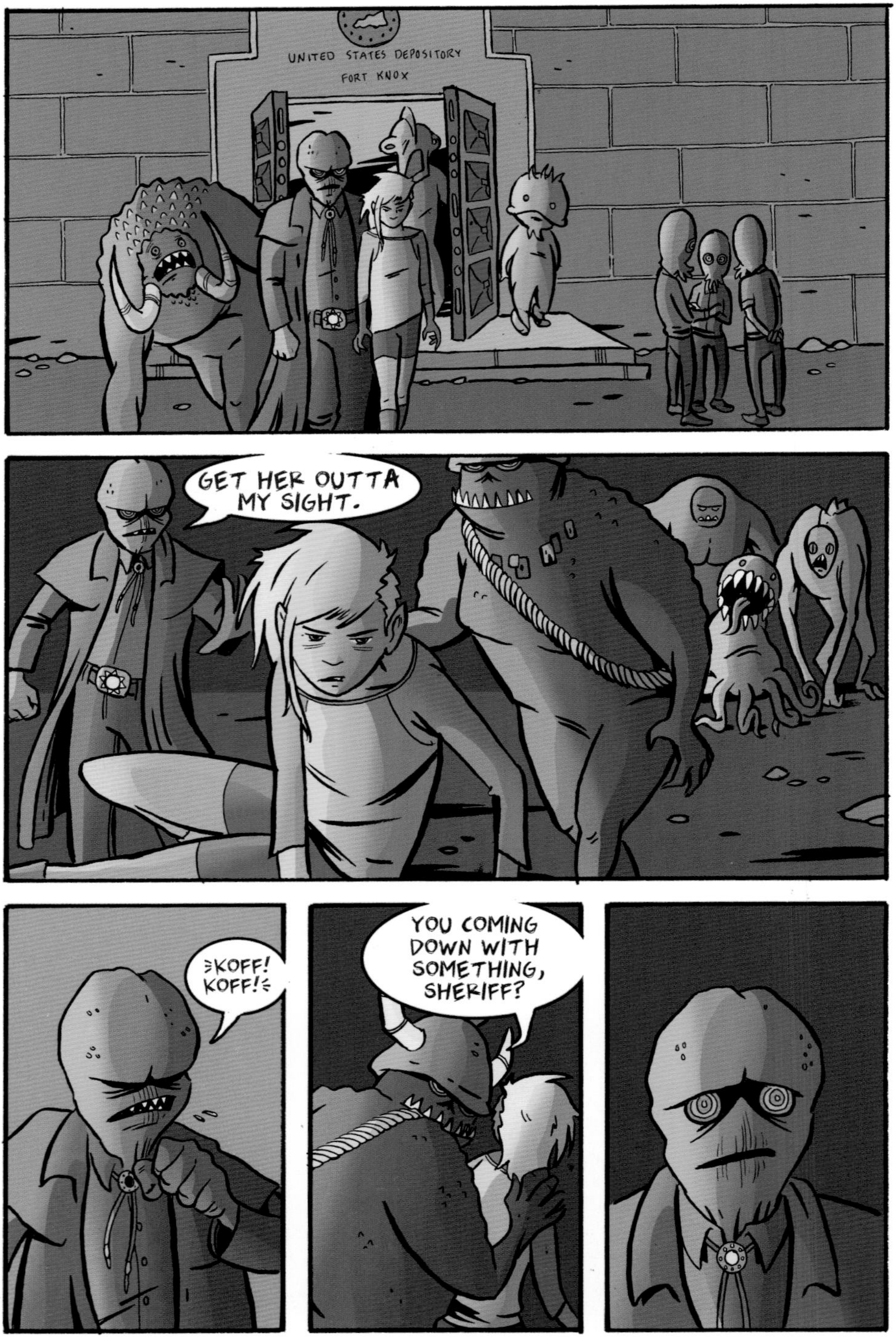
UNITED STATES DEPOSITORY
FORT KNOX
GET HER OUTTA MY SIGHT.
KOFF! KOFF!
YOU COMING DOWN WITH SOMETHING, SHERIFF?

SAM!

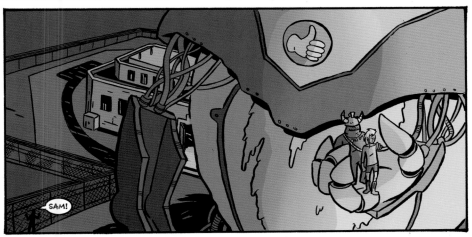

SAM!

I'M **HERE**! TAKE ME, TOO!

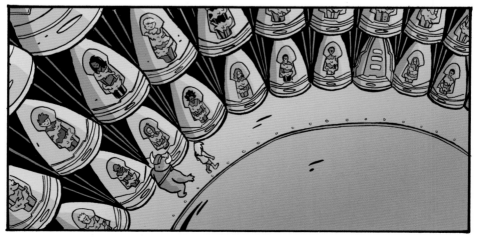

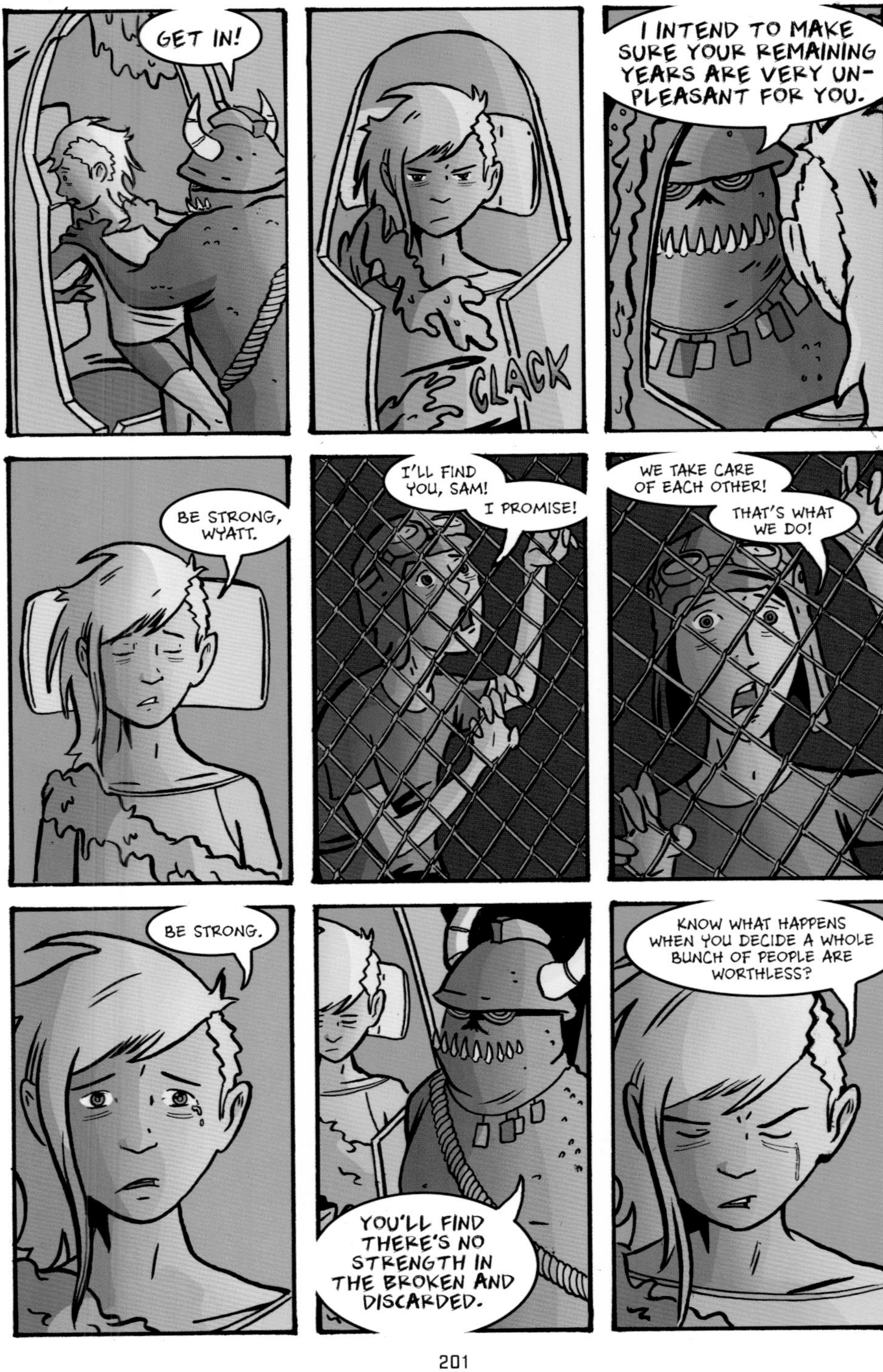
GET IN!
CLACK
I INTEND TO MAKE SURE YOUR REMAINING YEARS ARE VERY UN-PLEASANT FOR YOU.
BE STRONG, WYATT.
I'LL FIND YOU, SAM!
I PROMISE!
WE TAKE CARE OF EACH OTHER!
THAT'S WHAT WE DO!
BE STRONG.
YOU'LL FIND THERE'S NO STRENGTH IN THE BROKEN AND DISCARDED.
KNOW WHAT HAPPENS WHEN YOU DECIDE A WHOLE BUNCH OF PEOPLE ARE WORTHLESS?

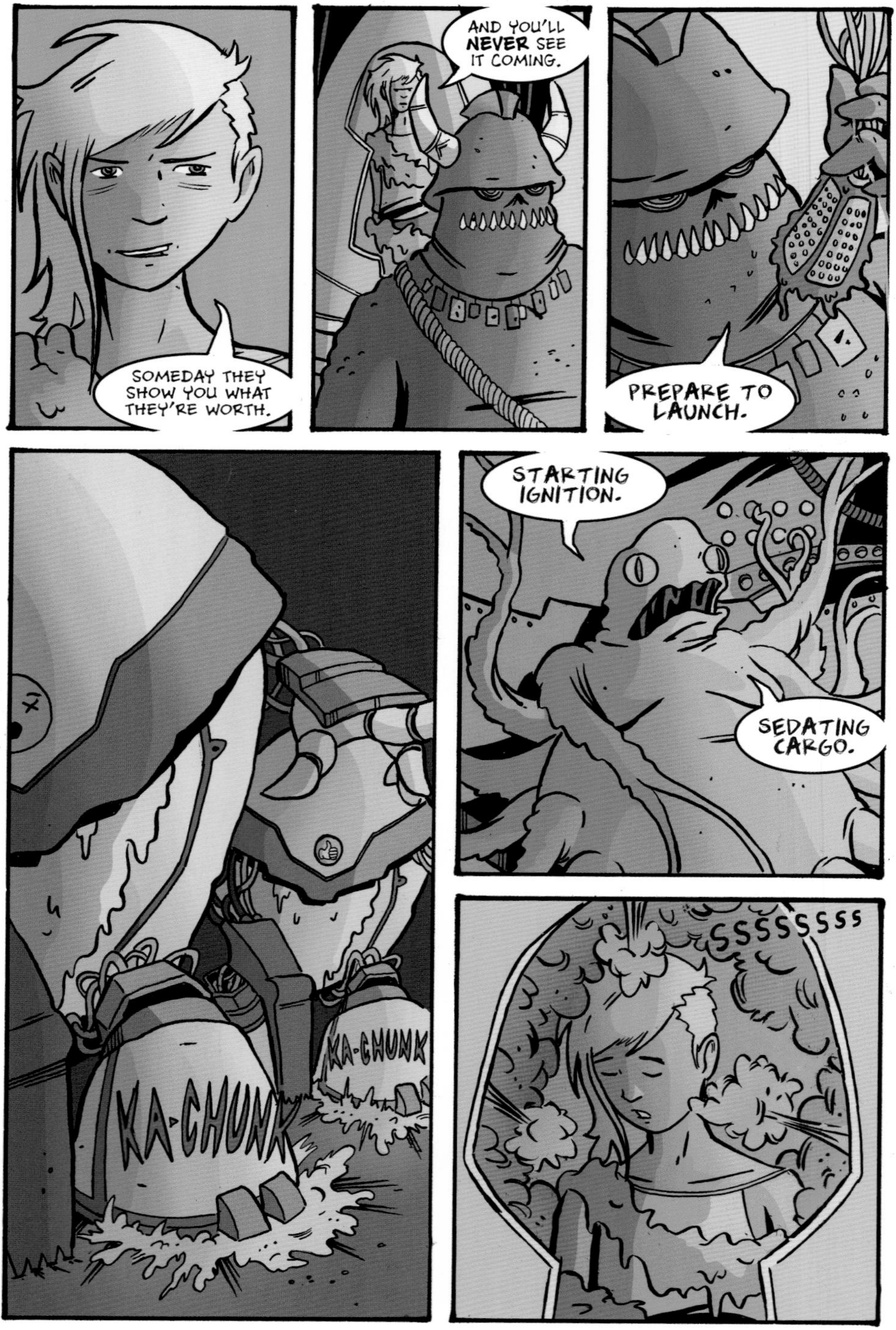
SOMEDAY THEY SHOW YOU WHAT THEY'RE WORTH.
AND YOU'LL **NEVER** SEE IT COMING.
PREPARE TO LAUNCH.
STARTING IGNITION.
SEDATING CARGO.
KA-CHUNK
KA-CHUNK
SSSSSSSS

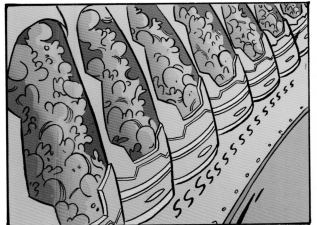

GET ME OFF THIS DIRT PILE OF A PLANET.

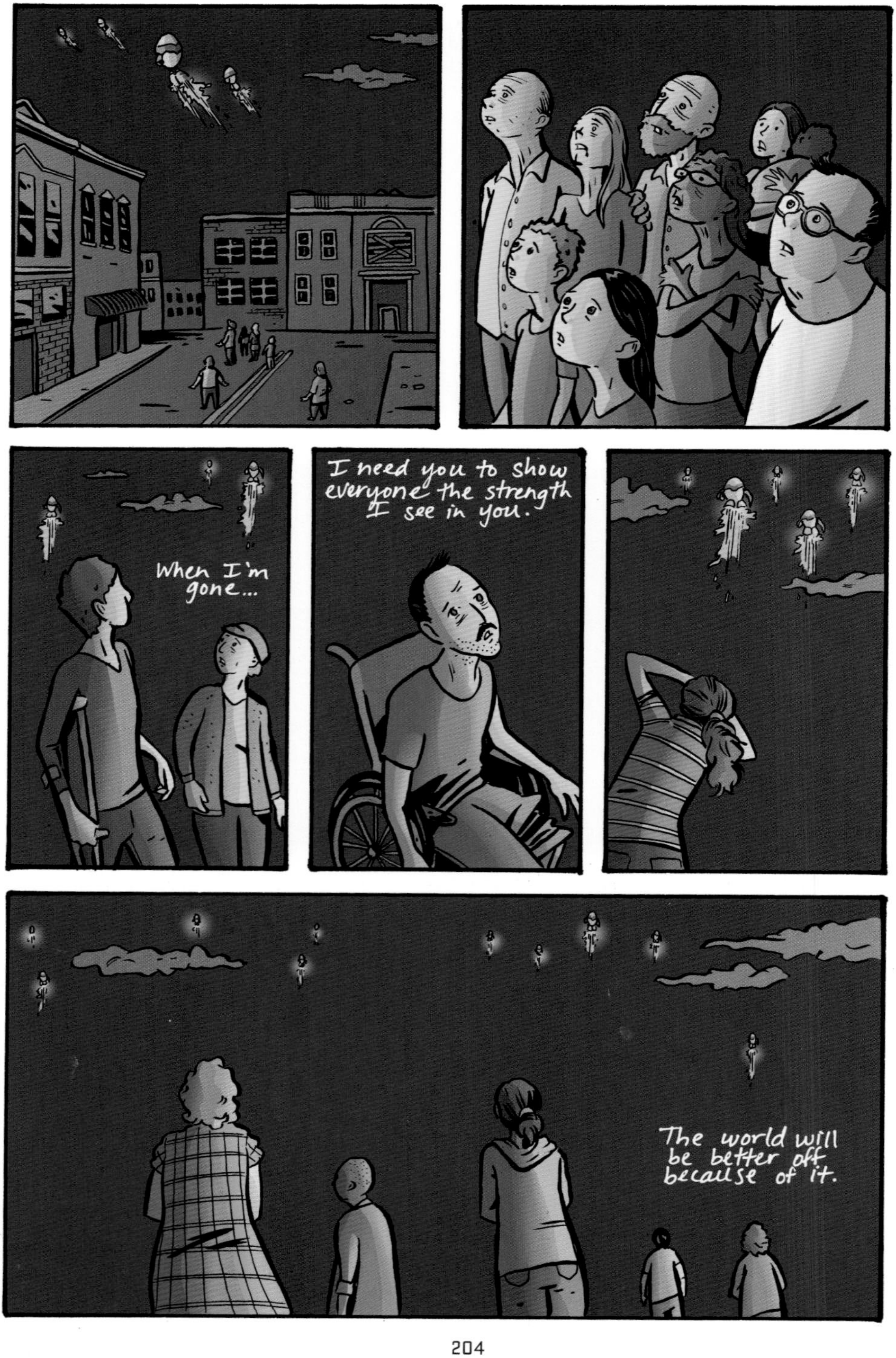
When I'm gone...
I need you to show everyone the strength I see in you.
The world will be better off because of it.

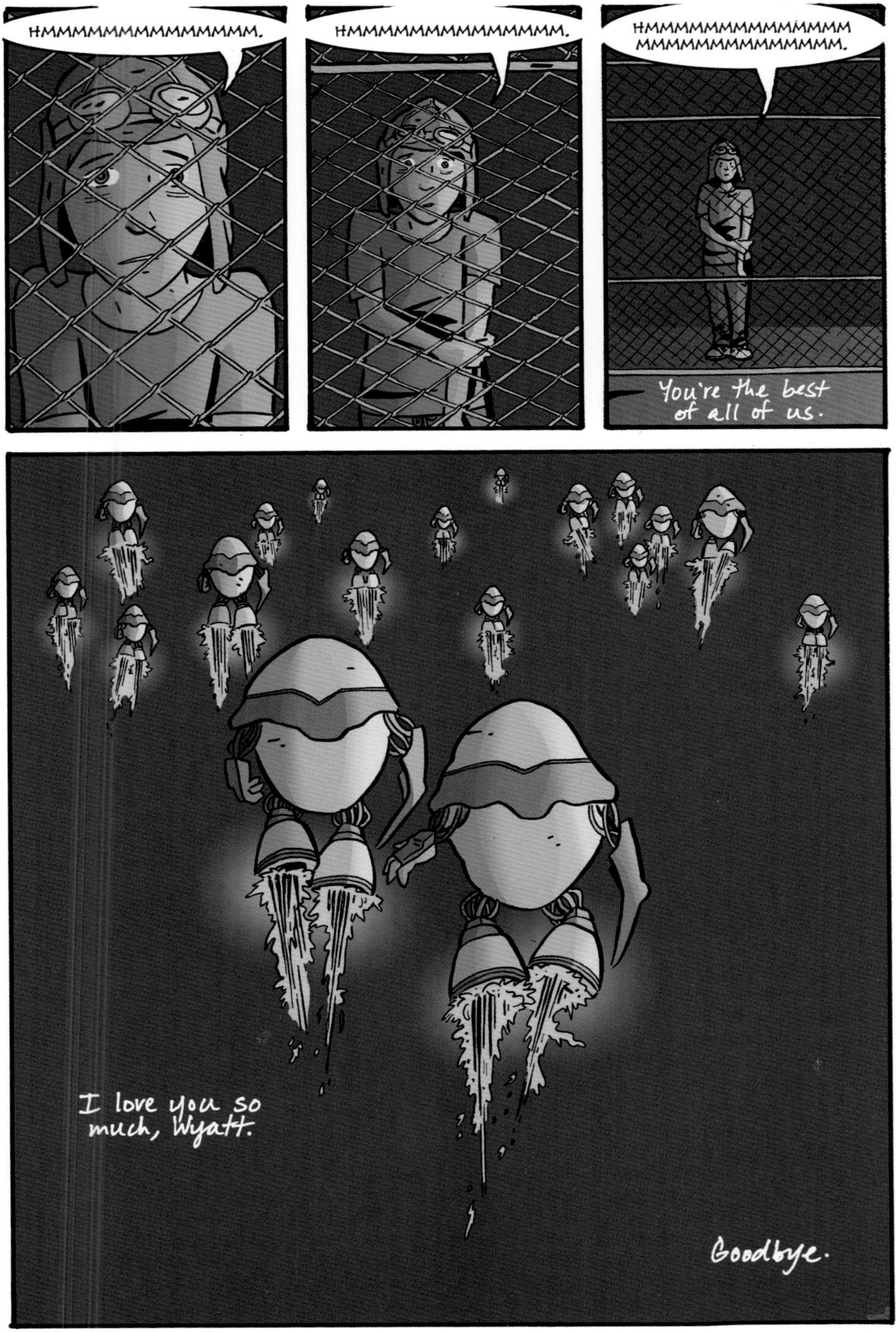
HMMMMMMMMMMMMMMM.
HMMMMMMMMMMMMMMMM.
HMMMMMMMMMMMMMMM
MMMMMMMMMMMMMMM.
You're the best of all of us.
I love you so much, Wyatt.
Goodbye.

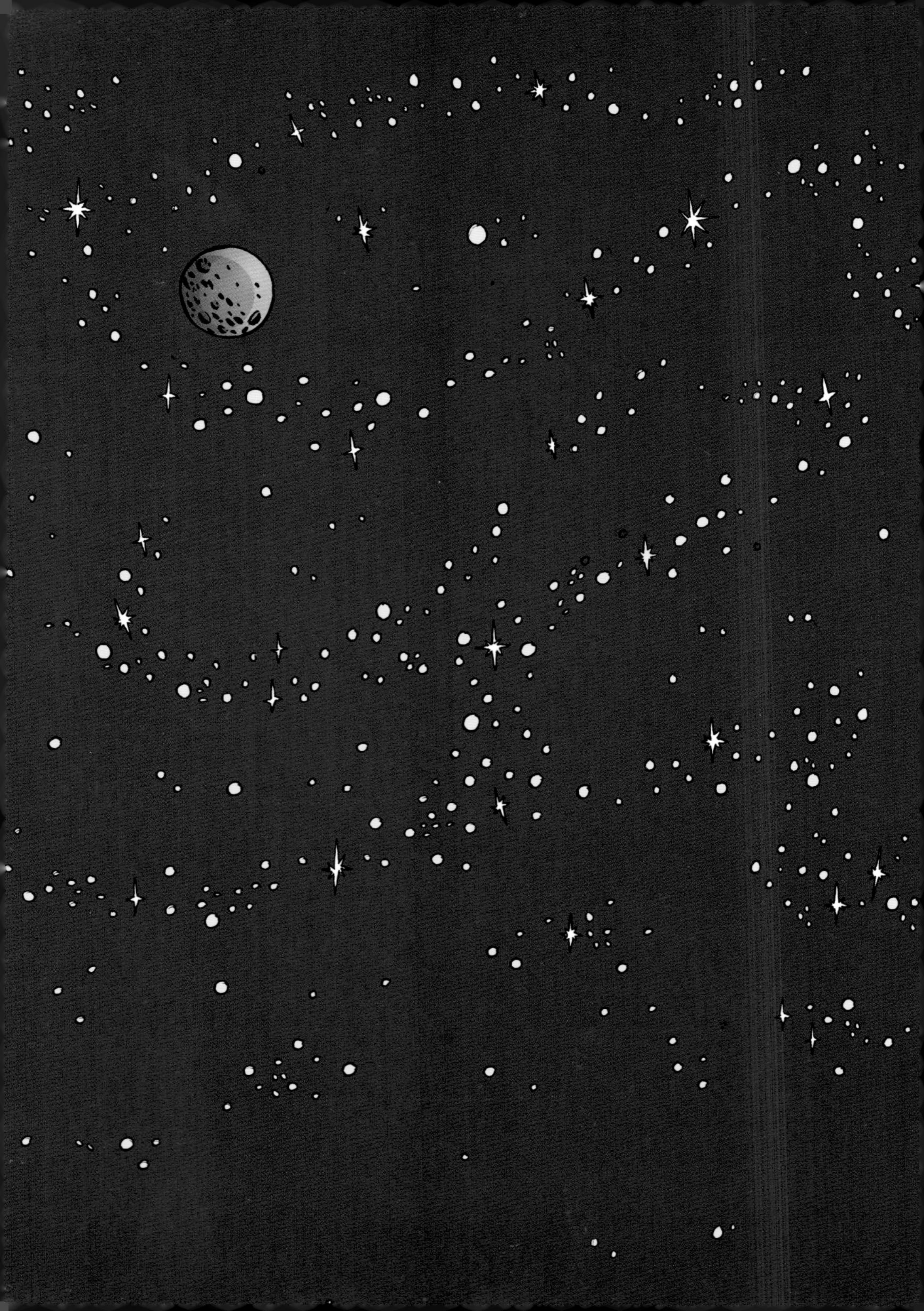

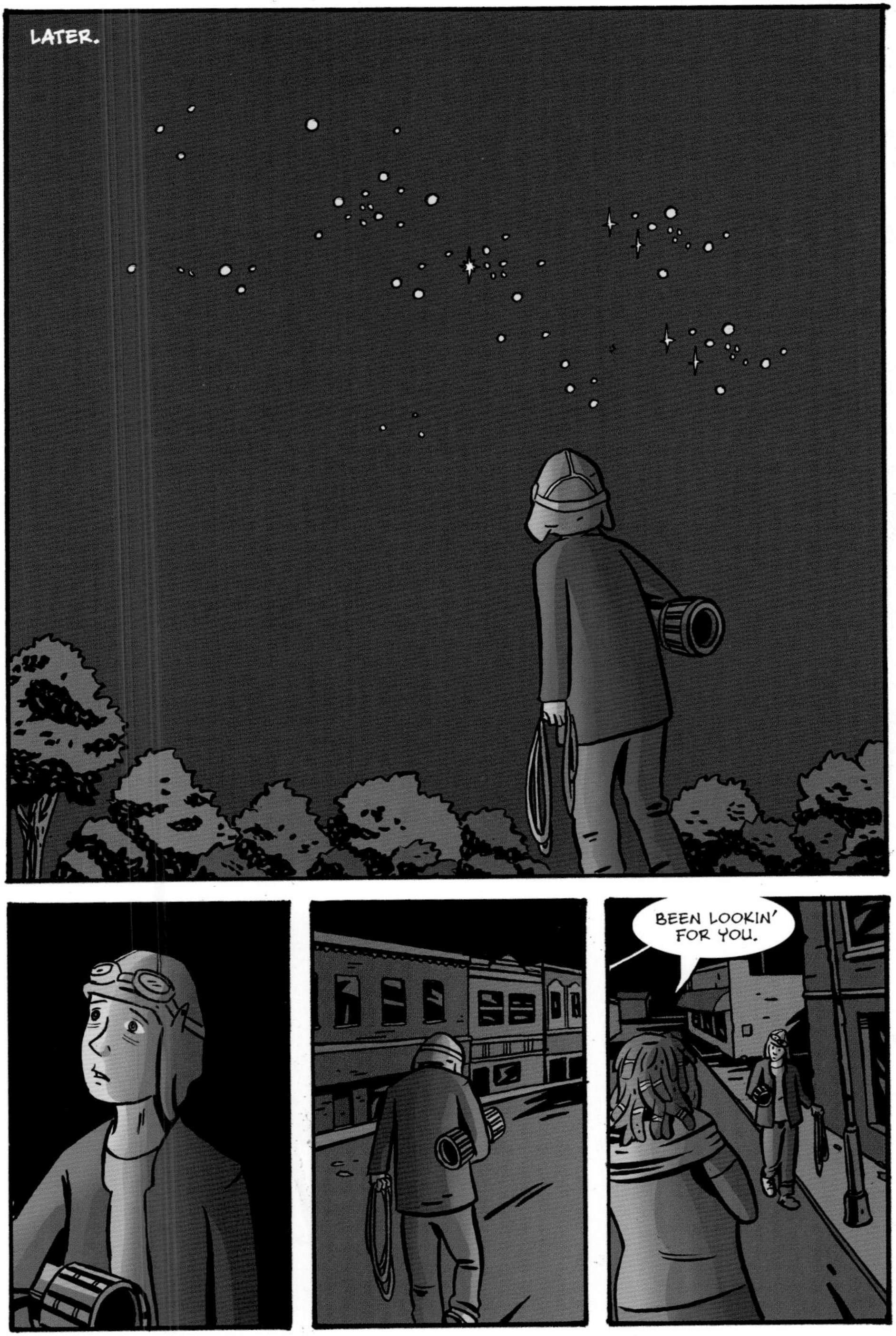
LATER.
BEEN LOOKIN' FOR YOU.

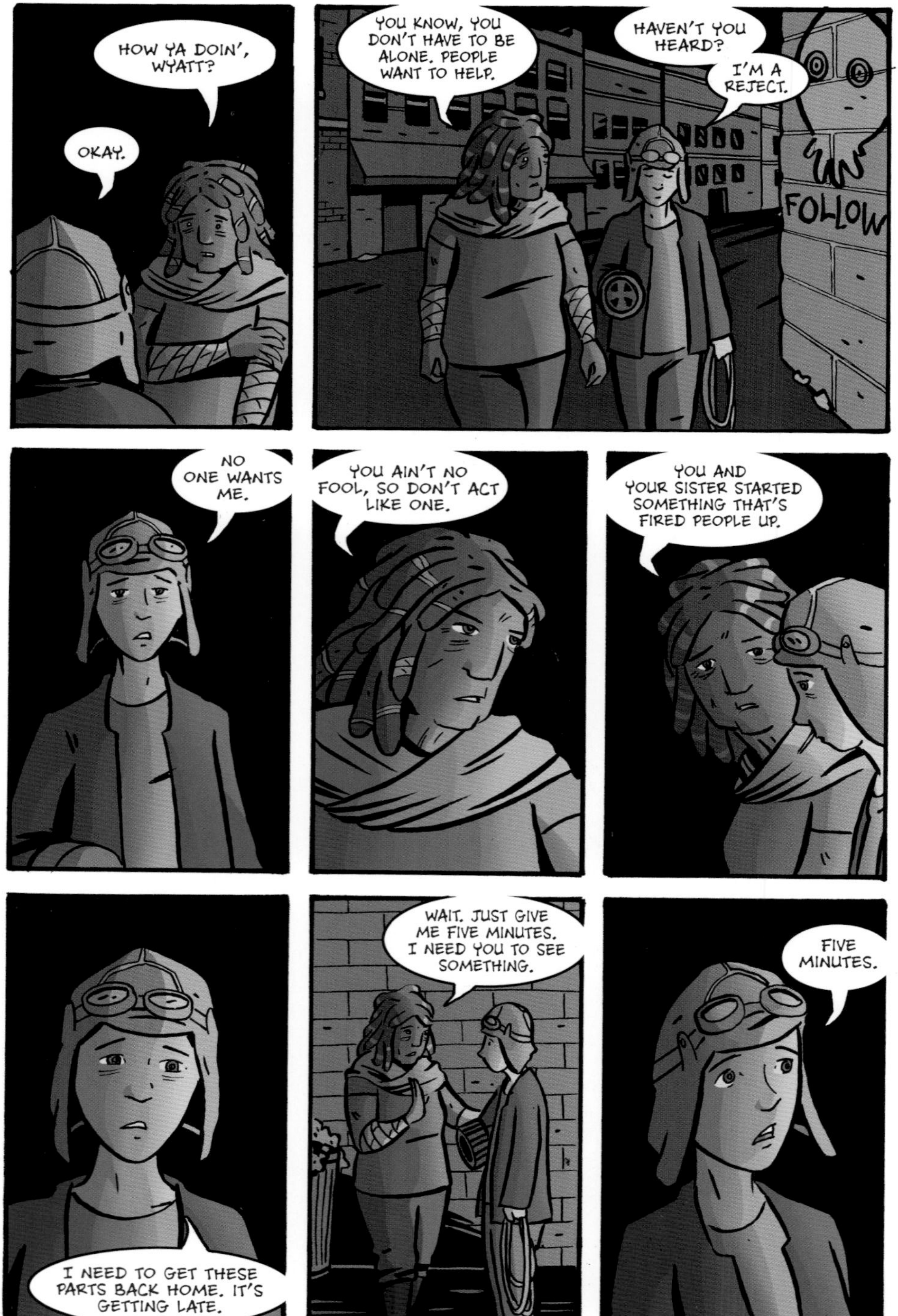
HOW YA DOIN', WYATT?
OKAY.
YOU KNOW, YOU DON'T HAVE TO BE ALONE. PEOPLE WANT TO HELP.
HAVEN'T YOU HEARD?
I'M A REJECT.
FOLLOW
NO ONE WANTS ME.
YOU AIN'T NO FOOL, SO DON'T ACT LIKE ONE.
YOU AND YOUR SISTER STARTED SOMETHING THAT'S FIRED PEOPLE UP.
I NEED TO GET THESE PARTS BACK HOME. IT'S GETTING LATE.
WAIT. JUST GIVE ME FIVE MINUTES. I NEED YOU TO SEE SOMETHING.
FIVE MINUTES.

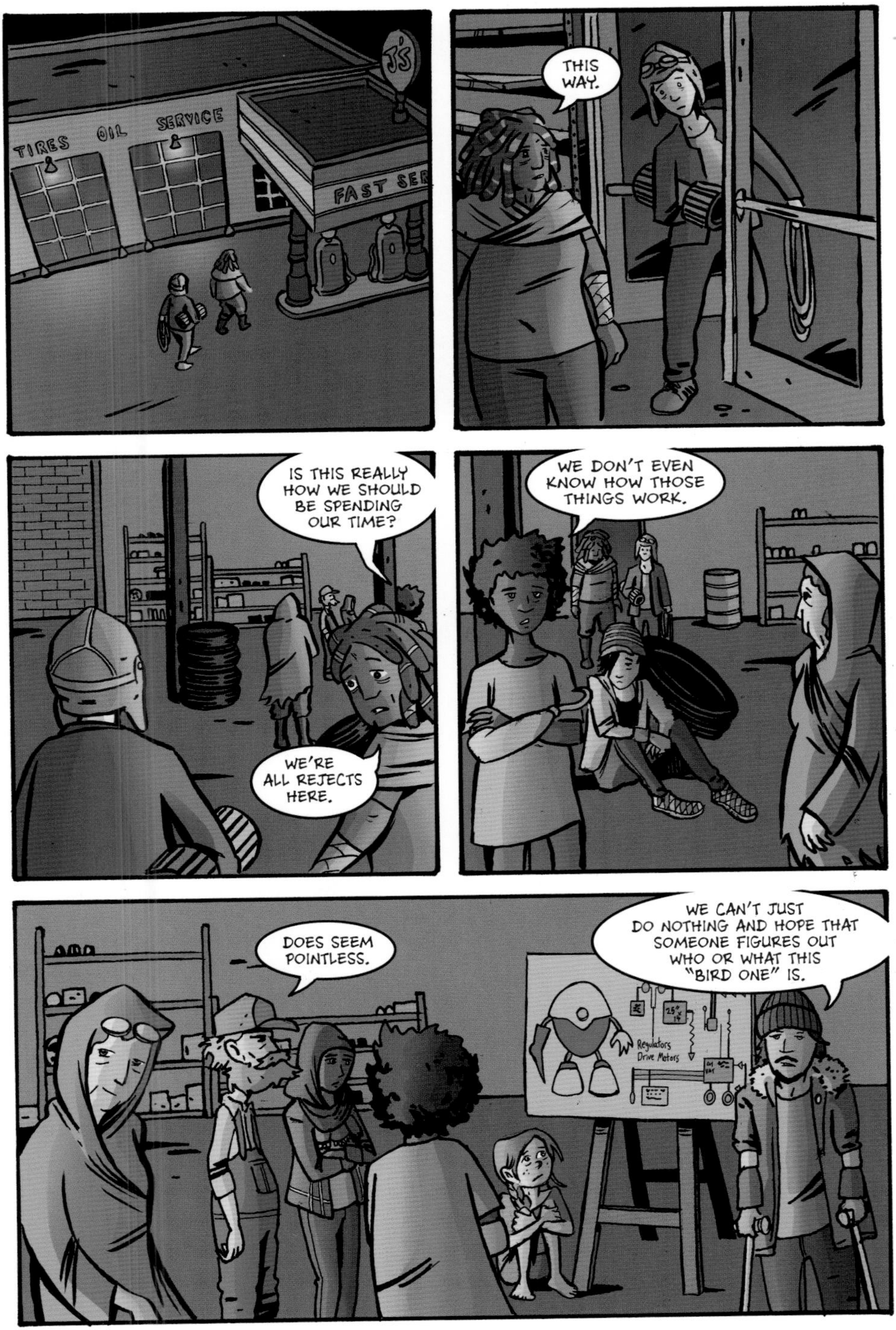
J'S
TIRES OIL SERVICE
FAST SER
THIS WAY.
IS THIS REALLY HOW WE SHOULD BE SPENDING OUR TIME?
WE'RE ALL REJECTS HERE.
WE DON'T EVEN KNOW HOW THOSE THINGS WORK.
DOES SEEM POINTLESS.
WE CAN'T JUST DO NOTHING AND HOPE THAT SOMEONE FIGURES OUT WHO OR WHAT THIS "BIRD ONE" IS.
Regulators
Drive Motors

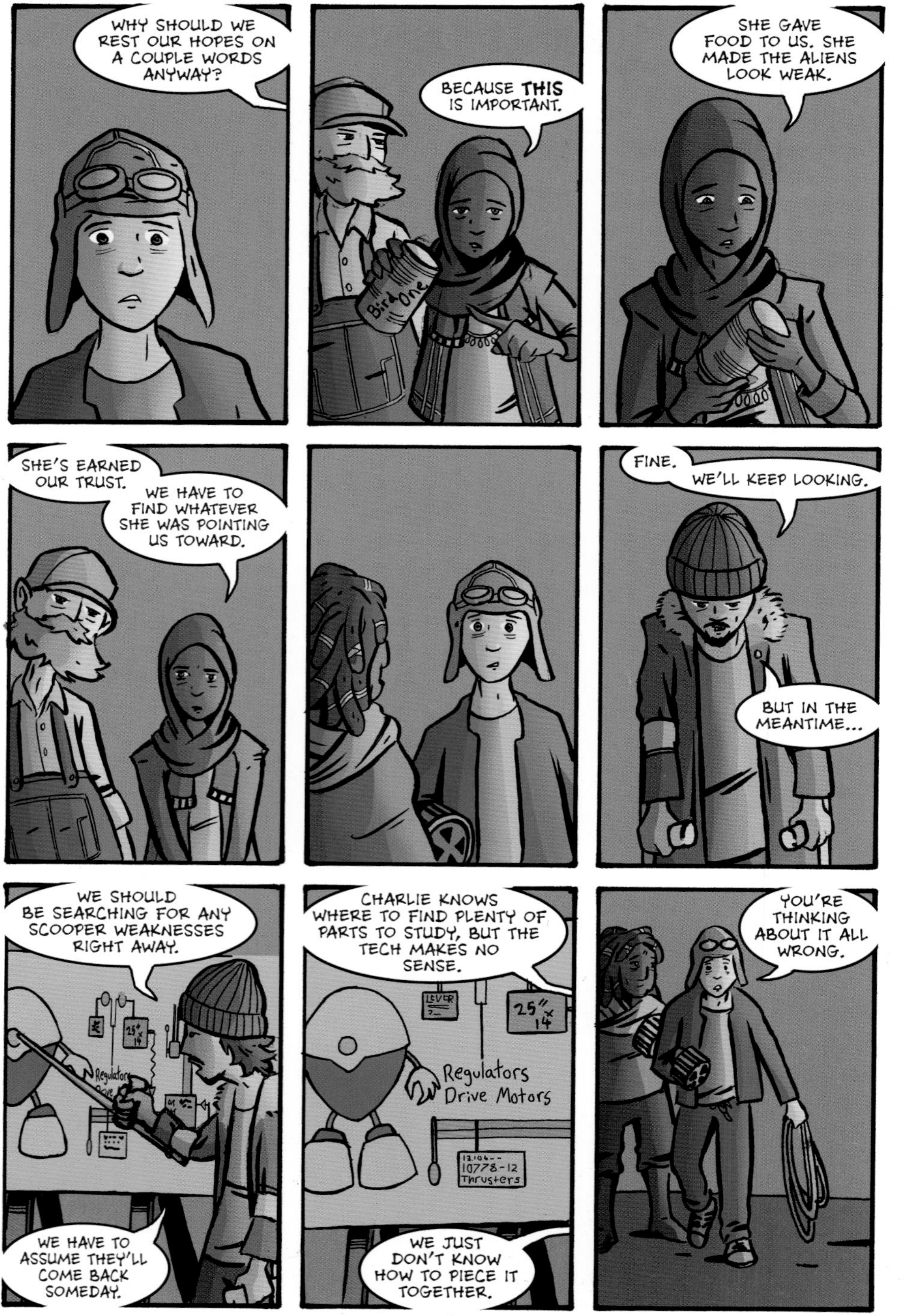
WHY SHOULD WE REST OUR HOPES ON A COUPLE WORDS ANYWAY?
BECAUSE **THIS** IS IMPORTANT.
Bird One
SHE GAVE FOOD TO US. SHE MADE THE ALIENS LOOK WEAK.
SHE'S EARNED OUR TRUST.
WE HAVE TO FIND WHATEVER SHE WAS POINTING US TOWARD.
FINE.
WE'LL KEEP LOOKING.
BUT IN THE MEANTIME...
WE SHOULD BE SEARCHING FOR ANY SCOOPER WEAKNESSES RIGHT AWAY.
WE HAVE TO ASSUME THEY'LL COME BACK SOMEDAY.
CHARLIE KNOWS WHERE TO FIND PLENTY OF PARTS TO STUDY, BUT THE TECH MAKES NO SENSE.
Regulators Drive Motors
10778-12 Thrusters
WE JUST DON'T KNOW HOW TO PIECE IT TOGETHER.
YOU'RE THINKING ABOUT IT ALL WRONG.

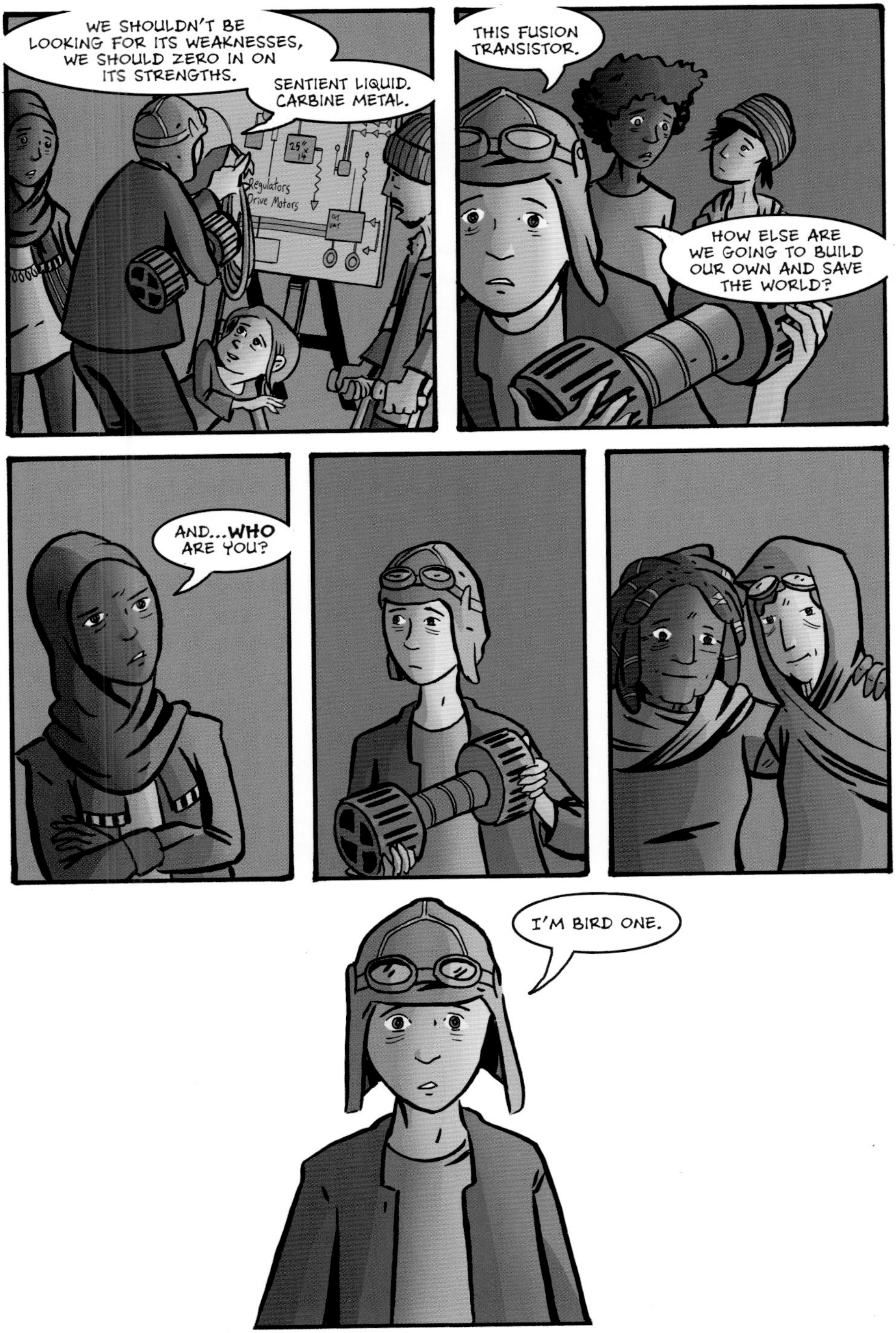
WE SHOULDN'T BE LOOKING FOR ITS WEAKNESSES, WE SHOULD ZERO IN ON ITS STRENGTHS.
SENTIENT LIQUID. CARBINE METAL.
Regulators
Drive Motors
THIS FUSION TRANSISTOR.
HOW ELSE ARE WE GOING TO BUILD OUR OWN AND SAVE THE WORLD?
AND...**WHO** ARE YOU?
I'M BIRD ONE.

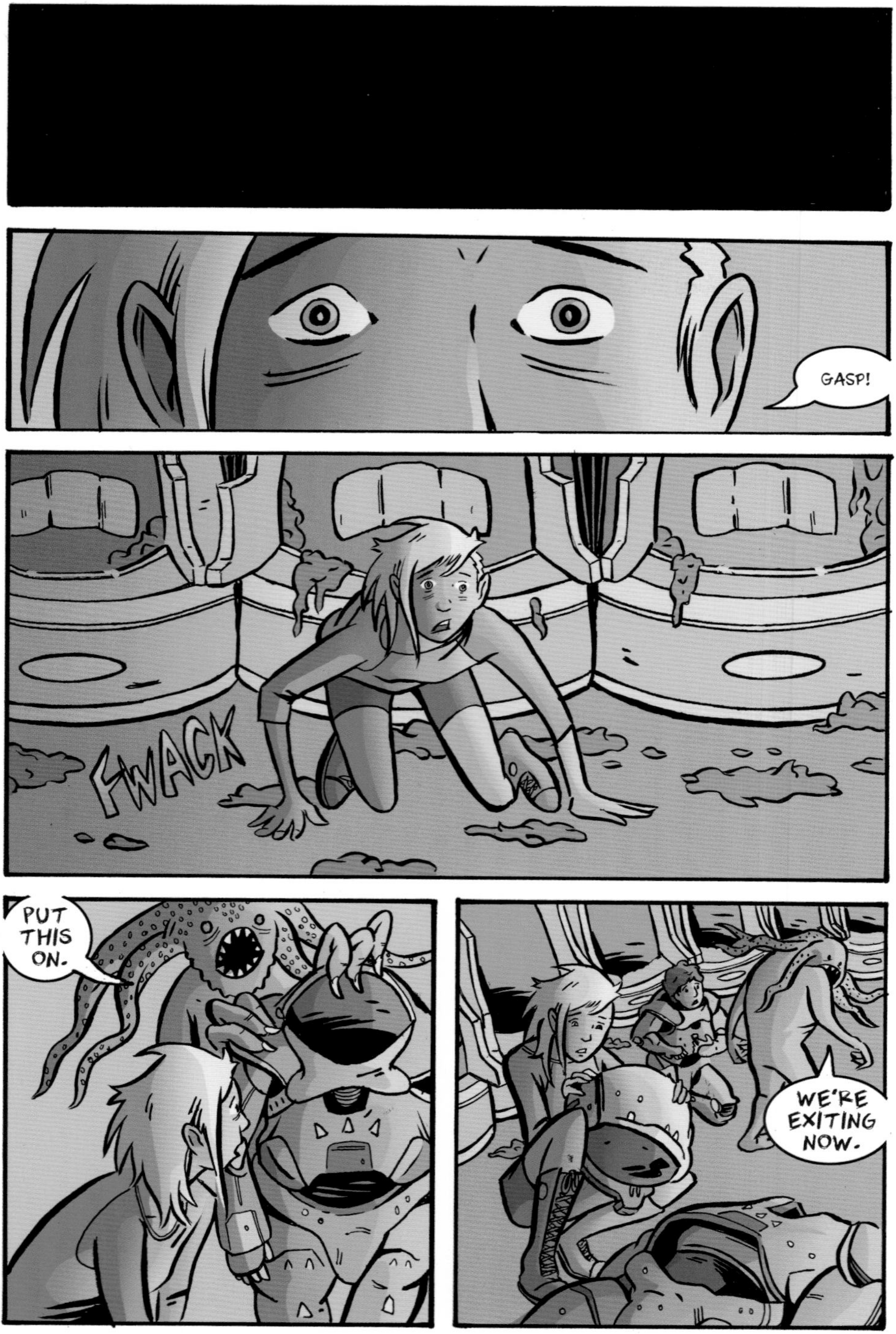
GASP!
FWACK
PUT THIS ON.
WE'RE EXITING NOW.

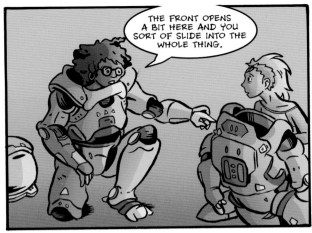

THE FRONT OPENS A BIT HERE AND YOU SORT OF SLIDE INTO THE WHOLE THING.

THERE YOU GO.

VERY FASHIONABLE.

WHY AM I THE LAST TO GET THIS STUPID THING ON?

THEY'RE MESSING WITH YOU. MOST OF US HAVE BEEN AWAKE FOR A WHILE.

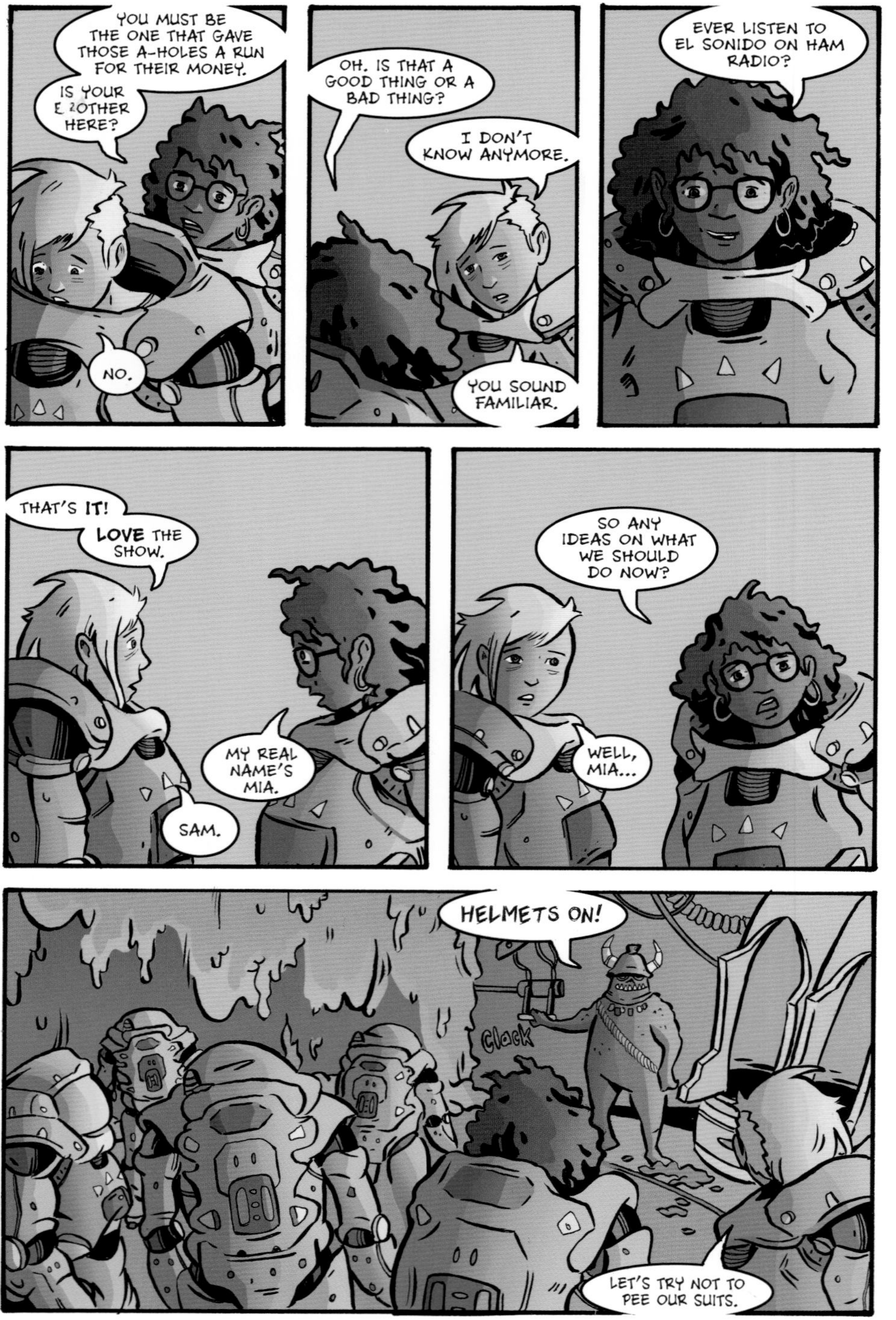
YOU MUST BE THE ONE THAT GAVE THOSE A-HOLES A RUN FOR THEIR MONEY.
IS YOUR BROTHER HERE?
NO.
OH. IS THAT A GOOD THING OR A BAD THING?
I DON'T KNOW ANYMORE.
YOU SOUND FAMILIAR.
EVER LISTEN TO EL SONIDO ON HAM RADIO?
THAT'S IT!
LOVE THE SHOW.
MY REAL NAME'S MIA.
SAM.
SO ANY IDEAS ON WHAT WE SHOULD DO NOW?
WELL, MIA...
HELMETS ON!
Clack
LET'S TRY NOT TO PEE OUR SUITS.

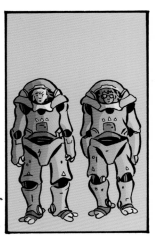

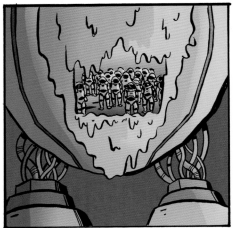

TO BE CONTINUED...

A SECRET MESSAGE FOR YOU (THE READER)

Psst. You!
Yeah, you.

Lean in close, becaue I've got a secret for you. You're not going to like it, but sometimes the truth is hard. Here it goes.

The world is set up so that there will always be losers.

Pretty terrible, right? I mean, it's great for the winners, but what about everyone else?

I've been a teacher for nearly sixteen years, and I've taught immigrants and refugees, students on the autism spectrum, and young people with mild to severe developmental disabilities. Among them have been some of the bravest and most interesting and creative people that I've ever met. All I want is for each of them to have a chance at happiness and access to the same opportunities as everyone else.

Unfortunately, the world often has a narrow view of what success looks like. There are people out there that need all of us to look and act in very specific ways, which means that some of my students are at a severe disadvantage. The arbiters of what qualifies as success don't realize that thinking and acting differently is what makes living on planet Earth so exciting and that we could all use a bit more of it.

But you don't have to carry a label that shouts to the world your "disability" to see how we constantly create new winners and losers. When was the last time you remember everyone getting an A+ on the same test?

You're probably thinking, "Whoa, Jason. Pretty bleak way to fill these final pages." Here's where I tell you the world doesn't have to be this way.

You, dear reader, are the hope for change. You might someday find yourself in a position to equalize the playing field in some small or large way by just taking the time to see what the person in front of you has to offer. Forget whatever real or imagined label has been placed on them and just take the time to see that spark within that looks at the world from a fresh perspective.

You might be surprised to find that whatever the world sees as "different" is exactly what the world needs more of.

ABOUT THE AUTHOR

Dad. Husband. Comic creator.

Jason Walz is the creator of the Eisner-nominated graphic novel *HOMESICK* and the short comic *A STORY FOR DESMOND*. Additionally, he created the online comic anthology *CRAP SHOOT*.

Visit Jason at **www.jasonwwalz.com**.